VENGE

BY:

WILL ISENBERG

FERAL CAT PUBLISHERS
Melbourne, FL USA
2021

Published by Feral Cat Publishers, Melbourne, FL
www.feralcatpublishers.com

Edited by Jill Hand (www.jillhandauthor.com)

Version 1.0, February 2021

KDP Print ISBN: 978-1970-087178

IngramSpark Print ISBN: 978-1970-087161

ebook ISBN: 978-1970-087154

TABLE OF CONTENTS

FOREWORD

When I was twelve, I had a nightmare that menacing terrorists took over my school, and I had to defeat them and rescue my classmates. The dream was so vivid that I decided to spend two years writing it out into a story: 100 pages, handwritten, in which I fought off terrorists using bows and arrows from the athletic department, and dismantled a twenty-foot tall bomb they had built in our gym. The tale was packed with gratuitous explosions, superfluous adverbs, and the deepest social commentary my tween mind could hack together. Writing that story on college-ruled paper was the most fulfilling task I'd accomplished until that point, and that includes the time I placed top six in our 4th grade Spelling Bee.

One of the most exciting parts of that project was adding complexities to the plot. It wasn't enough to defeat the terrorists with brute force. I had to outsmart them. I had to discover secret passageways underneath the school's foundation that allowed me to outmaneuver the terrorists. I had to strategically choose whether to liberate the hostages in the science room or the art room first. I had to find food and water for my freed classmates so we could stay hidden in our secret passageways. I had to spy on the terrorists' conversations in the locker room to figure out how to evacuate the students and destroy the bomb without getting killed. (In what I considered to be a clever twist, the only way to survive the blast was to be as close as possible to the bomb when it went off.) I found that the process of developing these plot points was almost as exciting as actually living them out would be.

When I finished that first draft, I fantasized about rewriting it, publishing it, and one day turning it into a movie. (This was before I watched *Air Force One*, and realized that Harrison Ford and Gary Oldman had already accomplished in an airplane what I'd attempted to do in a Junior High gymnasium.) But even though I soon abandoned that handwritten story for more advanced projects such as Venge, I've never forgotten the excitement of spinning a new tale out of nothing.

I'm pleased to share *Venge* with you all. I hope the explosions are more nuanced, the adverbs more tempered than they were in my terrorist story from long ago. Style and perspective change, but the passion never goes away. Somewhere I want to believe there is a 12-year-old boy snapping awake from a thrilling dream of bows and arrows and hostages. Somewhere there is a novice writer drying out pen after pen on college-ruled paper. And somewhere, hiding in a stack of faded pages on a dusty shelf, there is a seventh grader who accepts with grim reluctance, if not absurd contrivance, that the only way he can thwart the terrorists in his school is by crawling inside their bomb before detonating it.

I wish to express many thanks to Amy, the first person I spoke to about *Venge*, and who gave me invaluable feedback and encouragement on my first draft. And to my good friends Tyler and Jason, who inspired my crowning achievement, even when I was running out of toner.

Will Isenberg - 2021

Chapter 1

Two Giraffes

Sunday, April 15

The sign read "GIRAFFE STEAKS:100% ETHICALLY SOURCED."
On it was an electric cartoon animal with a long yellow neck. It faced the
street with a broad smile, apparently content with being killed as long as
it was killed ethically. Then the creature blinked, sensing motion in the
otherwise empty night, and its animated eyes glanced toward the building
across the street.

On the roof sat a young woman, her feet dangling over the edge.
Her face was wrapped in a black gaiter mask. Her hair, black and glossy
under the light of the cartoon giraffe, was combed straight back from her
forehead and pinned into a knot behind her head.

A security camera several feet away was pointed at her, zooming in
and out suspiciously, seemingly frustrated at being able to make out her
features beneath the mask. The woman tilted her head back and
coughed, swishing spit around her mouth until a warm sticky gob had
formed at the tip of her tongue. She adjusted her mask and spat, and the
security camera whirred, focusing and refocusing, smearing the slime
around its own lens.

Across the street, the glowing animatronic giraffe seemed to be
laughing. The woman flashed it a thumbs-up. At least someone, or something, appreciated her aim.

As the camera gave up and turned downwards, the woman pulled
the mask off, and raised a strip of dried meat to her mouth. Chewing,

she grimaced. They could grow giraffe in a lab, but they couldn't figure out how to make it any texture other than that of shoe leather. The woman choked down the rest of the jerky, and flicked the wrapper off the building. The glowing giraffe across the street illuminated the tiny identical giraffe on the plastic wrapper, which turned somersaults as it fluttered into the night air.

The tiny giraffe shrank and disappeared from sight, blown away down the street. The electronic giraffe narrowed its pixelated eyes at the woman. "Do you mind?" it seemed to say. Whether it was judging her for littering or being so careless with a copy of its own face, the woman didn't know.

The street was still empty. The woman kicked her heels against the wall of the building, and pulled out a black device, rereading the same message for the twentieth time that hour. Straining her eyes, she glanced between the device and the street signs down below.

There was a flutter by her side. Another empty wrapper, this one from a candy bar, had slipped out of her pocket. The woman grunted, diving to the side and slapping the plastic against the roof.

As the woman righted herself, the giant giraffe stared at her in disbelief. "Was littering twice in the same minute too much for you?" it seemed to ask.

"It's sentimental!" the woman called out to the advertisement. She held up the wrapper. On it was a drawing, in dried nail polish, of two stick figures: the taller one with long hair, and the smaller one standing on one leg, the other leg ending at the knee, balancing on crutches. Printed underneath in wobbling letters was: "Can we go to the park tomorrow?"

"Park's a bright idea," the woman said to herself.

The light shifted. The electronic giraffe changed its gaze from the woman down to the street, where three young men had appeared, singing loudly and strutting like peacocks.

The first man had teeth of silver, which glinted whenever he smiled. The second man had shaved only half of his head, with a greasy ponytail dangling from the other side. The last of the three was apparently under the impression that his face would be incomplete without a dozen metal fixtures pierced through his nose, ears, and lips.

"Silver, Ponytail, and Piercings," the woman said, surveying the men. Some said that giving your targets nicknames made it easier to keep track of them. Ponytail was the biggest. Silver and Piercings both held glass beer bottles. If they were drunk, that was to her advantage. But that advantage came at a cost: the bottles themselves, which could easily be smashed and turned into weapons.

The woman chewed on her lip, letting the sharp pain focus her attention. She kicked her heels faster against the side of the building, planning how it would play out. Crawl down the fire escape from the roof to the street. Hit Ponytail first, then Silver, then Piercings. Don't worry about the bottles. Those goons are high on puke-cheap beer and testosterone; they won't even see you coming.

She closed her eyes, imagining herself knocking out Silver's fake teeth, grabbing hold of Ponytail's oily hair, ripping the metal bits from Piercings' face.

The flavor of the giraffe jerky was still on her tongue, and as she bit harder, another taste, coppery and juicy, trickled through her mouth. She put the mask on and reached behind her, grabbing a brick with a rope coiled around it. It was time.

CHAPTER 2

THE MEDALLION

The three men, Silver, Ponytail, and Piercings, sang loudly and with a total lack of regard for any sort of harmony. Silver closed his eyes, swaying side to side, bumping into his companions with each step. Then his foot caught on a crack in the sidewalk, and he stumbled forward into Piercings. Piercings shoved him off with a grunt, and Silver elbowed him back.

Within seconds, their fists were swinging into each other's chests. The bottles slipped from their hands and shattered on the sidewalk. Silver wrapped his veiny, tattooed arms around Piercings' neck, squeezing until the man's eyes bulged. Piercings gasped. Spit bubbled out of his mouth, as he flailed his arms. His fingernails dug into Silver's arms, scratching deep grooves into the skin. Ponytail watched, egging them on in low grunts.

Then something caught Ponytail's eye.

"Hey!" he called to the others, staring across the street. "Plug it. Plug it!" he hissed.

The two scuffling men broke apart, Piercings massaging his neck, and Silver examining the scratches on his tattooed arms.

Ponytail grunted, pointing a finger across the street. A woman was standing by a wall, lit up by the light of the electronic giraffe. She had tangled blonde hair and her makeup was smeared. She wore red high heels and a short shirt, which showed off her long, coltlike legs. Her thin shoulders shivered underneath her jacket.

Silver smiled, his metallic teeth clinking against each other. He looked at Ponytail, and nodded.

The woman eyed them nervously. She walked away, her heels clomping on the concrete. Above her, a state security camera whirred, zooming in and out, trying unsuccessfully to focus on the scene. The only other sound was a lone rat lapping from a puddle of water by the sidewalk.

Piercings picked up his broken bottle, and the three men ran forward, their shoes slapping against the ground. Then a sound like a whip cracked through the air. One of the woman's heels had snapped, and her flight was reduced to a chaotic hobble.

Piercings reached her first. Pulling her into an alley, he threw her down on the concrete. Then Piercings was on top of her, flipping her on her back and pinning her hands underneath his knees. Silver grabbed her jacket and tore it open. Buttons popped and rolled to the ground as the woman struggled to get out from under them.

Ponytail leered, clapping his hands together, jumping up and down, and grunting like a gorilla.

"Plug it! All of you plug it!"

Another figure had approached, a man wearing a blue uniform, a badge on his belt. His face was thick like a ham, and his eyes were tiny and suspicious. He whipped out a baton with a glowing white tip. "Plug it! The whole cucking block can hear you!"

Silver looked up, his eyes narrowed. "Get cucked, Badge," he spat.

The officer lunged, jamming the baton into Silver's face. He yelped and rolled backward, his throat gargling with curses.

Ponytail and Piercings stared at the officer. "We're plugged, Badge. We'll stay plugged," Piercings promised in a meek voice. He mimed zipping his lips shut.

The officer motioned to the woman's purse, which had fallen when Piercings slammed into her. "Give that to me."

None of the men moved. The woman panted in short bursts, tears further smearing her makeup. Her hands, red and shiny from the rough concrete, were still pinned down by Piercings' knees.

"Help me!" she gasped.

The officer ignored her. "I said, give it to me!" he repeated, waving his baton.

Ponytail tossed the purse to him. He turned it upside-down and shook it open. A stack of bills fluttered to the ground.

"Share them, Badge?" Piercings suggested hopefully.

The officer gathered the bills into his fists. "5 Grams Gold," he read on one of them, before stuffing them in his pocket and letting the purse drop to the ground. "Flash up, all of you. And stay plugged."

The officer passed Silver, still lying on the sidewalk, and kicked him in the ribs.

"You heard the badge, flash up!" Piercings flicked a knife toward the girl's waist, cutting through the fabric and baring her skin.

There was a loud crack, and Piercings slumped to the side, blood trickling down his forehead. Ponytail and Silver looked around, confused. They saw the brick swinging on the end of a rope only moments before it connected with their faces.

All three men lay stunned and whimpering on the sidewalk.

"You shielded?" A woman wearing a black gaiter mask approached them. Coiling the rope around her arm, she bent over Ponytail, pulled open his shirt, and felt his bare chest.

"No shield." The woman held out a vial, uncorked it, and jammed it into his nostril. Ponytail went rigid then he became limp, as spit fizzled across his cheek.

She went through his pockets, removing a wallet containing plastic bills, then moved on to Piercings. His cheeks were bloody, and some of the metal fixtures had been completely torn out by the brick. Ripping open his shirt, she uncovered a copper-colored metal medallion and tapped it on the sidewalk. It made a hollow, emasculated sound, like fingernails clinking against an empty can.

The vial squirted a second time, and the metal piercings shook on his face.

The woman rifled through his pockets, then moved on to Silver, turning him on his back with a grunt of effort. Another copper-colored medallion slid out from his shirt and landed on the sidewalk with the ripe clank of solid metal. When the woman went through Silver's pockets, she stole nothing, but rather wiped the drool from his metal teeth and helped him to his feet. Murmuring, the man stumbled into the night, leaving his two friends where they lay.

Farther down the street, the rat stopped lapping water and disappeared into the sewer.

The woman took out a small black device, beeped it several times then bent down to the blonde woman on the sidewalk and gently wiped blood from a cut on her face.

"This complimentary rescue is sponsored by Balkon Death Insurance Agency."

CHAPTER 3

BLOOD MONEY

The street was no longer empty. People poured from every door and approached the bodies of the man with the ponytail and the man with the piercings. First with caution, then with purpose, they sifted through their pockets and shoes like vultures picking at meat. Then they retreated, disappearing as quickly as they had come. A dozen state officers arrived and examined the bodies for themselves, looting whatever was left of any value before leaving.

"That would have been me."

Those were the first words the blonde woman had spoken since being rescued. Her voice sounded like she had swallowed a mouthful of chalk. She was sitting in the Gyro Valley restaurant across from the alley where the men lay, the cut on her face slowly drying. A cold gyro sat untouched on a plate in front of her.

"You don't have to look at them. They're not your concern." The woman who had rescued her appeared to be in her mid-twenties, with tan skin, dark eyes and black hair. She'd already finished her gyro. The only remains were under her fingernails and in the corners of her mouth. The brick with the rope neatly coiled around it lay on the table next to her, as did the fake copper medallion and the two wallets she had stolen.

"Hey, look at me, not them. You have a name?"

The blonde woman tore her eyes away from the alley, and stared at her rescuer. "Harriden."

"Harriden. Solid name. I'm Lemma Quartz." Lemma wiped her hands on a napkin, and then on her jeans, before reaching out and extending a hand. Harriden did not return the handshake.

"Why did you help me?"

"Balkon Death Insurance Agency likes to be a good neighbor."

"But why were you there?"

Lemma pulled out the black device. "Balkon intercepted a message. Someone was planning to attack one of our clients. Said they'd be on this street. So I came to scout around, and lucky for you. You going to finish that?" Lemma nodded at Harriden's gyro. "Because if not…"

Harriden pushed the plate toward Lemma.

"Don't look at them," Lemma warned again, as Harriden turned to face the window overlooking the alley. "You'll make yourself pukey."

"I'm already pukey; I just saw two goons get ghosted."

"No," Lemma shook her head. "I didn't ghost them. I dropped them, but they're not dead."

"They're alive? What's going to happen to them?"

"Balkon will lift them," Lemma checked the black device. "If they're on our list, then we'll ghost them. If not, we'll turn them loose back on the streets."

"What list?"

"You know what a death insurance agency is, don't you? If someone ghosts one of Balkon's clients, we put them on a list, scout them, and ghost them back."

Harriden whimpered like an injured dog.

"If you want—" Lemma gagged, spitting out her first bite of Harriden's gyro onto the table. "Sorry," she apologized, brushing the clump of food to the floor, and gargling water from her cup. "Has yogurt in it."

"You don't like yogurt?"

"I'm allergic."

"You're allergic?" Harriden's full attention was on Lemma; only the absurdity of such a remark could make her forget what she had just experienced in the alley across the street. It was as if a physician had admitted to using leeches.

"Yeah," Lemma nodded. "Since birth. One in a billion, probably."

"But they cured allergies, didn't they?"

"Mostly. I'm a special case. Used to be allergic to nearly everything. I would have starved if they hadn't invented labbed food. That's food grown in a lab."

"I know that."

"Without labbed food, I'd have starved. I remember the first time I could eat broccoli. Thought it tasted delicious, thought it was dessert." Lemma chuckled at her own joke, but Harriden had gone back to staring out the window at the prone bodies of the two men.

"You have family?" Lemma said, hoping the conversation didn't feel forced.

Harriden shrugged. "A brother. No one else. You?"

Lemma pulled out the candy wrapper with the drawing of the boy on crutches. "He's not mine, but I help take care of him. If anything happened to me, or him, or his parents, I'd want justice. I told you I'm from Balkon. Death insurance," Lemma continued. "You shielded? Because after tonight... well, you saw for yourself. It's bloody out there. But if you're shielded..."

"I don't want it."

"You should. If goons see a medallion around your neck, they won't touch you. That third goon who attacked you? I had to let him go, because he was shielded." Lemma chuckled again. "I don't want his agency coming to ghost me."

A white vehicle with the words "Balkon DIA Ambulance" had stopped next to the mouth of the alley. Workers in white uniforms emerged and lifted the two men onto stretchers.

"Or the badges could just do their job. Cucking badges," Harriden spat, shaking her head.

Lemma snorted. "That badge didn't help you tonight, did he? He lifted your purse. How much was in it?"

Harriden looked down at the table. "Twenty-five grams gold."

Outside, the Balkon ambulance drove away.

"Sorry," Lemma said. "That's really cucked. But if you had Balkon, we could scout him and make him give your gold back. If you don't have Balkon, you really shouldn't be out at night."

Harriden glared at Lemma, and pulled out a card from the pocket of her skirt. The card was imprinted with her name and a smiling photograph of her face. Her wheat-blonde hair was styled and her makeup was expertly applied. The card read "State-Issued Intimate Contact License."

"Intimate contact. You're a conk?" Lemma asked.

"I'm a sex worker, a licensed sex worker," Harriden said firmly.

"If you're a conk, then you need Balkon even more."

Harriden ignored that, putting the license back in her pocket. As she did, a food wrapper slipped out. Lemma reached for it, reading the words that were scribbled on it.

"This a list of your chads?" she asked.

"Don't!" Harriden pulled the wrapper away from Lemma's fingers. "Don't look at that."

"If you give referrals, you can earn gold. Or silver. Or whatever you want."

"I'm not telling you who my chads are." Harriden stuffed the wrapper in her pocket. "And you can go. Leave me alone."

"I want to make sure you're safe."

"Safe?" Harriden scoffed. "All you care about is pitching me death insurance. And this is just sick." She pointed to the candy wrapper with the drawing of the one-legged boy on crutches. "Using a crippled kid for advertising."

"That's not true." It was true, but Lemma would never admit it. She rose, and placed two plastic sheets of currency on the table. The first read, "Balkon: 10 Grams Silver," and the second: "Balkon: 10 mL Human AB positive."

As she left the restaurant, Lemma called out, "I hope you change your mind, Harriden. It's bloody out there."

***

Back in her apartment, Lemma sorted through the two men's wallets, pulling out several contra bills, then checked the black device she had used to summon the Balkon ambulance. She reread one of her messages:

> *[Intercepted communication. Parties claimed to be scouting and sketching Balkon member residence, made plans to meet by Gyro Valley on 83rd street 23:30]*

Lemma sighed. She had certainly found the three goons on 83rd street, but their wallets had contained only currency, nothing to suggest which Balkon member they had supposedly been scouting. She wrote some notes in red nail polish on a Gyro Valley wrapper and waved it dry. Nail polish, while messy, couldn't be traced, unlike electronic communications, which were routinely monitored. Writing materials such as pens and pencils and notebooks were available on the black market, for those who could afford them, but such luxuries were beyond Lemma's means. Instead, she used food wrappers and nail polish.

The polish having dried, she stuffed everything under a loose corner of the carpet.

Massaging her neck, she lay down on the pile of sofa cushions which served as her bed.

The walls of Lemma's apartment were bare, except for two items. There was a framed newspaper article from sixteen years ago, headlined, *"Lions, Tigers, and Giraffes, Oh My! Labbed Exotic Meat to Hit Markets"* Next to it was a photo of a young girl, her mouth full of broccoli, giving the biggest smile her stuffed cheeks would allow. In the corner of that photo was the label: Licensed by the Department of Electronic Images.

Chapter 4

Human Resources

Monday, April 16

Lemma typed with one hand, her other hand tapping the fake medallion in her pocket.

> [*Received alert at 23:00 on Sunday, April 15. Balkon had intercepted message which indicated unknown parties were scouting a Balkon member and sketching their residence. Parties were apprehended on 83rd street around 23:30. Consisted of three males. They were attempting to assault a licensed sex worker. First name Harriden. Last name unknown.*]

Lemma mentally kicked herself for not recalling the surname printed on the card Harriden had showed her. She hoped it might come back to her, but the memory remained buried in the exhausted haze of a dozen other moments from last night. She shook her head and went on typing. "All three males dropped and searched. No drawing or images of any residence found. One was released after proof of death insurance found. Other two were collected by Balkon agents. One of them possessed a counterfeit death insurance medallion. Offered death insurance coverage to Harriden. She declined."

Lemma stretched her fingers and yawned. She tapped the screen, making the text turn green and then disappear.

"What's the count this week?"

Lemma turned from the computer to see a man with red cheeks and a bald head which shone under the fluorescent lights in the office ceiling.

"Howsie, Dr. Schwartz," Lemma greeted him. "Dropped sixteen. Pitched to twenty-seven."

"Any of them actually bite?" Schwartz asked.

"Twenty said they would. Six actually got shielded."

"Claps to you! Well done," he said, and gave her a robust pat on the back. "Six out of twenty-seven, almost twenty-five percent."

Lemma smirked. "Like I say, I'm Balkon's best agent."

"Contractor," Schwartz corrected her with a wink. "Also, Lemma," Schwartz lowered his voice, glancing around to make sure none of the occupants of the surrounding cubicles were listening. "Just heard from payroll division that you've been getting into food ration fraud? Please tell me you would never do such a thing."

Lemma snorted, reaching under her desk for a bag labeled "Disenfranchised Assistance: Dairy Rations. Manufactured by Phronesis Tech."

"All sheep cheese this time," she said.

"Bright, bright." Schwartz searched through the bag, sniffing like a hungry rodent. "Smell that, Lemma? Maximized value density. Sheep cheese costs the same rations as cow cheese, but resells for twice the rate."

"We talked about that last week. I was the one that convinced you, remember?" Lemma said.

"Definitely one of our ideas."

"It was mine."

"A solid team effort."

Lemma snorted again. "And my gold?"

Schwartz offered her a single dyed plastic bill bearing an image of his own face.

"Redeemable for 1/20,000 of a kidney transplant. Oh, Dr. Schwartz, you shouldn't have!"

Schwartz beamed. "Printed them off the other day. Always dreamed of spitting out my own currency."

"This will be perfect for when I need 1/20,000 of my kidney replaced."

"Ah, but that's the beauty of it. You save up another 19,999 of them and you have yourself a free transplant."

"But the beauty of gold is that it's what we agreed on."

Schwartz sighed, taking back the bill and replacing it with several plastic leaves which read, "Balkon: 0.25 Grams Gold."

"Bright," Lemma said, pocketing the bills with satisfaction.

"If you happen to know anyone," Schwartz said, again lowering his voice. "Got a fresh new set of organs the other night."

"Did he have half his head shaved? Or a jackload of metal in his face?"

"It was a goon with piercings. He was yours?"

"Yes," Lemma smiled.

"Bright, Lemma! Not a single organ damaged. Healthy, pink…"

Lemma closed her eyes, trying not to imagine the men from last night on Schwartz's operating table.

Schwartz slipped Lemma another plastic bill. "Bright," he murmured. "Keep the bodies flowing."

"You know I'm only dropping actual murderers, right?" Lemma stressed. "I'm not going to target a random just for their organs."

"Cuck no!" Schwartz was horrified. "But if you do, tell me, gel? And for now, I'm also offering a discount on mammograms. Two for the price of one."

"If I see any mams, I'll let them know."

"And, uh, how's the little one doing?" Schwartz patted his belly. "Started kicking yet?"

"Ha ha," Lemma said coolly.

Schwartz winked and left, as a young man approached Lemma's desk.

"Howsie, Lemma!"

"Jax." She returned to her computer, and pretended to type.

"Heard you ghosted someone last night. How was it? Was it scary?" Jax Yedra, from the Evidence and Documentation team, was a few years younger than Lemma. He had a baby face and a wispy mustache that looked like he'd glued dryer lint under his nose.

"I didn't ghost anyone, I dropped them. Balkon does the ghosting." Lemma hoped it wasn't Schwartz doing the ghosting, and forced herself not to think of him pushing a syringe into an unconscious body on a table.

"Oh. Have you ever ghosted someone?"

"No. I'm a contractor. Contractors don't ghost." Lemma pretended to concentrate on typing, but Jax wouldn't take the hint.

"You spect you could? I've always spected what it would be like ghosting someone, right?" He mimed firing a gun.

Lemma stood up. "Jax, I'm choked right now; I have to talk to Curio."

"I have to meet with her, too." Jax followed Lemma. "You spect you could, though? If you had to? Ghost someone?"

Lemma grimaced, the insides of her mouth becoming slick. "Can we talk about literally anything else?"

"Could you show me how you dropped them? Martial arts? Jujitsu?"

Lemma sighed. "Yes. Raise your fists."

A cluster of Balkon employees had paused what they were doing to watch them.

"Now bend your fist toward you, and stick out your elbow toward me. Bright. Your fist should be almost touching your chin…"

The door nearest them opened, and a dozen men and women walked into the office.

"Jax, stop being a twank," one of the men said.

"She's teaching me—"

But whatever reply Jax had planned was drowned out, first by Lemma pushing his elbow and driving his own fist into his face, then by a chorus of laughter from the observers.

"There. How to make your opponent hit themselves," Lemma announced, giving a mock curtsey.

His face throbbing painfully, his pride injured, Jax wanted to dish out a comeback, but couldn't think of a witty reply.

"Quartz!"

At the sound of her boss' curt voice Lemma stopped smiling. The crowd of employees dissipated, leaving her and Jax alone.

"Quartz. My office." Curio Agarwal wore her waist-length black hair in a thick braid. A red bindi was glued above her eyebrows, which sloped downwards in permanent dissatisfaction.

Lemma entered, closing the door behind her. Balkon headquarters was set up in an abandoned refrigerator factory called Facility 9381, and the single window in Curio's office boasted a breathtaking view of a crumbling brick wall.

"Claps to you." Curio's voice did not sound congratulatory.

"Claps? For what?"

"Schwartz tells me you're going to be a mother."

Lemma rolled her eyes. "He told you? That's private!"

"If I'm going to send you assignments, I should know if you're swelling. Is it a boy or a girl?"

Lemma scoffed. "It's a guaranteed seat on the CityBus. You should try it. Brighter tax bracket, too."

"I'm not going to fake a pregnancy for tax purposes. It's called integrity."

"That's bright," Lemma replied. "I'd hate for a company that ghosts people not to have integrity."

Curio smiled stiffly. "I read your report."

"I dropped two goons. One was a Balkon target."

"Claps," Curio said sarcastically. "What about what I told you to look for? Did you learn who they were scouting?"

"No."

"And what about the fake medallion?"

"One of the goons I dropped had a fake Axiom medallion. It was the color of copper but I spect it was tin or aluminum. Spelled out Axiom Death Insurance Agency, painted to look legit."

"Sounds like Axiom's problem, not Balkon's."

"But Curio, if people can make fake Axiom medallions, they can do the same with Balkon. And everyone will wear those instead of buying ours, and we'll be cucked."

Curio glared at Lemma. "Did you keep it? Can I see it?"

"Lost it on the street." Lemma forced herself to stare into Curio's eyes without blinking.

Curio sighed. "Are you finished? As I said, I'm choked."

"One more thing…" Lemma weighed how favorable Curio was feeling. "Since I have the highest record on sales, I was specting I could start training to be an agent."

"You have the highest record?"

"Highest rate. I pitched twenty-seven people this week, and got six to bite. That's over twenty percent."

"I don't care what the rate is," Curio said. "You got six new members to bite. Pathetic. That's one of the weakest totals in the office."

"I'm trying!" Lemma leaned forward. "But no one will bite when Axiom has brighter rates, faster response times, and they still manage to pay their agents brighter."

"Time's up. Bounce. If you have complaints, you can give them to Human Resources." Curio jerked her head toward a waste bin, which was labeled "Balkon HR."

CHAPTER 5

DIPSOCENE

Lemma wrinkled her nose, wading through a swarm of children old enough to smell like chicken broth, but not so old as to master the art of regular showers.

"Howsie, Lisa," a school security guard said, not taking his eyes off his tablet.

"Lemma," she corrected, pressing her thumbprint on the glass slide in front of her. The security guard waved her past without bothering to correct himself.

"Lemma!"

A boy hobbled toward her on crutches, smiling so broadly that Lemma almost forgot her exasperation with Curio.

"Howsie, Milligram."

Milligram released the crutches and threw his arms around her ribs. "Lemma, scope this! Today we painted a horse." He pulled out a glass tablet, and tapped the corner to bring up a collection of smudges that, when viewed creatively, could be interpreted as a horse.

"That's bright!" Lemma said, holding it close. "That's real bright, Milligram."

"And then during recess, I found a bug, scope at this."

Milligram reached into his pocket, and pulled out a black beetle the size of a grape.

"It's— wait, it was moving earlier."

"It was alive earlier," Lemma corrected grimly. "Doesn't look alive now."

Milligram inspected the beetle.

"Excuse me?" a woman approached them, eyeing Lemma with a tight smile. "Howsie, I'm subbing for Gram's homeroom teacher, I don't think we've met."

"Lemma Quartz."

"Are you a parent, or…" the teacher raised her eyebrows, leaving unspoken the glaring difference between Milligram's dark complexion and Lemma's lighter skin tone.

"Registered childcare provider. I lift him from school when his mother works late." Lemma held up a visitor's badge that showed both hers and Milligram's face, along with their names and descriptions:

> Annalemma Quartz:
> CityLink: 7214853.
> Age: 26
> 162 cm
> Asian
>
> Gram Mills:
> CityLink: 7348271
> Age: 11
> 140 cm
> African

The woman examined the badge. "Have a good afternoon," she said, and walked away.

"Milligram?" Lemma asked. "Could we scope your classroom? Real flash?"

"I have my stuff here." Milligram tapped the strap of his backpack, and collected his crutches, which had been balancing upright on self-correcting feet since he had released them to hug Lemma.

"Bright, but I want to see what your room looks like."

"You've seen it a hundred times."

"Milligram, don't edge me. I'll even give you a treat."

Milligram straightened, his eyes widening in excitement. He bounced down the hall on his right foot, his shorter left leg swinging.

Halfway down the hall, Lemma stopped at a door. "Milligram, this is the science room?"

"Yes."

"Can we squat here? Just for a mite?"

"You said you wanted to see my classroom."

"I know, I flipped. Want to scope your science room," Lemma opened the door. "Milligram!"

He turned around and followed her into the room.

Lemma looked through shelves of beakers and bottles. "How often do you have class here?"

"Mondays, Wednesdays, and Fridays."

In the corner was the largest desk, the teacher's. Lemma tugged the middle drawer open. Inside was an envelope filled with plastic notes, each reading "Balkon: 10 Grams Silver."

"Sometimes we go outside, but in here we always have to wear aprons, unless we're scoping a video."

Lemma took off her left shoe.

"…and then he put the vinegar in, and it went real fizzy."

Lemma pocketed the envelope, and pulled a small vial of pills out of her shoe, setting it on the desk.

"Excuse me?"

Lemma snapped around, so fast that she felt a spasm of electricity zing up the side of her neck. It was Milligram's substitute teacher.

"Can I help you?" The sub was approaching, eyebrows raised in suspicion. Lemma hastily shut the drawer as Milligram joined them at the desk.

"I was just… Milligram was just…"

"You're not supposed to be in here, Ms. Quarter," the woman said.

"Quartz," Lemma muttered. She stuffed her left foot back into her shoe.

"You scoping for something?"

"No."

"Maybe the front office could help?" the woman pulled out a glass rectangle. "Should I call them?"

"I…"

"Because if we see any people where they don't belong, we're supposed to report it. The state doesn't jack around with security. We can get fined."

"Fined?"

"Very hefty fines." The woman spoke slowly, nodding her head for emphasis.

Lemma's hand dipped into the envelope in her pocket and reached forward timidly. The substitute teacher shook her hand. Finding a slip of plastic currency in her palm, she smiled.

"But I spect you're gel, so I'll bounce. Have a good evening, Gram. You did real bright today."

Pocketing the slip of plastic, the teacher left the science room.

"Now, Milligram, you don't need—" Lemma turned to the boy, but her attempt to explain herself fizzled. The plastic vial she had left on the desk was unscrewed, and Milligram was putting something into his mouth.

"Oh cuck, Milligram, spit it out. Spit it out!" She grabbed his jaw, pinching his nose until his jaw opened. He gagged, coughing out a small white pill to the floor.

"Come here." Lemma grabbed him, kicking away his crutches, which remained upright as she dragged him to the sink.

"Wash your mouth out. Don't swallow." She pulled him up by his pants, pushing his face into the water.

"Lemma!" he gasped.

She set the boy back on the floor, standing back as he coughed water down the front of his shirt.

"I'm so sorry, Milligram."

She hugged his small body against hers, feeling him shake.

"Lemma!"

"I'm sorry, Milligram, but you can't pop chemies in your mouth without asking."

"I spected it was my chemie."

"I know, Milligram, but lots of chemies look the same. Yours are right here." She pulled open his backpack and opened a pill case which read,

"Dipsocene. To alleviate phantom pains. Manufactured by Phronesis Tech."

"Pop that," Lemma said, handing him a pill.

As he swallowed, she crawled on her hands and knees, pressing her cheek to the grimy floor until she saw the pill he had spat out. She washed it down the sink, then placed the pill vial in the middle drawer of the desk. She pulled out a black device from her pocket, and sent a message to a client.

[*Made delivery in science room. Collected payment*]

"Lemma? Is that a blink?" Milligram asked.

"No, it's…it's…" Lemma sighed. "Yes. It's a blink."

"Mom said blinks are contra. That only goons use them to talk to other goons."

Lemma sighed again. "Milligram?"

He looked at her, water dripping from his chin and down his chest.

"I'll give you an ice cream if you don't spill about this to your mom, gel?"

CHAPTER 6

WILCO RESIDENTIAL ZONE

"Milligram let's bounce here," Lemma suggested, as the CityBus slowed to a halt.

"This isn't where I live," Milligram said, between licks of a double-scoop ice cream cone. He had somehow managed to get pink smears on both cheeks as well as the top of each crutch.

"I know, but I want to take a walk. It'll be bright."

"Lemma…"

"Don't edge me, Milligram. Flash it."

Milligram stood obediently, balancing on his crutches. He was still licking the ice cream as Lemma led him through the empty bus section, past a cracked sign which read, "Expectant Mothers Only." The section reserved for pregnant women was at the back of the CityBus, near the exhaust fumes which billowed out like a noxious fog. No pregnant woman who cared about her baby would ever dare make use of these seats, so Lemma, whose pregnancy was only a checkbox in some government tax file, had the section entirely to herself and Gram.

"Won't Mom scope that we're gone?" Milligram asked. They were walking through a neighborhood of duplex houses.

"Your mom works late tonight, right?"

"Yes, but—"

"So we'll get back before she does; she won't even know. Gel?"

Milligram narrowed his eyes, trying to determine how to wring another ice cream out of the situation. Lemma examined the red nail polish scribbles on the Gyro Valley wrapper from the previous night.

"Are you steady you know where we're going?" Drips of pink tricked down Milligram's chin as he tried to lick the ice cream in sync with his steps.

"Yes, we're almost there."

"Can I have another chemie? My phantoms are coming back."

"Milligram, I'm sorry, but you can't pop another chemie when you just had one."

"Why?"

Lemma bent to his level. She licked her thumbs and rubbed the ice cream smears off Milligram's cheeks. "Because if you take too many they can jack you up. Make you paralyzed, or even ghost you. Gel?"

Milligram nodded, his brown eyes wide. "Gel."

Lemma looked at the Gyro Valley wrapper. "We're here. Careful!"

Milligram's crutch slipped into a pothole, and Lemma grabbed his shoulder before he could fall.

"This road is cucky," he grumbled.

"Don't say that word, Milligram."

"Why not?"

"It's not a nice word."

"You say it all the time."

"It's a bad word. So don't say it."

"This road is… clucky," Milligram said with gleeful emphasis.

"Milligram, don't!"

"I didn't! I said clucky; it's not the same."

They were standing on the front porch of one of the duplexes. Lemma knocked on the rightmost door.

"What are we doing here?" Milligram whined.

"It's a secret. Can you lock a secret?"

"I spect? Maybe I'll spill to my mom."

"Don't be a twank, and don't say that word either."

"What word? Twank?"

"Milligram!" Lemma sighed. "Have you ever pitched something for a fundraiser for your school?"

"For church we do. We pitch cakes."

Lemma tensed at Milligram's mention of his church. "Cakes. That's what we're doing. We're pitching cakes."

"For church?"

The door opened. A middle-aged man stood there, a frown on his face.

"Howsie. Can I help you?" He stared at Lemma, and then at Milligram.

Milligram looked up at Lemma expectantly.

"Howsie, my name's Lemma Quartz." She put out her hand, which hung in the air awkwardly. "Do you have a mite to talk?"

"Talk about what?"

"We're with the Tiresian Church, whipping support for our Fall Intervention Program."

"The Tiresian Church," the man sneered, then hastily replaced his disdainful expression with a polite smile.

"Lemma, we're not…" Milligram began, but Lemma nudged him. "If you already supported our Fall Intervention Program…"

"I didn't. You're the first to scout Wilco."

Lemma looked around. This neighborhood, Wilco Residential Zone, was a paradox: well-kept duplexes rather than cheap apartments, but the street was filled with potholes, and on the sidewalks there were more cracks than pavement.

"Your zone looks bright." Lemma made herself smile. "Can I pitch you a selection of cakes?"

"What kind?"

Lemma chuckled awkwardly. "We, uh— Milligram, what's your favorite?"

"Strawberry-banana."

"Strawberry-banana. Is that bright?"

"That's bright," the man said, his voice empty of excitement. "Do I fill out a form?"

"If you give me your name and CityLink, I can give you a reminder."

"Name: Fremen Orea. CityLink: 7178635. You going to write that down?"

"No."

"How are you going to remember it?" Fremen asked.

"This isn't a very safe zone, is it?" Lemma lowered her voice, gesturing to the street.

Fremen's eyes narrowed.

"Have you ever spected about getting shielded?" Lemma asked.

"You need to bounce," Fremen said curtly, and started to close the door.

"We have a referral program. A friend referred you, so you can get a discount on our first month of insurance."

"Who referred me?"

"Harriden."

Fremen Orea winced. "Harriden? How— how do you know— I don't know anyone named Harriden."

The Gyro Valley wrapper with Fremen's address burned in her pocket.

"That's gel. It could be a mistake. We can go through our records to scope who it was that referred you."

She stopped. The sound of metal banging on metal came from several houses away.

"Are those goons?" Lemma asked.

"Get in. Flash it, come in." Fremen pulled Lemma and Milligram inside. "Be steady with me. How do you know Harriden, and why did she tell you about me? Which agency are you with?"

"Balkon Death Insurance Agency. Harriden is one of our members, and she referred a list of about a dozen people who might be interested in coverage. I assume you're a friend of hers?"

Fremen scanned Lemma's face, trying to read her mind. "Friends," he muttered darkly.

The sound of banging metal continued, getting louder.

"I know what you're pitching, but you can't help us here."

"Balkon shields lots of zones throughout the whole city," Lemma said.

"Not Wilco. It's jacked up here. Goons everywhere."

"Goons won't edge you if you're shielded with Balkon. We can give you better security for your home: monitor, cameras, alarms."

"Fremen?" A woman was walking downstairs. She paused and stared at Lemma in surprise.

"Referral program for—"

"Tiresian Church, whipping up money!" shouted Fremen, cutting Lemma off. "I'll buy us a cake, gel?"

"Gel." The woman turned and went back upstairs.

"Do not tell her about death insurance," Fremen warned. "And I can't buy it. I'm sorry, but I can't."

"Just try it." Lemma pulled out the fake medallion from the previous night. "Keep this for a week. Wear it around the zone, see if the goons edge you."

Fremen examined the medallion. "What if my wife scopes me with it? You'll shield me from her?"

Lemma snorted. "I'll be back for it in a week." She shepherded Milligram to the door, saying loudly, "We'll send you your cake. The Tiresian Church appreciates your support!"

CHAPTER 7

EDEYONG

Tuesday, April 24

A blink buzzed in Lemma's pocket, with a message from a contact named "NewTulip786."

> [*Target will arrive in ten minutes. With two men and three women*]

Lemma pocketed the blink, and placed a printed photograph on the glass counter in front of her, letting it soak into her eyes, drowning out the chatter and clinks of glasses from the rest of the bar.

"Howsie. Howsie?"

She looked up at the bartender, and hastily covered the photograph.

"Raspberry Blush." Lemma pulled out a bill worth twenty grams of silver.

"Put it away," the bartender hissed, pretending to stare at the ceiling. "That's six thousand leisure rations."

Lemma grimaced, whispered an apology, and pressed her thumb to the glass counter. At the touch, an image of her own face appeared, with the message "The Edeyong Bar thanks you for your purchase. 6000 Leisure Rations."

She sipped the can of fizzy raspberry drink, and observed the venue. In front of her, within the glass counter, swam a school of fish. Their scales glowed as they observed a world of elbows and knees, darting away whenever someone set down a drink too roughly. To her right was a man, missing an arm, who was persuading a friend to come to church with him. To her left were several women whose seats glowed blue. The seats at The Edeyong Bar followed a color code: a lady in a blue seat wished to be left alone, while a lady seated in red expected strangers to buy her drinks. A man in red was in for a night of lonely disappointment.

"Twank. Can he go a rimming day without twanking off about what a saint he is?" the one-armed man to her right said loudly.

Lemma followed his gaze; he was watching a screen on the wall display an interview with several businessmen. Text crawled across, "New Growth for Phronesis Tech."

"That's Wade Syan," she said.

The two men turned to her. "Claps to you," the one-armed man said mockingly. The other sniggered and added, "We know who he is. He's a twank."

"He is not a twank," Lemma pushed her can of Raspberry Blush away, and raised her shoulders to seem more intimidating. "If it wasn't for him, you wouldn't be popping any of this." She gestured to the plates which had accumulated between the two men.

"What do you care, sushi?" The men looked at each other and chortled.

Lemma felt her face getting hot, but before she could retort, someone called out, "Lemma Quartz!"

It was Fremen Orea, with the fake Axiom medallion around his neck. He stumbled toward her and pulled her into a hug. "Lemma!" he repeated happily. He set down a glass on the counter with a loud clink, and the glowing fish scattered.

"Howsie, Fremen." Lemma pried his arms off her, and stared in disbelief at the woman at Fremen's side.

"You know Harriden, right?" Fremen backed away from Lemma, putting his arm around his conk.

"Lemma said you referred me," Fremen told Harriden, tapping the medallion. Harriden threw a resentful look at Lemma.

"Should you be here?" Lemma asked. "Is your wife going to scope you?"

"No, we're gel," Fremen said, and Lemma wished she owned a camera to capture the bravado on his face. "Wife's staying in tonight, we are gel!"

"All gel," Lemma muttered, and swiped her finger against her stool, turning it blue. "Fremen, it's bright to scope you here, but—"

"This medal," Fremen pressed on, hugging Harriden tighter. "Bulletproof! No one edges me when I'm wearing it."

"I know," Harriden said coldly.

"Two or three nights ago, a goon passes me in Wilco. Pulls out a knife, about to ghost me. I swing this at him, he bounces like a twank," Fremen said joyously.

"It's been over a week. You going to bite on the death insurance?" Lemma asked, removing the medallion from around his neck. "Cause I'll need this back."

"I'll bite, I'll bite," Fremen said. "Wait! I'll be back in a mite." He staggered toward the bathroom, leaving the women by themselves.

Harriden leaned over to Lemma, the cut from a week ago still faintly visible on her cheek. "If you ever pitch to my chads again, I'll have you ghosted, you squint," she hissed.

"Don't call me a squint," Lemma retorted, as her pocket buzzed twice. She pulled out two blinks. One had another message from NewTulip786, alerting her that the target had entered Edeyong. The other was from Curio Agarwal, demanding that all agents and contractors report to Balkon headquarters immediately.

Lemma cursed to herself, looking through the crowd of badges and conks, until she saw the man from her photograph.

"Scope at that," Harriden said with disgust, staring at a badge who had planted his nose in the neck of a teenage girl, running his fingers through her red hair. "Even younger than I was when I started. What are you doing? Lemma!"

Lemma was already off her seat, brushing past the badge and the underage girl. As NewTulip786 had promised, the man from the photograph was with two men and three women. A server with bare shoulders beat Lemma to the table. Lemma cursed, straining her ears to hear what they were saying as the group bantered and ordered drinks. She returned to the bar.

"Have some wine!" Fremen slammed a jug of wine on the counter, as the fish fled once more. "Lemma?"

Her blink was buzzing with more messages from Curio. She fought her way to the other end of the bar, waiting as the server set out six drinks on a platter.

"Could I have another Raspberry Blush?" Lemma asked.

The server gave her an irritated look. "I'm choked now, wait a mite."

"I'd like to report an unliced photograph," Lemma said loudly.

The server's eyes widened. "What? Where?"

Lemma pulled out the photograph of her target. "Here. See?" She pointed to the corner, which was blank.

"You have to contact the city," Lemma said smugly, as the server gave her a look of pure venom. Calling her a 'squint' he retreated behind a curtain to report the violation.

Lemma glanced around, removed a vial from her shoe, and splashed some into each of the six drinks. Within several days, the target, along with his five friends, would be rushed to the hospital, where NewTulip786 would be waiting.

Lemma threw down a bill of Balkon silver, and left Edeyong, Curio's blink buzzing in her pocket like an enraged hornet.

CHAPTER 8

THE ASSIGNMENT

"I'm here!" Lemma shouted, flushed and out of breath. "Howsie? Curio?"

As she entered, the squares of light on the ceiling flickered on, illuminating her path through the empty cubicles.

"Curio?"

"Over here," Curio answered from her office.

"I got your messages," Lemma said, wiping sweat from her forehead. "I flashed over here. Where is everyone?"

"They're all choked tonight." Curio's face looked tired without her usual makeup.

"What happened?"

"There's been a death, a possible murder. One of our top clients. I need you to scout."

"You're making me an agent?"

"I am assigning you to scrape evidence on a scene. If you perform bright, I will consider putting you on track for agent training."

Curio continued talking. Even though Lemma was certain she was missing out on vital information, she was so caught up in a vision of herself as a full agent that she could not focus on Curio's words. She saw herself scaling rooftops, tackling faceless men, whipping bricks at their skulls—

"Lemma?"

"Yes, I'm listening."

"You'll be accompanied."

"By you?"

Someone knocked the door, and Lemma turned to see Jax. He wore an apron covered with rusty brown smears.

"Howsie, Curio, Lemma. Sorry for being late. I was helping Dr. Schwartz sew up a stabbing."

"You're apron is inside out," Lemma told him. She turned to Curio. "Are you steady?" she asked in disbelief. "Him? He's accompanying me?"

"You'll need someone to show you protocol."

"I know how to scrape a crime scene!"

"Oh?" Curio raised her eyebrows. "When was the last scene you examined?"

"I read the manual."

Curio glared, and rubbed her forehead. "Jax, get cleaned up and take her. Ingo is waiting for you. We have a private car ready. If you have any complaints…" She pointed at the Human Resources waste bin.

***

"When scraping a scene, the most important thing…"

"Plug it, Jax."

Lemma had not been in any vehicle other than a CityBus for over a decade, and she wanted to savor the clean air in silence.

"Curio said I'm supposed to train you," Jax protested.

"I scoped the manual a hundred times. I know how to lift prints, question witnesses, all of that."

"But you've never done it in real life."

"Then I'll learn from scoping you. In the betweens, plug it."

Jax fell silent, and the car hummed through streets, passing clusters of people sleeping on the sidewalks, badges with electric batons, and girls waiting in alleys for hungry chads.

"Jax, give me the camera."

He grumbled, "Curio said only I get to use it."

"Jax, come on!"

"No, it's too valuable."

"I haven't had one in years. Jax, please?"

"I'm sorry, Lemma," Jax turned to her. "I really am. But Curio's going to ask, and I'm jack at lying."

Outside their car was a conk lying on her side below an electronic sign warning about unlicensed chemie dealers. It would have been a perfect image to photograph, Lemma thought ruefully.

"You used to take photos?" Jax asked.

"When I was a girl. Had a camera. Dad ran a studio."

"You have a lice?"

"No," Lemma murmured. An image of children jumping in front of a church flashed through her mind. "Lost it five years ago."

Jax didn't ask what had cost Lemma her Electronic Image License, so they continued in silence until they approached their destination.

"You have arrived," the car said politely, as the doors opened.

They were at an apartment building that reached hundreds of floors upward. On its side hung dozens of glass elevators which allowed a full view of the city.

"Never been here before," Jax said. "What do you spect this costs? Billion housing rations a year?"

"Please do not ask them."

"Wasn't going to," he murmured.

Jax touched his thumb to one of the glass elevator doors. "Jax Yedra and Lemma Quartz, here to visit Ingo Syan."

Lemma's entire body went numb.

CHAPTER 9

THE DEBT

Ingo Syan.

The name hung in Lemma's ears, and her mouth drenched itself with saliva as she bent forward, unable to prevent herself from emptying her stomach over the elevator floor.

Jax cursed and stood on his tiptoes, trying to avoid the reeking puddle. Lemma didn't care; she was so dizzy that without her slick palm pressed against the glass wall she would have fallen into her own mess.

Ingo Syan.

This is a joke, she told herself. How had she not heard the full name when Curio mentioned it? She prayed a desperate prayer that there was another Ingo Syan, that this was a mistake, but she knew there was no chance of it. There was only one woman in that whole world with that name, which meant that the death they were investigating was—

Wade Syan, CEO of Phronesis Tech.

Lemma leaned her burning cheek on the glass. When she opened her eyes she saw not her own current reflection, but the face of a nine-year-old girl, the same girl as in the photo in her apartment, but gaunt and puffy-eyed, with raw, cracked skin.

"Lemma?" Jax asked cautiously. "What's wrong?"

Against the hum of the ascending elevator, Lemma heard the crunch of her first slice of bread, tasted the first drippy, fleshy bite of a peach that didn't inflame her mouth. For the first time in her childhood, she was free to eat almost whatever food she wished, and meals went from dreaded experiences to exciting adventures. She had been the first child in history to fall in love with broccoli, and the first carrot she ate was so sweet and cool it was like a rich dessert. She had stuffed herself at every meal, and skyrocketed past her classmates, growing a tenth of a meter that summer.

In a cardboard box in her childhood room, buried beneath a photo of a sunset and other mementos, was a letter, handwritten in purple marker, addressed to the same apartment she and Jax were now about to visit.

'Dear Mr. Wade Syan, thank you for making food that is good for me to eat. My favorite is broccoli or meatballs. Please make milk that I can drink, it still makes me pukey. Love, Annalemma Quartz'

"Lemma, what's wrong? Should I blink Dr. Schwartz? Or Curio?" Jax fought for her attention.

Lemma's parents had never mailed the letter; she found it while cleaning out her room several years later. She had dreamed of one day meeting him in person, delivering the letter by hand, or at least telling him how his company's labbed food had finally allowed her to grow from a skeleton into a real person.

"Lemma?" Jax asked.

"I can't do this. Tell Curio we're going back." Lemma wiped her lips.

"What's happening?"

"Bring us back down!" she hissed.

The elevator stopped. They were on the top floor.

"We've been assigned to a case, Lemma! If you're pukey, you have to go back, but I can't— they need me here."

The glass doors opened, and Lemma and Jax stared inside Wade Syan's apartment.

CHAPTER 10

TESSELLATIONS

Lemma refused to believe that she was really here, after watching his interview at Edeyong less than an hour ago. The apartment didn't even seem real, but dreamlike, decorated with exotic statues from every century and culture. There were cold marble Caesars and screaming Hindu gods with blue faces. From the walls hung proud heads of the animals Wade Syan had engineered away from extinction: elephants, rhinos, and giraffes. Skins of cloned leopards and zebras were draped over sofas, whose armrests were lined with pangolin scales. The floor was a parquet pattern of ivory tiles, not from an actual elephant, but rather cultivated in a Phronesis Tech laboratory.

"Howsie— uh, good evening," Jax corrected himself, and Lemma snapped back to the moment, focusing on the people Jax addressed. They were two men in uniforms with gold and blue badges which read "Phronesis Tech Security" and a pale woman with hair so blonde it was almost silver.

"You're from Balkon?" the woman asked.

Lemma had seen Ingo Syan many times on the news. She was rarely away from Wade Syan's side, always standing several feet behind him, smiling silently in the flashes of a thousand cameras pointed at her husband. It was bizarre to see her in person, and even more so without her man before her. Her face, usually artfully made-up, was bare, her eyes puffy, her lips thin.

"Yes," Jax said, nodding. "From Balkon. I'm Jax Yedra, and this is Lemma Quartz. Lemma?"

Lemma swallowed, forced saliva into the back of her mouth, and said, "Good evening."

"I'm sorry for your loss," Jax mumbled awkwardly.

Somehow, beneath the numbness of the moment, Lemma found just enough contempt to glare at him.

"You found your husband in the bathtub?" Jax asked. "Would you show us?"

They snapped on rubber gloves, and Ingo led them and the security guards through the living room and hall, past twenty years' worth of framed articles chronicling Wade Syan's journey, from his design competitions in Renning University, to his first patent at only twenty-one, to founding Phronesis Tech.

"I have that same one," Lemma whispered to no one, pointing to the article about exotic animals grown in laboratories.

The bedroom had even more framed articles on the walls, with headlines such as, "*Underground Urban Farms?*" and "*First Artificial Rhino Embryo a Success!*" One was an opinion piece Wade Syan had written himself: "*Meat Without Pain: the New Vegan Diet?*"

Lemma licked her teeth, the bloody taste of the first meat she had ever tried returning to her mouth.

There were articles describing companies he had acquired: Mabel Corporation, Sphix, and Omnibus Industries. Other articles boasted of Syan's politics and philanthropy, next to photos of him standing with congresspeople, governors, top journalists, the pope, the president. One photo showed him wearing sunglasses, surrounded by a crowd of adults and children, some with sunglasses and canes, some with crutches. "*Syan pledges new building for Tiresian Church.*"

Lemma passed a nightstand, which held a pair of sunglasses and a pitcher of water.

"He wore those inside?" Lemma asked.

"To shut out the light. He used them for meditation," Ingo replied.

They arrived at the bathroom. The door had been forced open. A large window overlooked the galaxy of streetlights and apartments below. The room's spacious interior was covered in shiny ceramic tiles in turquoise blue, gold, black, and emerald green. The pieces were all the same shape: an oblong pentagon with each side a different length. They fit together in an elegant tessellation, no two tiles of the same color touching.

On a raised dais was a bathtub big enough to fit at least two people comfortably. There was one person in it now: Wade Syan.

There was no blood, no sign of violence. His skin was unmarked, soft and pale. His hair swayed in the water like seaweed. His knees were the only part of him exposed to the air, two doughy mounds which emerged like young islands from the primitive oceans. His head rested on the bottom of the tub, his face distorted by the water, his eyes open but unseeing.

Lemma didn't want to look, but she couldn't look away. She had often imagined meeting Wade Syan face to face, shaking his hand, smiling into a camera with him rather than watching Jax point a camera at his lifeless body. In the years since her first piece of broccoli, she had rehearsed entire conversations with him, sometimes even in dreams. She had written school reports on him, watched his interviews and speeches, cheered every new innovation from Phronesis Tech, never imagining that her first encounter with him would be in this tub of water.

"Ms. Syan," Jax said, his voice wavering. "When did you find him?"

"Two hours ago," Ingo said.

"What were you doing?"

"Reading in the living room. He'd gone in. Said he'd take a bath. That was the last thing he ever said to me."

Jax snapped photos of the rest of the room, including the bathrobe lying on the tiled floor, the last article of clothing Wade had ever worn. "We'd like to be alone here, that gel?"

Ingo and the guards left and closed the door.

"Lemma, you gel?" Jax asked gently.

Lemma shook her head. "You?"

"No, not at all." Jax stared at the body in the water. "That has to be the worst way to ghost off."

"In a bathroom?"

"No. Drowning. Almost drowned when I was seven. Never swam since."

"I'd always hoped to meet him," Lemma said quietly, wiping her nose, and rubbing her dry eyes. "Never spected it would be like this. I used to be allergic to everything, before Phronesis Tech, and labbed food. I'd have starved if it wasn't for him."

"We should scrape for prints, gel?" Jax asked.

Lemma nodded.

When every smudge of every fingerprint was black and visible, they went back into the living room, where they questioned Ingo and the security guards. None of them said they'd seen Wade go into the bathroom, or suspected anything was wrong. Not until Ingo had entered the bedroom, calling out to her husband, asking how long he would be, and hearing no reply.

"The door only locks from the inside?" Jax asked. "And it was locked when you found it?"

Ingo nodded. "They had to break it open."

There were only two entrances to the apartment: the glass elevator which Lemma and Jax had arrived in, and the balcony door in the living room.

"Are there surveillance cameras?" Jax looked at the guards.

They said every room in the apartment was under video surveillance, except the bedroom and the bathroom.

"Could someone see into the bathroom from another building?" Lemma asked.

Jax remained in the living room, lifting prints, while Ingo and Lemma returned to the bathroom. The window was large enough that she could view other apartments, and allowed others to see inside.

"No privacy?" Lemma asked, feeling the edges of the frame. The window shifted slightly. "Does this open?"

"Usually. It's been jammed shut for several months. Never got around to fixing it. Is it important?"

"It's only important that no one was able to get it and out," Lemma told her.

Then she heard the buzz of a blink. On instinct she checked the one in her pocket, but neither Curio, nor NewTulip786, nor any of her other clients had messaged her. She looked toward the bathtub, trying to find where the noise was coming from.

"Ms. Syan," she said. "Would you show the surveillance records to Jax?"

Ingo left. Lemma approached the bathtub, staring at the tiled wall where the noise seemed to be coming from. It took her a few seconds to spot a tile whose grout was missing. She gingerly reached over Syan's body and dug her gloved fingernails under the tile. It came loose, revealing a small hiding space. In it was a blink. The blink had only one message, a long string of numbers:

[11590114811322012081125611486014070140011 45011596015960160211651117080192501816018 60119020195412104020520210412155122001244 20244202709024041254602505125591263412652 12723027520281902883029111298603008130511 3115131501352603723033031336413581034581 36510]

"Lemma?" Jax had silently entered the room.

Startled, Lemma dropped the blink, sending it splashing into the tub. Without thinking, she plunged her hands in the water. Her knuckles brushed against Syan's chest as she felt around for the blink. Even through her gloves she could feel his cold, wet skin. She gagged, finally fishing out the device, but the water had already done its damage. The blink was dead, and the message was lost.

CHAPTER 11

CLOSED

Friday, April 27

"Lemma?"

Someone knocked on her apartment door, calling to her, but Lemma pulled her head under her covers, balling her body as small as she could on the sofa cushions. Whoever this was, it wasn't worth getting up in the middle of the night.

They knocked again. "Lemma, I know you're inside. Don't edge me, Lemma!"

Lemma recognized Jax's voice. Her legs itched, rough and prickly to the touch. How long had it been since she had shaved?

"I'm coming in, Lemma. I'm sorry, but Curio wants me to be steady you're alive. Gel? I'm coming in."

The door rattled and opened. Footsteps approached, and Lemma felt a timid tapping on her shoulder through the covers.

She stuck one eye out, and her pupil shrank in the harsh light. "What time is it?"

"Uh, four in the afternoon," Jax said.

"Jax," she said, her voice as bristly as her shins. "Bounce."

"Sorry, but Curio sent me to scope you."

Lemma rubbed golden crumbs from her eyes, and scowled at him. "How did you find me?"

"Curio gave me your address. And your door doesn't lock."

Lemma kicked away the covers, not caring that she was half naked, not really caring about anything. Jax turned away in embarrassment. She pulled on pants that were too big for her and a jacket without bothering to put on a shirt.

"Do you want to clean up? Jax's nose twisted and he blushed. "Or wash?"

"No."

"Or shake some scents?"

Lemma felt around the carpet for a deodorant dispenser, whose rough plastic edge scratched her arms. It was empty. She tried to detangle her hair, which hung flat against her skull, but as she raked her fingers through it, her nails collected oily white flakes like a combine in harvest.

Lovely, she thought.

She staggered past Jax to a screen on the wall, and sifted through three days' worth of messages, wincing with guilt at the ones from Milligram's school and Milligram's mother, demanding to know why Lemma hadn't been there to pick him up.

"You have city rations available," Jax said, pointing to a series of five identical alerts, but Lemma was too busy searching her blinks to come up with a sarcastic response. There were a several dozen messages from Curio, NewTulip786, and the rest of her clients, offering her assignments which must have been given to someone else by now.

"Syan had the same news article in his bedroom," Jax mumbled, pointing to one of the two framed clippings on Lemma's wall.

***

Something was different about Balkon headquarters, Lemma thought, but she was unable to tell what it was right away. Nothing had changed physically. The cubes and desks remained as dull as ever, with interns and contractors filing boring reports on which targets had been ghosted and dead clients had been venged.

Then Lemma noticed it. Before now, she had never interacted with anyone save Curio and Schwartz, and Jax if she had to, but today she was distinctly visible. All eyes pivoted toward her, and whispers followed her like statically charged hair clings to clothes. At first, she blamed her chaotic appearance and unwashed hair, greasy enough to fry donuts. But then an intern dropped a mug in front of her, followed by a contractor spilling a stack of fingerprint ink as she passed him.

"Jax, did you tell them about Syan's blink?"

Another employee, one of the accountants in the Bribery and Persuasion Department, made a large show of dropping a stack of copper certificates. The other Bribery accountants laughed.

"Curio might have mentioned it," Jax mumbled, as yet another accountant approached her.

"Howsie, sushi, you need help carrying anything?"

"Wipe off," Jax said angrily.

Lemma bit her lip and avoided eye contact until she passed Schwartz, but even he gave her only a stiff grimace of recognition.

"I'm sorry, Lemma, I told them it was an accident."

"It's gel, Jax," she muttered. For the first time, she approached Curio's office with relief. Here, at least, she could count on Curio treating her exactly the same as always.

"Oh, claps. The noble heroine reports to her post," Curio sneered as Lemma walked in without knocking. "Can't you scope I'm choked?"

Lemma looked at the man sitting in the office.

"Fremen. Howsie."

"Curio was just showing me different options," Fremen Orea said. "You didn't say it would bleed me so much."

"Sorry." Lemma grimaced.

"I came here to get shielded because badges won't even come into Wilco, then I find out no badges means higher rates. Where's the logic in that?"

"It's jacked, I know." Lemma happened to believe it was very logical. Unfair, but as mathematical as one could get.

"I understand this option may be out of your price range."

"Price range? My taxes are already out of my rimming price range, you'd spect they could give us some badges now and then."

"If the death insurance bleeds you too much, you can hire me freelance," Lemma suggested.

"Plug it," Curio hissed. "Don't pitch in my zone. Fremen, I'll contact you later, I'm steady we'll scout a solution."

Fremen left the office, and Lemma sat.

"I referred him," Lemma emphasized.

"Claps. You want to tell me where you have been for the last seventy-two hours?"

"Working."

"Working? Busy finding other pieces of evidence to destroy? So choked in the field you couldn't answer a single rimming blink?"

"I was in bed."

"In bed? You limp little squint. Absolutely rimming pathetic. Are you even wearing a shirt? I can scope your mams poking out." Curio leaned closer and sniffed, her face twisting into a look of repugnance. "At no time during the last three days did it strike you to take a bath?"

Lemma didn't say anything.

"Or, maybe you spect that drowning in bathtubs is contagious?"

"Don't!" Lemma's face felt hot. "Wipe off," she said with clenched teeth. She hadn't even been in a bathroom since Wade Syan's. She hadn't done anything after leaving his apartment that night beside collapse onto her sofa cushions. She wasn't sure if she could handle a bathroom. In the three days of her self-imposed seclusion, she'd been tormented by recurring visions of Wade Syan's ghastly white body bobbing under the cold water, his hair floating, limp as seaweed.

"What do you want from me? I'm here. What do you want?"

"Your report. Jax gave me his."

"I needed to be alone."

"In bed, wallowing."

Lemma shrugged.

"Is your wallowing over yet?"

Lemma mimed checking a wristwatch. "I still had some scheduled for this evening."

"Schedule some report writing. The fact that it's already been three days is unacceptable."

Lemma squirmed. "Gel."

"As soon as you give me that report, we can close the case."

"Close it? What about venging him?" Lemma yelled.

"Venging who?"

"Wade Syan!"

Curio laughed harshly. "Lemma! You and Jax found only Syan's and his wife's fingerprints in that apartment. There were only two possible ways to enter, and the bathroom window was jammed shut. No alcohol or chemies in his blood. No bruises. He fell asleep, slipped under the water, and left this rimming world the same way he entered it: naked and wet. Now, if there was something Jax forgot to report, maybe a piece of evidence that you didn't drop into a tub of water, we can reopen the case. Until then, wipe off."

Miserable thoughts chased Lemma the entire bus ride home, and somehow, the empty expectant mothers section seemed emptier that it had ever been. It had been three days since Wade Syan's death, but she had grown no closer to accepting it. When she finally stepped in her shower, she turned the handle all the way to the left, letting the water scald until her skin screamed out in angry pink botches. Desperate to feel anything except for crippling numbness, she turned off the shower, and ran a razor over her legs, without shaving cream or soap, again and again, until her shins looked like pepperoni.

CHAPTER 12

SIO4OUR

Sunday, April 29

Wade Syan's funeral was held two days later, and Lemma found the strength to watch the live footage on CityNews. Politicians, journalists, and businesspeople from all over the world poured in to pay their last respects. Many religious leaders from different traditions spoke, including a man in sunglasses seated in a wheelchair, whom Lemma recognized from photographs in Syan's apartment. He quoted from Syan's autobiography, *Thirsting for the Future*, and noted his many years of generosity. When the service was over, Lemma, and perhaps the entire world, felt a little more at peace.

Curio hadn't contacted Lemma since she had finished the report on Syan's death, which Lemma was perfectly gel with. It was painful enough having to sign a statement agreeing that his death was nothing more than an unfortunate accident. Now that all of Balkon knew her as the girl who had jacked up Syan's investigation, there was no reason for her to ever show her face there again. So she distracted herself from death agency work, devoting long hours to babysitting and tutoring Milligram, leaving all of her blinks unanswered in a pile in her room. She might never have taken another assignment if Fremen Orea hadn't sent her a message on her legit CityLink account.

[Getonia will be at Edeyong tonight. Make sure she stays safe]

It was refreshing to have an assignment that didn't involve dropping a target, Lemma thought, as she sat at the bar and ordered a can of Raspberry Blush. She hoped the bartender had forgotten about her unliced photo from last time. But she didn't need to worry; every server and patron alike was focused on only one topic of discussion.

"Death agencies ghosted him, from what I heard."

"I heard a business deal went cucky."

"Drowned? Wipe off, he didn't drown."

Not a single person could go more than two mites without tossing out a new theory about Syan's death. One drunken twank was convinced Wade Syan had never even existed in first place.

"But did you ever scope him in real life? No! Only on CityNews."

"Lemma Quartz? Is that you?" A woman broke Lemma's concentration. It was Fremen Orea's wife. "Howsie. I'm Getonia Orea. You were in Wilco, weren't you? Two weeks ago? You came to our house, pitched my husband a cake."

"Howsie. Join me, pop a drink." Up close, Lemma could see a tattoo of a red flower below Getonia's collarbone. It rippled on her skin as Getonia reached forward to wave at the server.

"What brings you here?" Getonia asked. Lemma realized that Getonia hadn't expected to meet her here. She opted not to mention that Fremen had hired her to protect her for the evening.

"Wade Syan," Getonia muttered, looking around Edeyong. "That's all they're talking about."

"It's jacked," Lemma agreed. "None of them know what they're talking about."

"Everyone's stringing out too much. Talk of conspiracies. Fremen— that's my husband— actually asked me if we should get death insurance. Can you imagine? Death insurance," she repeated with disgust, as Lemma squirmed.

"Your husband is specting about getting shielded? By a death insurance agency?" Lemma asked.

"I told him absolutely not. You know they ghost people? They actually go into people's homes and ghost them. No trial, no oversight. And the state doesn't edge them at all."

"Terrible," Lemma said. "Rimming terrible."

Something buzzed at the end of the bar, and Lemma turned to see Jax standing by a dartboard, which buzzed again.

"Jax, why are you here?"

Jax threw a dart into the board, which buzzed again as a display prompted him to input 1000 leisure rations to begin a real game.

"If you pay them, you won't have to sound like a twank," Lemma suggested.

"This version's free." Jax buzzed another dart.

Lemma scoffed, and pressed her thumb on the glass slate by the board. It responded with, "Annalemma Quartz. CityLink: 7214853. Gambling license expired. Please contact local Department of Entertainment and Sports for more information."

"Try to be quiet? Gel?" Lemma slinked away and rejoined Getonia, who was tapping her nails on the glass counter, making the glowing fish dart.

"Tell me about yourself," Lemma said, as drinks were poured. "What do you and your husband do?"

"I'm a journalist. Write for CityNews. Fremen used to be a badge."

"Used to? Why? Did something happen?"

Getonia gave a hollow laugh. "Couldn't keep his mouth shut. Didn't know when to wipe off."

"What did he say?"

"Told someone from CityNews about how death agencies were better at dropping goons then the badges were. The rest of the badges didn't clap for that one mite. They asked him to resign, and when he didn't, they accused him of possessing contra goods: gold, silver, blink, an unliced camera."

"They made a false accusation?"

"No, it was real. But all of them were doing it. He was the only one who was cucked for it."

"What does he do now?"

"He works in maintenance for the state," Getonia said scathingly. "Makes sure the buildings don't get too hot or too cold. What about you?"

"I'm unemployed, but I do community service. Childcare and tutoring. Used to be a photographer, but then they lifted my lice, the twanks."

"What happened?" Getonia asked, but before Lemma could answer Jax interrupted them.

"Howsie. Sorry I'm late."

Lemma touched the glass counter, and the seats changed color from red to blue. "We're talking, Jax. Wipe off."

"Do you know him?" Getonia asked.

"Curio told me to shield her starting at eight!" Jax said. "Why are you here?"

"Fremen asked me to shield her," Lemma said through clenched teeth.

"You're back at Balkon?" Jax asked.

"Balkon!" Getonia gasped. "Is he one of them?"

"Jax!" Lemma hissed.

"New death insurance agent, as of today." Jax pulled out a silver medallion, angling it so the light reflected into Lemma's eyes.

"Curio made you an agent?" Lemma asked, glaring at him.

"You're with them too?" Getonia stood up. "I'm going to be sick!"

"Ms. Orea, it's all gel, it's safe. Fremen hired us— me— to keep you shielded," Lemma assured her.

"Then why didn't he tell me?"

"He spected you would string out."

"Can't imagine why he would spect that," Jax muttered, returning his badge to his pocket.

"Getonia, we can explain everything," Lemma said.

"You're with the death agents?" Getonia demanded.

"Yes, but don't spill it for the whole bar. You're safe, Ms. Orea. We're just shielding you for the evening."

"Why?"

"Because your husband wants to keep you safe!" Lemma suspected the real reason involved Harriden or a different conk, but she didn't feel the need to mention that.

"If you want to keep me safe, scope that twank over there," Getonia said hotly, pointing.

Lemma and Jax turned to scout the bar. One figure dropped his gaze immediately.

"That man?" Lemma murmured. "You spect he was scoping us?"

"He's been scoping me since I came in," Getonia replied.

"If he makes you feel stringy, I can speak to the manager."

"I've scoped him around our zone. He walks through Wilco every day, and now he's here."

"I'll talk to him." One of Lemma's blinks buzzed. It was NewTulip786.

[*Sio4our, you're in Edeyong?*]

The skin on the back of her neck tingled. Until now, this number had only been one of many invisible clients, who issued assignments from afar and knew her only by her code name, 'Sio4our.' This was the first time any contact other than Curio had indicated they knew Lemma's location, and, by implication, what she looked like.

[*Yes*] she responded, rattled but grateful she had decided to bring her blinks with her.

[*Behind you in a booth is your next target. Beard. Missing tooth. Dark shirt. Sitting alone*]

Lemma allowed herself a surreptitious glance. NewTulip786's description matched. The target was the same man who had been watching Getonia.

[*I scope him*]

[*Drop him but be quiet. Top priority*]

Lemma's fingers were already reaching for the vial in her shoe, when NewTulip786 added: [*He's a suspect in Wade Syan's death*]

CHAPTER 13

BAIT

"Stay here, and stay safe." Lemma gripped a pill tightly in her palm.

"What?" Getonia asked. "Is it him? You said he wasn't dangerous."

"Things changed. Jax?"

"What?"

"Shield her."

Lemma pushed between a pair of badges trading gold, stopping beside the red-haired girl she had seen the night of Syan's death.

"Howsie."

The girl looked up at Lemma, her skin soft as a baby's beneath its garish makeup. She couldn't have been more than 13 or 14.

Lemmy asked, "You choked or open?"

The girl smiled flirtatiously, and Lemma's stomach turned. "I'm open." She pulled out a plastic card. It read, "State-Issued Intimate Contact License" It was issued to Ruby Rhodes, age 19.

The lice was legit, but the photo was so obviously of someone else, Lemma was astounded that the girl hadn't already been caught.

"Don't scope yet, but there's a man behind you. White skin, full beard, in a dark shirt and pants. Missing a tooth. Pointy nose like a mouse's. I need you to go over to him and distract him."

"Distract him how?"

"Sugar him. Whatever you're gel with."

The girl nodded, and Lemma pressed a pill into her hand. "Get him to pop that."

The girl shook her head.

"Name your price," Lemma pleaded.

The girl calling herself Ruby remained silent.

"Two grams gold?" Lemma pulled out a wad of notes.

The girl nodded slowly, and her fingers closed around the money and the pill. Then she walked out of Edeyong. Lemma returned to Getonia and Jax.

"What's going on?" Jax asked.

"Don't move, face forward," Lemma hissed.

"Why were you talking to that girl?" Getonia asked. "She's a child! Why is she allowed in here?"

Ruby had reentered the bar from an alternate door. She squeezed through a sea of grinning badges, whose fingers poked and pinched her, before approaching the target with the missing tooth.

"Lemma, you're using her?" Jax asked, astonished.

"Be quiet," Lemma ordered. "Don't scope her. Turn around. It's all gel."

"That's disgusting. You really shouldn't have—"

"It's gel," Lemma repeated, focusing on the distorted reflection of the girl and her target in her shiny silver can of Raspberry Blush.

Ruby had taken a seat next to the bearded man with the missing tooth. She leaned toward him, smiling.

"I can't believe this," Getonia said. "You people only care about ghosting, and you don't give cucks when children get hurt."

"That's not true," Lemma said, as the memory of Milligram spitting out the pill darted through her mind. "You don't know what you're talking about."

"Pull her away. Tell her to stop."

"So he can go back to scouting you?"

"I'm not going to let a rimming kid die to shield me."

"Plug it," Lemma hissed. The red-haired girl was on the man's lap, her body pressed against his. He nuzzled his bearded face against the back of her neck, whispering moistly. Lemma forced herself to watch. She would endure every moment of this with Ruby, while hating herself for letting it happen, and hating Getonia for judging her. The last thing she needed was Getonia thinking Lemma would force a child into this without knowing exactly what it was like to distract a man by sugaring him, sitting on him, squirming on his lap as you felt him rise to the occasion, letting him invade you just enough to lower his guard.

Ruby's fist was tightly balled, still holding Lemma's pill, but the target stood up before she could use it, pulling her by the wrist toward a set of stairs leading to the bar's lower level.

"Don't let her go down there, Lemma, don't!" Getonia begged.

Lemma didn't reply. She pushed past Jax, reaching under the electronic dartboard, which buzzed as she pulled out a brick wrapped in a coil of rope. Then she followed her target.

CHAPTER 14

TARGET

Lemma made her way down stairs slick with spilled liquor and vomit, and pushed through a weighted curtain into the basement. She was instantly hit with the raw, harsh scent of sweat. She pulled the neck of her shirt over her nose, as she stumbled over three unconscious patrons.

In this level were provocatively dressed women and men wearing half-unbuttoned silky shirts. There were badges pouring glasses of liquor over conk's backs and lapping it up like dogs; journalists whose eyes stared euphorically at the ceiling; people tearing clothes off or clumsily putting them on inside-out, faces pressed against chests or between legs. There was smoke pouring from lungs, and liquid pouring down throats.

Moving unobtrusively between the mass of people were the service staff. They were dressed in black, nearly invisible as they cleaned up spills and attended to the unconscious.

"What the rim's going on?" Jax's voice came from behind Lemma, muffled by his pulled-up shirt, as he tried not to vomit.

"Bounce upstairs. Get back to Getonia, shield her."

"She made me follow you."

"Jax, bounce."

"No!" He refused to budge. "Tell me, who's that twank? Why are we scouting him?"

"They spect he was mixed up with Wade Syan."

"Who spects? Curio?"

"No. A client. Now help me. Target's in one of these."

The basement walls were lined with curtained booths, each large enough to permit several people to lie down inside. Lemma held the brick, alert and ready, as she approached the nearest booth and ripped open the curtain. Inside, a tangle of bodies sweated and squealed like pigs at the feeding trough. The girl and the target were not among them.

Lemma dropped the curtain and moved to the next booth. *Please be safe,* she found herself praying. *Please don't be hurt because of me.*

Another curtain, another badge, or judge, or inspector. Some Lemma thought she recognized from the Department of Electronic Images, or the Intimate Contact License Department. Some of the booths were empty except for a state-issued poster pinned to the wall. In large red letters, it read, "*Ask to see their Intimate Contact License. No License = No Consent!*"

Blinking sweat from her eyes, Lemma threw open another curtain and found the target and Ruby wrapped in an embrace, their arms slithering over each other. The girl's fist was balled around an unseen pill.

Lemma entered the booth and Ruby and the man broke apart, startled. In the dull light drifting through the open curtain, Lemma saw with relief that neither of them had removed their clothes yet.

The man grinned stupidly, lying sunk between two cushions. Lemma drew closer, able to spot details in the low light: the missing tooth that NewTulip786 had mentioned, a hand which had lost its pinky. Up close, the target's nose looked less like a mouse's and more like a greedy rat's as he panted, his eyes moving up and down Lemma's body.

"Howsie, sushi!" he said, saliva dangling from his beard. "Come on, jump in and we'll make it a sandwich."

In reply, Lemma whipped her arm upward, sending the brick at the end of the rope crashing down. The man jerked as the brick landed next to his head, shattering a bottle and splashing liquor everywhere. The man screamed. Ruby twisted away, whimpering in confusion.

"What are you doing?" Jax shouted, as Lemma retreated, answering him with by pointing a finger pointing at the man's chest.

Around his neck was a copper medallion.

"Is he one of ours? Or a different agency?" Jax asked.

Lemma pried the capsule from the girl's fist.

"Shield him," Lemma whispered, thrusting the brick and the rope into Jax's hands. "Don't let him bounce, but don't hurt him. I'll blink for help."

Tripping over piles of abandoned scarves and dresses, Lemma pulled Ruby out of the den and up the stairs, breathing the sweet, clean air with desperate relief.

CHAPTER 15

HOUSE CALL

[TARGET CORNERED. NOT DROPPED. SHIELDED BY AXIOM]

Lemma stared at her blink, waiting for NewTulip786 to receive the message.

"Am I done?" Ruby asked, looking over the customers in the bar. "Because if I'm done I need to get back to work."

"Yes, here." Lemma pulled out a stack of contras.

"You can't do that!" Getonia had found them. "Don't give that to her; it's illegal."

"Getonia, if you don't shut your rimming mouth—"

"She needs to get help."

"I'm gel, give me my gold!" the girl spat, reaching for Lemma, but Getonia grabbed her wrist.

"What's your name? Do you have parents?"

The girl shook her head, as Lemma checked her blink, praying for NewTulip786 to arrive soon.

The curtain at the bottom of the stairs opened, but it was only a cluster of girls wearing wine-soaked scarves and barely zipped dresses, coughing and gasping as they escaped the fog of sweat from below.

"She needs to get help, she needs to go to Minor Aid," Getonia insisted.

"Minor Aid is a rimming joke. They're only there to look gel, like they're helping, but they don't," Ruby said.

"There are laws for a reason," Getonia said sternly, tightening her grip on her. "Laws named after the children who were killed!"

The girl was getting restless. "Let me bounce!"

"So more chads can spread you? You could have been killed down there," Getonia told her.

"Then name a rimming law after me. Laws named after dead girls are smoother to pass, anyway."

"You can bounce if you want," Lemma pressed the notes into her palm. "And wear this." She pulled the fake Axiom medallion from her pocket and set it around Ruby's neck.

"You can't let her go," Getonia shouted.

"It's her decision."

"I live at State Housing Facility 9316, Room 87," Lemma told the girl. "Ninety-three sixteen eighty-seven. You can remember that?"

The girl nodded, and ran out of Edeyong. Getonia's expression turned savage. She was about to rant at Lemma, but was cut off as the curtain at the foot of the stairs opened again. Jax stumbled upstairs, cupping his nose while blood spilled from between his fingers.

"Lemma, he got away!" he shouted. "He's wearing a green dress. Where did he go?"

Lemma frantically turned her head, looking in all directions for the target.

One of the cluster of giggling girls broke from the group, and exited the bar, shedding a scarf to expose short hair and a beard.

"Stay here," she told Jax.

Lemma ran, past screams of anger and indignation from patrons as she pushed past them, fighting to maintain her focus on the target in the green dress. She burst out the door, onto the street, into a jungle of squealing tires and barking honks. A car screamed to a halt, brushing her thigh after burning a rubber stripe into the street. In the chaos of vehicles, it wasn't until Lemma was a block away that she began to internalize how close the car had been to shattering her against the pavement where it had etched the dark streak of tire.

Lemma's thigh throbbed in perfect rhythm with her heart. She forced herself to breathe quietly, staying in the shadows as much as she could, only a block behind her target.

The traffic lessened as Lemma crossed into a residential zone, running between houses, dodging shrubs and waving her hands in front of her in case a chain link fence decided to jump out from the dark. She locked her eyes on the target's back, swiftly moving her feet so only her tiptoes hit the ground.

Then they were on an empty street between two rows of houses. The area looked familiar, but between Lemma's burning thigh and sore lungs, she couldn't focus her thoughts enough to recognize which zone it was.

The man in the green dress knocked on the door of one of the houses, and Lemma crept toward him, stumbling over potholes in the street.

Stay gel, stay quiet… Lemma fought the urge to panic. In any moment someone would open the door. An accomplice? An ally?

The target knocked the door again, harder.

Still approaching the target, Lemma pulled out the blink, and texted NewTulip786.

[*Out of Edeyong, unknown zone. Target knocking at door*]

The door opened, and a man's face appeared. His hands were wrapped around something small and dark.

In that moment, Lemma suddenly recalled the street, its potholes, the house itself, and the man who lived there. She remembered what Getonia had said about the target stalking her, and Lemma wanted to cry out, but the words jammed in her throat as she ran toward the house, her toes and ankles rubbed raw inside her shoes.

A noise she hadn't heard in almost a decade shattered the air. Lemma slapped her ears to protect them, but the noise was already finished. The target's head sprayed blood, and the green dress, now stained red, thudded on Fremen Orea's porch.

CHAPTER 16

STANDOFF

"Fremen! Fremen!"

Lemma's mind was stuck. The shock of seeing someone ghosted had numbed her brain. She wouldn't remember the scene properly afterwards, so scattered were the next series of events. In some versions of her shredded memories, Lemma was already running toward Fremen Orea when he had shot the intruder; in others, she didn't move until the intruder's body had landed on the porch, ground beef splattering out the back of his head.

"He had…he was shielded." Lemma's hands trembled as she felt under the man's dress for the medallion. It read "Axiom Death Insurance Agency."

"He was shielded?" Fremen asked, and cursed. "How? Get Curio! Blink her and send her here."

"Balkon can't help you."

"Then why do I pay them so cucking much!" Fremen shouted, stuffing the handgun into his belt and pulling a Balkon medallion from his shirt.

Lemma pulled out both blinks.

[*Target was ghosted in Wilco zone*] she sent to NewTulip786.

[*Send Balkon agents to Wilco zone, member Fremen Orea ghosted an Axiom member*] she sent to Curio.

"They're going to ghost me," Fremen said hollowly. "Axiom's going to ghost me."

"They are not going to ghost you, Fremen. Listen, you are shielded by Balkon. We'll hide you. Axiom won't touch you. We'll scope a remedy. Now get inside. Get in the house, now!"

Cars arrived, and agents spilled out, brandishing guns, knives, whatever weapons they possessed.

"That Balkon or Axiom?" Fremen asked, his whole body trembling as he peered out the window. There was a flurry of knocks on the door.

"Axiom Death Insurance Agency!" someone shouted.

"Give me your gun." Lemma took Fremen's gun, still hot from the blast that had killed the target. She had not held a gun in over a decade.

She approached the door, as a man outside shouted, "Axiom Death Insurance Agency, open up and let us in!"

Lemma took a deep breath, and shouted back, "I'm Agent Lemma Quartz of Balkon Death Insurance Agency. This house is occupied by a shielded member of Balkon. You are trespassing. Bounce!"

The man replied at the same volume, "One of our members was ghosted on this property. We are allowed to be here. Open the door and let us in!"

Lemma waited.

"How did they get here so flash?" Fremen whispered. "Who blinked them?"

"No one blinked them; their members have implants in their hearts. The mite he died, Axiom got the alert," Lemma said.

They waited for ten agonizing minutes, as the Axiom agents shouted and threatened, but didn't dare to enter.

Then another cluster of cars arrived, and Balkon agents as well as Curio herself poured into the street. The group from Axiom turned to face them.

Lemma could hear Curio berating them with the same furious tone of voice she used on Lemma daily.

"What are they saying?" Fremen asked.

There were flashes of light, and through the window Lemma saw Axiom and Balkon agents alike taking images of the dead body. Then the Axiom agents hoisted it, zipped it in a bag, and carried it into one of their cars.

The car drove away.

[*Lemma, are you alive?*] Curio blinked her.

[*Alive with Fremen. Did Axiom leave?*]

A firm knock came at the door, followed by Curio's voice. "Lemma, open up."

Curio and several Balkon agents came into the room. A few Axiom agents remained standing on the porch.

"What happened?" Fremen asked.

"What happened?" Curio said. "Didn't you hear? A Balkon member ghosted an Axiom member and created a jackload of paperwork for me!"

"I'm sorry, but he was trying to ghost me!" Fremen's voice was still fearful, but now it carried an edge of anger. "What's going to happen to me? Is Axiom going to venge him?"

"We haven't decided yet," Curio said. "This is the first time one of our members has ghosted one of theirs. We need to take you and your wife with us and shield you, and both of you need to be interviewed."

"Who's going to interview me?"

"Axiom and Balkon together."

"How long are you going to keep me?" Fremen asked.

"Until the trial."

CHAPTER 17

THE MESSAGE

Jax and Lemma stayed at Balkon headquarters for several hours, each being interviewed separately by Balkon agents, then Axiom agents, then one last time with all parties present.

"What were you doing at Edeyong?" Curio asked.

"Shielding Getonia Orea." Lemma's voice was ragged. She couldn't remember, but she suspected she had screamed when Fremen had shot the target.

"And who gave you permission to do that?"

"Permission? Fremen posted me! I don't have to ask you for permission to take a post."

"Getonia Orea is a member of Balkon, and we had a Balkon agent assigned to her." Curio pointed at Jax.

"Why did you make Jax an agent and not me?"

"We are not discussing that, we are discussing your actions tonight."

"I saved Fremen's life from those twanks over there." Lemma pointed at the Axiom agents sitting by Curio.

"Why did you attack a target at Edeyong?" Curio asked.

"Another client posted me. Wanted him dropped."

"So you abandoned Getonia, whom you had promised to shield, to drop a target?"

Lemma didn't answer.

"This is why I can't make you an agent," Curio said. "Along with your habit of dropping evidence into bathtubs."

The Axiom agents laughed.

"And because you took an alternate post, we have this rimming mess to clean up."

***

By the time the interviews were over, it was almost dawn. Forcing her eyes to stay open, Lemma stumbled toward a CityBus.

"Lemma!" Jax said, running up to her. "Lemma, I know Curio won't say it, but you did bright. You saved Fremen's life."

"Curio's right," Lemma mumbled bitterly. "If I hadn't sent that girl to sugar the target it wouldn't have happened." The thought of Ruby getting spread by other chads somewhere in the city filled Lemma with sour guilt.

"I lost your brick at Edeyong, sorry," Jax said, shame-faced.

"Jax, you twank!"

"I said I was sorry. Listen, I have something else for you. I spoke with Curio. She wouldn't post you as an agent, but when she wasn't looking, I lifted this." He handed her a blink.

"Bright. Now you can message me when you're able to give me a new brick," Lemma said sarcastically.

"Lemma, this was the one you scoped at Wade Syan's."

"The one that fell in the water?"

"I gave it to one of other agents; they were able to unjack it."

"So it works?"

"Yes."

Lemma turned Syan's blink over in her hands. "What am I supposed to do with this?"

"You said there was a message on it, before it fell in the water. It might help you venge Syan."

Lemma activated the blink. It had exactly one message, the same series of numbers that Lemma had seen the night of Syan' death:

[11590114811322012081125611486014070140011
4501159601596016021165111708019250181601 86
0119020195412104020520210412155122001244 20
2442027090240412546025051255912634126521 27
2302752028190288302911129860300813051131 15
1315013526037230333031336413581034581365 10]

"I have no idea what this means." She looked at Jax. "But I'm going to find out."

CHAPTER 18

NEWTULIP786

Tuesday, May 1

But the secret message in Wade Syan's blink remained an enigma. Lemma spent hours staring at the string of numbers, hoping they would magically transform in meaningful words. She tried replacing the numbers with letters, but each iteration only led to nonsense. She asked other agents at Balkon for insight, but none of their recommendations produced any fruit. Lemma even scoured CityNews, watching every report, in case the state discovered something new regarding Syan's drowning. But the surge of gossip surrounding his death had mostly died down. The world had finally accepted that he was gone.

So Lemma found ways to distract herself from Wade Syan. She carried out short assignments as her blinks buzzed, traded more dairy rations with Schwartz, and tutored Milligram in the afternoon. In the evening she visited Fremen, along with Getonia, in their safe rooms at Balkon headquarters.

"Any update on the trial?" Fremen asked several times. Their safe rooms consisted of a bedroom, a bathroom, and a sitting area where Getonia could continue her writing for CityNews. Getonia refused to acknowledge Lemma, but merely sat and typed. Fremen, however, could not go more than five minutes without pacing nervously around the room.

"Curio and I are still working things out with Axiom," Lemma assured him.

"Have they set a date for the trial?"

"No."

Getonia was also on edge, but chose to bury her concerns in a series of articles about the pros and cons of death agencies, and of underage conks.

"Did you read my article this morning? About unlicensed sex work?" Getonia asked, finally agreeing to speak with her when Lemma visited the next day.

"Even worse are the citizens who stand idly by, content to dismiss the issue as something beyond their control instead of taking action to fight it," Lemma quoted from memory. "Was that about me?"

Getonia sniffed and returned to her tablet and began to type, her expression icy. Lemma launched into an explanation of why she had chosen to let Ruby go rather than call the authorities, and mentioned how she herself was worried about her. But all this accomplished was to inspire Getonia to begin a fiery opinion piece about the rising incidents of food ration fraud, which she had learned about earlier that morning when Schwartz had made a visit to the Oreas and attempt to sell them some of Lemma's cheese.

"I'm sorry Schwartz bothered you, I promise Curio won't let him do it again." Lemma stopped, feeling a buzz in her pocket. NewTulip786 had sent her a message.

[*Let's meet in person. Tonight*]

***

"You steady this is the place?" Jax nervously cut his giraffe meat into smaller and smaller pieces.

"Yes. Going to actually pop that, or just edge it?" Lemma asked.

Jax slid his plate toward her empty one. "You spect he forgot?" he asked, looking around Gyro Valley.

Lemma sighed, and examined Jax's leftovers for yogurt or cheese.

"Spect it's him?" Jax nudged his head toward a man seated between two children.

"Do I spect NewTulip786 brought his children? No, Jax, I don't."

"Maybe he brought kids as a distraction."

"To distract who?"

"Us. To catch us off guard when he ghosts us."

"He's not going to ghost us."

"How do you know?"

"He knows what I look like. He could have followed me home if he wanted to ghost me. And you think he's going to let his kids scope him ghosting us?"

"Maybe they're not his kids. Maybe he borrowed them, or rented them as part of his disguise."

"Jax, what's edging you?"

"Can't stop thinking about Syan," he said, after a pause.

"Spect that makes you special?"

"You think about him too?"

Lemma pulled out Syan's blink. "Every mite of every day."

"You ever dream about him? Cause I do. I have nightmares where I'm drowning in a tub, the water rising over my chin and covering my mouth."

"I told you how I always wanted to meet him. When I was a little girl, I wrote him a letter saying thanks for inventing food I could eat. Like this giraffe, right here." Lemma stabbed a bite with her fork. "Because of Syan I can eat this. The idea of him dying by accident. It's… it's humiliating. He deserved better. And no one cares. It's only been two days since his funeral, and everyone already forgot."

As Lemma chewed on the piece of labbed giraffe, the door to Gyro Valley opened, and a man walked in.

CHAPTER 19

IRRATIONAL

"Which one of you is Sio4our?" The man asked, setting a briefcase by the table. He was Hispanic, in his mid-forties, with a thick beard.

Lemma raised her hand.

NewTulip786 sat down. "Want to explain to me how Ennerd Vik got ghosted?"

"Ennerd Vik?" Lemma asked.

"Your target at Edeyong. I asked you to drop him so I could question him, and instead, his head got popped like a water balloon."

Lemma cringed. "I'm sorry."

"Sorry? Bright start," the man snorted. "Say 'sorry' enough times and maybe he'll come back to life."

"Sorry," Lemma repeated. "I tried to follow him."

"It was my fault," Jax said. "I was scoping him."

"I asked you to scope him," NewTulip786 said to Lemma. "Who's this twank?"

"Jax Yedra." Jax put out his hand. "Lemma and me, we post at Balkon together."

"Balkon?" NewTulip786 asked.

"The other night," Lemma said. "Your message said you thought the man— Ennerd Vik— was a suspect in Syan's death. How?"

"He'd been scoped near Syan's apartment several times three weeks ago. After Syan died, we wanted to question him, but now he's gone forever."

"Sorry," Lemma mumbled.

"Me too. You said you both post at Balkon. Did you scrape Wade Syan's apartment with her?" NewTulip786 asked Jax, jerking his chin at Lemma.

Lemma and Jax exchanged a glance. "How did you know?" Lemma asked.

NewTulip786 smirked. "The night Syan died, you'd been taking tasks that whole evening, and you'd said you'd be free all night. Then you stopped replying. Went cold. Must have been important, right?"

Lemma nodded slowly. "What do you want from us?"

"I scoped Balkon's report on Syan's death, as well as the official state report. You were there, you scraped the scene. Tell me what really happened."

"If I tell you…"

"You'll be paid for every new detail."

"How much?"

"As much as I spect it's worth."

Lemma poked at the pieces of giraffe.

"Sio4our, I promise, I'm steady. And I spect you're steady. We can trust each other."

"Why do you care about Syan?" Jax asked.

"Because everyone cares about him. If we venge his death there'll be a jackload of publicity."

"If you want publicity, stop using a code name, NewTulip786," Lemma said.

NewTulip786 looked around the restaurant. "Can I trust you to lock a secret?"

Lemma and Jax nodded.

"Balkon and Axiom have done bright. The past four years, death insurance agencies have redefined criminal justice. You venge murders where badges give up; you ghost the goons the badges are too limp to touch. You've embarrassed every government organization in the country by doing their post for them."

"And?" Lemma asked.

"But you can be brighter. Someone can always be brighter. New kids are moving into the zone, and they want to play ball."

This was news to Lemma. "There's a new death insurance agency?"

"Yes. Mine. Balkon and Axiom, they venge murders. My agency will offer everything: security systems, law enforcement, legal mediations, even garbage collection."

"Like a government for hire?" Jax asked.

NewTulip786 smiled. "When's the last time the city fixed a street this side of downtown? People want justice, and law enforcement, and city maintenance. I'm going to give it to them at a steady price."

"What does Wade Syan have to do with your new business?" Lemma asked.

"Advertising. Imagine: the richest man in the world dies. Everyone thinks he drowned by accident. But you know that's not what happened. Scope it." He pulled a tablet from his briefcase, and swiped past several graphs. One had been labeled "Sio4our."

"Is that me?" Lemma asked.

"It's a list of all the locations of your assignments, and how long you took to complete them, and the timestamps of your messages. It's how I spected that you post at Balkon, how I know where you live."

"You know where I live?" Lemma was indignant.

"Scope this data," NewTulip786 found the graph he was looking for. "Number of murders in the city from the past eight years. Death insurance agencies have been operating for the past four."

"Murders dropped. Death agencies are doing bright," Jax commented.

"Murders as defined by the city have dropped, but scope this."

With several swipes, a new graph appeared.

"This purple line and the blue line are deaths by chemie overdose and rates of chemie use. Chemie overdoses have gone up. But chemie use has stayed the same. Why? Scope it like this: how does Balkon ghost a target? Do you plow into their home, firing guns and playing trumpets?"

"No. We make it look like an accident."

"An accident," NewTulip786 said, raising his eyebrows and nodding.

Jax frowned. "These chemie overdoses... some of them aren't accidents?"

"Claps." NewTulip786 smiled. "If you want to ghost targets and stay loose, make it seem accidental. It's easy to ghost someone with an overdose. So, because of your death insurance agencies, murderers are becoming cleverer. They still ghost, but they keep it quiet."

"But Syan didn't have an overdose, he drowned."

"Rates of drownings of adults in the past eight years," NewTulip786 said, showing a new graph. "Again, a sharp increase within the last four."

"But Syan's apartment was closed off! There were only two doors. We scoped the surveillance footage. Ingo was there, but she was nowhere near the bathroom. And the window was jammed shut!" Lemma said.

"Jammed shut?" NewTulip786 asked. "That's not what I heard."

"Your report said the window didn't open," Jax reminded Lemma.

"Yes," she replied. "It was jammed shut, therefore it didn't open."

"Jammed shut versus designed to stay shut. That's an important difference! Details like that can be crucial! That's what I need you for, to tell me if the report was missing anything," NewTulip786 struck the table with his fist.

"Jammed window or not, Wade Syan went in, took off his clothes, drew a bath, and drowned. Show me all the graphs you want, no one could have done that to him," Lemma said flatly.

"Which is why his murder is so important. Think about it. If someone had the power to make someone drown remotely, by hypnosis or voodoo doll, or whatever, then every murder becomes an accidental drowning, and no one is venged. Death insurance will be useless. No one will buy it."

Lemma thought of Syan's eyes staring dully up at her from the bottom of the tub.

"Which is why I need you," NewTulip786 said. "Syan's death might be a new type of murder. Something completely foreign. Maybe the first of its kind in human history. If my new agency can solve it and venge him…"

"You want us to solve Syan's murder for you, as part of an ad campaign for your new death agency?" Lemma asked.

"Does that sound too callous? If it makes you feel better, I also want to learn their method so we can ghost our own targets."

Lemma grimaced.

"I'm going to trust you both to lock this to yourselves. If you want the post, I'll pay handsomely. Both of you." NewTulip786 nodded to Jax.

Jax cleared his throat. "Maybe we should think about this."

"I'm in," Lemma said. "I want to solve Syan's murder, if it was murder, but not for the money. Syan's inventions saved me from starving."

"I respect that," NewTulip786 said with gravitas. "So you'll take the post for free?"

Lemma scowled.

"We don't even know this twank," Jax muttered.

"I know him," Lemma insisted. "NewTulip786 is a regular client of mine. He's steady. Pays on time, no drama."

NewTulip786 smiled. "Thank you, Sio4our. Now, do you have any information for me?"

Lemma pulled out Wade Syan's blink. "We found this in Syan's apartment."

The man's jaw dropped. "The report didn't mention a rimming blink."

"I…" Lemma's face reddened. "I dropped in it the bathtub. We left it out of the report. We only just unjacked it."

"I unjacked it," Jax muttered.

"Anything on it?"

"One message." Lemma displayed it. "A string of numbers, maybe a code. I burned several hours trying to crack it."

"Show me." NewTulip786 touched the blink to his tablet, and the numbers appeared on his screen:

[11590114811322012081125611486014070140011
450115960159601602116511170801925018160186
011902019541210402052021041215512200124420
244202709024041254602505125591263412652127
230275202819028830291112986030081305113115
131501352603723033303133641358103458136510]

"Interesting. You scope any patterns?"

"They're all random," Lemma said.

"Not entirely," NewTulip786 said slowly. He made several strokes on the tablet, and the string split up into sets of five digits.

[11590 11481 13220 12081 12561 14860 14070 14001 14501
15960 15960 16021 16511 17080 19250 18160 18601 19020
19541 21040 20520 21041 21551 22001 24420 24420 27090

*24041 25460 25051 25591 26341 26521 27230 27520 28190
28830 29111 29860 30081 30511 31151 31501 35260 37230
33031 33641 35810 34581 36510*|

"Scope every fifth digit," NewTulip786 said.

"Every fifth is always a one or a zero," Jax said.

"Yes." NewTulip786 nodded. "I've scoped similar codes in the past year. Every set of five, every quintet, refers to a letter of the alphabet."

"Gel, but almost none of them repeat. There's only twenty-six letters in the alphabet," Jax said.

"Different quintets could match to the same letter. 'Death agent' and 'twank' are different terms, but they both describe you." Lemma snorted. "How do we know what quintets correspond to what letter?"

NewTulip786 stared at the string of numbers. "Every code needs a key. The codes that I've scoped recently, they liked to use irrational numbers."

"Go on," Lemma said.

"They do, forever. Pi, Euler's number, root two, root three. Suppose the key was Pi. 3.14159, the one the Greeks invented."

"I don't spect the Greeks actually invented it," Jax said.

NewTulip786 ignored him. "Our first quintet is 11590. We'll focus to the first four digits, which takes us to the 1159th position of Pi. The digit there is 7, so convert that to the alphabet, which would be 'G'" As he spoke, the tablet adjusted its display, automatically displaying the number Pi.

"You like that?" NewTulip786 said with a smile. "New software. It listens to my voice and illustrates what I'm saying."

A cartoon of a man with a speech bubble over his head appeared on the tablet.

"What about letters after 'I'?" Jax asked. "M is the thirteenth letter of the alphabet, but if we scoped '13' we would translate it to 'AC,' not 'M.'"

"That's what the one or zero at the end of each quintet is," NewTulip786 answered. "A zero means you're scouting for a single digit, from 1=A to 9=I. A one means you're scouting for a two digit number: from 10 = J to 26 = Z. Maybe. Still a guess."

"So we have to try every irrational number we know? And hope whoever sent the message to Syan actually used this code?" Lemma asked.

NewTulip786 nodded. "We have to start somewhere. Let's try Pi as our irrational." He tapped the screen, and the entire code translated.

[GIG-YGE—II—BAD—FB—FFD-A—V-B——T—RAG—EJA]

"I'm going to take a wild guess," Jax said. "And say it's wrong."

"Why are there blanks?" Lemma asked.

"Because there are only 26 letters in the alphabet. If the code gives us a 27 or a 28, there's no letter to match," NewTulip786 replied. "I'll try the other way. Where one means single digit, and zero means double digit."

[—FB—GD—HHXL-IFG-ZFIH—FMGDBBEUFEIIBEDAS-CD-AP]

"Claps!" Lemma exclaimed with mock excitement. She and Jax smirked to each other.

NewTulip786 was unruffled. "So we've ruled out Pi. I'll jack around with other numbers. Blink me if you have more info. And go scope your report again. Tell me if you missed anything — any rimming thing — at Syan's apartment."

He stood up. "You have a name, Sio4our? Now that we've had to endure each other's faces, there's no reason to use codes."

"Quartz. Lemma Quartz."

"And I'm Haydis Donovez. Also, I'm going to keep Syan's blink, in case anyone sends another code. In exchange…" He pulled out two devices and set them in front of Jax and Lemma. "Phones, not blinks. Unlicensed and fully encrypted, in case we need to make live calls. Welcome to the team."

CHAPTER 20

GOLDEN RATIO

Thursday, May 3

Milligram's apartment was five times the size of Lemma's. It had white walls, empty except for paintings of triangles from an artist who had made a specialty of drawing various polygons. One of the paintings was a golden spiral within a golden rectangle. It was supposed to be the only spiral the artist had ever produced.

On a white sofa sat Lemma and Milligram. Milligram busied himself with his school-issued tablet, while Lemma examined two of her blinks, deciding whether to smuggle a kilo of silver into a church, or deliver chemies to a chef at a rhino lab.

"Gram, can I give you a snack?" asked Cheri Mills, Milligram's mother, walking in from the kitchen. "I got a bonus dairy ration today, so I lifted a wheel of brie."

"Brie!" Milligram sang to himself. "Brie brie brie!"

"Gram will have some, none for me, thanks," said Lemma, stuffing the blinks into her pocket before Cheri could see them.

"Sorry, I forgot you don't eat cheese."

Milligram looked up from his tablet, dropping his jaw in exaggerated shock. "You don't pop cheese?" he asked Lemma, clapping his palms to his cheeks. "Why?"

"Gram, we don't ask why people eat or don't eat foods, it's impolite," Cheri admonished. "Remember what we talked about at church?"

77

"It's gel, you can ask me," Lemma said firmly. "It's because I'm allergic."

Milligram looked between Lemma and his mother, unsure which side to take.

"Lemma, Gram and I are practicing not criticizing other people's food choices," Cheri said.

"He wasn't criticizing, he was just asking."

"Part of making people feel empowered with their food choices," Cheri spoke louder as she set down a plate of soft cheese, whole grain bread with seeds the size of beetles, and orange jam, "is letting them decide whether or not to tell you about them, gel?"

Milligram nodded and mumbled, "Sorry, Lemma."

For a moment, Lemma wanted to flick the jam into Cheri's short blonde hair, but Cheri handed her a tablet before she could, adding, "I left some bread without the cheese."

"Thanks." Lemma touched her fingerprint against Cheri's tablet, and her own face and information appeared, along with the words "Renew existing waiver?" Lemma swiped several times, confirming that she had once again inspected Cheri's kitchen and found no domestic health hazards.

"What's that?" Cheri asked, narrowing her eyes. Lemma's heart hiccupped, and she pushed the blinks farther into her pocket, before realizing Cheri wasn't addressing her.

"It's nothing," Milligram mumbled, rubbing at his forearm, where Lemma saw a long, dark scrape. "Fell at recess."

"Did a student push you? Are you being bullied at school?" Cheri asked.

Milligram shook his head.

"Because, Gram, if anyone hurts or harasses you, or makes you feel unsafe, you have to tell me. You know that, gel?"

Milligram nodded.

"And if you see any evidence of anything like that, you have to tell me too, Lemma. I'm not going to let my son be bullied. His father was abusive. I told you about that, didn't I?"

"You've mentioned it."

"His father was abusive. He's in prison now, but it's important to talk about it and discuss it thoroughly, otherwise these systems perpetuate. Gel, Gram?"

Milligram nodded.

"Cheri, could Gram and I continue with his lesson? Thanks for the snack."

Cheri smiled tightly, gave Milligram a Dipsocene pill, and left the living room.

"The reason I don't pop cheese, or anything made from milk, is that I'm allergic," Lemma told Gram, speaking softly so Cheri couldn't overhear. "It's like poison to me. I get very sick."

"Would you die?" Milligram's eyes were wide.

"Probably not."

"So you could pop it if you wanted."

"But I'd get sick. So why would I want to do that?"

"If the only food you had was this," Milligram licked brie off his fingers, leaving a streak of saliva and creamy cheese on his dark skin. "Would you pop it?"

"I spect I'd have to, in that case. When I was a little girl, most food made me sick. Now, do your math."

Milligram licked his fingers again, and turned to his tablet, tapping cartoon slices of a pie as numerical fractions danced across the screen.

Lemma bit a slice of whole wheat bread, gagging as she realized the seeds were not only beetle sized but also beetle flavored.

"Are you sad that you can't have cheese?" Milligram asked, as he finished a level, causing an anthropomorphic fraction to appear and congratulate him.

"I spect. Never tried it. Don't know what I'm missing."

"What are you sad about?"

Lemma gave a dark laugh. "Do I seem sad?"

Milligram shrugged, and started another level, as Lemma checked one of her blinks. Jax had sent a message: [*Went to Edeyong again. Didn't scope the girl*]

Lemma sighed. She had scouted Edeyong for the past several evenings, but she had not seen the girl who called herself Ruby since the night Fremen shot the man on his porch.

"Sorry for asking about you and cheese," Milligram said quietly. "They said at church we shouldn't do that, but I forgot."

Lemma leaned forward and touched his shoulder. "Milligram, what your mom said? And whatever they told you at church? Don't bother with that. It's not wrong to ask someone about what food they like, gel?"

Milligram nodded. "Do you want to come to church with Mom and me sometime?"

Lemma tensed. "I… I'd rather not."

"You should. They're nice people." Milligram ate a cracker dipped in jam, then asked, "Why don't you and my mom like each other?"

"I'm gel with your mom. Does it seem that we don't like each other?"

Milligram shrugged, and began the next lesson, rubbing his forearm.

"Milligram," she asked gently. "Where did you get that? What happened."

"Um. I fell at recess."

"Milligram."

"Don't tell Mom," Milligram whispered. "Please?"

"I won't spill. What happened?"

"One of the girls in my class, Corandy. She tripped me outside of gym." Milligram slid closer to Lemma. "She said it was an accident. Don't spill to Mom, gel?"

"Milligram, if someone's bullying you…"

"It was just once. Don't tell Mom, she'll talk to my teacher." Milligram's face twisted as he fought for control. "Please don't, gel? Remember, I didn't tell Mom about the chemie you brought to school? The one you made me spit out?"

You little twank, Lemma thought. She'd hoped Milligram wouldn't remember that incident. "Yes, but if this Corandy edges you again, tell me, gel?"

Lemma's skin prickled, she could already see herself at the next childcare audit, facing the same questions she had to answer four times a year. "Have you known a child in your care to have endured bullying, religious harassment, or verbal assault in the past three months? Did you alert the child's parents and teachers, if applicable?"

Cheri Mills entered the room again, brushing a feather duster against a window that was already immaculate. Lemma and Milligram exchanged a look, and slid apart.

At that moment, one of her blinks buzzed. Lemma stifled a gasp, coughed loudly, and waited until Cheri had left the room.

"You have a blink!" Milligram whispered.

"Plug it!"

It was a message from NewTulip786, or Haydis Donovez, as Lemma had to remind herself.

[*Solved it. It used Fibonacci's number phi as the key*]

Lemma replied: [*What was the message?*]

[*MASIDONBARREAUXNATISRAFEZZSHWACHINNYVI NIDAENTIEREZ*]

[*Those are names of people*] Lemma replied.

Most of the names Lemma had heard occasionally on the news, but it was the first name, "Masidon Barreaux," that made her blood rush. She stared at Milligram, who was rubbing the space where his left shin should have been, once again experiencing phantom pain.

"Milligram," Lemma said. "I want to visit your church."

CHAPTER 21

MASIDON BARREAUX

Friday, May 4

The word had been painted on the side of the Tiresian Meditation Center in ugly deep purple paint. A large crowd had gathered outside. Journalists and badges were collecting information and taking photographs. A janitor was spraying the graffiti with a water jet, and when Milligram, Lemma, and Cheri approached, he had just finished scouring off the '*R*'.

"Eezy," Milligram read aloud, pushing through a group of people on his crutches. "What does '*eezy*' spell? And who's that?"

"It spelled Reezy, Gram," Lemma said. "You know what Reezy means, don't you? How it's not a nice way to refer to Tiresians?"

Milligram nodded somberly.

"That's rimming horrible," a woman said, shaking her head. "I hope they catch him."

The janitor had finished spraying off the '*Y*', and moved to the other half of the graffiti: a grotesque cartoon face whose eyes had been replaced by x's.

"Let's go inside," Lemma whispered to Gram.

They entered a vast hall filled with what looked like a thousand chairs. In front, a woman in a white robe was giving a lecture. On the wall behind her was a pair of ovals, where soap bubbles the size of soccer balls formed and sank to the floor, gently bursting to release clouds of vapor.

"It's supposed to be a pair of eyes," Milligram whispered loudly, as Lemma put her finger to her lips.

More bubbles fell, and the woman finished her speech, and walked away from the podium with a help of a guide. Then the service concluded, and the congregation began shaking hands and hugging, some pointing toward the outside doors with hushed voices.

"Where is Masidon Barreaux's office?" Lemma asked Cheri.

Cheri led Lemma and Milligram out of the lecture room, past a gift shop and a lounge. They ascended in an elevator, and walked down a hall toward a pair of glass doors etched with the same double oval symbol Lemma had seen downstairs.

"Visitors for Mr. Barreaux?" a secretary asked, seated in front of the doors.

"Cheri Mills and Lemma Quartz," Cheri replied.

The secretary ran her fingers across her desk, which glowed in response.

"Mr. Barreaux will admit you now."

The glass doors slid open behind her. It was dark inside, but the light from hall penetrated far enough for them to see the silhouette of someone seated behind a desk.

"Masidon?" Cheri called out. "Cheri here, with a guest."

The three entered the office. A symphony was playing from a speaker.

"Lights on," a man's voice said, "and music down."

The symphony's volume lowered. The room filled with light, and they saw a man wearing dark glasses. Lemma recognized him from Wade Syan's funeral and the photographs in Syan's apartment.

"Cheri," the man smiled. "It's been too long."

He adjusted a control on the armrest of his wheelchair. It slid out from behind the desk, facing Cheri as she walked around and hugged him. Lemma blinked. Both of his legs were missing below the knee.

"And how is Gram?" he asked.

"Howsie, Mr. Barreaux," Milligram said, waving his arm. "I'm waving, but you can't scope it."

The man laughed. "Well, thank you for letting me know. That was very considerate of you. And Cheri, you said you would bring a friend?"

"I'm Lemma." Lemma cleared her throat. "Thank you for agreeing to meet me."

"The pleasure is mine, Lemma. My name is Masidon Barreaux. How do you know the Mills family?"

"I tutor and supervise Gram in the evenings. For five years now."

"Wonderful. I understand you had some questions about Wade Syan?"

"Yes, I did."

"Gram and I'll be outside," Cheri said. They left the room, leaving Lemma alone with Masidon.

"Besides childcare, are you employed elsewhere?" he asked, driving his motorized chair back behind the desk, and gesturing for Lemma to sit.

"No. I'm unemployed. Used to be a photographer, but they took my lice away." Lemma couldn't avoid putting an edge into her voice.

"That is regrettable, but they are a wonderful family. Cheri is a very involved woman. I'm certain she appreciates your assistance."

"I like posting with Gram. He's a bright kid."

"Families like that are why I love my work so much. And people like Gram are the reason we exist, to provide aid to those who need it, especially when their families do not aid them. I presume Cheri told you about his father?"

"Often. Mentioned he was abusive. Sent to prison six years ago."

"A shame when those closest to us don't support us." Masidon's fingers reached out to a figurine on his desk, a bust of a teenaged boy, and explored the face with his fingers. Lemma saw that the office was filled with figurines and statues. On the walls, instead of paintings, three-dimensional reliefs had been hung.

"Interesting artwork," Lemma mentioned. "Three-dimensional, so you can feel them?"

"Indeed." Masidon's chair glided to a wall, and he ran his fingers over one of the plates, a relief of a street view of a house.

"Cheri told me that you chose it for yourself," Lemma said. "Do you ever miss it?"

"Miss what?"

"Being able to see?"

"I can still see," Masidon replied. "I see with my fingertips, my nose, my ears. I enjoy music and songs more. I have a deeper sense of reality now that I no longer depend on my eyes."

"If you don't mind me asking, why did you decide to go blind?"

"Please, we prefer to use the terminology 'vision non-dependent'."

"Sorry. Why did you choose to be vision non-dependent?"

"It helps to limit the distractions of the world."

"Wouldn't being bl— being vision non-dependent be a mite distracting?"

"Around us sit a million distractions already, Lemma. Advertisements. Images trying to pitch you delicious food, better housing, more fulfilling sex."

"But isn't there a way to ignore that without going blind? Isn't it extreme? Having no sight at all?"

"For some. Not all members of our congregation opt for permanent vision non-dependency. Many wear corneal shields."

"Contact lenses?"

"A silicone circle, not unlike a contact lens."

Lemma was getting sidetracked, but she couldn't resist asking,

"Does anyone get the surgery and then decide they want to go back? Get cured?"

Masidon frowned. "'Cured' implies an illness or injury. It suggests that we are defective. Do you think I am defective?"

Lemma thought of Milligram's leg. "Maybe some people would rather be able to see and walk. Some are blind, sorry, I meant vision non-dependent from birth, or from injury."

"You are familiar with the founder of our church? Filbing Tires?" Masidon gestured at a statue in the corner of the office.

"I heard about him in school."

"A man who suffered a fall while riding a horse. Rendered completely independent of his limbs."

"Paralyzed."

"Again," Masidon said with firm patience, "Your term carries a bias. Tires' inability to move led him to study others who had learned to live without their limbs, or eyes, or ears. His landmark research revealed that people who live such lives are often happier. Finding more fulfillment and meaning. This revelation was what led him to found his movement, and eventually, his church."

Lemma clenched her jaw to avoid scoffing at the word 'movement.'

"Some members of our church, like our founder or your friend Gram, join after an accident or illness alters their body. Others, like myself, realize the benefits of living without eyes or feet, and choose surgery for ourselves. But I understand that our life is not for everyone. There are many who wish to see, but cannot. When my eyes were removed, I was able to grant partial sight to two individuals within our church. I gave them something they had longed for since birth."

"You donated your eyesight?"

Barreaux lifted his shaded glasses, and Lemma inhaled sharply. His eye sockets had been filled with white balls of lab-grown ivory. Each contained a black inscription: 'Consciousness' on the right and 'Freedom' on the left.

Lemma felt her face grow hot. "But altering yourself, in such a permanent way…"

"Plenty of people get orthodontics to straighten their teeth. Cosmetic surgery. Ink tattoos. Are these not also permanent?" Barreaux asked calmly.

"I…"

"Lemma, as you can guess, I am limited to knowing you only by your voice. Would it be intrusive of me to request to read your face?"

He lifted his hands, palms facing the ceiling, fingertips patiently extended.

"Gel. You may." Lemma took his hands, guiding them to her cheeks, her chin, her forehead, her eyes.

"You are of Eastern descent?" he asked, as his fingers glided over her eyelids.

"Yes, the Democratic Monarchy of Central Korea."

"But your accent says otherwise."

"Adopted at birth. I spent my entire life in this city."

Masidon replaced his shaded glasses. "For many, eyesight is a crutch. You would be surprised how much you can learn about the world, about yourself, by isolating your senses. May I interest you…?"

He had the eerie ability to find the exact drawer he wished without moving his face in the slightest. He extended his hands once more, offering a clear plastic vial, inside which floated two dark discs.

"Corneal shields. Try them."

Lemma hesitated.

"Please take them; I wish for you try them on. Do it and I will answer your questions about Wade Syan."

"Oh, gel. How do I…uh…wait."

She pulled open her left eyelid, and inserted the first corneal shield. Her left eye seemed to be turned off.

"Oh!" she said, her heartbeat fluttering. "This is—"

"Freeing?"

"I was going to say insanely rimming weird."

Masidon laughed quietly. "Put in the other one."

"Gel. It's in."

"Lemma, please do not be dishonest with me."

"What?"

"Put the other corneal shield in."

Lemma's right eye scanned the room, looking for some way Barreaux could have known she was lying, but found nothing. She touched the second lens to her eye.

Everything went black, but it also seemed to have grown louder. In the absence of light, she could hear her own heartbeat and Barreaux's, hear the hum of the lamps around them, feel the background symphony's drums and violins, smell the chemicals which had been used on the carpet, and her own deodorant. The chair where she sat felt more rigid, and her feet within her shoes were cold and damp.

"And in only a few moments, you have learned why so many choose this lifestyle for themselves. You are now a Tiresian."

"Uh, no, I'm not."

"To be a Tiresian is not to cease to be anything else. Some of us are Evangelicals, or Muslims, or Hindus, or even without any form of spirituality. We are not a religion with rules or supernatural beliefs, but a practice. A lifestyle of intent, of consciously isolating ourselves from outside influences."

Lemma's hands gripped the desk as dizziness pulled at her head.

"You are adjusting to a world with only four senses. It is quite acceptable to rely on sound and touch."

"I need to take these out."

"Patience, Lemma. Leave them in. Enjoy this moment. And now, ask your questions."

CHAPTER 22

IN THE DARK

"First question is…"

She couldn't see anything, but she could hear Masidon breathing with anticipation. The symphony was still playing gently.

"What can you tell me about Wade Syan?"

"Ask your first question again, but with more specificity," Masidon said, sounding amused.

"Gel. How well did you know Wade Syan?"

"Wade and I met privately about once a month. In addition, he and his wife attended fundraising events for the church several times a year."

The darkness highlighted certain features of Masidon's voice. His 's' sounds carried a sharp cusp, a combination of a whistle and a razor.

"So he was a member of the church?"

"As I told you before, anyone who strives to free themselves from the distractions and pressures of the world can be a Tiresian. You, in this very moment, are enjoying the Tiresian philosophy of independence of sight. Listen to the music." He paused. "You know who composed this?"

"No."

"Our good friend Mr. Beethoven. Some say his best music was composed after he became independent of his ears. You could say Ludwig van Beethoven was a Tiresian ahead of his time." Masidon sighed. "Syan developed a love for sight-independent meditation. He went so far as to learn Braille, and was able navigate this entire church building with his eyes covered. But he was never a registered member of the Tiresian Church. I believe he was affiliated with the Evangelicals, as he found their health plan and food plan to be the best fit for him."

"What did you talk about during your private meetings?"

"Lemma," Barreaux's smile was evident in his chiding tone. "Has no one explained to you the meaning of the word private?"

Lemma cleared her throat, but Barreaux wasn't finished.

"I provide counseling for a number of people, inside and outside the church. They come to me with their fears, their doubts, and I help them to understand options for helping themselves."

Lemma adjusted her position in the chair. The sound of the friction of her pants against the leather was amplified in the darkness.

"I understand the meetings were private, but was there anything Wade Syan ever said that strung you?"

"Strung me?"

"That made you concerned for him."

"Concerned? I wouldn't say concerned. Syan was a complex man, both gifted and cursed with a thirst for experimentation and invention. Everyone knew it. What few people know is how harsh he was on himself. No matter how many animals he rescued from extinction, or how many countries he saved from environmental destruction or economic collapse, he never found fulfillment. Through countless meetings, and calls in the middle of the night, he confessed his disappointment in himself."

"But he prevented mass starvation. He gave food to the whole world."

"You are not the only one who holds him in high regard, but he always thought he could achieve more, and even the great feats he had achieved he refused to take satisfaction in. My guess is he carried the weight of some memory… some guilt."

"Guilt for what?"

"It's only my guess. He never told me what it was, but every time he and his wife made a donation, I couldn't help but suspect some desire for atonement lay beneath the generosity."

"Or maybe he had more money than he could use for himself, and wanted to help others with it," Lemma suggested.

"Perhaps."

Lemma cleared her throat. "When was the last time you spoke with him?"

"Sunday, April 22. Two days before his death."

"Did you scope anything different about him?"

Barreaux paused. "I don't think so. Syan was the same driven, passionate man as he always was."

"I found a list of names. I'd like you to explain each of their relations to Wade Syan."

"Agreed."

"Natisra Fezz."

"Ah… Ms. Fezz. Formerly a city journalist, now the current head of CityNews. A steady advocate of the Tiresian Church, and a good friend of mine. She's currently writing a biography of Syan, so I imagine she can tell you even more than I can."

"When you say she's an advocate, what do you mean?"

"She reported on some of the earliest cases of religious persecution against our church. Her research helped to expose the hatred and even violence our community was facing. I take it you saw the most recent attack outside our building today?"

"The vandalism? That was cucked. I'm really sorry."

"Thank you, Lemma. I am grieved as well, especially for whoever the vandal was. That sort of action does not come from a happy person."

"Another name. Shwa Chinny?" Lemma asked.

"I am not familiar with that person."

"Gel. Vinida Entierez?"

"Ah, Ms. Entierez. She was not connected to Wade Syan, but is as influential as Ms. Fezz. Ms. Entierez is one of the most anti-Tiresian voices in the country. She earns money by writing books and giving speeches full of lies about us. A professional bigot, if you will. She is fond of propagating the rumor that we remove the eyes and limbs of our children."

"I…" Lemma hesitated. "I scoped a jackload of children in your church service today. With crutches, or walking sticks, or support animals."

"Of course," Barreaux said. "Our church goes out of its way to welcome adults and children who have been injured through no choice of their own. If your child loses their ability to walk, what better resource than a church founded by a man who himself was unable to walk? I assure you no church leader ever had more compassion for those without eyes or legs than our own Filbing Tires. But people like Entierez see injured children joining our church, and accuse us of causing the very injuries we seek to help them overcome. Her most recent work, 'Scalpel,' inspired a fresh wave of hatred against us." Barreaux's voice was grim.

Lemma stared into the dark.

"Do you have other questions?" Barreaux asked. "If not, you are welcome to keep your corneal shields. We have extras available in the lobby, should you wish to introduce the experience to your friends. Just don't share shields that you have already worn, due to the risk of contamination. And may I ask you a question?"

"Yes."

"Why the fascination with Mr. Syan? And Fezz, and Entierez?"

Lemma took a deep breath. "They say he drowned by accident, but I spect someone murdered him."

"Oh? And what led you to that conclusion?"

"It's just a guess."

"Interesting. If you have any more questions, I would love to assist you. I can even arrange a meeting with Fezz, if you would like."

Lemma nodded, forgetting it was a useless gesture. She felt for the desk, and stood. "One more question."

"Ask away."

"If there was any chance Syan was murdered, who would you spect it was?"

CHAPTER 23

RATIONS

Friday, May 11

"Farmers?" Jax scoffed. "Barreaux thought farmers ghosted Syan?"

Jax had stated this about a dozen times in the week since Lemma had visited Masidon Barreaux.

"I didn't say I agreed with it." Lemma scoped the refrigerator shelves underneath the sign which read "Dairy Rations. Manufactured by Phronesis Tech." Behind them, Milligram stood, humming to himself.

"Because that's stupid. Syan invents new ways to grow food, so seventeen years later, some farmer decides to ghost him?"

"Labbed food did put a jackload of farmers out of business." Lemma cursed, staring at one of the empty shelves. "How is all the sheep cheese gone?"

"How is the product with the highest resale value gone?" Jax repeated with mock curiosity.

Lemma cursed again. "Getonia's article. Now everyone knows what to buy. Schwartz will be rimmed."

"Salted butter," Jax suggested. "Best value. Resells for six grams silver. Also, even if a farmer wanted revenge, how could they get into Syan's bathroom and drown him? That building's got jackloads of security."

Lemma filled a basket with salted butter. "Maybe it wasn't farmers, but Barreaux had a point. We need to scout people who were edged by Syan. Twanks at Phronesis Tech who were terminated. Business rivals."

Jax didn't answer, but Lemma knew what he was thinking. After dozens of interviews with current and former Phronesis Tech employees, not a single likely suspect had emerged.

Lemma and Jax had now spent several evenings analyzing these interviews as well as their own reports, searching for anomalies. Messages from her other clients went unanswered. Syan's death was her priority. She even brought notes scribbled on food wrappers when tutoring Milligram, promising him an extra treat in return for him not spilling to Cheri. Lemma and Jax would have also continued their work while at Balkon, if not for the looming trial with Fremen Orea and Axiom.

"Trial's May 25, that's less than three weeks away!" Curio would say several times a day, storming past Lemma's desk to demand why things weren't moving faster. Even more stressful was the fact that Balkon membership was in steep decline, as Curio also made sure to bring up during her frequent rants.

"They're all going to Axiom," Curio had shouted, to no one in particular except a poor intern who had happened to be in her line of sight. "Axiom moves into town and cucks out honest community-minded mom-and-pop death agencies before we can even pull our rimming pants up!"

"Lemma," Jax asked, interrupting her memory of Curio. "You said Masidon made you blind?"

"He gave me blacked-out lenses."

"What was that like?"

But Lemma couldn't put it into words. She had left Masidon's office in complete darkness, unsure how to take the discs out of her eyes. Masidon's secretary took pity on her, leading her by her hand to the nearest bathroom, where she helped her remove them.

"It was… disorienting. Everything was louder." Lemma turned her attention to a purple stain on her hands. She couldn't remember how long it had been there or where it had come from; she owned nothing containing purple ink or paint. But then again, she couldn't even remember what she'd eaten for breakfast, so consumed was she with the Syan case.

"Lemma?" Milligram asked.

"What?"

"Can I have a treat?" Milligram pointed at a shelf of ice cream under the Dairy Rations sign.

"Sorry, Milligram. I'm not your parent. There's a limit to how many rations I can bleed for you."

"What about him?" Milligram pointed to Jax. "Does he have a limit?"

"Yes, he has a limit. His limit's zero. He's not your registered guardian."

As Milligram turned away, pouting, Lemma caught sight of a dark bruise on his arm.

"Milligram…" she began, reaching for him, but as he moved, his sleeve shifted and covered the bruise.

"Lemma?" he asked, wincing and massaging the stump of his left leg, "Is it time for my chemie?"

Lemma put the bruise out of her mind, telling herself it was only a shadow, and handed him a Dipsocene pill. "Here."

"Medicine," scowled Jax, watching Milligram swallow it. "Why does everyone have to take chemies?"

Several days prior, Curio had instructed Schwartz to give every Balkon employee a daily assortment of vitamins, which only served to add to the stress of the upcoming Orea trial and declining membership rates.

"Maybe if you bled less money on chemies, you could match Axiom's prices," Jax had made the mistake of saying. Curio did not appreciate this feedback, and had thrown a bottle of the pills at Jax's face before making him pick them up from the floor.

"You can't make us pop these!" Jax had hissed.

"Fun fact of the day," Schwartz had replied, watching Jax collect the pills on his hands and knees. "There is more than one way to get a pill inside someone."

Jax reconsidered his position, and agreed to pop the pills.

"I liked Schwartz better when he just asked for our kidneys," Jax muttered, as Lemma set the dairy rations in front of the cashier. "And why does Milligram need pills? He doesn't even work at Balkon."

Lemma sighed. "Milligram's chemies are different from ours, he's always taken them. Ours are vitamins or jack knows what. His prevent phantom pains in his missing leg. Every Tiresian who's been amped takes them."

Lemma's words stuck in her throat, as she stared at the cashier who was pointing the scanner at the products without looking at them. Ever since Lemma had spoken with Masidon, she noticed more people with amped limbs around the city. But it was the ones with dark glasses, like this cashier, that stood out the most to her, reminding her of what it was like to walk in complete darkness.

"You're gel," the cashier said. "Have a bright day."

Lemma checked a message on one of her blinks, and cleared her throat, unsure if the cashier could recognize her voice. "I also have something for you? A delivery?"

The cashier pulled off his glasses, blinking as his eyes adjusted to the light, and glanced at the package in Lemma's hand. He took it, smiled, and slipped her several cubes of silver in return.

"And there's another mystery," Jax said, when they were out of earshot of the cashier. "Who's the real twank, someone who chooses to be blind, or someone who just likes pretending they're blind?"

"Vision non-dependent," Lemma corrected, smirking as Jax rolled his eyes.

CHAPTER 24

LIGHT FROM DARKNESS

Saturday, May 12

When Lemma had entered Masidon Barreaux's office eight days ago, she had gone in already knowing what she had learned from Cheri and Milligram, and what she had read in the news over the past several years. But now, entering the CityNews building, a vast structure whose windows stared gloomily outward, Lemma was armed with only a few details on Natisra Fezz. She knew from Barreaux that Natisra's articles had helped the Tiresian Church, and she had also obtained Getonia's opinion during her last visit with the Oreas in Balkon's safe rooms.

"Fezz," Getonia had said, curling her lip and exhaling sharply and turning back to the article she was writing.

"Care to elaborate?" Lemma had asked.

"No."

"You said you used to juggle a camera? Wanted to be a photographer?" Fremen interrupted, looking up from a bowl of cold soup.

"Yes. Why?"

"Oh," Fremen smirked. "You'll love Natisra Fezz."

***

The inside of CityNews was as dull as the outside, Lemma thought, as Natisra Fezz's secretary beckoned her to enter the office.

"Ms. Fezz is ready?" Lemma asked, but the secretary didn't answer, instead pointing to a sign which read 'Independent of Hearing.' Next to the sign was a portrait of Masidon Barreaux, and another of Filbing Tires, and a third, the same teenage boy whose bust Lemma had seen on Barreaux's desk.

Lemma's first instinct was to scan Natisra Fezz for any clue that she might be affiliated with the Tiresian Church, but all her limbs and senses appeared to be intact. She was in her mid-thirties, with a round face and a rounder body.

"Lemma Quartz. Thanks for having me."

"Howsie, Lemma. Call me Natisra. Masidon told me you'd be coming."

Fezz had a slight accent, as if a German were doing a poor impression of a Russian. Or it could have been the gum she chewed.

"I like your office," Lemma lied politely.

Natisra shrugged. "It's got a view of the hospital and fountain. Nice, isn't it? They're renaming it after Wade Syan. Dedication ceremony is on Friday." She gestured out the window to a building across the street. The walls of the hospital were glass, and inside there was a fountain where jets of water shot in graceful parabolas into a pool of water.

Lemma decided that she had made adequate small talk, and sat down opposite Natisra. "I'm actually here to gather information on him, Wade Syan."

"Well," Fezz smiled, twin dimples forming in her cheeks, "Don't think you'll be getting my book before everyone else."

"Masidon mentioned you were Syan's biographer."

"His official biographer. The book hits the screens in twelve days."

"I look forward to reading it. My whole life, I crawled for Syan."

"The whole world crawled for him; he saved us from global starvation," the journalist said.

"Especially me. I was allergic to all the chemies farmers were putting in food," Lemma said, shuddering at the memory. "Every single meal made me pukey. You could label every bone through my skin."

"And when laboratory food was engineered to not need pesticides—"

"I could finally enjoy eating. In my apartment I have a picture of me, the first time I had broccoli."

Fezz nodded, a hungry look in her eyes. Never breaking eye contact with Lemma, she reached for her desk and starting typing on the glass surface.

"Keep talking. This would make a bright story. 'Once an emaciated pile of bones, Lemma Quartz is now a well-built, attractive woman. She owes her health to Wade Syan's innovations in food science.'"

Lemma's face reddened. "I spected your biography was finished."

"I can always use side articles." Natisra chewed her gum loudly.

"If you want to schedule a meeting later, I can tell you everything about how Syan affected my life. I wrote my final school essay on him. Every time Phronesis Tech cracked open a new molecule, my family had a feast."

Natisra's fingers tapped the desk, which flashed and glowed as she typed.

"Can we talk about Wade Syan?" Lemma managed to keep her tone gentle.

"Book's out on May 24," Natisra said in a singsong tone. "You can read it then."

"I'm more interested in the parts you left out. The boring details. Anything that might help shed some light on his last days."

"You read the state report. We all did."

"Did the state report mention the first person to investigate?"

"The state detectives?"

"Before the state detectives."

Natisra's eyes narrowed, she stopped typing to peer at Lemma.

"He had death insurance. You've heard of Balkon? They sent a team of investigators before the state detectives were ever there."

Natisra spat out the piece of gum into the garbage bin. "How do you know that?"

"I was one of the Balkon investigators."

Natisra leaned back in her chair, partly thrilled and partly afraid. "You're a death agent?"

"I post for Balkon."

"What did you see in his apartment? Was his wife sad? Angry? How did she react?"

"Can you tell me about Wade Syan?" Lemma smiled. "When did you meet him?"

"During the Ovian Hodeft case." Natisra glanced at a photo of a teenage boy on the wall. It was the same boy whose likeness was on her secretary's desk, as well as Barreaux's.

Lemma's smile went away. She had heard this name before, in one of Milligram's school assignments. Cheri, too, had a picture of the boy in her apartment, opposite the paintings of triangles and the golden spiral.

"Ovian Hodeft?" she asked.

"I was the lead journalist on the story. You're familiar with him?"

"He was one of the first victims of an act of anti-Tiresian violence, right?"

"The first." Natisra reached to a shelf, past a copy of Syan's *Thirsting for the Future,* and pulled out a book titled *Ovian Hodeft: Light from Darkness.* On the back was a close-up of Natisra, looking solemn.

"Bullied, because of bigotry and ignorance. This was ten years ago, before they were even a state-recognized religion." Fezz's voice was cold enough to make leaves fall from their branches.

"He became blind, right?" Lemma asked.

"He was not permanently vision non-dependent," Fezz corrected. "He wore darkened glasses. The church doesn't allow surgery on children, and it never has." She spat out another gob of gum to join the first.

"Yes," Lemma said, wondering why Fezz had been chewing two separate pieces of gum.

"Ovian Hodeft fell victim to the unkindness of his fellow students, who could not understand why he attended Tiresian meetings or practiced vision non-dependent meditation. His teachers did not attempt to protect him, or prevent his peers from tormenting him. During one occasion, one of his classmates forced him into a supply closet. There were lawn mowers in the closet, along with cans of fuel. One of them spilled fuel on his clothes. Another pulled out a lighter. This was before licensing laws on flame devices. And then..."

Lemma had seen the photos. Ovian had been burned so badly he could only be identified by his dental records.

"Ovian was killed, and the bullies were sent to prison, except for one, Teskir Mong. He was injured in the same fire that killed Ovian, and suffered irreparable brain damage. He's been in a coma ever since. And then came the lawsuits. That's where Mr. Syan entered the story. He offered to pay for Ovian's family's litigation against the school, and eventually their lawsuit against the country. Hodeft's brutal murder helped inspire a wave of support for the Tiresian Church, which was finally recognized as a full religion alongside Islam, Evangelicalism, Humanism, and the rest. Also there were tighter laws regarding privacy." Natisra pulled out a pack of cinnamon gum, and one of mint, and placed one stick of each into different corners of her mouth.

Lemma swallowed, feeling ill at the thought of how it must taste. "Privacy?"

"I had been writing about the need for stronger laws regarding privacy and electronic images before that. Photos taken of Ovian without his permission, showing him wearing his sunglasses, played a large role in his bullying. It was high time lawmakers worked to ensure people used cameras responsibly."

"So you're the reason I need a photography license?"

"Photography licensing laws were one aspect of Ovian's Law, that's correct."

"Ovian's Law," Lemma mused. "Laws named after dead kids. Smoother to pass."

CHAPTER 25

THE DOOR WITH NO HANDLE

Tuesday, May 15

Wilco Residential Zone had still not received any attention from the city, and a large pothole, hidden in the quickly dimming twilight, grabbed Lemma's ankle as she and Jax walked toward Fremen Orea's house.

"I want to watch a realtor try to pitch a house here," Jax's said, dodging potholes. "Two beds, two baths, but if the baths are busy, you can go out and piss in any of the potholes, and don't string out about your favorite pothole going away, because the city never… Cuck!" His toe caught in a crack. He flailed his arms, barely managing to keep his balance.

"You're leaving out the best part: gangs, goons, and occasional murders." Lemma tried to smile at her own joke, but with every crumbling, potholed step towards Fremen Orea's house, the memory of Ennerd Vik being shot on the porch drilled louder in her head. Her nightmares about Wade Syan were nothing compared to the raw visions of Ennerd that attacked her in the night. Sometimes they were so vivid that she would soak her sheets with sweat, unable to close her eyes without seeing his mangled skull.

"You want to say what we're scoping for?" Jax asked.

"Fremen said not to spill."

"Just a hint? We scraping evidence for the Axiom trial?"

"I wish."

Fremen's trial was in ten days, and despite countless hours of discussion late into the night, they couldn't find a single redeemable reason for Fremen to have shot a complete stranger on his porch. Curio was losing her temper, shouting at Lemma and Jax that if Fremen didn't provide a better excuse, Axiom would insist on ghosting him.

The only time Curio wasn't ranting about Fremen's trial was when she had been ranting about Lemma's meeting with Natisra Fezz. The day Lemma first met Natisra, the journalist had refused to tell her anything else about Wade Syan until Lemma agreed to give an interview about her childhood food allergies. When Lemma mentioned her work tutoring a child who attended the Tiresian Church, Natisra had insisted on interviewing Milligram as well the following day.

Natisra had yet to fulfill her promise to answer Lemma's questions about Syan, but both Lemma's and Milligram's interviews had been published, and became the top-viewed articles of the week. Within hours, both Lemma and Milligram had received invitations to the dedication ceremony for the newly named Wade Syan Hospital. Only Curio seemed to be unhappy with Lemma's interview.

"How do you spect to carry out assignments when everyone has scoped your rimming face!" she had yelled, loud enough for the entire floor to hear, calming down only when Jax defended Lemma by saying that the Syan Hospital dedication would be a valuable opportunity for Lemma to spy on the state's top government officials.

"This is it," Jax whispered, breaking Lemma's train of thought, and gesturing at Fremen Orea's house.

The porch had been wrapped in plastic tape of two colors. The orange ribbon held the words "*Under Balkon Protection. Do Not Enter*" while the yellow one read "*Axiom Death Insurance. Do Not Cross*"

"This place strings me out," Jax said. "Vik was right there. We had to clean up his rimming brains."

"I know. I was there when Fremen ghosted him."

"Plug it." Jax put a finger to his lips then pointed down the street. A cluster of goons were standing around a metal barrel in which they'd started a fire.

"Were they here before?" Jax asked. "Spect they're in a pack?"

"Don't know."

"Lemma, I spect they can scope us."

"Howsie, cucks!" one of the gang members shouted. "Want to get spread?"

"Back of the house, flash it!" Lemma grabbed Jax's wrist, pulling him around the side of the house, as the gang ran toward them, contra baseball bats clanking on the asphalt.

Lemma dug her fingertips between the bricks on the wall, ignoring the sharp pain as her nails tore off. She climbed to a window. Fingers going numb, she pried open the glass, and threw her fist into the mesh screen.

"Lemma!" Jax cried.

Rocks pelted the window, glass shattered, shards stung Lemma's forehead. The gang was screaming below, but Lemma's eyelids had fused together. She felt behind her for Jax's hand, and rolled through the window, dragging him with her into house.

Lemma opened her eyes and felt her forehead, wincing at the blood.

"Lemma, come on!" Jax grabbed her hand and they stumbled away from the window.

"Where— what—Jax?"

A door opened and shut. They were now in a closet. Fabric and zippers rubbed against her face.

"We're in the wrong half of the duplex," Jax said bitterly. "I told you, Fremen's place is the other side."

"Fremen told me to go in this side. His was locked, and these twanks always have their window popped open," Lemma said.

"But how do we get out? Jax cursed. "Someone's here!"

The gang was still shouting and throwing rocks outside, but a new voice could be heard coming from within the house. A man was muttering something, too quiet for them to hear. Then everything was still.

Jax counted to a thousand before opening the closet door. Stepping softly, they surveyed the shards of glass and rocks on the carpet.

"Twanks," Jax said. "We should leave money for him, or something."

"Absolutely not."

"It's our fault the window got broken."

"Then he'll know someone was inside! We cannot be scoped."

"Too late for that," Jax said bitterly. "Cuck, my fingernails got torn off."

Lemma's own nails began throbbing the moment Jax mentioned it.

"What did he say? To make the goons bounce?" Jax asked.

"I don't know. Want me to wake him up and ask?" Lemma pressed her fingertips into her palms, trying to suffocate the pain, as she groped along the wall. Her fingers rubbed against a door, which she unlocked by turning the deadbolt. Opening it, she revealed an identical door.

"There's no handle," Jax said.

"Claps. You should be a detective."

"How do we get out?"

Lemma shushed him, and pulled a cube of cold metal from her pocket.

"Lemma, please tell me what the plan is."

"But that would ruin all the suspense."

"Because that's what my life needs: more rimming suspense." Jax put his throbbing fingers in his mouth.

Lemma placed the metal cube on the door, at the height where the handle would normally be. She moved it around, and pushed on the door.

"It didn't open," Jax said.

"Thanks for your input."

She swiped several more times, finally feeling the magnet drag in her hand, an invisible force tugging against her. The lock on the other side clicked, but when she pushed, the door refused to open fully.

"Fremen said there would be a bookcase in the way. Jax, I need you to kick it down."

"You need me?"

"You're heavier."

"Because earlier, when you thanked me, it sounded a mite sarcastic."

"Jax!"

Jax raised his foot, slamming his heel against the door, with his other foot firmly planted on the ground. The door budged, and the bookcase on the other side creaked.

"Almost got it," Jax grunted, pressing his back to the door and rocking his body against it.

"Flash it."

"I'm trying!"

"And be quiet," Lemma whispered.

Another door opened in the hall, and a man walked out.

Jax and Lemma froze, staring at him.

"What do you want?" he asked. It was the same voice that had spoken to the goons outside the window.

"We, uh…" Lemma tried to come up with an explanation that wouldn't give them away.

"Please," the man said. "Anything. You can use my house, do whatever you want."

Lemma had expected him to shout, to threaten. She had not anticipated the stammer in his voice, or his broken pleas for peace.

"Just don't edge my family anymore."

"We won't edge your family," Jax promised.

"That house is empty. Abandoned." The man pointed to the door they had been trying to break into. "You can sell your chemies out of there."

"We will. Just stay out of our way," Lemma said.

The man nodded, and retreated into the bedroom.

"He thinks we're part of the gang." Jax pushed once more, and the door surrendered, as the bookcase blocking it fell with a thunderous crunch.

Lemma and Jax entered Fremen's half of the duplex.

Chapter 26

Uniform

They were in another hall, a mirror image of the first, except the man begging for the safety of his family was replaced by a shattered bookcase, whose fall had knocked several framed paintings to the floor.

"Lemma, tell me, what are we scouting?"

"Fremen said there was a chest in the basement full of contra goods. We need to lift it and shield it."

"When did he say that?"

"When I visited him and Getonia this afternoon."

"He's been at Balkon for over two weeks. Why now?"

Fremen hadn't told her exactly, but from his worried questions that he repeated each time she visited, Lemma realized he hadn't expected to be away from home for such a long time.

Lemma and Jax descended the stairs and walked through the same living room where Lemma and Milligram had once pitched death insurance to Fremen.

"Scope them." Jax pointed out the kitchen window at the flickering silhouettes of the goons, who still prowled around the house.

"How do we bounce if they're shielding the yard? And— oh, cuck!" Jax put his hand to his nose.

The kitchen cabinets had been emptied and forks, knives, and plates littered the floor. The refrigerator door hung open. Food, dripping and rotten, puddled on the floor.

"Those twanks broke in," Jax said.

"No. The door and windows were taped off. We're the first ones in here since the night Fremen shot Ennerd Vik."

Eyes watering from the smell, Jax and Lemma waded through a cloud of flies back into the living room. They descended the basement stairs and halted.

In the dim light from a narrow, dirt-streaked window, they saw five men curled up asleep on the floor, despite the noise from the goons outside. All were hairy and smelled like soap was against their religious convictions. Two of them were wrapped in sleeping bags, like giant domestic caterpillars. The rest slept on piles of clothes.

"How long have they squatted here?" Jax whispered.

"Should I wake them and ask?"

"You just said the house was taped off! How did they get in? From the other half, like us?"

"And put the bookcase back exactly where it was?" Lemma scoffed.

"They're asleep."

"Or clouding." Lemma pointed to a syringe lying next to one of the men.

"Quiet. Don't wake them." Jax cautioned.

"No, I was going to practice yodeling." Lemma spread her hands out, following the wall blindly, praying she wouldn't trip over anything or anyone as she navigated toward the far side of the basement where Fremen said the chest was located.

One of the vagabonds snored, and Lemma tensed, pinching her nose shut, holding her breath until her head throbbed.

She bent, feeling along the floor until her fingers slipped into a groove in the cement. She pulled, and a panel opened, exposing a cavity. Inside was a wooden chest the size of a microwave oven.

They lifted the box out of the hole, their muscles straining, and placed it on the floor. Jax wiped sweat from his forehead.

"Scope, Lemma. That's how they got in."

He pointed to a shattered window, just wide enough to crawl through. Against Lemma's whispered protests, Jax went over to it, staring up through the window well outside.

"It's the front porch," he said, feeling around the window well.

Lemma's arms prickled with goosebumps at the memory of Vik's head exploding as the bullet hit it.

"Jax! Come back here," she hissed.

He returned to her, and they carried the chest across the basement and up the stairs, trying to keep quiet as the steps creaked beneath them.

"Ung," muttered one of the sleeping men, and began to stir.

"Go, go!" Lemma hissed. They pushed out of the basement into the living room.

"Those goons are still out there." Jax jerked his head toward the taped-off windows.

Lemma's sore fingers gave up, and the chest slipped to the floor with a crash that rocked through the entire duplex.

Jax cursed to himself, and they waited. The silhouettes shifted outside the windows, and someone began scratching at the front door.

Jax looked at Lemma in panic. "Flash it! Move!"

"We have to shield this chest first!"

One of the windows shattered, as the goons cut through the tape and forced their way inside. Jax dragged the chest into the kitchen, slipping on the scattered cutlery. He reached into the open refrigerator, splattering handfuls of rotten mush onto the chest. Then he and Lemma ran up the stairs, splitting up as they reached the top level.

Lemma threw herself into a closet, and waited, as feet raced through the house. The goons forced open doors and turned over furniture. The door to Lemma's closet opened, and through the gaps in the clothes hanging in front of her, she recognized one of the goons from the street, brandishing a contra knife.

She waited, motionless, her heart pounding.

Then another wave of people entered, loudly announcing themselves as Balkon agents. They searched the house, tackling goons to the floor and arresting them.

Lemma counted to a hundred, then two hundred, then five hundred, then a thousand. Her bladder tightened and she emptied herself where she crouched, hot, damp, itchy, and smelling like rancid pickle juice.

Somewhere in the house was a clock, or some sort of kitchen timer. It beeped every hour or so. She counted three or four beeps before dozing off.

Finally, she saw a sliver of pink light seep under the door of the closet, growing steadily brighter. She gathered her courage and crawled out of a pile of clothes and into the hall.

There was no one here.

"Jax?" she called out.

"Mm." Jax came out of the bedroom, his eyes sunken and blood-shot. "You gel?"

"I spent the whole night lying in my own piss, but I'm alive."

They hugged tightly.

"Lemma…"

"What?"

"You need to scope this."

He motioned her into the bedroom and crawled under the bed, dragging out a bundle of clothes.

"What's that?" Lemma bent down.

It was a blue uniform, with a utility belt with handcuffs and a flashlight.

Lemma snorted. "So Fremen and Getonia like to play dress up."

"Lemma, scope it closely— where did Fremen say he posted?"

"As a janitor for the state." Then Lemma saw the gold and blue badge bearing the words "Phronesis Tech Security."

CHAPTER 27

HOPPING

Thursday, May 17

Cleats dug into artificial grass, dancing between shin guards and striking at soccer balls. An automated goalie zoomed between the posts, darting to the left or the right as it sensed balls approaching. On the bleachers sat a boy with one leg, his crutches standing on their own by his side. In his lap was a glass tablet, showing the words "*Soccer Essay, by Gram*" Nothing else had been written.

The soccer ball struck behind Milligram, sending a hum through the metal seats.

"Gram! Ball!" one of the girls shouted. Milligram leaned over, scooping up the ball and throwing it. The stump of his left leg rose into the air.

The girl caught it without saying anything.

"You're welcome," Milligram muttered. Saying this when someone forgot to say '*thank you*' was a joke he had learned from Lemma, although it was funnier when she said it.

Milligram wrote several words with his finger tip, and then erased them, drumming his hand on the bleachers until a ball bounced toward him again.

"Gram!" the girl shouted.

Milligram bent over his tablet and pretended to work.

"Gram!" Now it was the coach.

Milligram threw the ball with little effort, smiling as the girl had to run for it.

Recess ended, and Milligram hobbled past the goal, stopping in front of the same girl who'd demanded he return the ball. Now she blocked his path.

"Excuse me," he said.

The girl didn't move, and as Milligram stepped to the side, she mirrored him.

"Corandy, please. Sorry about the soccer ball. Please let me go by."

"I scoped you on the news," Corandy said.

Milligram shifted on his crutches.

"You going to be famous now?"

Milligram stepped in the other direction. Corandy blocked him again.

"Let me past!" He walked into her, trying to push her over, but she was twice his weight. "Move! Let me get by!"

She retreated, and he stumbled forward, falling and hitting the ground. Snickers fluttered around him.

Milligram blinked, fighting to keep from crying, and pulled himself up.

"He'll spill to his mom," one of the boys said. "Wipe off him."

Corandy stopped her taunts, hopping on one foot to shake a pebble out of her shoe, before turning back to Milligram. "You're going to spill to your mom?" she asked. "Going to bounce bounce bounce back to your mom?"

The kids were laughing harder.

Corandy moved towards Milligram. "Maybe your dad…"

Milligram swung one of his crutches like a baseball bat, striking her in the face and falling to the ground from his own momentum. Corandy clapped her hand to her jaw then dove for Milligram, who had no time to roll away. She turned him over, grabbing his coarse mop of hair, and dragged his nose against the grass. His arms whipped around, trying and failing to hit her. Milligram screamed into the ground, as Corandy reached down, digging her fingers into the elastic waistband of his shorts, and pulled.

His shorts slid off, along with his briefs, all the way to his right ankle. His left stump kicked helplessly.

Kids were screaming, falling down with laughter, waving cameras at him. Milligram closed his eyes and tried to shut out their jeering voices. The grass scraped against his bare buttocks as he reached for his pants, but Corandy had pinned them to the ground with her foot, trapping his ankle in them.

Then Corandy was gone, and Milligram's foot was free. He wiped the grass from his eyes and mouth, and saw Corandy lying on the ground, underneath someone whose hands were around Corandy's neck.

The students were no longer laughing, but they hadn't stopped filming either.

Teachers were shouting, sprinting toward them, blowing whistles. The person who had pinned down Corandy stood up, and turned toward Milligram.

"You gel?" Lemma asked, lifting him up and pulling his shorts back on with one motion. His briefs lay abandoned on the grass.

"Milligram, are you gel?"

The air slammed out of Lemma's lungs as Corandy planted her foot into her back. Lemma snapped around, and seized it before Corandy could retreat.

"Let go!" Corandy spat, but Lemma gripped tighter, holding onto a goalpost for balance. The automated goalie wheeled toward them, humming in confusion, scanning left to right for a soccer ball that never came.

"Let go of me, you rimming squint!"

Lemma swung the girl's foot against the goalpost, the knob of her inner ankle striking the metal with a nauseating clacking noise. Corandy's mouth sprang open, and she collapsed to the ground, gasping for air like a gurgling drain, but Lemma wasn't finished, smacking the ankle against the post again and again, rubbing the skin raw.

Teachers were shouting, and two security guards appeared and clapped their hands on Lemma's shoulders.

***

Lemma and Milligram were in the school office, staring blankly at a row of angry adults, as Milligram's mother forced her way into the room, demanding to see her son.

"Gram!"

She pulled Milligram into a tight hug.

"Careful!" Lemma hissed. "He's bleeding."

Cheri was about to retort, when a man with a shaved head and a thick neck addressed Lemma.

"Ms. Quartz, Corandy's family is considering pressing charges against you."

"There was just a sexual assault on your school premises, which your staff did rimming nothing to prevent! Maybe we should talk about that!" Lemma shouted.

"Sexual assault?" the bald man glared at her. To his left, the substitute teacher Lemma had bribed after being discovered in the science room raised her eyebrows.

"The little twank— Corandy— pulled off his pants. Forced exposure at an educational institution. That's fourth degree sexual assault. And she called me a squint. Ethnically motivated verbal assault, first degree. And Milligram is a member of the Tiresian Church, which makes Corandy's attack religious harassment in the second degree."

"It had nothing to do with him being Tiresian."

"I scoped her hopping around. Hopping on one leg in front of a Tiresian missing a leg is a form of religious harassment. She was mocking him. Right, Milligram?"

Milligram nodded quickly.

"But Ms. Quartz, you have yet to explain why you were even on campus in the first place," the bald man said.

"On campus? I— I don't need..." Lemma flushed, and tightened her grip on something in her pocket. "Half your students had unliced cameras that they were using to record Milligram's harassment, violating Section 5.14 of Ovian's Law."

The man exchanged an awkward glance with Cheri.

"Here's what's going to happen," Lemma said. "You're going to expel that girl. Make whatever calls you need, but get that twank out of this school. And you will forget that I was here. Understand?"

Everyone in the room stared at her.

"Or we can get CityNews involved. I'm sure Natisra Fezz would love to hear how your school treats Tiresians."

***

As they walked off the school grounds, Cheri looked at Lemma. "I'll take him home myself. He'll take tomorrow off, so we won't need you to visit."

Lemma nodded.

"What were you doing there this early in the day?" Cheri asked.

Lemma didn't answer. Instead she touched Milligram's shoulder. "I'll see you tomorrow evening at Syan Hospital for the dedication ceremony, gel?"

Cheri pulled Milligram away from Lemma, and cleared her throat. "Well? Why were you at the school this early?"

Lemma moved so close to Cheri that she could see her own reflection in Cheri's pupils. "You're welcome. For me being there for your son."

Through his tears on his green-stained face, Milligram smiled at Lemma.

CHAPTER 28

MOTHER

Friday, May 18

Wade Syan stared at Lemma with a broad smile which flickered as Lemma moved her hands through the holographic beams at his feet. She had never found holographic portraits enjoyable, but this one was especially difficult to stomach. This image, smiling at Lemma without seeing her, was the closest she would ever get to meeting him.

The Syan Hospital dedication ceremony was filled with guests from all over the city, laughing and gossiping, taking cocktails from hovering automated servers, playing at roulette wheels and blackjack tables for charity. There was a table draped in immaculate white linen with a pyramid of champagne-filled flutes stacked so high that no one could reach the top one. Lemma looked around the banquet hall, feeling pitifully underdressed in her jeans and hooded sweatshirt. She glanced at one of the hospital security guards, wincing at the memory of the Phronesis Tech uniform she had seen in Fremen's bedroom. She tried to think of something else.

Then Lemma's ears pricked at the sound of a familiar voice, and she turned to see Ingo Syan, posing with a tasteful smile, one that she had no doubt spent hours, if not a lifetime, crafting. It had the perfect ratio of lips to teeth, balancing the appropriate amount of grief with a dash of glamour.

"Remember, you want to be sad that your husband drowned, but also sexy enough to remind viewers that you're single again," Lemma imagined herself coaching Ingo, while aiming a camera whose flashes of light echoed off Ingo's flawless white teeth, blue eyes, and glittering necklace.

Ingo was as beautiful tonight as she had been during her first photoshoot as a young model, before she had ever known Syan, at an age when no man was allowed by law or decency to admit his desire for her. Lemma both despised her smile, and wanted one just like it.

"Agent Quartz, I'm so glad you were able to attend," Ingo said, as she turned away from the cluster of photographers who were documenting the hospital dedication ceremony. She approached Lemma with her arms outstretched.

"Just 'Lemma' is gel."

"Thank you for being here; it means so much to me," Ingo said, embracing her. This poised woman was not the same as the one Lemma had met in the apartment. That Ingo was flesh and blood, puffy-eyed and vulnerable, helpless in an angry, uncaring sea. This was a mere copy, constructed by careful artists, as artificial as the flickering image of the man who had once been her husband.

"Is there anything new with the investigation?"

"You scoped Balkon's report, and the state report. I'm sorry, Ms. Syan, I wish there was more we could do."

Ingo blinked, the light from the hologram bouncing off her dewy eyelashes. "It's all gel. You investigated, that was your duty. I was stupid to think there was anything else that could be discovered."

Many questions clawed at Lemma's throat, but she restrained them with a determined swallow.

"I can still hear his voice. He would make these silly jokes. On one of our anniversaries, he gave me a card. On the outside it said, 'Some people say the best things in life are free.' Then on the inside it said, 'But I say the best things in life bring a high return on investment.' And inside was a single printed share of Phronesis Tech stock. That was his idea of romance. I think I'll mention that in my speech. Do you want to read through my speech?"

"I'm not good with speeches, sorry."

"I could accept it…" Ingo's voice wavered, as if her shell was starting to crack. "I could accept it if I only knew what happened. He didn't have anything to drink, there was no note, he gave no indication that… How can someone…how can that happen so quickly?" She looked at Lemma, pleading for an answer.

"Can I ask you about some of your husband's friends?"

"Which ones?"

"Masidon Barreaux."

"What about him?"

"Was he close to you or your husband?"

"Close? Not exactly, although we saw Masidon frequently. He encouraged Wade to wear the dark lenses to meditate." Ingo gave a bittersweet smile. "I could never get into it. Kept banging my knees on furniture. I only really knew him through fundraisers at the church."

"What about Natisra Fezz?"

"She wrote his biography. She must have interviewed him a dozen times. She interviewed me once or twice. We didn't know her before that. Maybe— Oh, Quinn!" Ingo waved to a server who was leading a woman on his arm. As the server whispered into the woman's ear, the woman turned her face toward them, and Lemma saw that she wore dark glasses.

The woman, led by the server, approached Ingo and Lemma.

"Quinn, it's me, Ingo."

"Ingo! How good to find you here."

As the two women recited their respective lines of greeting, Lemma fought to remember where she had heard the name. Quinn… Quinn…

"Have you met Lemma Quartz? She was one of the investigators for my husband's accident. Lemma, this is Quinn. Quinn Hodeft."

Lemma felt a chill run up her spine. She held out her hand automatically, retracting it in embarrassment when Ingo cleared her throat. "Pleased to meet you, Quinn."

"And you as well. It's wonderful we can all come together to celebrate and remember Wade."

"I met Natisra Fezz on Saturday," Lemma said, not sure what her plan was for this conversation. What do you say to a woman so haunted by her son's brutal murder that she relinquished her eyesight in pursuit of the same tranquility that her son was killed trying to find? "Natisra told me all about… well the whole story involving your son… anyway, I'm sorry for your… I'm sorry."

Ingo pressed her lips together and looked around, as if hoping for a distraction that would end this uncomfortable line of conversation.

"Thank you. That means a lot to me," Quinn said. "Even after ten years, I'm still astounded by how much Ovian meant to everyone. Not a day goes by that I don't miss him dearly, but in a way he helped guide me on my journey. Because of what happened to him I found the Tiresian Church, and because of them I found a deeper peace than I could ever imagine."

Lemma wondered if she should hug her, but thought better of it. "It's terrible what they did to him, but I think it's really good how you're being an advocate for… your advocate work. Advocacy work," she said.

Lemma did not need to see Ingo's grimace; she was perfectly embarrassed all by herself.

"It's just awful," she continued, ignoring Ingo, ignoring how clumsy the words sounded in her own ears. "People, children especially, take any difference, anything that sets someone apart, and they turn it into a reason to make you an outcast."

Quinn nodded, her somber expression inviting Lemma to continue.

"You heard of Gram Mills? Natisra wrote an article about him earlier this week. He's the gentlest kid you've ever seen, but his classmates edge him. They trip him in the hallways, and elbow him in class, just because he was amped. Just because his mom takes him to a different church than theirs."

Ingo was looking around, searching for a convenient way to exit the conversation, but Quinn's attention was locked on Lemma, giving her a sense of understanding that Lemma had not felt in years.

"I didn't even know Ovian was being bullied," Quinn muttered. "Not until he was already… oh." Her breath fluttered, but her words were still smooth. "I never would have guessed he wanted anything to do with any church. He'd been teased when he was younger. His first day of kindergarten, they called him 'Duck Feet.' I never forget how he cried that day."

"Duck Feet?" Lemma asked.

"Here, I'll show you." Quinn adjusted her weight on the server's arm, pointing down at her own sandaled feet. Both of her feet had a fleshy web of skin between the second and third toe.

"I was bullied for it, as a girl. Then Ovian got his feet from me. We always joked how he got his father's nose and my toes. Thankfully he was able to get over it and find hobbies and friends. Marksmanship and acting, he loved those."

"Kids thought I was different too," Lemma returned in a low voice. Ingo had not yet departed, and the server who was guiding Quinn around had remained silent during this conversation. Lemma guessed he had heard all sorts of gossip between people who relied on him as a sighted guide. "Until I was nine, I was allergic to most foods. The pesticides and preservatives did it. Spent most of my childhood sick or hungry. It wasn't until Wade Syan…"

Ingo's head snapped back toward Lemma.

"He actually saved my life. I wanted to mention that earlier. That's why I wanted to come here today and be part of this. My whole life I wanted to one day see him in person, in order to tell him to his face how his food saved me."

"Phronesis Tech… the labbed food," Ingo marveled.

"It didn't just help people save money, and help to save the planet. It really saved my life. That's why I had wanted to meet your husband. I wanted to thank him. And I wanted to ask if he would ever invent a labbed version of milk."

"You can't drink milk?" Ingo and Quinn asked in unison.

"It's the only thing they can't grow in a lab. So it still has too many chemies in it for me to drink without getting sick."

"I wish he could be here," Ingo said wistfully. "Even just for a moment, just so he could hear how much of a difference he made to you."

Lemma glanced at the hologram behind Ingo and Quinn, also wishing that he would come to life, just for a second.

I'm going to venge you, she silently promised him.

CHAPTER 29

THE GOVERNOR

"Ingo! Quinn!"

A lady with crisp iron-gray hair inserted herself into the circle. She had a strong jaw and nose, features which Lemma recognized immediately from the news and the photos in Wade Syan's apartment.

"You're Governor Kawling," she said.

The woman finished her embrace with Ingo and Quinn, and turned to Lemma. "Governor Kawling I am. You'll forgive me if we've met before, I once memorized the name of everyone in the city, but I can't always recall them perfectly."

Ingo and Quinn laughed.

"Raemin, this is Lemma Quartz. Lemma, Governor Raemin Kawling," Ingo said.

Lemma shook hands with the governor, wondering if she had suddenly shrunk several inches. Wade Syan's hologram was taller than in real life, but it was this casual familiarity between his widow and the governor of one of the biggest states in the country that made Lemma feel so small.

"Lemma was one of the investigators when my husband passed away."

Lemma tensed, throwing an urgent glance at Ingo. Governor Kawling's eyes had narrowed, and she asked, "An investigator? With the state?"

There was a beat of silence.

"I meant, Lemma worked for…" Ingo's face was desperate and apologetic, as she looked to Lemma for help.

"She means I did an interview about him, after he died. Natisra Fezz interviewed me," Lemma said quickly.

"I saw that Natisra was writing pieces about what Syan meant to the city, I look forward to reading it," Kawling said.

"That's a relief. I thought you might be with one of those death insurance agencies." Quinn smiled, moving her head as if to sense whether her joke had landed.

"Well, I hardly doubt Wade Syan's family would consort with criminal gangs." Kawling's smile had returned.

Lemma spun a thousand ideas in her mind, searching for a way to change the subject. She had not expected to speak face to face with any government officials, and had no desire to give herself away.

"Can you believe people actually buy it? Death insurance?" Quinn asked. It was lucky for her she was blind. Had she seen Lemma's and Ingo's expressions, like cats ready to claw at her, she would have hastily retreated.

"It baffles me, innocent citizens risking their lives for some cheap theater of safety. Can you imagine, inviting goons to protect you?" Kawling shook her head grimly.

Lemma searched the room for a reason to escape the conversation. She bit down hard on her lip to keep from retorting.

"Are you feeling nervous about your speech, Raemin?" Ingo asked, and Lemma felt relief wash over her.

"Nervous? I wouldn't say so."

"I'm feeling unsure about my own speech. Could I get your thoughts on my opening line?"

Lemma spotted Milligram and his mother near the fountain in the center of the room, and turned in their direction. Milligram had cleaned up nicely, wearing a black suit one size too big for him, and Lemma wished she could hold a state journalist's camera and tell him how very handsome he was. But as Cheri made eye contact with her, she took Milligram's wrist and pulled him in another direction. Lemma tried to ignore the hurt.

"Do you know that death insurance agencies commit more murders than any other criminal industry?" Quinn said, jolting Lemma back to the conversation. "And over forty percent of their targets are the wrong one?"

"That's not true." Lemma answered too loudly, as if someone had held an invisible microphone to her lips.

Ingo cleared her throat warningly.

"You're not defending this corporate vigilantism, are you?" Kawling asked. "Businessmen who care for nothing but profit? Basing people's worth on how likely they are to be a victim?"

Ingo's expression urged Lemma to hold back, but the weight of years' worth of criticism would not be restrained so easily.

"Twenty percent of the population of this city has some form of death insurance. That's how little faith they have in your courts."

Kawling's smiled was strained. "Disregard for the law isn't a reason to break it further."

"Just a month ago, I saw a woman being assaulted by goons in the street, and a city badge walked past her," Lemma pressed. "Didn't help her for a rimming mite."

"Which is why we must continually invest in building up our law enforcement and legal system." As Kawling spoke, Quinn nodded enthusiastically, while Ingo watched with growing discomfort.

"Build up your legal system all you want, no one's going to trust it," Lemma retorted. "The citizens don't trust you; that's why they turn to death agencies. The food rations run out, so they turn to wolf packs to get food and water and chemies, and they can't pay for those so they have to use contra gold."

"So what solution are you proposing?" It was Quinn who spoke, her motherly tone gone. "You're making complaints, with no actual fix."

"You— you could…" As Lemma struggled to respond, she realized she had no answer.

"We should what? Cancel the food rations? Force people to buy from the gangs?"

The four women stood awkwardly. Then Quinn asked, "Where was it you posted, Lemma?"

"I'm unemployed, but I do service hours as a tutor. Used to be a photographer. Then the Department of Electronic Images lifted my lice and my camera."

"Oh! What happened?"

"Someone was edged by an image I took," Lemma said, allowing ice into her voice.

Kawling laughed awkwardly. "Well, I hope you can get your license back."

"You know, when I was a girl, we didn't even need a photography lice. People were taking photos left and right, absolute chaos," Lemma said coolly.

"Photography licenses did improve things," Kawling said, pretending not to notice Lemma's sarcasm. "Imagine a camera falling into the hands of voyeurs or spies! Sensitive information leaked, lives put at jeopardy. Lives and reputations ruined by chance photos with no context, left to the masses to decide who is in the right or in the wrong. Both child voyeurism and youth suicide rates dropped when we first required licensing for cameras."

"The other day I scoped half a dozen students, each with an unliced camera."

"More important than ever to enforce. You want goons taking photos of you without your knowledge? Young men, flooded with hormones, stalking you late at night on the street? Hiding behind your curtains, peeking through the cracks in your bathroom?"

"Maybe if I could fix the cracks in my bathroom— Oh wait! I can't, unliced home repair is illegal."

"Lemma," Kawling said gently. "I understand your concern. But we need to focus on finding solutions, rather than dwelling on our troubles. For example, the photography license laws are changing."

"So I can buy a camera without a course on why scouting people's bedrooms is wrong?"

"We are increasing the required hours for a license from 100 to 120."

"How will that help?" Lemma scoffed.

"How will it help?" Kawling laughed. "Lemma, are you being difficult? Of course it will help. Besides raising the quality of photography, it will safeguard your own profession. More required hours mean fewer people to clog the market to steal your hard-won customers. You'd earn more money."

"So the money I earn with the lice can help me afford the lice."

"I'm not your enemy, Lemma. I understand your frustration. If I had my way, licenses would be good for three years, not two. Maybe even four or five."

How generous, Lemma thought.

"But as it stands, we must take a hard stance to defend privacy. I will not have the state overrun by voyeurs and perverts."

"Privacy. Like when the DOEI sees every photo we take?"

"Lemma, there are people in this world who would do anything for a profit, including exploiting children and the vulnerable for the twisted gratification of those willing to pay. Supply to meet demand. Have you ever seen wolves ripping at a deer? Greedy animals, devouring their kill until there is nothing left? Businessmen, gangs, they'd find a way to profit off clean air if we let them. They'd charge a fee just to allow you to watch the sunset."

At that moment, an automated platter of cocktails flew up on whirring blades and halted by the women.

"Drinks?" it asked politely.

Kawling held out a glass to Quinn's attendant, and one to Ingo. Lemma reached for one, but Kawling warned, "Careful, those contain milk. Here, take this."

Lemma sipped a can of Raspberry Blush, as the music coming from speakers overhead changed.

"Aenna Mae," murmured Kawling. "I could never stand her voice."

"She's one of my favorites," Lemma said. She also hated the singer.

Ingo was about to start a new conversation when someone entered their circle and took Lemma by the wrist.

"Lemma," Natisra Fezz said. "I need you to come with me."

CHAPTER 30

TESKIR MONG

"Natisra!" Kawling said. "Wonderful to see you, we were just talking about your interview."

"Howsie, Governor. I'll just be a mite, and then I can chat. Lemma, walk with me."

Lemma stammered a quick goodbye as Natisra led her away.

"Natisra?" Lemma said sharply, pulling her wrist away from the journalist's grip. They were standing by a large flag, which rippled in the breeze of the room's ventilation system, its forty-eight stars swaying above the two women.

"Natisra, are you going to give me any info on Wade Syan?"

"I will, but we have to find a quiet place to talk. Are you going to drink that?" the journalist asked.

"I..."

"Thanks." Natisra grabbed the can of Raspberry Blush and poured it down her throat. She coughed, as two pieces of gum, one pink and one blue, ejected onto the floor. "Shouldn't have popped that so flash," she mumbled, wiping her chin.

"Natisra, are you all right?"

"Plug it, we'll find a safe place to talk."

Natisra pulled her past the stage, where people were gathered, studying notes on their tablets, preparing to make speeches, and past a mural on the wall, which displayed the Phronesis Tech logo, along with Syan's motto, "Thirsting for the Future."

"I read your article about Gram and his mother," Lemma said.

"What'd you think of it?"

Lemma had too many thoughts to share at once. She had felt it didn't focus enough on Milligram's bullying, instead extolling the benefits of living with one leg.

"I spect you changed some details around."

"Changed details?"

"The article was supposed to be about him dealing with bullies."

"I didn't make anything up; it's all the questions he answered."

"But it seems like you have an agenda."

"This way, Lemma," Natisra said, directing her out of the hall, and down a flight of stairs to a quieter section of the hospital.

"I was scoping my notes for my Syan biography," Natisra said. "And I found some details which might be of interest to you."

"Details? Ow— twank—" Lemma had stumbled over a set of orange ridges in the floor. "What the cuck?"

"They're for vision non-dependent patients to guide themselves. Watch out for them," Natisra said.

"What details?" Lemma asked, struggling to keep up with the journalist.

"Possible enemies of Syan."

"Oh?"

"Apparently, he had a habit of lifting credit for ideas."

Lemma narrowed her eyes. "Lifting credit?"

"For his employees' ideas. Some former employees thought he was a thief."

"What?" Lemma couldn't believe what she was hearing.

"A number of his innovations, labbed meat especially, had been designed by others. He copied them and scraped the patents before they could bring it to market."

"He didn't." Lemma stopped. "Wade wouldn't do that. He— he never lifted someone else's ideas."

"I know this is hard for you to hear."

"How could you even suggest that? And at the dedication ceremony for his hospital!"

"Lemma, don't be ridiculous, if there were people he cucked, they'd have had reason to ghost him. Now, I have a list of former employees who attempted to file lawsuits against him. I'll give it to you later."

They were halfway down the hall, almost at one of the entrances to the hospital.

"I also wanted to ask, have you scoped organ grinders as suspects?"

"Organ grinders?"

"You know, they buy and pitch people's organs?"

"Uh…" Lemma tried desperately not to think of one particular individual with whom she had done business.

"Because in some of our private interviews, Syan mentioned that Phronesis Tech was working on growing human organs in a lab, things like kidneys, livers, and lungs."

"Steady?"

"Think about it. If he were to start growing and selling commercial organs, who would be hurt by that? People who pitch organs! Imagine gangs trying to compete when Syan could grow them with a snap of his fingers?"

"I'll… I'll consider that. Natisra, why are we here?"

They had reached the end of the corridor, and were standing by a large glass box. Inside was a man lying in a hospital bed, and dressed in a hospital gown. The figure had a multitude of tubes and hoses sprouting from his body, making him look like an artificial weeping willow. In the corner of the box was a metal plate. On it, Lemma read, "Teskir Mong, who went into a coma after fatally injuring Ovian Hodeft in an act of brutal religious intolerance, which spurred lawmakers to pass Ovian's Law and legally recognize the Tiresian Church as a regulated religion."

"You remember I told you about Ovian and Teskir?"

"Wipe off!" Lemma hissed. She could not think of anyone, conscious or not, that she would be less willing to visit than the murderer of the son of the woman she had just spoken with upstairs.

"I told you how Teskir was in a coma, that the hospital kept him on life support all these years," the journalist said.

"Natisra, I don't want to be here. I want to go back upstairs and scope the speeches."

A message buzzed in Lemma's pocket. It was from Donovez.

> [*Are you at the hospital ceremony? Intruder in the south wing. Ghosted guards. Armed with a knife*]

Chapter 31

PHANTOM PAINS

"Lemma!"

Lemma ignored Natisra's shout, sprinting away from the ghastly box where Ovian's killer lay, almost tripping on a set of orange ridges.

"Donovez!" She whipped out the phone Donovez had given her and initiated the first telephone call she had made in many years.

"Where you now?" Donovez's voice asked.

"Main entrance, by Teskir Mong."

"I'm scoping you on the surveillance screens. Take the first elevator on your left."

"Anyone else know?" Lemma hit the elevator button a dozen times, willing the door to open.

"Just us. Drop him before he causes any more jack."

"Who is he? Why is he here?"

"Keep him breathing so we can find out."

The elevator door slid open, and Lemma entered.

"Target's moving down the hall. Still on opposite side of the building from you." Donovez cursed. "Twank ghosted another guard—cuck— he lifted their uniform. He's disguised as a guard."

Lemma bounced on the balls of her feet, urging the elevator to move faster. She screamed and kicked the door. The elevator continued ascending at the same smooth pace, but the shiny metal now bore a round dent, distorting Lemma's face like a ghastly carnival mirror.

"Target is on the third floor, approaching the event hall," Donovez said.

"Third floor now," Lemma said as the door opened.

"To the left, down the hall, and take another left."

In the windows on either side of the hall, Lemma's reflection sprinted along with her, flickering whenever it was interrupted by brick or wood.

"Flash it, Lemma!" Donovez growled.

Lemma's rubber soles squeaked on the floor tiles as she turned. Another long hall stretched in front of her. At the end a door was opening.

"Lemma, he's in the same hall where you are."

Through the door walked a man in a security guard's uniform.

"He's walking toward me."

"Walking, or running?"

"Walking." Lemma threw her phone into her pocket, frantically turning her head until she found it: a food tray, left standing in the hall. On it was a metal coffee pot that felt firm and weighty in her hands.

Donovez's voice was muffled as it came from her pocket.

"Plug it," she whispered. The man was less than twenty feet from her.

"Ma'am," the man said, touching the side of his belt. "You belong back here?"

Lemma raised the coffee pot. "Yes," she said. "I'm a nurse."

"Show me your card."

"Here." They were only a few feet apart, as Lemma pulled out her wallet.

"This is only a citizen's—"

Lemma's knee jerked up, slamming into the soft flesh between the man's thighs. Before he hit the floor, she whipped the pot down against his temple.

The man was sprawled on the floor, motionless.

She spoke into the phone, "Donovez, I got him."

Donovez was screaming at her.

"Gel, Donovez, tell me what's—"

"Wrong target! You have the wrong target, you twank!"

"He's not the intruder?" Lemma pulled the guard's ID from his belt. Except for a dent in his skull and a flow of blood, the faces matched. "I spect I have the wrong one," she said.

"You rimming twank."

"I know you can't hear me, but I'm real sorry," Lemma told the unconscious man. "Donovez, I just dropped the wrong person."

"Lemma, ahead of you…"

Lemma tensed.

The door at the end of the hall opened a second time, but it was only a hospital patient in a white gown. He walked slowly, his toes cautiously exploring the ridged path along the floor.

"Sir?" Lemma shouted. The man said nothing. He kept one hand in front of him, waving it through the air, as if feeling for obstacles in his path. He ran the other hand against the walls and windows, feeling his way down the hall.

"Donovez, it's only a Tiresian. Blind and deaf." Lemma walked briskly to the blind man, snapping her fingers in his face and getting no reaction. He shuffled past her, his eyes open but unseeing, unaware that there was another person close to him.

"The target's nearby. Stay alert— cuck— turn around! Follow him!" Donovez shouted.

Lemma spun around. The man was now running at a full sprint, his white gown billowing until it slipped off, revealing a stolen security uniform. He jumped over the motionless body of the guard and charged down the hall.

Cursing, Lemma chased him, her feet pounding against the tiled floor. The man maintained his pace, but Lemma was faster. As she gained on him, she saw why: an artificial metal limb had replaced his left leg below the knee.

The man's limp became more pronounced. He threw open a pair of doors to a room and slipped inside. Lemma crouched outside, watching and listening as the intruder raised his stolen ID badge and mumbled several words.

A computer's voice spoke, "Welcome, Officer Holloway. How may I assist you?"

"Send out a Public Health Crisis Warning. Input text: I'll be avenged."

"I have your message: 'I'll be avenged.' Is that correct?"

"Send it."

The computer's screen turned red, displaying the three words of the man's cryptic message. The man turned to leave, but jerked to a halt as a sudden spasm of pain crossed his face. He gasped, massaging the stump where his leg connected to the metal replacement. Hopping on his good leg, he reached into his pocket, pulling out a single white pill. As he brought it to his mouth, it slipped from his grasp, falling to the ground and rolling out of sight. The man screamed, denting a table with a blow from his metal leg. Then he limped out of the room through a door on the opposite side.

Lemma went inside and approached the computer screen.

"Computer," Lemma said. "Cancel the Public Health Crisis Warning."

"Please enter your ID number."

Lemma keyed in her CityLink ID.

"Unfortunately, I can't verify your ID. Please contact an administrator."

Lemma bolted out the door behind the man, catching a glimpse of him as he rounded a corner.

She followed him, pushing through a set of double doors.

She was back in the main banquet hall, at the top balcony overlooking the crowded floor below. The party had continued as if nothing was wrong: cameras flashed, roulette wheels spun, Wade Syan's hologram glittered, and the fountain sent jets of water splashing into the air. Outside the glass walls the city billboards had all changed to the red medical alert, but the guests were too absorbed in their cocktails and conversations to notice.

Lemma ran down the steps three at a time. She pushed past servers and hovering automated platters carrying hors d'oeuvres, fighting to keep sight of the target in the jumble of guests.

But the man had disappeared.

Lemma jumped, trying to see over the crowd, but she had lost him. Cursing to herself, she cased the perimeter, passing the table with the pyramid of champagne glasses.

Lemma threw her weight into it. The resounding crash brought everyone's attention to her, and they stared in awkward horror, motionless as statues. Lemma focused her attention on the one man who hadn't ceased moving. Now wielding a kitchen knife, he limped toward a woman with iron-gray hair.

"Governor Kawling!" Lemma shouted and ran toward her, her feet sliding on shards of wet glass as people dove out of her way.

A guard jumped out from the crowd, whipping his electric baton at the intruder's face. The man ducked, and thrust his metal leg into the guard's chest. The baton clattered to the floor.

The intruder lunged at Kawling. The knife swung down on her shoulder, but as he raised his arm for a second strike, his body trembled, and he grabbed for his metal leg with an agonized cry. Lemma was on him, wrapping her arms around his neck and shoulders, smothering him before he could complete his attack. The knife was flailing, guests were screaming, cameras were flashing—

Then Lemma was struck by a bolt of lightning.

Chapter 32

Father

Saturday, May 19

Help me.

"Lemma."

I'm dead.

"Lemma, dear."

Cool wetness tickled her forehead and cheeks.

"Can you hear me?"

She groaned and opened her eyes.

"That's a relief," said Dr. Schwartz with a matter-of-fact tone. "I have enough paperwork without you dying."

"Good to see you, too," Lemma said, as a stream of memories rushed in. "Schwartz! He's juggling a knife! He's going for the governor."

"It's gel, Lemma! Plug it," Schwartz hissed. "Everything's gel. Badges arrested him, the governor survived. You got a slight scratch from his knife, and a bit of a zap."

"A zap?"

"Shock baton, during your cuddle time with the attacker." Schwartz giggled. "Never seen an adult piss so much in my life."

Lemma scowled, and tried to move her right arm, which was wrapped in a bandage.

"Ow."

"Grow a pair."

"Sexist."

"—of ovaries."

Lemma snorted. "You get an offer?"

"Eggs by the dozen," Schwartz said, grinning. "But on a more serious note, I did a quick blood test while you were out. I know Curio said no more asking, but if you ever want to sell a kidney—"

"Where am I?"

"Syan Hospital. You chose a convenient place to get dropped, claps."

"How did you get in?"

"Jax pulled some favors, he has friends here. See this?" He dangled an ID badge in front of her eyes.

"That's a woman's photo."

Schwartz examined the badge. "Hmmm. So it is."

Lemma stretched and scratched her scalp with her free arm.

"I'll get you loosed. Curio wants a full report. Also…" Schwartz pulled out several blinks and Donovez's phone. "Lifted these from your pockets before the state doctors could scope them."

"Thanks."

"Does Curio know you're juggling all these?"

"Uh… I'd rather you didn't mention it."

"It's all gel. Doesn't string me. Just get your story steady for Curio's report. And you'll want a version to give the state badges, too." He stood and tossed the wet washcloth into the sink.

"Can't imagine what that twank was thinking, attacking the governor like that, and in front of his own son."

"The attacker had a son? Was he helping him?"

"Not helping. Lemma, you haven't heard?"

"I was unconscious, so I might have missed it."

"Your friend, the Reezy kid, Gram Mills. The attacker was his father."

The security guard might have tased Lemma a second time, so numb was she in both body and mind as she waited the rest of the morning. A thousand thoughts clamored in her skull, but there was no one to give her any answers. Finally, in the afternoon, security guards wheeled in a visitor.

"Governor Kawling," she said, trying to look less injured.

"Careful," the guard behind Kawling warned.

"Oh, wipe off," the governor told him. "She saved my life; she's not going to hurt me. Bounce!" The guard left. "I hope I'm not disturbing you," Kawling said to Lemma. Like Lemma, she was wearing a hospital gown. She wasn't imposing anymore, less of an iron lady and more of a frail grandmother.

"You can call me Raemin, you've earned that. It was very brave, what you did," Kawling said. "How did you know?"

"He passed me in the hall." Lemma had spent hours rehearsing her answer. "I saw his ID had someone else's face on it, and I followed him. Didn't know what he planned to do until I scoped him going after you."

Kawling didn't press her on the details.

"Raemin? Earlier last evening, we were talking and— I was a twank to you. I'm sorry."

Kawling smiled and winced as the bandages tightened around the stab wound in her shoulder.

"Don't string out about it. And I apologize, too, if I was rude at all. One of the aspects that make this country great is the freedom to disagree with one's leaders, and with one's fellow citizens. I should get better at listening to the people I represent."

Lemma nodded.

"Well… thank you again. Is there anything I can do for you? You mentioned a difficulty with your photography license. I'm certain I could expedite that."

"Photography lice. That'd be bright." Lemma grinned. "Also, can you introduce me to someone named Shwa Chinny?"

"Shwa Chinny?" Kawling answered slowly. "I believe he's a data analyst for the state. You wish to meet him?"

"Yes. It's a side project."

Kawling's eyes narrowed, but if she suspected Lemma of anything, she hid it well. "I'd be delighted to introduce you. Also, your ability to take down an armed attacker certainly caught the state's attention. Have you ever considered a career in security? Or law enforcement?"

"I— no. I haven't."

"Perhaps you should."

Lemma nodded.

"Consider it, and give me a call. I could give you my personal number?"

Lemma squirmed. "I don't have… I have a unliced phone. You're not going to turn me in, are you?"

Kawling gave her an amused look. "I'll pretend I didn't hear that."

Lemma fished Donovez's phone out from the pile of her clothes on the chair by her bed. As Kawling entered her information, she sighed.

"Lemma, did the attacker say or do anything to indicate why he wanted to hurt me?"

"Didn't have time to ask. Too busy getting stabbed."

"What about Natisra Fezz?"

"Fezz? Why would he say anything about her?"

Kawling's face grew somber. "Didn't you hear?"

"Hear what?"

"Before he attacked me, he got to her and pushed her into the fountain."

"She's— she's dead?"

Kawling nodded.

CHAPTER 33

QUERIES, SORT, AND FILTER

Natisra Fezz wouldn't leave Lemma's mind, no matter how she tried to distract herself. She spent the morning walking through neighborhood after neighborhood, rehearsing her last conversation with Natisra, cursing herself for not getting the information she sought sooner. But Natisra's clues remained unsolvable; even after hours of searching through lists of past employees and business associates whose work Wade might have stolen, Lemma was no closer to an answer.

Almost as impossible to solve was the matter of Fremen Orea, whose trial was now six days away, and who still refused to give any more details about the night of Ennerd Vik's death. Lemma had given up trying to help him; she no longer paid him and Getonia visits, except to confirm that she and Jax had safely hidden his contras somewhere in her apartment's single room. She refused to mention the Phronesis Tech uniform hidden at his house; she wouldn't even discuss it with Jax or permit herself to think about it. She had promised Fremen to keep him safe, and if she allowed herself to consider that he had played any role in Syan's death, she might have killed Fremen before Axiom could.

With no other lead to pursue, Lemma called Governor Kawling that afternoon, and requested an introduction to the next name on Wade Syan's list.

***

Shwa Chinny, data analyst for the state, was pale and tall. Slender except for a bulging belly, he had dark hair pulled into a ponytail which failed to cover his bald spot. In his office hung posters of aliens and space exploration. As Lemma sat across from him at his desk, she noticed his shelves, which held empty liquor bottles for decoration, as well as several bottles which had not yet been emptied.

"Raemin said you were the one who saved her?" Chinny asked. "You were in the middle of last night's, uh, unpleasantness at the Syan Hospital?"

"That's one way to phrase it."

"He hurt you?"

"Stabbed me." Lemma raised her bandaged arm stiffly. "And the badges buzzed me." Lemma sniffed. Chinny was wearing a pungent lemon-scented cologne.

"You wanted to ask about Wade Syan?"

"Yes."

"Last I heard, he was still dead."

"Did you know him?"

Chinny shook his head. "Never spoke a word to him."

"No interaction with him at all?"

"None."

Lemma sighed. "Maybe you can tell me something about some people he knew? Masidon Barreaux?"

"Barreaux." Chinny smirked. "I could clog a toilet with what I know about him."

"Steady?"

"For starters, he's not actually blind."

Lemma's mouth dangled open. "Are you jacking me?"

Chinny's smirk widened. "The look on your face! He's blind, but he has secrets."

"Secrets that connect him to Wade Syan?"

"You think he drowned Syan? Drove his scooter over him in the bathtub?" Shwa closed his eyes, and pantomimed steering a wheelchair. The lemon smell became stronger.

Lemma didn't smile when Shwa opened his eyes. "Do you know anything or not?"

"Masidon Barreaux used to rimming hate the Tiresian Church."

"Steady?" Lemma leaned forward.

"Yes." Chinny smiled knowingly, and Lemma suspected he got a rush from sharing this bit of gossip. "Everyone did. Syan, Governor Kawling, every politician and journalist did. This was fifteen years back;

you would have been too young to remember. The Tiresians were these weird little twanks. Every comedian rimmed on them. Easy targets. You remember the donut-Earthers?"

"I've heard of them."

"Convinced themselves Earth was shaped like a torus. That's donut-shaped, if you don't know."

"I know what a torus is."

"No one took them seriously; they were just good for a cheap laugh. Then one day ten years ago, some twanky kid with sunglasses catches fire, and suddenly we have to crawl for them."

"But Barreaux was already Tiresian before Ovian Hodeft died. What made him convert?"

"I could tell you, but it's easier to show you," Shwa said, turning his computer screen to face her. With a couple keystrokes, he displayed a jagged graph of blue and red pixels.

"Book sales related to Tiresian beliefs and practices. Three years before Hodeft died, they started to increase. It was still a weird cult to the rest of the world, but it was gaining popularity. There was a market for a new religion, and people like Masidon jumped in to capitalize on it."

"He amped his eyes and legs just for the money? Weren't there other religions to take advantage of?"

Chinny shrugged. "Maybe he had other reasons. Profound mental illness would be my guess for most Reezys."

Lemma gasped. "You can't… you can't say that. It's—"

"Religious harassment? Verbal assault?" Chinny sneered. "Only if you turn me in."

"What if I did?"

Chinny laughed. "You wouldn't. You're not so in love with the Reezys yourself."

Lemma swallowed.

"You volunteer for a Reezy family, but that's because of a court-mandated community service. You never donate to them, or attend their fundraisers." Chinny swiped at his desk, and the display changed. "Other than the Mills family, none of your close friends are Tiresians."

"How do you know all that? Where I donate? Who my friends are?"

"I'm one of the top data analysts in the state. I know everything about everyone."

"Then why didn't you know anything about Wade Syan?"

"I never said that. I only said I never met him in person."

"So do you have any data on him?"

"What? Like him cheating on his wife?"

CHAPTER 34

FAKE BABIES

Lemma tensed. "What?"

Chinny sneered. Lemma glanced at a mug on his desk imprinted with the words "Let Us Sphix Your Problems," and fantasized about the sound of ceramic shattering against his skull.

"You heard me. Conks, girlfriends, secretaries."

"That's not true."

"Oh? You have access to his messages?"

"That's illegal."

Chinny shrugged.

"Why would you tell me that?" Lemma's pulse was pounding.

"I read your interview with Fezz. Syan might have saved your life, but you can't let yourself be blind to his faults." Chinny's face looked greasier, and the lemon smell was making her nauseous.

"At the dedication ceremony Natisra told me Syan had a habit of copying other people's work. You think that's true?"

Chinny nodded. "Everything that came out of Phronesis Tech was something he copied from someone else. If anyone tried to spill on him he destroyed them in court."

"Maybe one of those people ghosted him? Out of revenge?"

"No. It was his wife."

"Ingo? His wife killed him?"

"If I had to guess."

"She knew about his— habits?"

"About him spreading conks and pinning secretaries? She knew. She hated him. Besides, who else was in the apartment with him? No one else could have done it."

Lemma swallowed. "What about Natisra Fezz? Any secrets about her? Could she have known something about Syan?"

"Natisra Fezz," he murmured. "Wrote some landmark articles, including the Ovian Hodeft story. She's head of CityNews, one of the youngest to run it."

"I knew all that. What about below the surface?"

He swiped on his computer, glanced at the screen, and smiled.

"What about her?"

"She fabricated some stories. Nothing to do with Syan."

"Did she get caught?"

"No. After she wrote the Hodeft story, she was bulletproof. She could say two plus two equaled cuck and the Tiresian Church would shield her."

"What about Vinida Entierez?"

"Entierez, Entierez… ah. Also a journalist. Hates the Tiresians. Fined multiple times for writing absolute ratjack about them. Claimed they were forcing kids to get amped."

Lemma fell silent.

"And what about you?" Chinny asked, smiling knowingly.

"Me?"

"I scraped more info on you. You used to juggle a photography lice, but had it revoked five years ago. Accusations of religious harassment against the Tiresian Church?"

The computer displayed a photograph of several children, each hopping on one foot. In the background was a Tiresian meeting center.

"The anonymous complaints took issue with the subjects hopping on a single foot, making a mockery of Tiresian Church members who opt for pedectomy," Chinny read aloud from the file. "Was it on purpose, Lemma?"

"The kids were playing a game. They didn't know about the church being there, and I didn't see it either."

"But they still took your camera and license." Chinny sneered. "And made you do community service. What else can I find out about you?"

The sharp, cloying smell of lemon was making Lemma sick. She resisted the urge to fan herself.

"Unemployed, receive state rations and food assistance. You spend your entire dairy rations on sheep cheese," Chinny said, reading from his computer.

Lemma swallowed. "So?"

"Highest resale value in the contra markets."

"I like sheep cheese."

"Natisra's article said you were allergic to dairy. But what's a little food ration fraud? So I dug deeper."

"You don't need to—"

"Health records. Turns out, you have been pregnant six times in the last six years. Officially, you're swelling with a little twank right now. Claps."

Lemma's face was burning.

"You had the pregnancies terminated, each at around five months. And the doctor who amped your babies… the majority of his clients go in at five months. Scope it!"

He displayed a graph of every pregnancy termination doctor in the state, and the average age of the fetus being terminated. There was a thick red line by Lemma's doctor around the five-month mark.

"Five months is the longest you can be swelling without a bump. Let me guess, your doctor gets a cut of your expectant mother benefits in exchange for pretending to amp your fake babies?" Chinny pulled more data. "But none of that is as damning as your work for Balkon Death Insurance Agency."

Lemma swallowed. "What makes you say that?" she asked.

"It's the power of data. Scope at this. I have a list of all city deaths this year that were labeled as accidents or unsolved murders. Let's narrow that down to people who had been accused or suspected of committing a murder themselves."

Lemma shifted in her seat.

"Now we'll narrow it down to those whose alleged victims had coverage with death agencies. Let's do Balkon, as an example. Now, if I ghost someone covered by Balkon, and then I die accidentally, it's only logical to guess I was targeted by Balkon, right? So let's scope at purchase records, and find every citizen who was in a bar or restaurant with any Balkon target less than forty-eight hours before that target was found dead. Now that is interesting." Chinny pulled up a list of several dozen people. "I'd guess it's a list of the most active death agents. Your name is on the list. Coincidence?"

"I visit bars a lot."

"Specifically with people who have murdered Balkon Death Insurance members and then wind up dead?" Chinny smirked. "What a coincidence."

Lemma couldn't resist stealing a glance at the list. Jax Yedra's name was there, as well as half the names of people she knew at Balkon.

"It's the power of statistics," Chinny said proudly. Lemma sniffed, and finally recognized the lemon scent. It wasn't cologne at all, but a citron-scented mosquito repellant.

Lemma wrinkled her nose. "Why are you doing this?"

"I could spill on you; there's always a reward for scouting death agents, but I bet I could get a bigger reward from you."

Lemma sighed. "Like a bribe?"

"Lemma, bribes are illegal. Besides, I need something else."

"What?"

"Data. Balkon's list of agents. I can guess from stats like this, but you'd have the full records."

"You want me to spy on Balkon?"

Chinny shrugged. "Think about it. I'd pay you, supplement your food rations fraud."

Lemma stood up. "I have to go."

She stumbled out from the office, pushing past dozens of state data analysts. Someone called out her name, but she put her head down and walked even faster.

CHAPTER 35

CORANDY

Monday, May 21

The bell buzzed, and children spilled into the hallways, some racing for lockers, others playing on tablets. One wore dark sunglasses, and moved around like a zombie with outstretched hands. This amused his peers, until a teacher pulled him aside, chastising him with angry words like "appropriation" and "religious mockery."

Through the waves of students limped a boy walking on crutches. His bag clung desperately to his shoulders, and with each hobble it threatened to slip off.

"Gram!" a girl called out. "I'll juggle that, gel?"

"Wipe off, Corandy," Milligram replied, dodging her.

"I'm helping you. Give me your bag."

"Didn't they expel you?" Milligram refused to make eye contact with her, aiming his face at Corandy's feet, one of which was bandaged thickly.

"Corandy! Get away from him!" A teacher with razor-thin lips joined them, stepping in front of Corandy.

Corandy protested, "I'm helping him; I'm juggling his books."

"Is she helping you, Gram?"

"I'm gel on my own."

"Corandy, you need to leave Gram alone, understand?"

Corandy exhaled heavily. "I have to. My dad is making me. I have to be nice to him."

"Your father told you to do this?"

"Yes."

The teacher smiled with satisfaction. "Gram, you should let her help. She's trying to say sorry for last week. Right?"

Corandy nodded. Milligram shrugged.

The teacher whispered a warning to Corandy, and observed as they walked away, both limping.

"How's class?" Corandy asked.

"Gel."

Corandy asked several more questions and received corresponding monosyllabic replies. She made frequent glances behind them until they reached Milligram's locker.

"Gram," she said quietly.

"What?"

"I heard you were at the fancy dinner when the governor was attacked."

Milligram shifted his body and held his crutches tightly.

Corandy set the book bag in Milligram's locker. "They're saying it was your dad who did it. That right?"

Milligram stared into his locker.

"Your dad stabbed the governor? Tried to ghost her?"

"I need to go to class."

"Drowned some people?"

"Go away."

"You want to know why?"

"Wipe off!" Milligram turned around, looking around until he met the teacher's gaze. She was walking toward them.

Corandy stepped backwards. "Don't you want to know why your dad did it? Didn't they tell you?"

Milligram glared at her. "What?"

"Did you read the news? My dad told me why your dad tried to ghost everyone."

"I…"

"You want to know?"

CHAPTER 36

ARTIFICIAL SOLE

For two days since she had met with Shwa Chinny, Lemma had been afraid to leave her apartment. Her head was still spinning from her conversation with him, his offer and subtle blackmail pressing down on her shoulders. She could sense him spying on her; every location tag, from her thumbprint in the empty expectant mothers section of the CityBus to her scan at the District 9384 prison, gave Chinny another morsel of data to analyze.

It wasn't until she was inside the prison that she was able to let go of her anxiety. Chinny could see where she scanned in and what she purchased, but he was not omniscient, or he would not have asked her to supply him with data he lacked.

She breathed more easily as she faced one of the prison workers.

"Howsie. I have an appointment with Perron Mills," she said.

"No appointments today. Schedule's choked," the worker said dully.

"I already made the appointment."

The worker shrugged.

Lemma sighed and pulled out several contra bills. She cleared her throat.

The worker nodded, took the money, and led her through the facility, pressing buttons as metal gates opened and shut, until they reached a cell.

"Your conversation is being recorded. Unless the recording device is broken," the guard said, adding, "It's probably not broken."

Lemma kept her commentary to herself, and took a seat opposite the man in the cell. They were separated by a plate of glass.

"Remember me?" Lemma asked, staring into the face of Perron Mills. His skin was darker than Milligram's, but his upturned eyebrows and prominent cheekbones bore a strong resemblance to his son's. "We met at the Syan Hospital dedication three nights ago."

"Met," Perron said hollowly.

"We didn't get a chance to toss names; you were too busy stabbing me. I'm Lemma Quartz."

Perron sighed.

"And you stabbed Governor Kawling, ghosted several others, and drowned Natisra Fezz."

Perron's lips twitched in a shadow of a smile.

"Anything you want to say about that?"

"What's there to say?"

"You must have had a reason to ghost people in front of your ex-wife and son."

Perron leaned forward. "My son? Gram was there?"

"Yes. He saw you stab me. He had to watch his father try to ghost his nanny."

"You're my son's nanny?"

"I watch him after school."

"So you know Cheri?" Perron asked.

"Yes."

"She told you about me?"

"She mentioned you."

"What did she say?"

"She—"

"What did that rimming cuck say about me?" Spittle flew from his mouth and struck the glass window.

"Said you'd been arrested for domestic abuse."

Perron laughed, baring his teeth like a hungry dog. "She still tells people that?"

"Why? Is it untrue?"

"She said it to get custody of Gram."

"So you didn't abuse her? But you ghosted four people at the Syan Hospital."

"That was a mistake."

"How do you drown someone by mistake?" Lemma yelled.

"All I cared about was Kawling."

"Why her?"

"That cuck is the Reezys' pet. She's going to run for president in four years. She'll make us all cut our eyes out. You know what they did to my son? Cheri ever tell you that?"

"Cheri told me that after Gram lost his leg, they joined the Tiresian Church."

Perron groaned, striking his metal foot on the floor of the cell. "Backwards! You have it backwards! She joined the church first."

Lemma knew what he was going to say, but she still asked, "Why would your wife join the Tiresian Church before he lost his leg?"

"He didn't lose it," Perron growled. "They amped it off. They took it from him."

Lemma leaned forward, pressing her burning forehead against the fingerprint-smeared glass. Her throat knotted; she couldn't swallow or cry or even breathe.

"I don't know how she joined. Maybe some of her friends invited her. They tried to get me to join too. Bunch of freaks. Cucked-out cult."

Lemma managed to take a breath. She asked, "How long was she in the church before she had your son get surgery?"

"Not surgery. Mutilation. Three months after she joins, she starts bringing home these ideas, and wearing those dark glasses. You've seen those? You can pretend to be blind. Half her friends were blind or deaf or they cut off their arms or legs. The delusional twanks said it helped them. She asked me why I cared if someone else scoops out their eyes? I said I don't. Cut off your eyes, your ears, pull out all your teeth. It's nothing to me. But then they started doing it to their kids."

Lemma swallowed.

"She never got amped herself. Too afraid. But she insisted on it for him. Said it would help him. I told her she shouldn't go to that church anymore, but she kept going. I tried to take Gram, to protect him from her. That's when she threatened to divorce me. I fought to keep him, argued that she couldn't be trusted with him as long as she was in that church. But the judge was friends with the Reezys. Judges are supposed to be neutral, right? No such thing. You're either with the Reezys, or you're not. I knew I was going to lose, so I surrendered. We stayed married, and his mother took him to get amped."

"Amping children is illegal." Lemma's throat was dry.

"Didn't stop her. Reezys can protect you. Gram was three, too young to understand. She told him later he'd been injured."

"You didn't tell him the truth?"

"I'd promised the judge not to."

Lemma wiped her eyes.

"Then it got worse." Perron's voice was low and gravelly.

"How?"

"Cheri got pregnant." Perron raked his fingernails across his cheeks, leaving bloody furrows. "Six years ago. Gram was five. I didn't want another kid, not raised by that twank. But we got drunk... Worst mistake of my life."

"But Cheri doesn't have another child. What happened to it?"

"Not it," Perron growled. "*Her.* Gram was going to have a baby sister."

Lemma's stomach was sour. "What happened?"

"Cheri and the Reezys had this idea to amp the baby before she was even born. Cut her eyes out. Make her blind from birth."

"No. Who would— how would someone know how to do it?"

"Pregnancy termination doctor. Give them some silver, schedule a regular termination. Except he goes in, and just takes out the eyes. Then he does the mandatory pre-termination screening, signs a statement saying the baby was found already blind, and by law—"

"You can't terminate a fetus based on handicap discrimination."

"Exactly." Perron's voice was bitter.

"Then what?"

"I refused. Wouldn't sign off. And by law—"

"You need a spouse's signed consent to get a pregnancy termination."

"But I wouldn't give it. Not going to let her gouge my daughter's eyes out."

"So?"

"So she divorced me. Sued, pretended that I hit her and Gram. Said that I'd pinned the baby into her."

"She accused you of rape?"

"I had to run. Took Gram with me, but we got caught. Gram went back to Cheri, and I was arrested."

"How did you get out?"

"Part of my sentence was mandatory counseling. Guess who my therapist is?"

"Who?"

"A Reezy." Perron laughed darkly. "A Reezy. Pushed his ratjack down our throats, had me wear shades, ear plugs. Told me how my dependence on my five senses was holding me back. Therapists at the prison could get you released if they spected you were rehabilitated. So I had to prove it to him. Showed them how committed I was."

"How did you do that?"

"Here." Perron lifted his left leg up, showing Lemma the metal foot that he had used to kill the guard at the Syan Hospital dedication. "Only way to get them to loose me. Maybe one day they'll invent labbed feet. And a foot was smoother to live without than an arm or eyes. My left one, just like Gram. Wrote a whole thesis about why surrendering my foot would help me find peace. Worst rimming thing I ever wrote it my life, but it worked. They decided I was rehabilitated and loosed me."

"And then?"

"I declared war on the Tiresians. First I tracked down the doctor who amped Gram. Did some amping of my own. Not so smooth to be a doctor without eyes or limbs." Perron smiled. "But according to their religion, it's what makes you happier, gel? Got a list of doctors who work for Tiresians. I've ghosted seven so far. Their church leaders, too. Some journalists—"

"You became a murderer."

"Is it murder to ghost someone in self-defense? What about to shield someone else? Every doctor, every priest that I wipe off makes a hundred fewer kids who get mutilated. Everyone hates the Reezys, but they're so strung out to do anything, because these days, even pointing out that it's wrong to amp a kid is verbal assault against their church. I'm the only one who's solving the problem."

"But you're not solving anything," Lemma protested. "The more doctors you murder, the more martyrs you make! You create more Ovian Hodefts. There's no way to win."

"You're wrong."

"I'm not going to start ghosting Reezys and doctors."

"Then fight back in small battles, Lemma. Tyrants depend on us thinking that only big changes matter. I didn't only ghost people. If I scoped a doctor's private car going into work, I slashed his tire. Just one tire, you can save a kid."

"What's the use? So you stop a doctor on their way into work? The parents will get their kid amped the next day."

"What if the doctor who amped Gram had been late that day? It would have been worth it even if it gave him one more afternoon with both his legs."

Lemma felt her stomach churn; she feared she would vomit onto the glass pane. "Why did you target Governor Kawling? She's not a doctor. She didn't amp your son."

"She's running for president. She's the Tiresians' favorite, she helped them out as governor. Gave them protection and extra funding. Imagine what she'll do when she runs the whole rimming country. We have to stop her. You can't change the past, but you can still change the future, Lemma."

"How did you get into the Syan Hospital dedication? How did you get through security?"

Perron sneered. "Same way I walked past you." He closed his eyes, mimed feeling for an invisible surface. "If you're a Reezy, you can get away with anything. You can close your eyes, go up to a badge, feel around with your hands, then when they let their guard down…"

Lemma jumped and yelled, but the harsh bang of metal against re-inforced glass was already nothing more than an echo in her throbbing ears. Spidery cracks blossomed from the center of the window, the only shield which had kept the sole of Perron's mechanical leg from driving into her face.

Perron pulled his leg back, and sat down, smirking, as Lemma's heart fluttered like a trapped bird. "Didn't realize how strong a fake leg is, huh? I could break open your rib cage, yank out your heart, and make an omelet from it." He winced, and massaged his leg. "Phantom pains. You juggling any Dipsocene? It's the chemie we take."

"I know what it is. I don't have any," Lemma lied. "What about Wade Syan?"

"What about him?"

"He was friends with the Tiresians. Gave money to them. Was he ever on your list?"

Perron shrugged. "Didn't have to be on my list. He drowned on his own."

Lemma had one more question. "Mr. Mills? What happened to the baby? Gram's sister."

Perron put his hands over his eyes, exposing a tattoo on one wrist which read *I'll be avenged.* "Doctor jacked up the amping," he said, his voice finally breaking. "The fake termination became a real one."

CHAPTER 37

SCHEDULE ONE

"They amp kids?" Jax whispered. "They amped Milligram's leg? You always said it was jacked from an infection!"

"That's what Cheri told me."

"But you believe the dad? He tried to ghost you."

"Plug it!" hissed one of the other Balkon agents. They were in the break room at Balkon headquarters, waiting for the governor's live address from the capitol.

"I don't know who to believe. I don't want to know. I'm trying to forget it." Perron's words had weighed on her all afternoon, as had Shwa Chinny's claims about Wade Syan, and Chinny's offer to buy Balkon's list of agents.

"You talk with Milligram since the dedication? Or his mom?" Jax asked quietly.

"I haven't talked with them since I jacked that girl's ankle."

"No childcare?"

"He's been staying home. And Cheri's been avoiding me."

"Plug it!" shouted Curio, as they watched Governor Kawling approach the microphone on the live feed.

"Several nights ago, I and several others at the Syan Hospital dedication ceremony were attacked by a deranged man intent on causing injury and terror to friends and members of our Tiresian community," Kawling said. Her arm was in a sling, which made for a powerful visual, whether or not she actually needed it. The licensed photographers and journalists stood around her, camera flashes reflecting off their badges, each one reading "State-Certified Photographer."

"Natisra Fezz, a beloved member of our community, and a powerful advocate for the Tiresian Church, was drowned in the Syan Hospital fountain by this man," she said. Behind her, a mug shot of Perron Mills appeared.

"Our hearts go out Ms. Fezz's family and friends," Kawling said, pausing and letting five seconds slide by.

"We are certain that this attack was prompted by a disturbing bias towards our Tiresian community. The attacker was known to harbor a deep resentment towards his estranged wife and son for their involvement with the church. This resentment manifested itself, as such feelings inevitably do, in a hateful and very public act of violence.

"This man utilized a kitchen knife as his tool of assault, and made use of a compromised security system to enter the dedication ceremony. His weapon was obtained despite lacking a chef's license, and was purchased with illegal, so-called 'contra' currency," Kawling said, her expression stern.

"I implore you, as members of our community, to regard this tragic incident with a determination to avoid anything like it in the future. There is no reason why any peaceful citizen with good intentions should make use of non-state-issued currency."

Lemma looked at Jax.

"If you currently possess any contraband of any kind, including non-state-issued currency, I implore you to surrender it to our police force. In accordance with our voluntary compliance laws, no one will be prosecuted for handing over illegal goods to a state officer or representative."

One of the death agents yelled at the image projected on the wall for Kawling to get cucked. Curio shouted at him to wipe off.

"If you suspect a friend or family member of owning and dealing in non-state-issued currency, you are obligated by conscience and by law to file a report. Every time you exchange any good or service for contra currency, you are fueling a dangerous trade of unlicensed goods. You cannot know whether your currency will next be traded for a weapon, an unlicensed blink, or a camera to be used by a sexual predator," Kawling paused again, letting that awful image sink in.

"Come and rimming get it!" a death agent shouted, waving a Balkon bill in the air. Curio threw a bottle at her.

"Furthermore, this attack is a grim reminder of the danger presented by a controlled object in the wrong hands. The attacker purchased his knife with the express intent to cause injury and death, and he had the safety edge removed in violation of state law. Starting tomorrow, our state legislature and I will discuss measures to require a chef's license for any knife longer than four inches in length, and to more tightly monitor any business or individual with the tools to sharpen knives. For those of you who are chefs, we do not hold a grudge against you. We fully realize the great responsibility and value you provide to us in our restaurants, hospitals, and schools. However, I urge you to always keep your controlled tools secured, and not lend them to anyone but licensed users. Safety is a responsibility we all share, and only by a joint effort on everyone's behalf can we keep our city safe.

"Furthermore, our best intelligence suggests that the attacker was working with one of the so-called death insurance agencies. Until now, the city has treated death agencies as any other illegal business. But on the recommendation of my attorney general, we are now classifying death agencies as a Schedule One domestic terrorist group."

The room erupted in shouts of outrage. Half the Balkon agents, including Curio, were demanding to know why Lemma had bothered to save the governor's life. Lemma and Jax backed away, as cartons of food and glass bottles flew towards the wall, breaking across Kawling's face. She had finished her speech and was smiling victoriously, waving her free arm toward the journalists and citizens that surrounded her.

CHAPTER 38

THE GOOD DOCTOR

"Claps Quartz, claps," an agent called out sardonically.

"Get rimmed." Lemma shouted back.

"You should have let the twank ghost her."

Someone threw a bottle at Lemma's face, but Jax swatted it away. "Let's bounce," he told her.

Jax and Lemma headed for the hallway.

"They don't know what they're stringing about, you did the right thing by saving her life," he assured her.

Lemma leaned against the wall. The noise from the break room was faint, but she could still make out insults hurled at Kawling and herself. "What if Kawling does step on us?"

"We'll deal with it." Jax reached out, patted her shoulder clumsily. "You cold?"

Lemma shivered, and Jax pulled off his coat. "Here, take this; I was too warm anyway."

A door opened, and Schwartz stuck his face out.

"Can we help you?" Jax said, pulling his hand away from Lemma's shoulder, as she clumsily pulled on the coat with her healthy arm.

Schwartz grinned. "You can help me by not pinning each other outside my office."

Lemma looked at the floor, heat radiating from her face.

"Or you can help me with this sample." Schwartz gestured into the room, where Fremen was sitting on a padded, sterilized table, his left shirtsleeve rolled past the elbow.

"You help him. I'll give you a shout when they've calmed down, gel?" Jax returned to the break room and Lemma followed Schwartz inside.

"Wipe his arm here, gel?" Schwartz pointed to Fremen's inner elbow, handing Lemma a swab and a plastic bottle of alcohol.

"How are you?" she asked Fremen.

"Surviving." Fremen winced as the cold liquid touched his skin. "Any breakthrough on the trial?"

Schwartz inserted a needle in Fremen's arm and the syringe filled with blood.

"This Friday. Four days from now," Lemma replied. "We're burning ourselves on it. Did you remember anything new?"

"But we'll win, right?" Fremen looked up at Lemma anxiously. "It was self-defense. I have a right to protect myself."

"Like I said; if you remember anything else let me know."

The memory of the Phronesis Tech uniform hidden under Fremen's bed burned in her mind.

As Fremen stood up to leave, Schwartz handed him a stack of bills. "Also, I'd appreciate it if you didn't spill this to Curio. For some reason she gets stringy when I buy blood on company property."

Fremen nodded.

"'Don't buy from our clients, it's against Balkon policy,'" Schwartz imitated Curio's voice with a high degree of accuracy, and Lemma and Fremen laughed.

Fremen left, and Schwartz and Lemma were alone.

"His trial. He doesn't have a rimming prayer, does he?" asked Schwartz, capping the blood-filled vial.

Lemma shook her head.

"If he's guilty, do we have to ghost him? Or do we give him to Axiom?"

"That's Curio's and Axiom's decision. Not mine."

"If they do ghost him, they better save his organs. I mean, it's better than letting them go to waste, gel?" Schwartz said. Seeing Lemma's expression of disgust, he added, "The man's O-neg. It would be irresponsible not to save his parts and his blood, if he's not using them. Bad for the economy. And the environment." He placed the vial of Fremen's blood in a refrigerator. "O-neg, Lemma, the universal—"

"Universal donor, I know."

"Universal seller," Schwartz corrected with a smile. "Anyway, you want an extra hundred grams silver?"

"I'd rather not."

"It's for science, and the enlightenment of man. And woman." Schwartz dangled an empty vial in front of her.

Lemma snorted. "What science?"

"The benevirus. 'Bene,' from the Latin, meaning 'good'. 'Virus,' from the English, meaning 'virus.'"

"Is this something Curio would get stringy about?"

"Not if you stay quiet."

"So what's a benevirus?"

"A good virus that can fight bad viruses. Suppose there's a mass outbreak of typhoid. Then a benevirus comes in handy."

"Typhoid?" scoffed Lemma. "What is this, the eighteen rimming hundreds? Going to leech my blood to fight my typhoid?"

"It's an example! Suppose there's an outbreak of anything, and I don't have time to manufacture enough vaccines to give to everyone. Instead, we build a good virus specifically engineered to kill the first one. You infect people with the good virus, and it spreads and saves everyone else."

"You can engineer a virus?"

"Trying to. Not much luck so far."

"I'm going to decline for now. Thanks for the invite."

Schwartz shrugged and put the empty vial back in his pocket. "If you won't help me out, can you at least convince Jax to get in here?"

"How would I convince Jax?"

Schwartz snorted. "You could bend him to do anything. You know he crawls for you, right?"

Lemma's face felt hot. "That's... I don't spect that's true."

"That's why he got those mustache transplants."

"You gave him mustache transplants?"

Schwartz groaned. "Maybe they weren't noticeable. Don't spill to him, or I'll have to refund him."

They both laughed.

"What?" Schwartz asked, as Lemma's face sobered.

She inhaled slowly. "I need to ask you something."

"If you're asking whether I have a two-for-one pitch on kidney transplants…"

"The night Natisra Fezz died she told me that Phronesis Tech was working on technology to grow human organs in a lab."

Schwartz's eyes narrowed.

"And she said that labbed organs would cuck organ grinders out of business, like what Wade Syan once did to farmers. So I was wondering, maybe organ grinders were the ones who targeted Syan? To protect their business?"

Schwartz popped one of Curio's mandated vitamins, and began wiping down the counter. "You spect I ghosted Syan?"

"I didn't say that."

"You really spect that I would go into his apartment, hold him under the water until he drowned, leave without a trace, and not even lift his kidneys?" Schwartz smiled darkly.

Lemma laughed, already breathing easier. The question had gnawed at her since the night Fezz died, and even though a million more questions still barked at her heels, she could assure herself that this suspicion was false.

"One more question."

"Aim and fire." Schwartz was restoring instruments to shelves and locking the drawers.

"Organ transplants, you're experienced with those, right?"

"Kidney, eyes, liver. But not lungs or heart."

"What about legs?"

"Legs aren't something I do, but I know some doctors who can do legs. Why, you want a third?"

"No, but I know someone, an eleven-year-old boy, who's missing his left leg."

"Hmm… if he's still growing, transplant can be tricky. Not so much the attaching part, but adjusting the leg to grow as he grows. That'll require additional surgeries. Titanium plates and screws that he'll need to turn every day in order to lengthen the tibia and fibula and femur. There'll be a considerable amount of what we doctors call 'discomfort,' which is our little way of saying agonizing pain. This boy, he's Tiresian I'm guessing?"

"Yes. And a man, in his forties. He also needs a new left leg. Both of them are African, so they'll need legs that match the color of the rest of them."

"Two left legs. That's a tall order. Give me their blood types and heights and I'll scout for them, gel?"

Lemma accepted a vitamin from Schwartz and swallowed it. She couldn't change the past, but she could still change the future.

CHAPTER 39

STRONGER IMAGE

The chaos in the break room had not subsided. Curio was engaged in a shouting match with several other agents, and there was a large dent on the wall where Kawling's face had been projected.

"Plug it!" Curio shouted. "Plug it or I will rimming—"

Lemma retreated into a side room. She took Donovez's phone from her pocket, initiating a call.

"Governor Kawling here."

"Howsie, Governor— uh, Raemin. This is Lemma Quartz. From the Syan Hospital dedication?"

"Lemma! A welcome surprise. Is your arm is healing?"

Lemma massaged the bandage. "Hope so. Your shoulder?"

"I'll manage."

Lemma's ears twitched. Curio's voice could be heard in the background, ranting against Kawling's speech.

"I scoped your speech tonight."

"Oh?"

"You said Perron Mills, the attacker, was a death agent?"

"That is what the police force determined."

"Because— because he wasn't. He's not."

"How would you know?"

Lemma's voice quivered. "I spoke with Perron earlier today."

"You actually met with him? In prison?"

"Yes."

"Why would you do that? The man tried to kill you— us!"

Curio's voice burst out again. "Schedule One terrorists! I'll show that cuck Kawling Schedule One rimming terrorists!"

Lemma hoped Kawling didn't hear that. "Perron tried to kill us, but he's not with a death agency."

"Of course he denied it."

"He did it because of his son. The Tiresians amped his son. Hacked off his leg and pretended it was for medical reasons."

"So he tries to assassinate the governor? Why not the doctor who performed the operation? Why not the doctor's assistant?"

Lemma gripped the phone tightly. "He already targeted his son's doctor, and others. But he also blamed you. Said you made it smoother for Tiresians to amp other kids."

"You know that's not true." Kawling sounded horrified.

"He said that you fought to make it illegal to criticize the Tiresian Church."

"Lemma, I pushed for the Tiresian Church to receive the same protection as Muslims, Evangelicals, and other religions. Verbal assault is illegal. The same standard applies for every religion. I find the idea that I show any religion preference offensive."

"That's— well, you shouldn't accuse Perron of working for Balkon Death Insurance Agency. I guarantee you, he's not one of— he's not a death agent."

"And how you would know that?" Kawling's voice was suspicious.

"I… he's not. Death agencies don't ghost politicians. They protect citizens."

"They kill people."

"Only proven murderers."

"Lemma, I fear we are merely rehashing our conversation from the dedication ceremony."

"Death agencies aren't all bad."

"Lemma, please. I appreciate your opinion, both as a citizen and as a friend, but let's not allow politics to get between us, please?"

Both women were silent for several moments.

"I scoped your sling during your speech. It was larger than the one you wore in the hospital," Lemma said.

Kawling gave a gentle laugh. "I was talked into it by members of my staff; they felt it presented a stronger image."

Curio stormed out of the break room, muttering. As a parting shot she threw an empty bottle at Jax.

"Raemin, you need to be careful," Lemma said.

"Careful? I'm always careful."

"I meant your speech. Death agencies won't be gel if you're chasing their flaps, they'll target you."

"Didn't you just say death agencies never attack politicians?"

"I— please be careful, Raemin."

"Are you threatening me?"

"No! I'm not making a threat. I don't agree with you, but I still don't want you to be hurt. But I can't be there every time someone tries to stab you."

There was another pause.

"Did you ever meet with the data analyst, Shwa Chinny?" Kawling asked.

"I did. Thanks again for the intro."

"What was your impression of him?"

Chinny's sneering face floated through her mind's eye. "Um… he uses bug spray as cologne."

Kawling laughed. "So I've heard. Is there anyone else I can put you in contact with?"

The Balkon agents had finally calmed down, or at least had ceased throwing things.

"I spect I'm gel for now." Lemma said.

***

The CityBus was quiet, the expectant mothers section empty and polluted as always, as Lemma's thoughts spun around in her head: Kawling's speech, Fremen's trial, Shwa Chinny's offer, Perron Mills' story…

There was a crack in the bus window, and Lemma shivered, pulling Jax's coat up to her chin. She inhaled, catching the faintest mite of his deodorant, some synthetic scent called Blue Iceberg, smirking as she remembered what Schwartz had said about Jax's mustache implants.

Don't be a silly girl, she warned herself.

It wasn't until she approached the door to her apartment complex that her concentration was broken.

"Where is he? Have you seen him anywhere?" a woman yelled, startling Lemma. It was Cheri Mills.

"Seen who?"

"He's missing! Is he with you? Did he come here?"

"Who?"

"Gram!"

CHAPTER 40

MISSING

Lemma's arm throbbed, pulsing as if Milligram's father father were stabbing her all over again. Cheri pushed into the apartment as soon as Lemma had unlocked it, overturning the table and the sofa cushions on the floor, shouting her son's name.

"Cheri! What are you doing?" Lemma asked.

"Have you seen my son?"

"No."

"He hasn't contacted you?"

"When did you last scope him?"

"I brought him to school today. Halfway through, his teachers told me he was missing from class. They had no idea where he was— my boy— my baby!"

Cheri was sobbing, but Lemma felt no sympathy for her. Her stomach churned with revulsion, recalling what Perron Mills told her.

"If I find him, I'll contact you."

Cheri turned an incredulous, tear-streaked face to her. "You're not going to help me look?"

"And where would we look? He's not in my apartment. He doesn't even know my address. If he's on the streets, the badges will lift him and tell you. If he's somewhere at school, they'll scope him. There is nothing you or I can do."

Cheri's eyes widened. "You don't even care. Gram is gone and you don't care."

"I don't care?" Lemma hissed, forgetting her injury as both her hands clamped down on Cheri's shoulders. "I have done everything for him! I'm more of a mother to him than you are!"

Cheri cried out, "Let go! You're hurting me!"

"I didn't amp off his leg because of some rimming cult, and I didn't ghost his baby sister. You did that!"

The stab wound caught up to her in a burning surge of pain, and she dropped her arms. Cheri stepped back in panic.

"Who told you about that?"

"His father."

"His father!" Cheri shouted. "His father was abusive! He beat me and Gram!"

"Why did you join the Tiresian Church?"

"I told you; Gram lost his leg from an infection. They took us in. They cared for us."

Lemma laughed harshly. "He lost his leg first? The Tiresian Church keeps records of when their members join. I can find those, and I have friends in the state Data Department who can find the date of your son's amputation. Should we compare which one came first?"

"You don't... don't..."

"Wipe off, or I'll call my friends."

"What friends?"

Lemma reached into the pocket of Jax's coat, and Cheri retreated in alarm.

"These friends." Lemma held up Jax's silver badge, angling it so the light bounced off the words 'Balkon Death Insurance Agent.'

***

After Cheri left, the thrill of intimidating her wore off. Lemma's sleep was delayed by worries about her response. Cheri could spill on her, especially now that Kawling had declared war on death agencies. Lemma could retaliate; it would be easy to prove that Cheri had joined the Tiresian Church before Milligram lost his leg. It all centered on whether Cheri would risk her own freedom to send the badges after Lemma.

Then, as Lemma tried to get comfortable on her nest of sofa cushions, a knock came at her apartment door. She pulled the covers over her head, but the knocking came again, louder and more insistent this time.

Cheri had turned her in.

"Lemma?"

Lemma jumped up, pulled her clothes on, and opened the door. She threw her uninjured arm around the boy whose voice she could never mistake.

"Lemma!"

"Your mom said you were missing. Does she know you're here?"

Milligram pushed into the room. "I'm not going back."

"You ran away?"

Milligram was sweating and shivering with exhaustion.

"You walked all the way from school? Milligram!"

He collapsed into her arms.

***

Lemma dabbed his forehead with a cloth soaked in warm water, and Milligram opened his eyes.

"Eat," she said, placing a bowl of soup in front of him, blowing on the steam to cool it down.

Milligram took a spoonful and didn't stop until he had devoured all of it.

"Thanks," he mumbled.

"Do you want to talk about why you ran away from home?"

"My mom…"

Lemma waited. Milligram stared at the floor, refusing to make eye contact.

"I went back to school today. They told me that my mom— that my leg never had anything wrong with it. They did it just because of church."

"Milligram." Lemma wrapped her arm around him. "Milligram, who told you?"

"Corandy."

"Corandy, who's that?"

"Girl at school. The one you jacked."

"How did she know?"

"She said her dad works for the state. He told her. Lemma?"

"Yes?"

"Can I stay here?"

Her threat to Cheri had been stupid before; it was a thousand times more stupid, even dangerous, now.

"Of course you can." She took the empty soup bowl from him, sliding it across the carpet toward the kitchen, and lay down on the sofa cushions next to him. He curled up into a ball, burying his face in the pillow next to hers.

"Do I have to go to back to school?" he asked.

"If you want to squat here, you can't go to school anymore. I can keep teaching you, all by myself. But we'll have to keep you hidden if badges come, gel?"

The apartment was quiet except for Milligram's breathing, which quivered in soft sobs. He pulled closer, his head nestling on her shoulder, his coarse hair tickling her cheek. After several minutes, his sobs turned to deep breaths, and his shoulders traded their jolts for deep, rhythmic cycles. Lemma lay there, absorbing his warmth and the smell of his hair, finding it almost as comforting as the Blue Iceberg scent of the coat which lay on the floor.

CHAPTER 41

REPLICAS

Tuesday, May 22

"Lemma?"

"Mm…" Her eyes still crusty, Lemma patted the cushions, but she was alone. "Milligram?"

"Lemma, is this gold?"

There was the soft clink of metal on the bathroom countertop.

Lemma jumped out of bed, sending a spasm through her back which would haunt her the rest of the day. Her eyelids tore apart and, blinking away the crumbs, she stumbled into the bathroom.

"Lemma, I'm over here."

The bathrooms tiles were securely in place; they kept their secret just as they had when Cheri had torn through the apartment the previous night.

"Milligram, you said you had gold."

"This." Milligram held up an Axiom bill for one gram of gold. "It says 'Gold' on it. What's it for?"

By his hand was a ceramic mug of water, which had sounded to Lemma's drowsy ears like metal when he'd placed it on the countertop.

"Milligram, give that here." She stuffed the bill into her pocket.

"What is it?"

Lemma sighed. "You know how people can print out a message on paper?"

Milligram nodded.

"You can also print out money. If I have a piece of paper that says one piece of gold, I can trade it in for a piece of gold. Or I can trade it for food or water."

Milligram stared. "But… why?"

"Why? If you print it out, you can buy stuff without other people knowing. Sometimes people like to have more privacy."

"I've never seen that before."

Lemma hesitated, trying to think how best to explain. "Well, it's illegal. Which is why you can't spill about this, gel?"

Milligram nodded. "Who prints it? Can you print money? If you print one would people just give you gold?"

She pulled a crumpled food wrapper from the garbage, and used her nail polish to write on it: "Trade for one ice cream, from Lemma."

"Scope it. Before, it was just a wrapper. Now, it's money. It's a promise that I'll trade you whatever it says on it. So instead of trading it for gold you can trade it for—"

"Ice cream!" Milligram's eyes sparkled.

"Exactly. But it only works with me, because I'm the one who wrote it." Lemma pulled on Jax's coat, and handed Milligram the contra ice cream currency. "Now I'll pay you this, if you work on your math facts while I'm gone, gel? When I get home, you can trade it back to me for an ice cream. And Milligram?"

"What?"

"Don't open the door for anyone."

***

Balkon was still on edge from Kawling's announcement the previous night. The agents and the other employees looked at Lemma with suspicion, dropping their voices whenever she walked past.

"Ignore them," Jax said, taking back his coat. "They know you won't cuck us out. Everyone's stringy, that's all."

Lemma remembered Chinny's offer, and avoided making eye contact with anyone.

Around lunchtime, Lemma called Cheri and left a message, using a legit Balkon phone.

172

"Cheri, Lemma here. I want to apologize for anything I might have said at my apartment that would have made you uncomfortable." She selected her words with caution; legit phones, even at Balkon, were monitored by the state. "The friends I mentioned are working with me, and we promise to help find your son." *So you'd better not turn me in.*

"Who were you calling?" Curio demanded, as Lemma ended the call. Lemma bit her tongue and listened meekly as Curio berated her for saving the governor's life, and for even going to the dedication ceremony in the first place. Then Curio yelled at everyone on the entire floor about the recent break-in at Fremen's house, blaming no one and everyone at the same time. When Curio had finished, Lemma returned quietly to her seat, now certain of her response to Shwa Chinny.

She copied data, as much of it as she could find. Names of clients, Balkon agents, lists of past targets, anything that Shwa Chinny might find useful, or anything that Curio would hate to have leaked. Then she encrypted it, using the same algorithm Donovez had shown her after having cracked the code on Syan's blink. She sent the coded message to Chinny, promising to tell him how to crack it if he would give her some data of her own: a list of every amputation a state doctor had performed, as well as enrollment dates of every member of the Tiresian Church.

[*Why?*] Chinny replied several hours later.

[*Because there's still time to change the future*]

It was as if someone had lit a fire in her chest. Lemma's interview with Perron Mills combined with Milligram escaping his mother had inspired her with a new energy. She would find a journalist willing to write articles against the Tiresian Church, and she would give them this new, damning data once Chinny delivered it, along with Perron Mills' account of what the church had done to his wife and children.

However, Lemma had to deal with a new issue: money, or rather the lack of it. Donovez had not yet found clients for his new death agency, and with Lemma's employment at Balkon hanging by a thread, she would need to find a new source of income to support herself and Mills. At first, she considered going back to her other clients, but the risk was too great. With Milligram staying at her apartment, she had to find a post that wouldn't get her killed.

She turned to the same idea she had brought up with Curio five weeks earlier: the false membership medals. She had given the fake to the girl from Edeyong, and had given up on ever seeing it or the girl again. But it was not difficult to manufacture her own medallions from cheap pieces of metal, cut into shape and painted to look like copper. She even enlisted Milligram's help, paying him ice-cream-backed contras in return for an hour of help in the evenings. During the day, she sold the replicas door to door to people who could never afford actual death Insurance.

When Lemma wasn't tutoring Milligram or pitching fake medallions, she was at Balkon. Curio had decided not to fire Lemma, at least not yet, and was driving her and Jax even harder on the Fremen Orea case, which was now only one day away.

CHAPTER 42

THE LOST CLIENT

Thursday, May 24

"I give up," Lemma said, on Thursday evening. In less than twelve hours, she and Jax would argue their case against Axiom in front of a panel of arbitrators. "Fremen's going to lose."

"Fremen should lie," Jax said glumly. "Just rimming pretend that he knew who Ennerd Vik was. Twank. Fremen's a rimming twank. Or…" he looked at Lemma. "We still haven't asked him about that uniform. You know, the Phronesis Tech one under his bed."

"Why would we do that? If anything, it means that he was involved with Syan."

"We still haven't venged Syan, either."

Lemma had asked Masidon Barreaux to introduce her to the last name on the list, Vinida Entierez. Vinida had agreed to meet with her after tomorrow's Balkon-Axiom trial, which she had expressed a deep interest in observing. Other than that, Lemma and Jax had no more clues to pursue.

She shivered, and Jax instinctively handed her his coat. Lemma had made a habit of borrowing it, even when she wasn't particularly cold, although she could have done without Schwartz smirking every time he walked past them.

"Fremen's finished. Syan's never going to be venged," Lemma groaned. As she put on the coat, the Balkon badge which she had used to threaten Cheri slid out.

"Why do you keep that in your pocket?" Lemma asked.

"It's gel."

"Not if it falls out so easily."

"It doesn't usually fall out."

"Really?" Lemma returned the badge to the pocket, and jumped up and down several times. The badge fell out again, as did a wallet.

"Oh claps, now your wallet fell out."

"It's not mine."

Lemma scoffed.

"I'm steady. Cucks, I forgot about this." Jax turned over the wallet in his hands.

"Forgot about what?"

"Found it in Fremen's basement. The window well under his porch."

"And you didn't tell me until now?"

"Got distracted when those goons woke up."

"So… it's Fremen's?"

Jax opened it, and out fell three contra bills, as well as several sketches of the outside and inside of Fremen's house.

"Did Fremen draw these?" Lemma asked, as Jax flipped through the sketches, finding a licensed photograph of a man and a woman.

"This isn't Fremen. It's the man he shot: Ennerd Vik," Jax said, pointing to the man in the picture.

"How did he get a sketch of the inside— oh my rimming cucking twank!"

The picture showed a smiling Ennerd Vik with his arms wrapped around a woman whom Lemma had seen before.

***

The sign advertising ethically sourced giraffe steaks had been replaced with a new notice.

"Observe Level Laws! 'Yes' to one means 'yes' to everyone!"

Accompanying the words was a cartoon of two women at a rationing store, one wearing sunglasses. Written on the notice in green spray paint were the words: 'Wipe off, Reezy.' Lemma smirked, entered Gyro Valley, and patiently waited.

In the early hours of the morning, a woman walked past, and Lemma threw open the door.

"Harriden!"

The woman gasped, whipping around and pulling out a kitchen knife. As her hand trembled, the reflection of the city lights wobbled on the blade. The knife had a sharp tip. Someone, maybe the same person who had once assisted Perron Mills, had filed off the safety edge.

"Harriden, it's me. Lemma Quartz. From Balkon. Remember me?"

Harriden put the knife away and pulled her jacket tighter across her slender shoulders. "I remember."

"It was right here where we first met."

"Don't rimming talk about that."

"I want to talk to you. Buy you a drink?"

"Don't want a drink."

"Food?"

"Not hungry."

"I'll buy a half hour slot from you."

"You're steady?"

"That's your post, isn't it?"

Harriden scoffed.

"I'll just be a mite," Lemma said, holding open the door to Gyro Valley. "Number nine for her," Lemma told the cook, tossing the rest of her own plate into the already overflowing garbage.

"What do you want to talk about?" Harriden asked.

"We could start with small talk. The weather. What chads you pinned tonight."

"You want to talk about your goons edging me every night?"

"My goons?" Lemma asked, startled.

Harriden didn't speak, but pulled down her jacket, exposing a copper medallion which read "Balkon."

"You got shielded. That's bright."

"It's not bright." Harriden put the medallion away with a sour look.

"Why not?"

"They won't let me quit."

"What?"

"I tried to cancel. Was bleeding me too much. But Balkon won't let me quit."

"Then just stop paying, they'll come and take your medal, and then it's over."

Harriden gave her a look of pure venom. "What about the cucking rocks through my window? Will those be over?"

"Rocks?"

"Day after I quit Balkon. Glass everywhere. Goons follow me on the streets. Grab at my flaps."

Lemma cursed. "You're steady it's Balkon?"

"Yes."

"We don't jack with our members. We'd never do that."

"No? Because it stopped when I got shielded again."

Lemma said nothing.

"I didn't even need it," Harriden continued. "I was gel without you."

"What about rough clients? Chads that get bloody? You don't want protection from them?"

Harriden laughed darkly. "And who protects me from Balkon? Badges? Another agency?"

The cook approached their table and set a sizzling plate between them. As the cook returned to the kitchen, Harriden stared at her plate with disgust.

"What part of him did this fall off of?" she said, pulling a gray hair out of the meat.

"Harriden, I need your help, and if you do, I can get you new coverage. With a different agency."

"I don't want new coverage, I want you to get Balkon off my flaps."

"Then I'll do that."

Harriden sniffed the giraffe gyro, and made her peace with the hair she had pulled out from it, stuffing half of it into her mouth.

"What do you want?" Harriden asked through the mess of giraffe.

"I want to ask if you know someone named Ennerd Vik."

Harriden's mouth fell open, and a bolus of meat fell onto the table. She slid her chair backwards and stood up.

"Don't— Harriden, it's gel. I'm not going to— Harriden, wait!" Lemma begged.

"I don't know what you're talking about," Harriden said.

"Don't be a twank."

"I need to bounce."

"Harriden!"

Harriden pointed the knife at Lemma, never lowering it as she backed to the door.

"Don't talk to me anymore."

"I'll help you with Balkon! I'll get them off your flaps, let me help—" As the door closed, Lemma cursed, kicking the garbage can until it vomited a pile of greasy scraps onto the floor.

CHAPTER 43

THE ASSASSIN

The door opened again, and Harriden walked back inside. She was shivering from the cold evening air.

"If that was you who knocked it over, clean it up," the cook called from the back room.

Lemma and Harriden stared at the pile of garbage.

"Who sent you?" Harriden finally asked. The knife had returned to her pocket.

"I just need some answers."

"How do you know about Ennerd? Are people scouting me?"

"It's just me. I promise I won't hurt you, I just need some details."

"If I talk, will you get Balkon off my flaps?"

"Yes. They'll give your money back. You'll be gel."

Harriden returned to the table, stepping over the overturned garbage bin. "How do you know about Ennerd?"

"He was ghosted by one of our clients, Fremen Orea." Lemma's mind flashed to Harriden's scribbled list from the night they had met. "Fremen was one of your chads."

"I know."

"We scoped a picture of you in Ennerd's wallet. Was Ennerd another one of your customers?"

Harriden stirred a piece of meat on the floor with her foot. A dark grimace crawled over her face. "Ennerd was my brother."

Lemma's mouth opened. "You're sure?"

Harriden narrowed her eyes in contempt. "Why would I not be sure?"

"I meant, can you show proof? I believe you," Lemma added quickly.

"You want proof?" Harriden spat, a look of defiance shooting from her eyes. Lemma leaned away in alarm.

"How about him losing a tooth when he dragged our step-father off me? Or his amped pinky when he gave me his pair of gloves because I lost mine in the snow!"

Lemma's stomach felt like it was dissolving in its own acid. She wanted to throw her arms around Harriden, to smother her soul with sympathy. When she finally spoke, her voice hobbled like Milligram's leg.

"Harriden — I— I believe you." A thousand thoughts clogged her throat. "I want to help you. Do you know why your brother was at Fremen's house? Did he ever say?"

"He was sent to ghost Fremen."

"How do you know?"

"I was helping him."

"You…" Lemma sat down, so numb that she didn't feel the chair beneath her.

"Fremen wasn't the first. Ennerd and I were a team. I found his targets, sugared them, spread my flaps and let them pin me. I kept their address, their schedule, the times they were home. Scouted the doors and windows, the weak points. Drew sketches of everything to show Ennerd."

"I found sketches in Ennerd's wallet. Yours?"

"Yes."

"The night I met you and shielded you from those goons, Balkon had intercepted a message from a blink. Someone was scouting a Balkon member. I spected it was the goons, but… it was you, wasn't it?"

Harriden nodded. "Ennerd asked me if Fremen was shielded by Balkon. I went to Fremen's house, made sure he was safe to ghost."

"And because you had Fremen's name on your list, I visited him the next day," Lemma groaned, piecing it all together. "I pitched death insurance to him, then later he hired me to shield Getonia at Edeyong, where I found Ennerd scouting her. Wait. Why was Ennerd scouting Getonia that night if his target was Fremen?"

"I don't know Ennerd's exact plan that night, I'm sorry."

"I cornered Ennerd in Edeyong, but loosed him because he was shielded by Axiom. Once he knew he was being scouted, Ennerd went to ghost Fremen as flash as he could. If I hadn't cornered Ennerd that night, maybe he wouldn't have tried to ghost Fremen… But I was scouting him because Donovez said he was a suspect… Harriden, why did you and Ennerd target Fremen in the first place?"

"Someone posted us."

"Who posted you?"

"If I tell you, you'll get Balkon off my flaps? No more rocks through windows, no more goons chasing me?"

Lemma took Harriden's hands in hers, noticing a smudge of green paint on Harriden's knuckles. "I promise."

"It was Wade Syan."

CHAPTER 44

TESTIMONY

Friday, May 25

The trial was not going well.

Lemma sat in between Jax and Harriden, as she and the representative from Axiom called witnesses to testify. Harriden was wearing sunglasses and slouching, refusing to make eye contact with anyone.

Lemma had not slept. After seeing Harriden at Gyro Valley, she had spent the entire night meeting with Curio and Donovez separately. Neither had appreciated being disturbed in the middle of the night, but Lemma had assured them both that it would be worth the loss of sleep.

Fremen's trial was being held in a neutral zone, in an abandoned warehouse. Both Axiom and Balkon agents were present. The presiding overseer was a Buddhist monk, the Venerable Phra Zang, whom both Axiom and Balkon trusted to act as judge and to arbitrate fairly. There were a number of journalists present as well. They had promised not to spill anyone's identity, in exchange for a chance to witness the first murder trial ever held by a death agency.

"What's happening?" Getonia whispered, from behind Lemma. "You said you had a plan?"

"Plug it," hissed Lemma, listening as the Axiom representative, a thin man named Mr. Encas, spoke. She fidgeted, her fingers twisting over a candy wrapper which read "One hug from Milligram."

"Stop crinkling that, you're stringing me out," Getonia pleaded. Lemma ignored her.

Lemma went up to testify, explaining how she had witnessed Ennerd following Getonia at Edeyong, and how she had followed Ennerd to Fremen's house. When she finished, Fremen was called to be questioned.

"Mr. Orea, had you ever seen Ennerd Vik before the night of Sunday, April 29?" Encas asked.

"I hadn't," Fremen said hollowly.

"So you had no idea what his intentions were when he appeared at your door?"

"He was trying to ghost me."

Zang cleared his throat. "Mr. Orea, are you a mind reader?"

Fremen glanced at the judge. "No."

"Then you are not allowed to talk about his intentions. Continue, Mr. Encas,"

"Thank you. Mr. Orea, you say you feared for your safety with this man?"

"Yes."

"You thought he was violent?"

"Yes."

"A threat to you and your wife?"

"He scouted my wife! He was at Edeyong, Lemma already told you!" Fremen pointed to the table where Lemma, Jax, and Harriden sat, and Lemma nodded to acknowledge her testimony.

"Does Fremen see me?" Harriden whispered.

"Fremen's choked, you're gel," Lemma assured her. She glanced at her blink, which had been silent for some time. She sent a message to Donovez: [*Trial still moving. HV is stringy. Update?*]

"Mr. Orea, you really shouldn't talk about things that happened when you weren't there." Encas' voice was oily. Lemma was certain she would dislike him even if he wasn't trying to ghost her client.

"So ask me about what I remember about the night he broke in." Fremen's forehead was shiny with sweat.

"But he didn't break in, did he? He died on your porch."

"Yes," Orea replied, defeated.

"You shot him, with a gun, on your front porch."

"It was self-defense!" Fremen shouted. "I'm not a goon!"

"Mr. Orea! Calm down!" warned Zang.

"May I display an exhibit? A photo of the Oreas' upstairs closet?" Encas asked, brushing a dangling lock of blond hair out of his eyes.

"How is that relevant?" Jax, who sat at Lemma's left side, had risen to his feet.

"Mr. Orea just claimed he's not violent. I'd like to disprove that claim."

"Show it to me first," the judge ordered. Jax and Encas approached his desk, where they whispered to each other.

"You may display it," the judge said, glaring as Jax cursed loudly. "But I will remind everyone that Fremen Orea is only on trial for one death. Any evidence that is connected to another violent crime should only be taken to disprove his claim of being a peaceful person."

As Encas motioned, an image appeared on the wall behind Fremen and Zang. It showed a Phronesis Tech uniform spread out on a bed. Lemma dug her fingernails into her palms.

"This is your bedroom, isn't it?" Encas asked Fremen.

"Yes."

"Axiom and Balkon agents found this while investigating a break-in at your house on May 15. You recognize it?"

"If there was a break-in, maybe someone left it there," Fremen said.

"I have reports from both Axiom and Balkon which confirmed it had your fingerprints on it, as well as strands of your hair, and flakes of your skin." Encas gestured, and images of fingerprints appeared on the wall next to the photograph.

Fremen said nothing.

"Do you want to explain why you possess a Phronesis Tech uniform, credentials, and badge? You don't work there, do you?"

"No."

"You never have worked there?"

"No."

"Did you visit Phronesis recently?"

Fremen didn't reply.

"Did you ever use this costume to break into Phronesis Tech facilities?"

"Flash it, get to your point," the judge said, acknowledging Jax's look of outrage.

"Both Balkon and Axiom agents contacted Phronesis Tech and asked about that badge number," Encas said, a glint of triumph in his eyes. "We learned that it had last been used on April 6. Were you there that day?"

Fremen didn't reply, but at another gesture from Encas, a surveillance image appeared of him, in the Phronesis Tech uniform.

"This was taken in Wade Syan's office the same day. You want to tell us why you were on the Phronesis Tech campus?"

Jax stood up again. "How is this relevant?"

"Mr. Encas, do you have any point to these questions?" Judge Zang asked.

"Mr. Orea, did you kill Wade Syan?" Encas shouted.

Jax, Judge Zang, and a dozen others shouted at once. Zang blew a whistle.

"Mr. Yedra, sit down. The rest of you will forget all about that, because Mr. Encas did not offer any proof. We are discussing whether or not Fremen Orea was justified in killing Ennerd Vik. Mr. Encas, do you have any more relevant questions?"

Lemma's blink buzzed with a reply from Donovez. [*Outside his apartment. State badges with us. Waiting for him to come out*]

Lemma showed the text to Harriden. She asked her, "You ready to talk?"

Harriden nodded, and Lemma stood. "Judge Zang, Balkon has one more witness, if Mr. Encas is finished."

Encas nodded, and the judge asked, "Name?"

"Harriden Vik."

Excited murmurs slithered through the room, as Lemma brought Harriden forward, passing Fremen on the way to the witness chair.

"Lemma!" said Fremen, his face drenched in worry. "Why is she here?"

"I'm sorry, Fremen, I would have told you," Lemma said.

"Ask your questions," Judge Zang told her.

"Harriden, do you know either Ennerd Vik or Fremen Orea?" Lemma began.

"Judge, she was a witness, she can't also ask questions," Encas said indignantly, jumping to his feet.

"She can ask her questions, but flash it, please," Zang said.

"I know them both," Harriden said, looking from Lemma to Zang.

"Here is Harriden's birth certificate and legal identification," Lemma said, as the damning images of Fremen were replaced with images of Harriden. "Harriden, how do you know Ennerd Vik?"

"I was his younger sister."

The audience grew silent.

"You have a post?"

"Self-employed intimate contact worker. Liced by the state," Harriden said defiantly.

"How do know Fremen Orea?"

"He was one of my chads."

Lemma forced herself to focus on Harriden. She could feel the weight of everyone's eyes on her.

"This affair, was it related to Fremen Orea shooting Ennerd Vik?"

"It was."

"How do you know?"

"Ennerd and I worked together as a team," she said. "If we had a target, I would visit him. Sugar him. Make sure he didn't have Balkon or Axiom insurance. Ennerd would then ghost him."

"How many times did you have contact with Fremen?"

"Once on April 15, and again on April 24."

"What about the night Fremen shot Ennerd? April 29?"

"No."

"Did you inform Ennerd of your meetings with Fremen?"

"I did. I used my time with Fremen to get all the information Ennerd would need so he could target him."

"Did someone hire you and Ennerd to ghost Fremen?"

"Yes. Wade Syan."

Judge Zang blew his whistle as the room broke out in a babble of excited conversations.

"Ms. Quartz, is this going to be important?"

"I promise, it is!" Lemma shouted. "Harriden, did Wade Syan ever pay you for intimate contact?"

"We never did that."

"Had you and Ennerd ghosted people for Wade Syan before?"

"Yes."

Lemma's blink buzzed with another message from Donovez: [*He hasn't come out yet. Not answering*]

"I want to clarify something," Lemma said. "If Wade Syan had died on April 24, why was Ennerd still targeting Fremen Orea on April 29?"

"After Wade Syan died, I told Ennerd we should stop. But Ennerd wanted to finish what Syan had hired us to do."

Lemma walked to Harriden. "Can you provide evidence that you and Ennerd intended to ghost Fremen?"

Harriden pulled out a folder. "Ennerd and I didn't have access to paper, we wrote all our notes on food wrappers. Both his and my handwriting are there. We have Fremen's address, times he and his wife would be home, and sketches I made of his house."

"Fremen said he had never seen Ennerd Vik before the night of the shooting. What do you think of that?"

"It's not true. Ennerd tried to ghost him once before, on April 21. Fremen was walking by himself on the street by his home."

"Why didn't Ennerd kill Fremen that night?"

"Fremen used a fake medallion to pretend he had death insurance coverage."

"Pretended? Why did I come here if he only pretended?" Judge Zang interrupted.

"Mr. Orea has true Balkon coverage now," Lemma explained. "But his coverage didn't begin until April 27."

Lemma turned back to Harriden. "Did Syan give you the reason why he wanted Fremen dead?"

Encas stood up. "Hearsay! I object!"

"Syan's dead; it's gel." Judge Zang waved his hand as if to swat away the objection.

"Wade said Fremen had lifted something from him," Harriden continued, after Lemma had repeated her question.

"Did he say what it was?"

"Wade didn't know. He just said that Fremen had broken into his office in Phronesis Tech."

"Is all of this true?" Zang demanded, staring past Lemma, who finally gave in to her burning curiosity and turned to face the Oreas.

Fremen's face had a defeated look, which was nothing compared to Getonia's expression of complete emptiness.

Fremen nodded glumly.

"Ennerd Vik tried to ghost you because you stole something from Wade Syan on April 6? That's what the outfit in your bedroom was for, so you could get into Phronesis Tech?"

Fremen nodded again.

"What did you steal?"

"Data," muttered Fremen. "Phronesis Tech secrets."

"Why?"

"Someone paid me to. One of Wade Syan's enemies."

"Who?" Judge Zang demanded. Every pair of eyes drilled into Fremen, waiting to hear what he had to say, but he refused to answer.

"He told me," Harriden announced loudly. "Fremen said it was…"

Then she uttered the name which she had told Lemma only a few hours ago, the name of the man whose apartment Donovez and his men were now waiting to ambush.

At that same moment, Donovez sent Lemma another message: [*Broke into the apartment. Shwa Chinny dead on arrival*]

CHAPTER 45

MANIFESTO

"Shwa Chinny?" Judge Zang asked, staring in confusion at Fremen and Harriden. "Who's Shwa Chinny?"

"Data analyst, works for the state. I don't know why he and Syan were enemies, but…" Fremen's reply was cut off by a sudden storm of exclamations from the crowd. Licensed phones and unlicensed blinks were buzzing with messages to check the news.

"Plug it!" Zang shouted. "Shut your rimming mouths!"

He blew his whistle, but it had no effect.

"CityNews!" a journalist yelled. "Show CityNews!"

Maybe Zang hoped that granting this request would win back the audience's attention to the trial, but the switch from Harriden's photos to live coverage from state authorities drove the proceedings even further out of Zang's control.

A news reporter was standing outside a building, facing the camera, a look of barely concealed delight on her face at delivering such a bombshell. "…was found dead in his apartment inside the building behind where I'm standing only minutes ago. He has been identified as Shwa Chinny, a state data analyst suspected in the death of Wade Syan. First reports indicate alcohol poisoning or drug overdose."

The audience in the warehouse, who until now had never heard Chinny's name except for Harriden's answer to the judge, stared with fascination as the image of Chinny's dead body appeared on the wall. He was naked except for a pair of boxer shorts, his body sprawled on the floor and surrounded by bottles, some lying on their sides, empty, some containing the same liquors that Lemma had seen displayed in his office six days earlier.

Lemma pulled her eyes from the screen. Getonia Orea was weeping, alternating gazes between the news story and her husband, who looked as though he might implode. Harriden was still sitting meekly in the witness chair, waiting for the judge to give her directions. Finally, Fremen made eye contact with Lemma.

"Lemma, what the cuck? Rimming cuck, Lemma!"

"I didn't have time to explain."

"Didn't have time?"

"I found Harriden last night, and she didn't even tell me everything until this morning."

The audience was out of their seats, pushing as close as they could to the wall. Zang blew his whistle in desperation, trying to restore order. Harriden took the opportunity to get out of her seat and run, disappearing into the crowd.

"Rimming cuck. How did you find her?" Fremen asked.

"You mean Harriden?" Underneath an avalanche of pity, mostly for Getonia, there a ripple of indignation that Fremen couldn't even say the name of the woman who had spent the entire morning fearing she would be killed for exposing Chinny.

"Ennerd left a wallet with her picture in it at your house. It fell out of his pocket when you shot him."

"What about my wife?" he hissed, turning to look at Getonia, the only audience member still in her seat. "What about her?"

"I'm sorry."

"'Sorry?' That's it? It's all gel now?" Fremen shouted.

Lemma glared at him. "You're welcome for clearing you of a murder charge."

"By telling my wife and everyone I'm a cuck! What am I supposed to tell her? Lemma!"

Fingers, hard and vice-like, gripped Lemma's arm. Curio fought through the mass of Balkon and Axiom members, dragging both Lemma and Jax into a side room.

"Lemma. Claps," she began, with a warm tone she had never used before with Lemma. "That was bright. Above and beyond. Both you and Jax."

Jax grinned. "I found the wallet and the picture."

"But I recognized Harriden. And scouted her, and flipped her to talk," Lemma retorted.

"Lemma's right, Curio," Jax said. "She did most of it. You should consider maybe… you know…"

"Say it," Lemma urged.

"Promote her. Make her a death agent."

Lemma looked hopefully at Curio, who broke into a smile.

"Of course, Lemma. You've earned that a hundred times over." Curio glanced back at the trial room. The tumult had only grown louder. "I need to find Judge Zang and confirm that Fremen can be released. And I need updated reports from both of you, and an interview with that girl, the conk."

"Harriden," Jax and Lemma corrected in unison.

"And you'll confirm that she'll be able to quit without being edged anymore?" Lemma stressed. "I promised her that."

"Certainly. I assure you, not a single agent will ever edge her again." Curio shook their hands, and returned to the trial room.

It was difficult to tell who made the first move. Jax was first to step forward, but Lemma responded faster and with more force. Then they were wrapped in a tight embrace, their arms around each other's necks and shoulders, bodies pressed together.

It was over before it could progress beyond a hug. They sprang apart, clearing their throats and sputtering excuses, pretending to ignore what had occurred, or nearly occurred, between them.

"You think Getonia flips her mind on death agencies?" Jax asked, after a moment of awkward silence.

"Tomorrow's headline will be, 'Balkon Agents Saving Lives, Cucking Up Marriages.'"

"Can't wait to— oh." Jax stopped, staring at a woman with straight, chin-length black hair and puffy eyelids who had entered the room.

"You have a moment, Lemma?" the woman asked. It was the same journalist who had shouted at Judge Zang to display the live report on Shwa Chinny.

"Vinida Entierez," she greeted, shaking their hands. "Didn't know if you would be able to talk."

"Entierez? From Syan's—?"

But Lemma had elbowed Jax before he could say anything damaging.

"Jax, could you bounce for a mite?" Lemma asked, and Jax left the room.

"That was fascinating," Vinida said, studying Lemma as Lemma did the same to her. It was hard to believe that this petite woman, who was even slighter and smaller than Lemma, was the same person who, according to Barreaux and Fezz, wrote such vicious articles about the Tiresian Church.

"When I received your message this morning, I knew I was in for an experience, but an entire trial, conducted without a single elected official! An entire murder case, conducted between two corporations!"

"Is that good or bad?" Lemma asked.

"It's a relief to scope a room without any political corruption, but I wonder…"

"Whether replacing it with private corruption makes it any better?" Vinida smirked. "Brilliantly phrased."

"I scoped your article about the attack on Kawling's life, and everyone's response to it."

"Ah, now I recognize you. You saved that twank's life, didn't you?" Lemma coughed and gave a startled laugh. "I did."

"Of course, she twisted it to be about death agencies. They didn't even mention that Perron Mills was a Reezy, oh no! We can't let people think that a Reezy could ever commit a crime."

Lemma remembered how Masidon had described Vinida.

"They wouldn't even let me interview him," the journalist continued. "I scheduled a meeting yesterday at the prison, then they canceled on me, the twanks. But did you need to see me for something? Masidon Barreaux said you wanted to talk about Wade Syan?"

"I wanted to ask about his death. If you thought it was more than an accident. But now we know," Lemma said.

"You should have found me earlier. I knew Wade and Chinny had a history. Wade stole Chinny's work years ago. Labbed meat was rightfully Chinny's invention, not Syan's."

Lemma's heart twisted. The idea that she owed her life to Chinny was repulsive, but not as repulsive as the fact that Wade had been a fraud.

"But I would never have guessed Chinny was out to get him," Vinida mused. "I was certain the Tiresians were behind it."

Of course, Lemma thought.

"But they still don't know how to make someone just drown like that. I wonder how Chinny did it? I'll have to investigate. Can I count on you for an exclusive interview? I'll pay whatever you want. And with Fezz dead, I'll be able to write my own biography of Syan, with the new angle of his relationship with Chinny. Come, I want to scope CityNews."

Vinida brought Lemma back to the main room, where the CityNews live report finally filled in the last pieces to Harriden's story. As the state detectives searched through Chinny's apartment, they uncovered a lengthy manifesto, written and rewritten by Chinny, detailing how Wade Syan had bought Sphix, the company where Chinny had been employed, then took credit for everything Chinny had worked on. Days, months, even years later the city would wonder how Chinny had managed to kill Syan without even entering his apartment, but after reading through Chinny's rant against the businessman, there was no doubt that he had spent nearly two decades dreaming of the perfect murder, which, without Lemma, would never have been solved.

Chapter 46

Abadon

"Can I be done?" Milligram asked, poking at his noodles with his knife.

"Are you done?"

It was evening, only hours since Wade Syan's murder had been solved. The entire county was gossiping about the news. Images of Shwa Chinny's ponytailed head and smirking face were broadcast into everyone's home. Natisra Fezz's biography of Wade Syan, published posthumously just yesterday, was already outdated.

"I'm asking you." Milligram spread his knife around the bowl, until no noodle was on top of another. "Like this?"

"If you have to ask, you're not done."

"Ugh, Mo—"

Lemma and Milligram stared at each other in awkward silence.

"What was that?"

"Nothing."

"You called me Mom," Lemma said gently. "You were about to call me Mom."

Milligram looked into his bowl, and poked the noodles with his knife. "Didn't mean to. Sorry."

"You can call me Mom if you want."

"Gel. Mom, can I be done?"

"Don't edge, Milligram." She scooped up the entire contents of the bowl into one large spoonful, and held it in front of him. "Mouth."

"I don't want to."

Lemma sighed. "See that picture?" She pointed to the photo on the wall of herself when she nine. "I used to not be able to eat a lot of food.

I'd get pukey all the time. My skin was itchy and red. And when they finally made food I could eat, I ate twice as much as the other kids. So, eat up." She pushed the spoon to his lips.

"Ew."

Lemma scoffed. "Dishes."

She looked down at a stack of fake Balkon medallions and a hand-written list of addresses to scout. Then she felt something on her waist: two hands, hugging her from behind. Milligram's face was warm against her back.

"Milligram?"

He mumbled something into her back.

She rose from her chair, turned to face him, and pulled him into her chest, her cheek pressed against his, her ear tickled by the tightly wound hair which spilled from his scalp like coarse black clouds.

"What did you say?" she whispered.

"I love you, Mom."

"I love you, too."

She sniffed, and her nose wrinkled. The air around his shoulders smelled like chili. "When's the last time you took a shower?"

"I don't take showers. I take baths."

"Hmm. When was your last bath?"

"Every Saturday."

"I don't have a bathtub here, just a shower. That gel?"

"Now?"

"And every three days from now on."

"Three days? Mom— my other mom— only made me take one on Saturdays."

"You're older now."

"Not that older."

"Go, into the bathroom! I'll give you a towel when you're done."

She pushed him toward the bathroom door. The door closed behind him, followed by the sound of the shower turning on.

Lemma turned to her phone, which was buzzing with a call.

"What is it, Donovez? Going to give me claps for venging Syan?"

His voice was warm. "A million claps, Lemma. Rimming bright work."

Lemma preened. "Balkon offered to onboard me as a death agent."

"I hear you, Lemma. Scope this: I just contacted our investors. We're getting our next round of funding. You and Jax will both get 250 grams gold for your work with Syan, gel?"

"Gelly gel."

"And even better news; I talked to the man from your trial, Fremen Orea."

"What about him?"

"He lives in Wilco Residential Zone. His entire street has goons squatting. You heard of Cobra?"

"They're a pack. They buy and pitch contra food rations."

"Yes," Donovez replied. "Residents rimming hate them. You remember what I said about my new death agency?"

"Your rent-a-government?"

"Fremen's going to talk to his neighbors. Wilco might be our first client. Flush out Cobra, shield Fremen and the entire street."

"Except that Cobra is shielded. The entire pack has death insurance from Balkon."

"You shield Cobra?" Donovez's voice was soaked with disappointment.

"Yes."

Donovez sighed and cursed. "I'll talk to my investors. Lemma, I need you to scout Fremen's conk."

"She has a name; it's Harriden."

"Scout if she knows how Chinny did it."

"How Chinny did what?"

"Ghosted Syan. Because if Cobra has Balkon coverage we'll need to make them drown in their own bathtubs."

Lemma's skin contracted into goosebumps. "I'll find her."

"Also, now that we are officially launching our agency, you should know our name," Donovez said. "It's Abadon. Abadon Death Insurance."

CHAPTER 47

NADIA

Someone pounded on the door to the apartment.

Lemma's eyes snapped open; she stared into the darkness, wondering if it had only been a dream.

The knocking came again, rattling the walls. Lemma scrambled off the sofa cushions, her shoulder hitting Milligram's jaw as she stumbled to the door. She wished for a gun, a knife, a brick, anything to defend herself.

"Wipe off!" she shouted. A thousand possibilities danced through her mind: badges, Axiom agents, Cobra goons.

"Lemma!"

"Wipe— who is that?"

"Lemma! It's me!"

"Who?"

"Ruby! From Edeyong!"

Lemma pressed her face against the crack of the door frame. "Are you with anyone?"

"No!"

Lemma opened the door, and there stood the girl, small and vulnerable, shivering under a torn jacket, her red hair matted.

"Ruby!"

The girl ran into the room and pressed her face into Lemma's chest, pulling her into an embrace.

"You said I could talk to you if I ever needed anything. I need somewhere safe to squat."

"You're safe here."

"Lemma, who is it?" Milligrams head popped out from under the covers.

"A friend of mine. Her name's Ruby." Lemma closed the door, and breathed on Ruby's hands. "You're freezing," she said, but Ruby wasn't looking at Lemma; her eyes darted to the ceiling, the bathroom, the corners, for signs of a threat.

"No one's here, Ruby, only Milligram and me. You want something to eat?"

"Can I have something?" Milligram asked.

"No, go to bed."

"But you're being loud, and I want food too!" he said, hopping towards them on a single crutch.

Lemma sighed. "Plug it, Milligram. Ruby," she added in a low tone. "Are you safe? Is there anyone who might want to hurt you? Anyone following you?"

"Um. I don't think so."

"Wait, why is she crying?" Milligram asked.

"Gram Mills." Lemma placed her hand on his shoulder and squeezing it. "You need to not talk, do you understand me? You need to sit back on the cushions and stay there until I tell you to get up, gel? Or I'll have your mother lift you."

Milligram opened his mouth and glared at her. Then he thought better of it and returned to the cushions.

"He's a friend of mine; he's staying here," Lemma explained. "There's room for both of you, but you have to tell me honestly, is there anyone following you?"

Ruby shook her head.

"Gel. Do you want to tell me why you're here?"

"You said if I needed to someplace to stay…"

"Yes. And you can stay. I meant is there anything that happened to you that made you want to come here?"

Ruby swallowed, and shifted her eyes away.

"Ruby, you can say as much or as little as you want, gel?"

Ruby nodded.

"I have some clean clothes. They'll be big on you, but we can get you better ones tomorrow. Come."

She led Ruby to the bathroom. "Shower?"

Ruby shook her head.

"You're filthy. Take a warm shower and change. It's free."

But Ruby's expression was not one of defiance. She looked at the shower, flinched, and shook her head, shrinking into a smaller, mousier version of herself.

"You don't like showers?"

The girl shook her head again.

"Is… did something… are you scared of them?"

Ruby shrugged.

"Did something bad happen to you in a shower?"

Ruby sank to the floor, tears flowing, her stomach pulsing with the force of her sobs.

Lemma crouched down and hugged her with her uninjured arm. "Whatever happened, you're safe here. I'll bring you a washcloth and shampoo. Can you use that and the sink to wash yourself?"

***

Ruby emerged from the bathroom, clean and wearing one of Lemma's shirts.

"Milligram and I sleep on these sofa cushions. I can find more. Tonight you can squeeze next to me, gel?"

Ruby nodded shyly. "Lemma?"

"Hmm?"

"My real name isn't Ruby. It's Nadia."

"Good to meet you, Nadia."

Lemma lay down, with Milligram and Nadia on either side. It was uncomfortable, but she was relieved beyond measure that these two were safe with her. Milligram nestled close as always, but Nadia kept her distance, putting her knees up against Lemma to share her warmth, her hair still damp and smelling like coconut.

The two kids breathed, like alternating pistons of an engine which ferried Lemma out of the room and into a private space where they could rest in safety.

CHAPTER 48

FAMILY BUSINESS

Saturday, May 26

"Excuse me, Lemma, we have a partial match on these fingerprints."

Lemma cleared her throat.

"I'm sorry, *Ms. Quartz,* would you examine these?"

Lemma cleared her throat with authority.

"*Agent Quartz,* would you please…"

Lemma's new name plaque bore raised metallic letters. She polished it every half hour or so, before returning it to the top shelf of her cubicle, where it would stare menacingly at whoever came to interrupt her for advice. Since the Fremen trial, Lemma had become the unofficial consultant for every Balkon case, to the point of embarrassment for Curio, who had already sent out three memos forbidding other agents from disturbing Lemma's work. Lemma didn't mind the attention; there was no greater satisfaction than hearing pleas for assistance from coworkers who only several days before had been throwing bottles at her for daring to save the governor's life.

But even though Balkon and Curio had forgiven Lemma for this, Governor Kawling's pledge to eradicate death agencies was still the most pressing issue at the office, with countless memos from Curio detailing plans for a counterattack. They practiced drills in case the police attacked Balkon headquarters, and each agent was required to make a list of five state employees they could either blackmail or bribe.

CityNews ran continuously, projected on the wall, and every agent watched impatiently for updates about the new laws.

"And it gets worse," Curio told Lemma, after shooing away an agent with a box of evidence. "You were right."

"I know," Lemma replied. "What about?"

Curio pulled out a sealed bag with three pieces of metal inside. "Counterfeit medallions. We're scoping more every rimming day. If people buy them, they might think they don't need actual insurance."

Lemma nodded solemnly, nudging her foot against a leather satchel hidden under her desk, and praying that no one heard the clinking metal inside. "That's serious. Do we know who's pitching them?"

"We don't, but you're going to scout them out. I know you'd rather be ghosting people, but I consider this worthy of your time."

"Yes, I'll do it," Lemma said hastily. "I'll scout them and drop them."

"Excellent. Also…" Curio set a miniature glass rectangle by the counterfeit medallions. "This slide was delivered. It has your name on the label. We spected it was evidence and scoped through it."

"What's on it?" Lemma's fingers fidgeted around the fake medals.

"Gigabytes of data about the Tiresian Church and every doctor in the state. I can't say it's not organized well, but I have no idea what it's for. Unless you wished to blackmail their church."

Lemma examined it, silently thanking Shwa Chinny for upholding his end of the trade. "Blackmail?"

"If you scope it, you'll see. The church claims they don't amp children, but it's impossible to deny that's what's happening."

Lemma gripped the glass rectangle. "I'll use it well."

***

In the evening, Lemma began to help Milligram and Nadia with their lessons. Thanks to Lemma's tutoring, Milligram had been a year ahead of his classmates. However, Nadia hadn't been in school for over a year, and had been falling behind even when she was still going. So even though Nadia was three years older than Milligram, Lemma was able to teach them both at the same level. She did her best to keep the lessons interesting as well as relevant, in case the children ever decided to pursue the family business.

"If there are eighty neighbors in a zone, and twenty-five percent of them have death insurance, how many don't have death insurance?" Nadia read aloud, writing out the numbers on an unlicensed tablet Lemma had purchased. The other day Donovez had paid her 250 grams of gold, which was enough to purchase either a gun or a camera. Lemma had decided the tablet was a more pressing need. With the remainder she had bought a sofa and a bed, both large enough to fit all three of them, even Nadia, who despite her small size would often swing her legs wildly in panicked nightmares.

"It's twenty. So eighty minus twenty is sixty. Right?" Nadia asked.

Lemma smiled, as she checked her state-monitored messages on the wall. So far, she had received no warnings about housing non-relative minors. And Cheri Mills hadn't contacted Lemma since the evening her son went missing. For now, Lemma and the children were safe.

CHAPTER 49

ROCK OF MONKEYS

Sunday, May 27

Two days after the trial, Donovez invited Fremen and the other Wilco residents to Abadon Death Insurance Agency's first informational meeting.

"How many residents are there?" Jax asked Donovez, as people poured into the room.

"Fremen said eighty lived in Wilco. You spect I should have booked a larger room?"

They couldn't hold the meeting in Wilco without the Cobra gang finding out, so Lemma and Donovez had rented a factory warehouse several blocks away under the pretense of starting a satellite Tiresian chapter. Lemma, now an expert at navigating the world independent of vision, had worn a cheap pair of black sunglasses, and the owner of the venue, eager to showcase what a Tiresian ally he was, asked no questions when they paid in contra gold.

"You can actually move around without seeing?" Donovez asked.

Lemma pulled out a case of black corneal shields, and ripped off the red plastic seal. "Try some for yourself. They gave me extras."

Donovez turned them over in his hands. "Maybe I'll wear them to Edeyong. If a conk says no, can I spill her out for religious persecution?"

Lemma laughed darkly. "Might work. I was accused of persecution just for taking a photo of kids jumping in front of a Tiresian Church. Twanks."

From the crowd of his Wilco neighbors, Fremen approached them.

"Fremen. Howsie?"

"Getonia's leaving me."

"Sorry about that." Lemma grimaced.

"The conk was trying to kill me! Harriden and her rimming brother were plotting to kill me," he said indignantly.

"We all make mistakes," Jax said.

"Chinny never even paid me. Gave him everything I lifted from Syan and I never got paid."

"Did Chinny ever mention what it was that he wanted to find out?" Lemma asked.

Fremen shrugged. "Everyone's asked me that. I don't know what the data was. Some Phronesis Tech secrets, I spect; it was all encrypted. And I don't know how Chinny drowned Syan."

"I understand. Is Getonia going to be here?"

"No. She's left the house. Moved downtown. Is my gold safe?"

"All of it. Gold, silver, chemies, bullets. All safe," Lemma assured him.

"I'll come for it. But shield it in the betweens, gel?"

"My pleasure."

Then Donovez cleared his throat over a microphone, and everyone took their seat.

"Thank you for coming," he said. "Welcome to the first official meeting for prospective Abadon Death Insurance members. My name is Haydis Donovez, and I represent Abadon Death Insurance. I know what's happened to Wilco. I've been to your zone; I've walked your streets. Goons everywhere. Squatting in your yards, even in your homes. You can't tell them to wipe off. You're too strung out to even talk to them. They buy and sell and lift as they please."

"One of those twanks came in my house!" a man shouted.

"They broke my window!" another shouted.

"They grab at me! Whenever I walk past!" a woman shouted.

"Please, calm down!" Donovez said. "I understand! And we are here to help you. Abadon will help you. Until now, when you hear the words 'death insurance,' you might think of the big ones: Axiom, or Balkon. If you're ghosted, they track down the twank and venge you. Abadon will do more. We'll not only dispense justice, but serve other government functions: settling disputes, security, even garbage removal. And our first move will be to wipe every single one of those cucks off your street.

"But it's your choice whether you hire us. Think of us like a rent-a-government. So I'm going to pitch our terms.

"First: we're going to remove the Cobra pack from Wilco. We will set up security measures, including armed guards, to ensure that no packs edge you anymore.

"Second: all of you will be shielded by our death insurance. It will cover murder, kidnapping, violent assault, and significant theft. We'll give you a full list of everything to read before we all agree to the contract.

"Third: we'll provide mediation for any disputes between residents. It can be anything from playing loud music to an actual crime. If you have an issue with a resident, we'll help you settle it.

"Fourth: we'll also provide street and sidewalk maintenance. What the city does, or at least what it claims to do."

Laughter broke out, but Lemma noticed with a chill that it was not friendly, but bitter, the sort that would usually be accompanied by pitchforks and torches.

"How much will it bleed us?" a woman asked.

"Twenty-five grams gold per month, per household."

A wave of grumbles spilled through the room.

"Wait!" Donovez continued. "Abadon is a business, and we have to make money."

"That's four times what I bleed for property tax!"

"But unlike the state, we'll actually deliver!" Donovez shouted back. "And that brings me to our fifth service. We will keep the city badges off your flaps. Kitchen knives, blinks, guns, cameras; Abadon does not care what you buy, or sell, as long as you don't hurt each other."

Everyone was shouting at once.

"No guns!" one shouted.

"Wipe off, it's my house!"

"No cameras at night!"

"No cameras at all!"

"Knives stay in the kitchens!"

"Tie up your dogs!"

Everyone's voices blended into an avalanche of noise.

"Plug it!" Donovez shouted, glaring at them until they had stopped. "Lemma, get up here. Everyone, this is Lemma— Agent Quartz, she'll be one of our death agents. She's the one that helped us solve the Wade Syan case."

At the mention of Wade Syan, everyone leaned forward, listening carefully as Lemma took the microphone.

"Howsie. I'm Lemma Quartz. I've been working for a death agency for two years. I've met a jackload of different people, and I know you all have different opinions on what you should be allowed to do, both in public and in your own homes."

She gestured, and a document appeared on the wall behind her and Donovez.

"This is a list of city laws. You all will vote on which ones you want us to enforce for Wilco. Guns, knives, cameras. Intimate contact licenses, liquor licenses. In three days, we'll meet again to discuss how you voted. Then you can decide whether you want to hire us, or whether you want Cobra to stay on your flaps forever."

***

"This is a nightmare," Lemma murmured, as the room emptied.

"Democracy is a nightmare?" Donovez asked.

"Even if we could get them all to agree on a list of rules, what if they decide they want to change the rules later?"

"Then we'll have more votes later. Governments vote to change laws; so can we."

"What if they want a really cucked-up law? What if they want us to allow them to ghost each other?"

"It's not like the badges are stopping that now," Donovez said. "But they wouldn't vote for that. No one wants ghosting to be allowed because no one wants to be ghosted."

"What about amping? Parents become Tiresian, want to amp their kid. We going to allow that?"

"If that's how our customers vote, then yes."

"So we'll base right and wrong on what most of them decide?"

"You just summarized all of human history." Donovez sat down and rubbed his aching forehead.

"If everyone in the city joined the Tiresians, and decided to amp you and your family, that would be gel?"

"Not with me or my family."

"So it would be wrong?"

"It wouldn't matter whether it's right or wrong, because if everyone wanted it to happen, they'd do it regardless."

"So right and wrong don't matter, just what people agree on?"

"I hate to say it, but… exactly that."

"No. Some things are simply wrong."

"But says who, Lemma? We're a bunch of monkeys on a rock trying not to starve. One day the sun will go dark, and it's going to get really cold. Right and wrong won't matter then, and they never have. Survival matters. We make laws against killing because killing makes it hard to survive. In this case, our company is trying to survive. And we survive by enforcing whatever laws Wilco pays us to enforce. Right and wrong is nothing but a contract, Agent Quartz."

Lemma tried to think of a counterargument.

"Quartz. Sio4our," Donovez said suddenly, watching the last Wilco residents leave the building.

"What?"

"I just realized what your alias meant. The one you used until we met in person. S-I-O-4. One part silicon, four parts oxygen. Chemical formula for quartz."

Lemma smirked. "Clever. What was yours? NewTulip786? What did that mean?"

"It means that NewTulips 1 through 785 were already taken."

CHAPTER 50

CHIPPED

Wednesday, May 30

Over the next three days, the Wilco residents submitted their votes, using their monitored state CityLink accounts. Some rules had unanimous support, but others, such as camera and guns, were so divisive Lemma couldn't understand how they would ever get the entire neighborhood to agree.

"They'll agree to compromise. We just have to remind them that we're the only option besides Cobra," Donovez assured Lemma.

But it was difficult for even Jax, Lemma, and Donovez to agree which rules to keep and which to throw out.

"You have to let them have cameras," Lemma insisted. "What are we, the state?"

"I agree, but thirty-six percent voted to keep the camera ban."

"That's not even half!"

"We could compromise," Jax said. "Cameras allowed inside, but not in the public streets. You've never heard of a compromise?" he said, as Lemma glared at him.

***

On the morning of the final vote, Lemma's blink buzzed every five minutes with updates from Donovez.

"Sounds like someone wants to get your attention," Schwartz said. They were in one of the triage centers in Balkon. "Is it Jax?"

"Wipe off," Lemma muttered. "You're gel, Nadia, you're gel."

Nadia's hands were trembling as she pressed a red-soaked cloth to Lemma's belly.

"Press harder. Keep holding," Lemma encouraged. "Don't be afraid to push hard."

Nadia's nose wrinkled and she turned her head away.

"You have to face me— don't— push harder, here." Lemma grabbed Nadia's hands, pressing them tightly against her stomach.

"Doesn't it hurt?"

"If this were real, I wouldn't feel anything. I'd be passed out."

"She'd have bled out, the way you're holding it," Schwartz interjected.

Nadia grunted in frustration, and pushed harder.

"You're doing— that's gel. Keep..." Lemma breathed deeply. "That's gel. Scope it? It's drying, turning brown."

Nadia pulled the cloth away to check her progress.

"Nadia! Don't! Keep it on, no matter what. You can't take it off even for a mite."

"It smells like ratjack," Nadia said.

"You know what smells worse? Dying," said Schwartz.

"You're not helping." Lemma glared at the doctor.

"Neither is she."

Nadia grunted, pushing so hard she forced a cough out of Lemma.

"Enough! Stop!" Lemma massaged her stomach, wiping blood from her hands onto her pants. "Get her a washcloth," she told Schwartz.

"Dr. Schwartz, have you seen Lemma? What the cuck?" Jax entered the room, and nearly vomited at the sight of them.

"It's just pig's blood, gel your flaps. And it's expensive, too. Who's paying for this?" Schwartz asked.

"Wash up, Nadia, you were bright. Jax, what is it?" Lemma stood and rinsed her hands in the sink.

"It's Curio. She wants you."

"Nadia, I'm going to be gone for a mite, can you help Dr. Schwartz clean up? And leave the door open."

Nadia and Schwartz nodded.

"What the cuck was happening in there?" Jax asked, still wincing at the rusty smears on Lemma's pants.

"Schwartz needs an assistant. Nadia wants to be a nurse. Today was the first day of her internship."

The blood on the front of Lemma's pants made no difference to the dozen Balkon workers who surrounded her as soon as she had left the triage center, holding out files and images, begging her to examine clues and give opinions.

"Wipe off!" Jax said, swatting them away. "Solve your own rimming cases!"

"Envious? Just a mite envious?" Lemma elbowed Jax's ribs playfully. "Don't cry; I'll save you some cases."

Jax stared at her, stone-faced.

"Jax, what's stringing you?" she asked.

"You heard about Kawling's new proposal?" His voice was flat.

Lemma tensed. "What?"

"The state just announced it. They're going to give every citizen free death insurance."

"What? Where are they getting the money?"

"They're partnering with Axiom."

Lemma couldn't believe it. "Axiom — but — Kawling said we're all Schedule One. She's stepping down on us!"

"She won't have to step down on us," Jax said grimly. "Every citizen is getting free death insurance from Axiom. We'll lose all our clients."

As they drew close to Curio's office, they could hear Curio's furious voice shouting from behind her closed door.

"And now Kawling's playing favorites, taking honest salt-of-the-earth death agencies and throwing them out on the street!"

Jax opened the door, and a trio of agents looked at him and Lemma with relief.

"Lemma. Just the one I wanted to scope. You and Jax squat. You three, bounce."

The agents hurried out of the room.

"Lemma, take a chair."

"Good morning to you, too," Lemma said.

Curio grunted. "Sit."

Lemma sat and looked at Jax, but he was focusing his gaze on his shoes.

"So," Lemma began.

Curio's hand whipped out. Lemma raised her hands, too late. Something cold and hard hit her in the teeth. She cried out in shock, her lips throbbing, the clink of metal still ringing in her ears. Her upper front teeth ached and stung. Lemma ran her tongue around her mouth, tasting salty rust as it caressed the rough chip in one of her incisors.

"Curio!" Lemma hissed, ready to pounce. "What the rimming cuck!"

"It was you!"

Lemma's anger was replaced by hollow unease. "What was me?" For a moment, her eyes flickered toward a leather satchel on Curio's desk.

Then Curio moved again, and Lemma threw her hands up as a barrage of metal objects flew at her. Round, shiny, fake medallions clattered on the table.

"Curio—" Lemma began.

"Shut. Your. Mouth. You lying cucking squint."

Lemma looked to Jax. He made no attempt to come to her aid as Curio continued her rant.

"You did this? You sold them? I have the state buying out Axiom. I have new agencies ambushing our clients in their own neighborhoods."

"What?"

"And then you, my own agent, selling fake rimming medals and flooding the rimming streets with them!"

"I— Curio—"

"Why Lemma? Why?"

"Only to people who weren't buying coverage. That way they still can protect themselves."

"Protect themselves. That's gel. And how does that help Balkon?"

"It... I'm sorry."

"You're sorry. Jax—"

Curio nodded to him and Jax stretched out his arm. From his fist the barrel of a gun stared at Lemma.

"Jax— no— Jax!"

"Give me one reason. One reason not to," Curio hissed.

"Jax, don't!"

"Don't scope at Jax, scope me in the rimming eyes and explain to me what you did," Curio said.

The thunderous sound of gunfire echoed in the room. Lemma's hands flew to her ears, her skin hot and cold at the same time. Visions of Milligram and Nadia alone in the apartment danced in her mind. She saw Nadia, wiping up blood from Curio's carpet, weeping as she wrung a blood-soaked rag into a bucket.

But at the last moment Jax had fired into the floor. A neat hole was drilled into the carpet, a thread of smoke rising from it.

"You get one more chance." Curio's whisper was far more menacing than her shouting.

"What?"

"I'm not going to ghost you. Yet. I have an assignment for you. One only you can do."

"An assignment. Yes, I'll do it. What is it?"

"A target." Curio pulled out a plastic vial, labeled "72 hours" in red letters.

"Yes. I'll ghost them. Who is it?"

"A dear friend of yours."

"A friend? Who?"

"Governor Raemin Kawling."

Chapter 51

Threats

Lemma's breath was heavy, her heart was pounding in her own ears. She could still see Curio, but the rest of the room was fading into a blur as she scrambled for something to say in reply.

"If you do this," Curio said, pressing the vial into Lemma's numb hands. "You will be forgiven. And what's more, Balkon will pay for your friend, the Reezy, to get a new leg."

Then Lemma was out of the chair and running, stumbling out of the office toward her desk.

"Lemma!" Jax caught up with her.

"Wipe off Jax, don't touch me."

"Listen to me!"

"I'm not listening, you—"

"I can help you, if you just listen."

"I don't need your help because I'm not ghosting Kawling."

"Then Curio will ghost you, Lemma, she'll make me ghost you."

"Oh, thanks for the help back there. Rimming appreciate it."

"What was I supposed to do? Curio made me!"

"She gave you a gun!" Lemma shouted, searching Jax's empty hands for the gun, fully aware that everyone on the floor was staring at them, afraid to interrupt. "You were juggling a gun, you could have rimming ghosted her right there!"

Curio's voice blared on the loudspeaker. "Lemma, I can hear you. If you're going to make death threats, I suggest you make them off the clock."

"Lemma, gel it, please," Jax begged.

"I'm not gelling, give me those!"

"Stop it!" hissed Jax. "Stop being emotional!"

Lemma threw her name plaque at him, missing him and striking the wall.

"Agent Quartz?" another worker asked timidly. "I have a file. Maybe you could help—"

Lemma threw a glass bottle, and the worker buckled to the ground, holding her face as red trickled from her fingers.

"Listen!" Jax said. "Milligram will get a new leg."

"Don't bring Milligram into this."

"But Curio promised!"

"You!" Lemma grabbed Schwartz by his shoulders as he attempted to walk past. "You told her about Milligram's leg."

"Please, Lemma! I'm late for surgery." He twisted out of her grasp. "I'm sorry!"

"Lemma, let's go." Jax grabbed her wrist, and pulled her out of the building into the street. Lemma breathed the fresh air into her lungs, recharging them for a new attack.

"Why didn't you tell me?" she screamed. The stitches in her right arm were throbbing against the bandage; she feared the knife wound would reopen. "Before dragging me into her office? Before she chipped my rimming tooth!"

"I'm trying to keep my post, Lemma."

"Your post? Did you forget that we have new posts with Abadon?" she hissed.

"You heard Curio, they know about Abadon." He kept the volume of his voice in check. "I don't know how, one of the Wilco residents spilled, or their kids did. But Balkon knows, and we have to choose. Abadon's cucked, Lemma. It's Balkon or be ghosted."

"Don't touch me. Don't talk to me. If I see you again, I swear I'll—"

"Lemma, please!"

Lemma jammed her knee upward. Jax recoiled, clutching his stomach, pressing his thighs together as he sank to the concrete.

"Lemma? What's going on?" Nadia had followed them outside.

Lemma grabbed the girl's hand, and ran.

CHAPTER 52

SOCIAL CONTRACT

"Lemma," Donovez asked, that evening watching as the residents of Wilco filed once again into the imitation Tiresian Church. "What's stringing you?"

Lemma shrugged. "Nothing. I'm gel."

"You're gel?" Donovez smiled at a cluster of Wilco clients, shaking their hands, and giving each one a blink.

"You're not gel," Donovez told Lemma. "Tell me, what's stringing you? And where's Jax tonight?"

Lemma didn't reply.

"Are you and Jax gel? Lemma, did Jax do something?"

"Jax isn't with Abadon anymore. And don't let him near me."

"What did he do?"

"I said, don't rimming let him near me."

Donovez nodded.

"I have a situation," Lemma cleared her throat, handing out more blinks as people filed past. "If you had the chance to help someone, but you had to do something ugly in return, would you?"

Donovez frowned. "Depends on how ugly. And how much money they offered me."

"Helping to ghost someone."

"I didn't think you'd have a problem with that."

"Not venging a murder, just an innocent person who was in the way."

"No one's innocent." Donovez said. "Who are they?"

"An elected official."

"Guilty enough for me."

"Guilty enough to deserve death?" Lemma asked.

"Is this person me?"

"No."

"Anyone with Abadon? Someone I know?"

"No."

"One of my friends or family, other than my father?"

"No."

"Then I really don't give a jack if you ghost them. I absolve your sins." Donovez waved his hands with sarcastic whimsy.

"Lemma," It was Fremen. "Lemma, can I come get my stuff tomorrow?"

"Yes."

Donovez ordered, "Fremen, get everyone to be quiet. It's time to start."

Fremen hissed at his neighbors, shushing them until they were silent.

"Welcome everyone. I want to thank you for submitting your votes over the last three days. You should all have been issued one blink per household," Donovez announced.

"Can we keep these?" a woman asked, holding up her blink.

"These are borrowed from a friend in the police force, and they need to be returned after this meeting."

Everyone grumbled in disappointment.

"What's that?" Another resident pointed to a large box by Donovez's side.

"That is a surprise for later. First, the results of the voting." Donovez waved his hand at the wall, displaying the list of rules that he, Jax, and Lemma had written.

"Some of the responses were straightforward. Everyone agreed that trespassing, theft, and violence were to be prohibited.

"Then we have contras. Everyone was split on guns, knives, and cameras. For that we proposed a compromise: you're allowed to store and use those objects in your own homes, but if any of you bring them outside, they'll be confiscated. Again, this is a compromise."

Then Donovez invited them to share their input. They discussed and argued. They argued what someone should be allowed to do in re-taliation if someone vandalized their house, or broke into their house, or if someone's pet caused damage in their yard.

The meeting went on late into the night. After five hours, they agreed on exactly fifty-seven laws. Thirty-six of these governed what the residents were and were not allowed to do. Twenty-one covered what Abadon owed them.

"I have a question," one resident said, standing. "How do we know that Abadon won't be the next Cobra? Squat in our houses?"

"Good question," Donovez answered. "Rule Four: no Abadon agent shall enter a peaceful resident's house without permission of the owner or lawful occupant, and shall leave upon request."

"What if you decide not to?" someone else asked.

"We're going to the best protection agency in the city. We're going to shield other streets, other zones, but first we have to prove we can treat you well."

"And if they don't," Lemma said. "You'll be allowed your knives and guns. If Abadon ever becomes like Cobra you can wipe us off yourselves."

A chill fell over the room.

At Donovez's instruction, they pulled out their blinks, and voted anonymously.

"Eighty-three percent agreed," Donovez sighed. "We're a business selling a product. If you don't unanimously agree to it, we'll leave. Who will protect you from Cobra? They don't rimming let you have knives, or guns, or blinks. They're too smart for that."

Fremen stood up. "Mr. Donovez, I spect some people are wondering how you'll wipe off Cobra. You'll drop them? Ghost them?"

Donovez gestured at the display behind him. "According to Rule Thirteen, we will keep our method of removing Cobra secret."

"Mr. Donovez?" Fremen asked again. "I was talking to some neighbors the other day. I spect people are worried about the contract lasting a whole year. None of us have ever rented a government before, and that's a long time."

"What if we kept the contract at the same price, but prorate it so it's just for a month?" Lemma suggested. "At the end of the month, we can discuss modifying our rules. If we cuck it up, you won't have to hire us back."

People nodded thoughtfully to themselves. Donovez looked at Lemma.

"We'll vote once more," he said. "Remember, every single one of you needs to vote affirmative. We won't sign a contract until everyone agrees. If it doesn't pass, my agents and I will walk out of these doors, and shield another neighborhood. You will return to your homes, giving your food to Cobra goons that sleep in your beds. You will pay them every time you want to leave or enter your house. They will use your property as they please, touch you without fear of repercussion. No set of laws will be exactly the way you want. I'm asking you a simple question. Do you want to be ruled by Cobra, or shielded by us?"

The residents of Wilco Residential Zone raised their blinks and voted again.

The contract passed unanimously.

"Claps," Donovez smiling. "In accordance with Rule Two, the first monthly fees will be due in three days. We'll have Cobra out within the week."

He motioned, and the large box at his side hummed, ejecting a bound paperback book. The book had a black cover, emblazoned in gold words: "The Community Contract Between Wilco Residential Zone and Abadon Death Insurance Agency, First Edition."

"Who wants the first copy?" Donovez asked.

CHAPTER 53

PEDECTOMY

The Wilco-Abadon contract was the first printed book Lemma had held in years. She kept it hidden under her shirt the entire way home, even in the empty expectant mothers section of the CityBus. Printed books were rare, and rare objects led to awkward interviews with badges.

Lemma heard loud voices coming from inside before she opened her apartment door. She rushed inside to find Nadia and Milligram yelling at each other.

"Plug it, both of you!" Lemma said, hiding the book under the loose flap of carpet with the other contras. "I told you, you have to be quiet; you can't let anyone know you're here! What's the edge?"

"She won't let me sit on the couch!" Milligram whispered loudly.

"What?" Lemma asked, exasperated. "Nadia, why do you care where he sits?"

"Can I just have one thing to myself?" Nadia returned, glaring at Milligram. "I just want to have a couch to myself."

"It's not your couch!" Milligram shouted.

"Plug it!" Lemma hissed. "It's my couch. Both of you share."

"Ha!" Milligram said, jumping on the couch next to Nadia.

"He keeps touching me!"

At these words, Lemma frowned. "What? What you mean, touching?"

"He keeps poking me."

Lemma looked at Milligram, who defended himself. "She was squatting on my side! There's a line." He pointed to the space between the two cushions, "and she was squatting over it."

"He doesn't need that much room anyway; he only has one leg," Nadia shot back.

"Don't say that," Lemma hissed. "Do not say that. Nadia, stay on your side. Milligram, don't poke her."

"What if she comes to my side?"

"Oh my rimming cuck, Milligram, she won't."

"But what if she does?"

"Then you can tell me. Both of you, sit."

They did.

"Lemma, Gram's humming!"

"I'm not!"

"You twanks!" Lemma pulled the book out from under the carpet, and Nadia winced, pulling her knees to her chest. Lemma felt a blade of guilt stab into her, but moved on.

"Milligram, call it: front or back?"

"What?"

"Like a coin. Not heads or tails; front or back."

Milligram called the front, but when Lemma tossed the book to the floor, the golden letters were face down.

"You lose. Bathroom."

"What?"

"You can squat in the shower. Nadia gets the couch."

"But Lemma!"

She grabbed his arm. "Milligram. Do you want to go live with your mother again?"

He glared at her. "No."

"Then sit in the shower."

"For how long?"

"Until I say you can come out."

Milligram gathered his crutches and limped into the bathroom, slamming the door shut.

"Lemma?" Nadia murmured.

"Mm?"

"Next time I'll sit on the floor. I don't want to go in the bathroom, gel?"

"Gel."

Nadia's knees were still pulled to her chest. "Tell Gram he can't poke me."

"I did. I'll remind him again when he comes out."

"I—" Nadia's eyes shimmered with tears. "I don't like when—"

"Nadia, I promise you, I won't let him do it again, gel?"

"Gel. Lemma? Are we going to see Dr. Schwartz again?"

"No. We can't go back there anymore. I'm sorry. Did you like being a nurse for Dr. Schwartz?"

Nadia nodded.

"I'm working for someone else now. They'll have doctors too. Maybe they'll need someone to be a nurse."

Nadia wiped her eyes on her sleeve and smiled.

"We're also going to move to a new zone. You gel with that?"

"Will anyone ask me to…?"

"No, Nadia. If anyone tries to touch you, I'll paint the sidewalk with their brains."

"Will Gram be there?"

"I promised to shield both of you."

Nadia's smile twisted.

"You don't want Milligram to come with us?"

"He's only got one foot. He's a Reezy, right?"

"Don't call him that. He's Tiresian, what's your edge with that?"

Nadia looked at her knees, pressing her face into the over-sized pants Lemma had not yet found a replacement for.

"They're not good people," Nadia mumbled into her knees.

Lemma's brow furrowed. "Hey, who told you that? It wasn't his fault he only has one foot."

"Reezys—" Nadia continued, her breaths coming faster. "You can't— you have to…"

"Have to what?"

"You can't say no to a Reezy," Nadia whispered.

"What do you mean?"

"If you're a conk, and you tell a Reezy no, they tell the badges."

"Level Laws," Lemma murmured.

"One of them was deaf."

"A deaf Tiresian?"

"He couldn't hear." Nadia sniffed and wiped her eyes and nose on her knee. "He was hurting me. Felt like… it really hurt. I told him it hurt, but he couldn't hear."

Lemma sat on the couch, and Nadia leaned onto her.

"I said no more Reezys. Then one of them went to the badges and said I had to let Reezys… or the badges would take me if I didn't."

Lemma remembered Donovez's joke about sunglasses. She felt a bitter taste in her mouth and she hugged the girl with her good arm.

"Nadia, how long have you posted? As a conk?"

Nadia sniffed. "Started last year. Lifted an inty lice so no one would spill me out." She reached into her sock and pulled out the intimate contact license Lemma had seen that night at Edeyong, the one issued to Ruby Rhodes.

Lemma's nose twitched. The card had a familiar lemon smell, but she couldn't remember what it reminded her of.

"You have parents?"

Nadia shook her head without answering.

"So why you don't like Gram? Because of other Tiresians?"

Nadia sniffed. "If he was older, and he asked me… I wouldn't be able to say no."

"But he won't, Nadia. He's a good boy."

"I don't know that."

"Nadia, Milligram is the sweetest boy I've ever met. He doesn't know what you've been through. If you want, I can explain it to him."

"No! Don't tell anyone! Promise?"

"I promise. Can you promise me something too?"

"What?"

"Promise to not be unkind to him. I'm not saying you have to be friends. But it's not easy for him. I'm not saying he's had it as bloody as you, I'm not saying that, but his mom had his leg amped off. She lied to him. Told him it was because of an infection. He has to take medication because of pains in his leg. Please don't fight with him. You're older than him; you need to be the one who stops fights before they happen, gel?"

"Did you know him then? When his leg came off?"

Lemma couldn't lie. Not after everything Nadia had shared. "I didn't know Milligram then. But I knew the doctor who did it. Actually, I worked for the doctor."

Nadia's face twisted in horror. "You worked for him?"

Lemma looked behind her; the bathroom door was still closed. "I wanted to stop it, but I let it happen."

Nadia swallowed. "You… you let them do it? Why?"

"Nadia, I promised to lock your secrets. I've never told anyone this, so you have to promise me not to spill, especially to Milligram."

Nadia nodded.

"It was eight years ago. I was eighteen. Before death agencies existed, I did lots of random jobs. As a courier, contra smuggler, bodyguard, anything. One of the people I worked for was a surgeon."

The memory was burned into her brain. She remembered the exact way the sun felt on her face as she sat next to Dr. Patel on the drive to the hospital, ready to jump in front of him at the first sign of a threat.

"What's scheduled for today?" Lemma had asked, already knowing the answer.

"Work for the Tiresian Church. Three-year-old boy's getting a partial pedectomy."

"Only three?"

Patel cleared his throat. "It's with his mother's permission."

Lemma had wondered what it would feel like to trample him. There was a pencil in her pocket; she could lodge it in his eye before he could do anything.

"I could have stopped him," Lemma told Nadia. "But I needed the money. So I shielded him. All the way into the hospital. Stayed with him all day. I worked for the surgeon for a while. Milligram wasn't his only patient. But you can't tell Milligram, gel? He can't know. I'm the only person he can trust anymore."

"When did you and Milligram finally meet?"

"Five years ago, I got in trouble for a photo I took near a Tiresian church building. Lost my photography lice. Was ordered to do community service hours for a Tiresian family. I specifically scouted the list of kids who got surgery from that doctor. And got assigned to the Mills family. Six-year-old boy named Gram Mills."

"What happened to his parents?"

"His father became Tiresian. Even got surgery, the same as Milligram. Eventually found Milligram's doctor and took revenge. Now he's in prison." Lemma flexed her bandaged right arm. "Milligram's mother doesn't know he's here."

"Do you feel bad?"

"I hate myself for it. Every time I scope him limp, I wish I could—"

Lemma's throat was thick, and her chest burned, hot and acidic. She reached for her blink and her phone, sending a message to Curio, and another to Governor Kawling.

CHAPTER 54

SENNACHERIB

Thursday, May 31

Lemma couldn't sleep. The two bodies on either side were no longer warm and comforting but suffocating, and every time she closed her eyes she saw a woman with gray hair, gasping for breath.

And then, after several agonizing hours of darkness, after countless stumbles into the shower, followed by gut-wrenching vomits until her stomach was shriveled like a raisin, it was morning. Lemma washed out the shower, cleaned the sweat and slime off her shivering body, forced herself to eat a piece of broccoli, vomited again, cleaned that up, and left the apartment.

She stared at her blink and phone the entire bus ride, begging it to show her a new message, a change of plans from Curio, a cancellation from Kawling. She scoured the expectant mothers section for an escape, a way to accidentally injure herself, but the bus ran as smoothly as ever, ferrying her to the capitol building at a record pace. Everything around her was a blur, and when she arrived at the front desk, she couldn't even hear her own words, which came out thick and rubbery as she asked to be admitted to see Governor Kawling.

"You have an appointment?"

Lemma didn't remember how she responded, or how she got into the elevator. She found herself suddenly halfway through a conversation with a capitol worker, trying to drown out her thoughts by focusing her attention on a black-and-white poster on one of the elevator's walls, pretending to be fascinated by the winged angel standing over a pile of corpses, sword in hand.

"It's '*Sennacherib's Army Is Destroyed*' by Gustave Doré," the worker said, nodding at it. "Not the most creative title, is it? Part of our city art project, we just installed…"

Lemma didn't hear a single word. She prayed for the elevator to slow, to malfunction, for the steel cables holding it up to snap, but it rose without a hitch, and the door slid open flawlessly.

"Where are you pointed?" the worker asked.

Lemma's mind skipped once again. Suddenly she found herself in front of a door, which opened to reveal—

"Lemma!" It was Governor Kawling.

The governor embraced her, smiling, her arm free of the sling she'd worn after Perron Mills' attack.

"Lemma! Come in, come in. Oh dear, you look exhausted. Would you like something to drink? Water? Coffee? Tea?"

Lemma's brain had stalled.

"Can I get you a drink?" Kawling repeated. "Goodness, you seem tired."

"Tea. I'll have tea."

"Come, take a seat."

The mugs clinked on Kawling's desk as she set out a tray of tea bags, rifling her fingertips through each label.

"I'm guessing you'll want one with lots of caffeine."

Lemma grabbed one without reading it.

Kawling smiled, poured water from an instant kettle into her mug, and added a tea bag. "What brings you here, Lemma? Your message last night sounded urgent, almost desperate."

"I…" Lemma realized she hadn't even considered a plausible reason for the meeting.

"Is this something to do with our call last week? After my speech about death agencies? You'd said I was in danger?"

Instead of answering, Lemma jerked her chin at Kawling's mug. "What kind of tea is that?"

"Golden Puer." Kawling lowered her nose to the surface, inhaling the steam's rich, earthy scent. "May I?" She gestured toward Lemma's empty mug.

"I'll just smell yours. I'm not sure if I want one, gel?"

Kawling gave a polite chuckle, and slid her mug toward Lemma. "Go right ahead. I wanted to ask, are you interested in attending the Governor's Ball tomorrow? Have you heard about it? I can issue you an invitation."

Lemma wasn't listening. She slipped her hand into her pocket, gripping Curio's capsule between her middle and fourth finger. She raised Kawling's mug, inhaling the aroma of the tea, as steam flooded her face. Her cheeks were sticky with sweat, and she feared she would pass out.

"Lemma, are you gel?"

Lemma could not do it. Kawling's voice had all the tenderness of a concerned grandmother, a favorite schoolteacher. Lemma's fingers were rigid, the capsule wedged in place.

"Lemma?"

Lemma thought of Milligram's leg, scarred and shortened, and focused on that image, echoing Curio's promise in her mind. She remembered Perron Mills' story, and stared into Kawling's face, forcing herself to hate her, to blame her for everything that had happened to Perron and his son.

Then something within Lemma shifted. Suddenly Kawling no longer seemed like a gentle grandmother but a cruel bureaucrat, a dangerous tyrant who had to be stopped.

Lemma's fingers spread apart, and the capsule plunged into the tea, stinging her palm with a drop of boiling liquid.

"What?" Lemma asked, sliding the mug back to Kawling.

"I was asking if you wanted to attend the Governor's Ball tomorrow." Kawling laughed, adding, "Hopefully neither of us will be stabbed by any death agent goons."

Lemma smiled. As long as she maintained a steady stream of hatred against Kawling, she could carry out this task.

Kawling lifted her mug, and Lemma tensed. But the governor was only blowing on the hot beverage, cooling it enough to drink.

She knows, Lemma thought. *Kawling saw you drop the chemie in, she's sending for security right now.*

"I hadn't heard about the ball." Lemma said.

"It's tomorrow evening. I'd like for you to attend. You saved my life. I believe the city would love to see you there. It would restore morale, boost confidence."

"Restore morale," Lemma echoed.

"We'll have better security than at the dedication, of course."

"Security. Yes." Lemma's gaze was locked on Kawling's mug.

"So you'd like to attend?" Kawling lowered her lips to the tea. Lemma held her breath, but Kawling was still only blowing on it.

"Yes. Governor's Ball. Sign me up."

"Wonderful. I look forward to it. Now, what was it that you wished to see me about?" Kawling blew on the tea once more, and then took a sip.

CHAPTER 55

KNEELING

Lemma hand moved on its own. In a single motion, the mug flew from Kawling's hand, shattering against the bookshelf.

Kawling screamed and jumped back, and Lemma rose, every muscle tense, heart convulsing, breath churning in her lungs. Kawling was in shock; her eyes alternated between the dripping bookshelf and Lemma, demanding an explanation but too shaken to even ask.

Then Lemma's eyes were spilling tears. She grabbed at her cheeks, tearing her fingernails into her own skin, and screaming into her palms.

"Lemma! What on earth?"

"Raemin, they made me! Oh cuck— Raemin, Governor, please don't be angry."

"Lemma?"

Lemma collapsed, and Kawling ran to her, but Lemma's face was pressed into the carpet and she only saw the governor's shoes.

"I didn't— please! I didn't want to."

Lemma was shaking. Her cheeks stung from where her fingernails had raked them. Breathing in shattered sobs, she grabbed the governor's ankles and pressed her forehead against her toes.

"I'm so sorry, Raemin!"

"Lemma! Tell me what's going on. God in heaven, Lemma, what is this?"

Lemma finally dared to look at Kawling, her face shimmering through Lemma's tears. She had hoped Kawling would be angry, would yell at her, but her expression showed nothing but tenderness and concern.

"Governor, please don't string at me."

"Lemma, just tell me."

"I did a bad thing."

"Lemma, please. Just say it. What?"

"They made me put poison in your tea."

"Poison? Where? Who?" Kawling's voice was fearful.

"They want me to ghost you." Lemma fumbled in her pocket, and pulled out the empty vial with the label which read "72 hours."

"You put poison in my tea? But you knocked it out of my hand before I could drink it. Who told you to do this?"

"Balkon. I'm… I'm a death agent with Balkon. They said… your law… they want you—"

"Lemma, Lemma." Kawling knelt, hugging her, squeezing out more tears. "You're a good girl, Lemma."

"I'm not— I'm not, I tried to ghost you."

"Lemma, it's gel. Listen to me."

"You're not going to turn me in?"

Kawling looked shocked. "Of course not, you've done nothing wrong."

"But the tea…"

"That's twice you've saved me, Lemma. Now be honest with me."

Lemma nodded, and hiccupped.

"The poison in the tea… How long does it take to kill?"

"Not right away. It makes you pukey, so you have to go to the hospital. They have agents who post in the hospital. They ghost you there."

Kawling considered, tapping her chin. "How long until I'm supposed to get sick?"

"The label says seventy-two hours."

"So we have several days before Balkon realizes you didn't do it?"

"I— yes. Yes."

"Lemma, I need you to do something for me."

Lemma blotted her eyes with her sleeve, and dared to hope. "Anything. Just name it."

"You need to help me end Balkon. Can you do that?"

"End them?"

"Balkon is a pack of goons that murder people for profit. You need to tell me everything you know: members, leaders, locations, number of weapons, contra currency, everything. Can you do that?"

Kawling pulled Lemma to her feet. Lemma's knees were still trembling.

"Lemma, this city needs to be rid of them. We can flush out them, and flush out the gangs. We can heal the city, but you have to help. Can I trust you?"

"I…"

"Can I trust you?"

Lemma swallowed. "Yes."

"Where is Balkon located"

"It's hidden in an old refrigerator factory, Facility Nine-Three-Eight-One. Balkon said if I did this mission they'd fix Milligram."

"Milligram?"

"The Tiresian boy, Gram Mills, the one from Natisra's article. He's missing a leg. The deal was they'd give him a new leg if I put the pill in your tea."

Kawling clasped Lemma's hands. "Lemma, if you help me wipe off Balkon, I promise you, we can get your friend a new leg."

CHAPTER 56

RECALL

"Agent Quartz!"

"Agent Quartz, excuse me, I have a client who was accused of…"

"Agent Quartz, scope these fingerprints."

"He says he's innocent, but Axiom detectives…"

Lemma swatted at them like mosquitos, but they continued to swarm around her, clamoring for help with evidence.

"Wipe off!" she hissed.

"Sorry, Agent Quartz."

"Forgive me, Agent Quartz."

They stepped out of her way, and she went to her desk. She swiped her finger, but her computer refused to unlock.

Lemma cursed and tried again before realizing that Curio had wiped her access.

"Agent Quartz—"

"I need you to let me into your computer," she said. "You, Agent Whoever."

"It's Agent Carter."

"I don't give a cuck. Get me an empty slide."

"I have several questions about evidence."

"Gel, open your computer. Everyone else, get back to work. Now."

She was the shortest agent in the office, but at her order everyone retreated.

"Pull up the list of all our members," Lemma told Agent Carter, pointing to his desk.

"But I'm asking about—"

"I know. Get the list of all current members, and export it. Now get a list of every agent, and all our current targets."

The query ran.

"Now search my name."

The profile for Lemma Quartz appeared. Her title was still set to agent, but a note had been added.

Agent Carter's brow furrowed. "It— it says your access privileges have been revoked. Agent Quartz, I'm not sure I'm allowed to give you this information."

"Plug it. Search Harriden Vik."

Harriden's profile appeared, with the label: Former member. Two notes had been added: "Assign to recall team" and "Drop coverage, end recall efforts."

"Recall…" Lemma muttered. "Search the database for that word. Recall."

"Agent Quartz I'm not sure I should—"

"Do it!"

Displayed was a list of members, each with a recall status. Every single member was one who had canceled membership, but a large percentage had renewed it soon after. In the notes were subtle references: "*Member saw agent breaking window, contacted badges.*" "*Member purchased contra weapon after break-in.*"

"Harriden wasn't the only one," Lemma murmured.

"What?" Agent Carter asked.

"Recall. It means Balkon edges members who try to leave." Lemma's mouth was sour.

"What does CA mean?" Carter asked, pointing to a number of notes: "'*CA approved extra measures*' '*CA instructed to reduce efforts*'"

"Curio Agarwal… she knows. Go to back to my profile. Pull up my history."

An account of Lemma's entire career at Balkon was displayed, from her early days running errands to her work as a scout, and her confirmation as a death agent.

"You were assigned to Wade Syan," Carter said. "I'd forgotten about that."

Lemma had not forgotten. Carter had been one of the dozen agents who had pretended to drop items in front of her.

"You and Yedra were the only available scouts?" Carter murmured, reading the notes about the investigation of Wade Syan's death scene. "That's wrong."

"What?" Lemma leaned in.

"It says here you and Yedra were assigned because every other agent was busy. I wasn't busy that night. I was at home."

"You're steady?"

"Yes. I was still at home when I heard about Syan's death from CityNews. Scope this."

Carter displayed a list of every agent's assignments on the night of Syan's death. Only half had been working.

"If we were all available, why did you and Jax go?"

Lemma stepped back, not hearing Carter's words. Her skin was cold.

"Agent Quartz?" Carter asked.

Lemma tried to focus, but her mind was spinning. Curio had lied the night she had sent Lemma and Jax to investigate Syan's death.

"Lemma!"

Lemma snapped out of her daze. Curio stood beside her.

"Well?" Curio asked. "You finished your assignment?"

"I poisoned Raemin Kawling," Lemma said loudly.

Every agent stood up from their desk and stared at her.

"Plug it. Follow me."

Curio led Lemma into her office, snapping her fingers as the windows frosted, shielding them from the gaze of everyone on the floor.

"We're alone. Speak. You popped her the dose?"

"Slipped it right in her tea."

"And she drank all of it?"

"To the last sip."

Curio nodded. "That's good. You've done well. Jax has contacts at the hospital who will finish her off. You're still under probation because of the medallions, but if you behave like a good little girl, you'll get everything back. And Schwartz has a new leg, fresh on ice, for your friend. Same blood type, skin color, size—"

"He found a new leg already?"

Curio shrugged. "Plenty of Tiresians, plenty of doctors."

"What?" Lemma shouted. "Milligram's leg— it's from— it's from a kid?"

"Oh, my mistake." Curio pretended to examine her computer. "My mistake, Schwartz harvested it from the leg tree. Ethically sourced and organic."

"You amped a kid?"

"Lemma, where did you spect we would get it? That a kid would drop dead right in front of us?"

"You amped a kid!"

"It wasn't us, it was a Tiresian doctor. The parents wanted their kid's leg amped. It would have gone to waste. Lemma, stop the dramatics. You're gel with Schwartz selling our targets' kidneys, but as soon as he buys an amped leg, he's a villain? Are you going to refuse it? Going to deny little Gram Mills his leg?"

"He can have mine!"

Curio scoffed. "Wrong blood type, wrong size, and your skin color will clash worse than stripes with plaid. Will you take the leg, or not?"

"You knew…" Lemma growled, changing the subject before she could lose the argument. "Harriden Vik. Every other twank who canceled. Recall. You sent goons to threaten them."

"Will you calm down?"

"I will not!" Lemma screamed so loudly her throat ached. "You edged your own members."

"We were bleeding out money!" Curio stepped forward until her nose touched Lemma's forehead.

"We agreed to protect them!"

"Which we can't do if they're not our members."

"What about Wade Syan?" Lemma shouted.

"Wade Syan? You're not making sense. First the boy's leg, then our members, now Syan! I'm choked, Lemma, I have a company to run!"

"Answer me. Why'd you send Jax and me that night?"

"What night?"

"When you had me scrape Syan's apartment!"

"Because you wanted an assignment."

"You said that night all the agents were busy."

"They were!"

"I scoped the records just now. Half your agents were free that night, but you sent me and Jax to investigate your top member. Now it all makes sense."

"What makes sense?" Curio hissed.

"You closed the case immediately. You declared it an accident."

"The family agreed it was an accident!"

"Did she help you? Ingo? Were both of you in on it?"

"In on what?" Curio screamed.

"You. Killed. Wade. Syan." Lemma's chest was vibrating. Saying the words aloud made her feel as if the office walls were closing in on her.

Curio's jaw dropped. "Oh?"

"Yes. You and Shwa Chinny. Maybe Ingo."

"And how could I have done that?"

"We'll never know, because you closed the case."

"Investigate all year if you want." Curio wrenched her computer screen towards Lemma. "The apartment door was closed and locked. His wife was the only other one there. The bathroom door was locked from the inside, and the bathroom window was jammed. So tell me, exactly how did you think I managed to do that?"

"What about the window?"

"I told you: it was jammed. No one could have opened or closed it." Lemma grinned triumphantly.

"No one ever said it was jammed," she said. "I wrote the report. I said the bathroom window didn't open."

"Jammed, closed, what's the difference?"

"If I say a window doesn't open, you spect it means built to stay shut. The only reason you would spect it was jammed is if you scoped it. In person."

"I—"

"I was the only one who scoped closely at it. You couldn't have heard it from Jax, and Ingo's statement didn't mention it. So who told you it was jammed?"

"No one told me."

"Because you'd been there. Maybe the day of the murder, maybe the week before. Maybe Ingo invited you in, as you made plans to ghost him."

Curio laughed. "Ingo— planning with me— Lemma, you— you're a rimming delight."

"Why Syan? Did he try to cancel his membership? You tried to recall him?"

"Oh, you're gushing all over him, the great Wade Syan." Curio's laugh soured, her face becoming mocking, cruel, scornful. "The philanderer, stealing work from his underlings and claiming it as own. You read Fezz's book, didn't you? He wasn't a saint; he was just like everyone else in this rimming city."

"Then why me?" Lemma felt as if her lungs were about to explode with the hate she poured into her voice. "Why me, Curio? Why did you set me on the case? Why did you want me to have to sit through every interview, hear those twanky things he did? He was my hero! You knew I crawled for Syan. You knew he saved me. You knew it jacked me the night he died. That's why you set me and Jax on it. You were hoping we'd jack up… hoping we'd miss clues, hoping I'd be so strung on it I wouldn't think straight. You planned all that. Blazing work, Curio."

Curio's lips pinched together. "Do you have plans for this little hypothesis of yours? You're going to run to the badges? CityNews? A death agency charged with murder, what a shock."

Curio moved, and Lemma jumped back, waiting for a blast of gunfire, but Curio hadn't even touched her weapon. She walked over to the door, and opened it.

"Here's the exit, in case you forgot. Come back when you want your next assignment."

"I already have one," Lemma whispered.

Chapter 57

The Banker

Wade Syan's death was finally solved. The final piece of the puzzle had been inserted: the jammed window which Lemma had thought too trivial to mention in the report had trapped Curio in her lie. Lemma sat down in the bus seat, her vertebrae uncoiling as the invisible burden slid off her back.

She called the governor on Donovez's phone and left a message.

"It's Lemma. Curio wouldn't let me scrape any data, but I remember I spilled a jackload of data to Shwa Chinny before he died. Your badges should have found it in his apartment. Also, I learned that Balkon harasses members who try to quit coverage. And I learned more about the Wade Syan case. Also, could you have the people at Minor Aid get me adoption forms for two children, an eleven-year-old boy and a fourteen-year-old girl? Message me when you hear this."

Curio would pay for what she and Chinny had done to Syan.

Lemma returned to find Nadia and Milligram sharing the couch.

"Lemma?" Nadia asked. "I finished my work."

Lemma shook her mind free of everything she had learned about Syan's death as Nadia held out Milligram's school tablet, showing a list of math problems.

"I couldn't get that one," she mumbled, looking down, her face reddening. "I'm sorry, I know you showed me how, but I forgot."

"Hey!" Lemma pulled her close. "It's gel to mess up sometimes. This is practice, not real life."

Nadia nodded, as Lemma read the problem.

"'If you can buy a contra blink and a contra gun for six grams, and you can buy two blinks and a gun for eight grams, how much does a gun cost?' Reason it out."

"The extra blink made it cost two more grams… oh, so a blink costs two. Which means the gun cost four?"

Lemma hugged her. "Bright. You know how to do it. You want another one?"

"Where were you just now?" Milligram asked. "Were you working on your mystery?"

"It's not a mystery anymore." Lemma sighed and then forced herself to smile. "I found the answer. Put all the clues together, and cracked the case."

Nadia asked, "Can you tell us what it was?"

"Remember Wade Syan? Milligram, you scoped his hologram at the hospital dedication. He was the one who invented labbed meat, right? He'd been killed, and we found one of the murderers, but there was someone else who helped."

"Who?" Nadia and Milligram asked in unison.

"My boss."

The children stared at her in awe.

"How do you know?" Nadia whispered.

"It's a thinking problem. You come into a room and scope a dead body. There's only one window, and it won't open. Later, you're questioning someone who says they've never been in that room before. You ask more questions, and they say they couldn't have done the murder, because the window was stuck shut. You tell me, did they do it?"

Nadia tapped her lips with her fingers, her eyes half-shut as she concentrated on the problem. "If they said they don't know how to break into windows…"

"I know it!" Milligram shouted. "Lemma, I know it!"

"Patience, Milligram, I was asking Nadia."

"Can I whisper?" Without waiting for permission, Milligram leaned in close to Lemma's ear, but started giggling before he could give the answer.

"You never said there were windows, but they knew the room had windows! So they were lying when they said they'd never been there!" Nadia said proudly.

"That's what I said!"

"You didn't say that, you were giggling."

"Lemma heard me, right Lemma? Didn't you hear me?"

"As I was saying," Lemma spoke loudly, "that's how I knew it was my boss who helped Chinny."

Nadia's face twitched. "Did you say…?"

A knock came on the door to the apartment.

Lemma gestured to the children. "Flash! Both of you go in the bathroom. Stay quiet."

Lemma approached the apartment door, asking, "Who is it?"

"Fremen. This still a gel time to get my contras?"

Lemma opened the door. "Howsie, Fremen. Kids, you can come out."

"Didn't know you had kids," Fremen said as Milligram and Nadia emerged from the bathroom.

"Look just like me, don't they?"

Fremen smirked.

"Milligram and Nadia," Lemma said, "I need you to take a walk, gel?"

"Where?" Nadia asked.

"Around the building. Don't talk to anyone, and don't leave the building."

"Do we have to?" Milligram pouted.

"Yes. Don't ask why."

Milligram pleaded to stay, but finally gave up and limped past Fremen.

"You too, Nadia."

Nadia hesitated, but then forced a smile, and left with Milligram.

"Sharp uniform," Lemma said.

Fremen looked down at his capitol maintenance uniform. "First day back."

"Back to keeping the air from getting too warm or too cold?" Lemma asked. "That's how Getonia described it."

Fremen grimaced. "I scoped you there, today. Tried to say howsie, but you were walking flash. Why were you there? Death agency stuff?"

"Just some errands. Let's get your contras. You juggling the knife?" Lemma led him towards the bathroom, as Fremen handed her a sharpened kitchen knife.

Lemma went to the shower and pushed the knife tip into the grout, making tiles pop out, revealing an opening.

"That's bright." Fremen said. "Never would have spected there was anything there."

Lemma reached in the opening and handed contra bills and grams of silver and gold to Fremen.

"I'm excited for Wilco," Fremen continued. "For you to wipe off Cobra. We're all excited, even the ones that weren't gel with it at first."

"Uh-huh," Lemma said, thinking about how much work it would entail to remove the gang from Fremen's neighborhood.

"I told you before, that was rimming amazing. Phenomenal."

"What?"

"Your work getting me free. Proving me innocent, finding that girl."

"Harriden."

"How is she?" Fremen asked.

"Why, you want to pin her again? Sorry," Lemma said quickly. The comment had jumped out of her mouth before she could stop it. "I haven't heard from her."

"Hope she's doing well. She was brave, coming forward about Chinny. Still can't believe it was him."

Lemma was about to mention what she had learned in Balkon headquarters, but thought better of it.

"What's your plan?"

"What plan?"

"The takeover. The coup. Flushing Cobra out of Wilco. We talk about it, secretly, so Cobra doesn't find out. We have a betting pool. My money's on poison."

Lemma stared at him in alarm. "Don't do that. Don't talk about it. Don't have a betting pool."

Fremen smiled and pulled a black and gold book from the back pocket of his uniform trousers. "Forgetting your own rules? Rule 58 says gambling is permitted between anyone sixteen years of age and older."

"That's— yes, it's allowed, but you can't talk about it. If you spill that we're attacking Cobra—"

"So it's an attack?"

"I didn't say that."

"I bet poison, but that would be hard, now that I think of it. They make us taste everything before they eat it."

"I need to repair this." Lemma gestured at the hole in the wall. "And then we can worry about Cobra."

Someone knocked on the apartment door. Lemma cursed.

"I told Nadia to stay out until we were finished."

A harsh voice shouted, "City Police Force. Open up!"

The tiles slipped from Lemma's hand and clattered on the floor.

"We know you're in there. Open this door!"

They knocked again. Then they kicked the door. There was a sound of splintering wood.

"Fremen, squat here and stay quiet," Lemma told him.

There was a crash as they kicked the door again.

"I'm here! I'm coming!" Lemma shouted, almost tripping over Fremen's feet. She closed the bathroom door, and went to face the badges.

CHAPTER 58

PROBABLE CAUSE

The door was so damaged Lemma had to drag it open. Panting, her heart pounding, she stared at three uniformed men.

"Lemma Quartz," the first said. He had thick lips, fat cheeks, and tiny green eyes which resembled olives in a loaf of deli ham. He looked familiar, but Lemma couldn't remember where she had seen him.

"Yes."

"We come in?" Without waiting for her to answer the badge pushed into the room. The other two men entered with him. "We have some questions."

Lemma forced herself not to look at the bathroom door. Thoughts buzzed through her skull. Milligram's mother had sent them, sensing she was hiding her son; either that or Curio had sent the badges after her, or it was something about Wilco.

"You have to bounce," she said, hating the timid sound of her voice. "You need to come back with a warrant."

"That liced?" the badge asked, pointing at the blink on the counter.

One of the officers, short, with skin the same medium brown as Lemma's, started opening drawers in the kitchen. He asked, "You know a man named Perron Mills, sushi?"

Lemma's skin rippled. "That's the man who attacked Rae— Governor Kawling."

The third badge, whose upturned nose desperately needed to be blown, leaned toward her. "You talked to him recently?"

"Uh, last Monday. May 21," Lemma said, after a moment of calculation.

The piggish one knocked the cushions off the sofa.

"He's not here. If you're scouting for him, he's in prison," Lemma said.

"*Was* in prison." He felt underneath the bed.

"What do you mean, was? He's gone? Escaped?" Lemma imagined Mills' metal foot smashing into Kawling's face.

"Not escaped. Dead." The piggish man approached Lemma, close enough for her to read the name "Garrity" on the badge on his chest.

"Dead? How?"

"What did you and Mills talk about?" Garrity asked.

Lemma stalled, wondering how much of it to reveal. Then she heard a dull scraping noise from behind the bathroom door.

"You should come back," Lemma said loudly. "I'll tell you everything, but I'm choked now."

"Choked with what?" Garrity leaned in close to Lemma. She could see flakes of dandruff on his shoulders.

"Please don't!" Lemma said, as the short badge pulled open her fridge. The man ignored her. "What happened to Mills?" Lemma kept her voice loud, praying it would drown out Fremen's continuous scraping.

"He was found seven days ago, face down in the toilet in his cell. Drowned," Garrity said.

Lemma stifled a gag. "Cuck. How?"

"We don't know. He was in there by himself."

Lemma felt sick. "I didn't have anything to do with it. I was here."

"You know what they found in his cell?" Garrity pulled out a tablet. On it was an image of a gray wall, with words scratched into it.

PH R0 NE SIS
HY DR A TE CH I LL
BE AV EN GED

"What do you think that says, sushi?" he asked.

"Phronesis. Hydrate, chill, be avenged."

"You know what that means?"

"Phronesis is Syan's company. Phronesis Tech. '*Hydrate*' and '*chill* ... I don't know."

"Mills ever say anything about Syan's company? Or venging anyone?"

"No."

The badge smirked. "You know a woman named Harriden Vik?"

The scraping sound stopped.

"What about her?"

"She's dead."

"Oh." Lemma was painfully aware of the silence coming from the bathroom. "How?"

"When did you last see her?" Garrity nudged her shoe with the toe of his boot.

Lemma thought. "Friday. May 25. What happened?"

As the badge spoke, Lemma remembered where she had seen him before. He was the same badge who had watched Harriden Vik being attacked that first night, who had stolen her contra bills instead of helping her. Lemma's teeth clenched.

"Weirdest thing, wouldn't you say?" Garrity turned to the other men, and Lemma took the opportunity to glance down at his hip, where a gun dangled from a holster. "They found her this morning in Food Rationing Center 9347."

"What happened?"

"She was inside the meat locker. Crawled in there in the middle of the night. Froze to death."

Lemma stared into Garrity's meaty face. His gun was only inches from her hand.

The scraping continued, as Fremen's moment of silence for his dead conk came to an end.

"You think their deaths might be connected to Mills' message?" Garrity asked.

"I don't know," Lemma said. Her back felt cold and sticky.

"Spect about it. '*Hydrate*'… Mills drowned. Drowning is like hydrating. '*Chill*' Harriden was found frozen. Maybe Mills knew how they'd die?"

"I don't know," Lemma said again.

"You have rats?" the badge with the snotty nose asked, jerking his head towards the bathroom door. "Scratch scratch scratch. They have poison for that. Makes the rats go stringy and run outside; then they die. Don't even leave a stink."

"Why was Harriden in the freezer? Who put her there? And how did you know I knew her?" Lemma asked.

"You've been seen together. She lived around here," Garrity replied. Lemma doubted he even remembered stealing from her.

"Well… that's all our questions," Garrity said. "There's the issue of the blink. There's a thick fine for unliced blinks." He looked at the other badges. "But maybe we could forget about it."

"Here," Lemma said, not wanting to learn how the badge preferred to be bribed. She went to the loose corner of the carpet, and pulled out a stack of bills, making sure to keep the Wilco-Abadon contract out of sight. "This gel?"

Garrity took the money, and the three badges walked toward the shattered door. "Have a bright day, sushi," Garrity said. "Better get this door fixed; somebody could break in."

His companions guffawed.

Then something crashed in the bathroom.

CHAPTER 59

SHARDS

"Who's there? Show yourself!" Garrity shouted. He drew his gun as the other two badges approached the bathroom door. "Come out!"

"I'm coming!" Fremen came out, his hands trembling above his head. The kitchen knife, dusty from fragments of grout, slipped from his hand and landed just outside the bathroom door. "Please don't shoot!"

"Orea!" Garrity shouted.

"Garrity."

"What you doing here? You friends with sushi?"

"Yes."

"What are doing— cuck! Colburn, Shawl, in there!" Garrity pointed at the dismantled shower wall.

Fremen stared at the floor, as Lemma's stomach boiled. The two badges pulled Fremen away from the bathroom, and stepped toward the shower.

"Contras…" Shawl said, scratching his wet nose. "How much?" He poked Fremen's stomach roughly. "How much?"

Fremen mumbled an answer, and looked pleadingly at Garrity. "Garrity, please!"

"Now you need my help?" Garrity asked. "I spected the death agencies were the only ones who could shield you?"

"Please!"

"Shawl, dig it out. Colburn, tear out the rest of the wall."

Shawl attacked the shower wall with gusto, using a metal baton to smash apart tiles, sending flecks of grout raining into the sink and toilet, some thrown so far they escaped the bathroom and landed in the living room.

Colburn went through the kitchen, emptying drawers, pulling out jars from the fridge and smashing them.

"Anywhere else?" Garrity turned to Lemma. "Hey, squint. Any more contras in here?"

Lemma shook her head.

"Shawl?"

"The wall's stuffed like a colon." Shawl beat the shower wall until every tile had come out.

The refrigerator scraped across the floor. Colburn had pulled it away from the wall, and dragged it toward the bathroom, examining the floor where it had stood.

It was then that Lemma dove for Garrity's gun, closing her fingers around his knuckles.

Garrity wrenched his hands away, and Lemma's body whipped forward. Garrity's elbow struck her head and she hit the floor, face-first. Garrity's heel stamped against the fleshy part of her back, between the ribcage and hip. The pain was tremendous, and she coughed so hard it felt like her stomach would tear. Whimpering, she pulled her body into a ball.

"You're going to give me any more edge?" Garrity asked. "Huh?"

Lemma shook her head, tears leaking into the carpet.

"Orea? You going to be a hero?"

"No," Fremen mumbled.

Garrity pulled Lemma's hands behind her, clicking metal cuffs around her wrists, and dragged her to her feet.

Fremen stared helplessly as Shawl, dusty from the grout, stuffed bills and gold cubes into his pockets. Garrity pulled Lemma toward the kitchen, which was littered with food and broken shelves.

"Shawl and Carter," Garrity began, holding Lemma's cuffed wrists. "Count what's there. Then—"

Lemma planted her foot on a broken cabinet and threw her back against him. He grabbed her around the waist in a desperate attempt to correct his balance. Lemma strained, pushing off the cabinet, and Garrity slipped, shards of glass crunching between his back and the kitchen floor.

CHAPTER 60

BLOCKADE

Garrity coughed, his breath hot and sticky, into Lemma's neck. Her head rang from the impact against his cheekbones.

Lemma braced herself as Colburn kicked her. Ribs throbbing, she planted her legs on the kitchen floor, but with her hands cuffed between her back and Garrity's stomach, she could do little more than flop like a fish.

"Help, I can't get up." She struggled on top of Garrity, her hands blindly feeling his belt until her fingers brushed against a key fob.

"Get up!" Colburn ordered, kicking Lemma harder. She rolled off Garrity onto the floor, crying out as pieces of broken glass sliced into her thigh.

Colburn raised a radio to his mouth to call for support, unaware that she had taken the key fob from Garrity's belt.

"Scrape the rest!" Colburn shouted at Shawl, who went back into the bathroom. Garrity's mouth was fizzing out red foam like a volcano.

"Lemma, let me help you up," Orea bent down, grabbed her by the armpits, and hauled her to her feet.

"Officer Garrity is bleeding and dropped," Colburn shouted into his radio. "State Housing Facility 9316, Room 87. Juggling a load of contras, at least five kilograms gold."

Lemma held out her cuffed hands behind her, gripping Garrity's key fob.

"Unlock them," she whispered to Fremen.

Fremen was trembling, his fingertips slippery. It took several tries, but then Lemma's hands were free.

"The refrigerator— block the bathroom door," she whispered, massaging her wrists.

She staggered to the pile of sofa cushions and lay down. Then she screamed.

She screamed louder than she had ever screamed in her life. Her limbs flailed, she buckled her back, and thrust her hips into the air.

"Plug it!" Colburn yelled, stumbling toward her, staring at her writhing body, not watching as Fremen grabbed the refrigerator, and heaved.

There was a crash, as it fell and blocked the bathroom door.

Colburn spun around, facing Fremen and pulling out his gun, not seeing Lemma roll toward him until her arms were wrapped around his knees. He whipped forward, the gun firing, his chest slamming into the carpet. From inside the bathroom, Shawl was shouting and pounding on the door as Lemma jumped up and down on Colburn's back, stomping her feet on his spine.

Another gun fired, and Lemma dove to the ground. Shawl had shot through the bathroom door, and was now thrashing his metal baton against it until it splintered, revealing his face and one of his arms. He forced his way through the shattered door, crawling over the fallen refrigerator, and pointing the gun at Lemma.

Fremen's hand moved before Shawl could retreat. Shawl's gun fired once more into the air, then slipped from his hand, as his head slumped onto the refrigerator. In his neck was the blade of Fremen's kitchen knife.

CHAPTER 61

HALFWAY

Garrity was still coughing, but Colburn lay on the carpet, broken and silent. Shawl was motionless, blood from the stab wound in his neck spilling onto the refrigerator.

"Fremen, get your contras," Lemma said. Her leg throbbed where the glass had cut into it.

Fremen staggered, vomiting onto his knees.

"Fremen, listen to me," Lemma said, more loudly. "Get your contras."

People were collecting in the hall, staring into the chaos that was her apartment.

"We need to find the kids, and we have to bounce. Fremen!" Lemma shouted. "Get your money. Go in there and get it."

Fremen said nothing, pointing to Shawl's shattered head.

"We're not leaving without it. Flash it!" Lemma ordered.

"Oh cuck—" Someone shouted from the hall, as Lemma ran toward them.

"Milligram? Nadia?" she shouted over their heads. There was no sign of the children. "All of you, wipe off," she told the onlookers.

"Lemma, I can't," Fremen was shaking. "I can't do it."

Lemma cursed at him. "Grab the fridge with me." They dragged it away from the bathroom door. With a grunt of effort, Lemma pushed Shawl's head through the hole in the door.

"More badges are coming, we have to flash it." Lemma stepped over Shawl's body and into the bathroom, grabbing as many bills as she could and stuffing them into her pockets. Then she picked up Shawl's gun.

"Move!" she shouted, pointing the weapon at her neighbors. They scattered like rats.

"Scrape the other two guns," Lemma ordered. Finding Donovez's phone on the floor, she made a call.

"Donovez?" she asked. "I'll debrief you later, but you need to send cars to my apartment. Housing Facility 9316. Badges are coming to ghost us, you need to send cars. Hurry!"

"It's done. They'll be there in a mite. Tell me what happened," Donovez said.

"Badges came to question me, found Fremen's contras. Tried to ghost us, we ghosted them first."

"Cuck. How many?"

"Two dead, one injured."

"Why were they questioning you? Do they know about Wilco?"

"They told me Perron Mills and Harriden Vik were found dead."

"What?"

"They knew I'd talked with them. They said Mills had drowned in his cell, and Harriden froze to death in a meat freezer."

Donovez cursed. "But why them?"

"I don't know. But Donovez…"

"What?"

"I spoke to Curio, my boss at Balkon. I spect she helped Shwa Chinny ghost Wade Syan."

"You think so? Why?"

"She said she'd never been to his apartment, but she said the window was — it's too long to explain, but trust me, I know."

"You spect she ghosted Mills and Vik too?"

"I don't know." Then a horrible thought crossed her mind. "Donovez, Curio might have other targets."

"Who?"

"That list on Wade Syan's blink— Barreaux, Fezz, Chinny, Entierez— half of them are already dead. What if Curio wants to ghost Barreaux and Entierez also?"

"Why?"

"I don't know, but we have to warn them." Lemma could hear Nadia calling to her. "I'm— Donovez I'll call you back."

"Lemma!" Nadia's voice grew louder, and with a clatter of footsteps she entered the apartment.

"Lemma— oh!"

Nadia stared at Lemma, Fremen, and the three badges, two dead, one injured, and began to cry.

"I'm gel. Look at me, Nadia," Lemma took the girl in her arms. "Orea, grab the gun! Nadia, where is Milligram? He with you? He in the hall?"

"Lemma! Lemma!"

"Nadia, where's Milligram?"

"I know you said not to tell, but…"

Fremen was at Lemma's side, each hand gripping a gun, his pockets bulging with contra bills and cubes of metal.

"But we started arguing. I'm real sorry," Nadia continued. "I told him about you and his mom and his leg. I'm sorry, I didn't mean to."

"Nadia! Where is Milligram? Where is he?" Lemma gripped Nadia's shoulders.

"He's gone."

CHAPTER 62

THE FREEZER

"She needs to go to Minor Aid!" Getonia Orea shouted.

Lemma, Nadia, and Fremen were in Getonia's apartment. Getonia was less than pleased to see Fremen.

"I'm choked," Lemma hissed, before turning to her phone. "Donovez, we didn't scope Milligram, we chased buses for an hour, but no sign of him."

"That's cucky, and I'm sorry, but you have to report in. I need you scouting Wilco."

"No, I can't leave Nadia alone."

"Then let me bring her to Minor Aid," Getonia interrupted. Lemma turned to her with a scowl and told her to wipe off.

"Donovez, I swear on my flaps I will post all day for you tomorrow, but I have to keep Nadia safe, and we need to shield Barreaux and Entierez."

Donovez gave a sarcastic laugh. "Are they members? Did I forget to give them medallions?"

"Whoever ghosted Syan is going to try to ghost them," Lemma said. "And if you're not going to help them, I will. You scout the CityBus for Milligram. I'll be at Wilco tomorrow."

Lemma threw the phone down. "Thank you for letting us squat here," she told Getonia, handing her the fistfuls of Fremen's bills she had salvaged from her apartment. Getonia looked at them with disgust, then pocketed them. Fremen seemed like he wanted to object, but he kept silent.

"She needs to go to Minor Aid." Getonia repeated, pointing at Nadia.

"No." Nadia said quietly.

"Why not?" Getonia pleaded. "They can help you; you won't know how they can help until you've been there."

"I've been there. They're run by Reezys. They tried to make me blind."

"You can't call them that!" Getonia gasped, looked to Lemma for support.

"Because that was the shocking part of what she said? Calling them Reezys, not them trying to amp her eyes?" Lemma snorted disgustedly.

"The Tiresian Church doesn't perform surgery on children. They wouldn't—" Getonia began, but Fremen cut her off.

"How did the boy outrun you?" he asked Nadia. "You have twice as many legs as he does."

"Fremen! Wipe off!" Lemma spat, then turned to Getonia. "Nadia's not going anywhere, she's staying with me. Now, I need bandages, chemies, tweezers, scissors, and a towel. Also, I need a legit phone with the contact information for Masidon Barreaux and Vinida Entierez. And something to eat, giraffe burger if you have it. Nadia, are you hungry?"

"No."

"Giraffe burger for her, too."

Getonia left the room before Fremen could ask for anything, pointedly avoiding looking at him. When she returned she served food and water only to Lemma and Nadia.

"Steady, I'm gel, don't string about me. I'll starve, it's gel," Fremen muttered under his breath.

"She seems to not like you. Some drama that I missed?" Lemma slid her plate to him as she took Getonia's phone.

"Howsie, Mr. Barreaux. It's—"

"Lemma Quartz," Barreaux's soothing voice said. "A pleasant surprise, especially since the call is from Ms. Orea's phone. To what do I owe the occasion?"

"You know it's me?"

"I never forget a voice."

"Mr. Barreaux, I think you might be in danger."

"Danger?" Barreaux replied, not sounding the slightest bit alarmed. "I'm always in danger. You saw the abusive graffiti they painted on our church. Those same people would throw me out of my chair and gleefully trample me if they had the chance. I live without sight in a world that demands it. The wrong step, a delayed reaction, could kill me instantly."

"Well, you're in more danger than usual."

"Then I'll indulge you. What is this danger of which you speak?"

Lemma took a deep breath. "Mr. Barreaux, the day that I first met you…"

"Ah yes, the day you first tried corneal shields. Have you kept them?"

"I use them to pretend to be Tiresian when I need special treatment."

"Oh, Lemma, that is rather vulgar, and a tad offensive."

Lemma ignored that. "You remembered the people I asked you about? Natisra Fezz, Vinida Entierez?"

"I do."

"They were on a list I found at Wade Syan's apartment."

"Wade Syan? Yes, you also asked me about him. Have you seen the recent news? It appears his death was no accident after all."

"Yes."

"I must say, I never would have guessed that the killer worked for the state government. Quite scandalous."

Lemma thought of Curio's taunting face. "But there were four names on the list: Natisra Fezz, Shwa Chinny, who killed Syan, Vinida Entierez, and you, Mr. Barreaux, you were also on his list."

"I was on the list?" For the first time he sounded rattled.

"And Fezz and Chinny are dead. I spect you and Vinida might be targeted next."

"You are certain?"

"More people have died, Mr. Barreaux. Perron Mills? The man who drowned Fezz at the ceremony? He was found dead in his prison cell last week. And Harriden Vik, who helped the state find Shwa Chinny's body, she was found dead today."

"They were murdered? By whom?"

"I spect Chinny had an accomplice. The head of Balkon Death Insurance Agency helped him kill Syan, and is targeting everyone else who was involved, including yourself."

"Even assuming that were true, I am safest here, in my home."

"They found a way to make Syan drown in his own bathtub! Perron was in prison, being watched by guards. That didn't help him! And they killed Harriden, too!"

"This Harriden person, how did they die?"

"She was found in a freezer at Food Rationing Center 9347."

"Found in a freezer?" Barreaux sounded horrified. "Did anyone see how she got in there? Is there a surveillance tape?"

"Uh, wait a mite. Getonia!"

Getonia looked at her from across the living room. "What now?"

"You heard about Harriden Vik?"

"Harriden Vik?" Getonia shot a dark look at Fremen. "She can't squat here, if that's what you're asking."

"She was found dead."

Getonia smirked.

"Do you have access to city surveillance footage?"

Getonia obliged, waving her hand as a portion of the wall became a large screen. She sorted through thousands of live feeds, before finding Food Rationing Center 9347.

"Did you find it?" Barreaux's voice came through the phone.

"We have the location, trying to see when— Getonia, there!"

Getonia had been rewinding the footage. She paused it, showing a cluster of badges standing outside the meat locker earlier that day.

"Tell me what you see," Barreaux said.

"We're rewinding… Getonia, stop. Play it. So, Harriden was in the store in the middle of the night. She's opening the freezer door. She's— she's climbing in. She closed the door."

"Was there anyone else there? Someone who pushed her?" Barreaux asked. "Or someone threatening her? Forcing her in?"

"No."

The footage continued. Store workers walked unconcernedly past the freezer without having noticed Harriden had gone inside.

"Well, there you have it. I don't mean to be crass, but it takes a special breed of idiot to attempt a nap in a freezer. Intoxicated, perhaps? I hope you will understand when I say that I am not in danger of making such a fool of myself. I appreciate your concern for my safety, Lemma, but again, I am safe in my own home."

"Gel. If anything does happen…"

"You'll be the first I ask for help."

Lemma ended the call. "Wipe the smirk off your face or I'll wipe it for you," she said to Getonia, who had observed the footage of Harriden's death with grim satisfaction. Getonia sniffed and left the room.

Then Lemma made another call. "Ms. Entierez? It's me, Lemma Quartz, from Fremen Orea's trial."

"Quartz! You helped get him acquitted. And you solved Syan's murder."

"Not yet. Chinny was working with the head of Balkon Death Insurance Agency. They ghosted Perron Mills in his cell. Harriden Vik's also dead."

"Harriden? She testified about Chinny."

"Yes. And I didn't mention it before, but I found a list at Syan's apartment the night he died. You, Natisra Fezz and Chinny were on the list. Since both of them are dead, I spect you're also a target. We have a place for you to squat to keep you safe. And this would be a bright time to buy some death insurance."

Vinida Entierez didn't hesitate. "I'll come. Tell me the address."

CHAPTER 63

OVIAN'S LAW

The sun set during the hour it took for Vinida Entierez to arrive at Getonia's apartment, where she handed Lemma a stack of plastic contra bills, and demanded to hear the full story.

Recounting the details was exhausting, but it provided Lemma with a distraction from the burning pain as Nadia helped remove shards of glass from her thigh. Sweating and cursing, Lemma pushed through with her account, beginning with the night she met Harriden to earlier that day, when she had learned about Perron's and Harriden's deaths.

"'Phronesis, hydrate, chill, be avenged,'" Vinida mused. "I have no rimming idea what that means, but you were bright with Syan's window. Your boss really showed her flaps on that one. What's next?"

"Still weighing options." Lemma had omitted the plan to oust Cobra from Wilco, as well as her attempt to assassinate Kawling.

"What about Barreaux?" Vinida asked.

Lemma winced, gritting her teeth as Nadia extracted one of the last shards from her thigh. "Barreaux assured me he was safe."

"Oh, I'd believe it."

"What do you mean by that?"

"I spect he's involved somehow."

"Yes, because you hate the Tiresian Church."

"They're not peaceful. You have no idea how many death threats I receive every day."

"True. But your articles…"

"Are you saying they merit death threats?"

"People think your articles cause trouble." Lemma gasped, forcing herself to breathe through the razor-sharp pain. "Twanks read them, and then they go out and harass church members."

"Because I point out obvious things, like how amping a kid's foot is child abuse," Vinida said indignantly. "Two decades ago that would have been something from a horror movie. Now amping children is one of the most serious issues of our time, but no one cares."

"I care," Lemma said quietly.

A car drove past the apartment, and they all started.

"Oh, now Lemma wants to protect children," Getonia sneered. "A death agent who hires underage unliced conks to help ghost targets for profit."

"Whose side are you on?" Vinida narrowed her eyes at Getonia. "The Reezys' side?"

"I'm a journalist; I report facts and remain neutral."

Vinida laughed derisively. "That's what the Reezys want: neutrality. That's how they win. They've built an empire off of people who are too polite to fight."

"They just want to be happy," Getonia said. "I can show you scientific studies that say people who lose a limb, even accidentally, are three times happier than twanks who win the lottery."

"Think of it this way," Vinida said. "If one person says they talk to an invisible being, they're labeled insane. But if a hundred do it? Suddenly it's a religion, and any criticism is verbal assault. One person pops out their own eyes, they're locked up in a hospital. If a hundred do it, they're praised for discovering enlightenment."

"I agree that amping kids is evil," Lemma interrupted. "Why does that mean Masidon is working with Curio? He was on the same list as you, Fezz, and Chinny!"

"Masidon has his own secrets to hide," Vinida said dramatically.

"Besides amping kids?"

"You've heard of Ovian's Law?"

Getonia barked a harsh laugh. "This again."

"Ovian Hodeft was bullied and eventually killed for being Tiresian. Fezz told me about him," Lemma said, recalling the nauseatingly sweet smell of the dead journalist's mint and cinnamon chewing gum.

"Fezz's article was complete ratjack," Vinida said.

"Says the woman whose book couldn't even make it past a single review at the Public Info Department," Getonia sneered. "She thinks Ovian spontaneously burst into flames on his own, right?" Getonia shook her head with contempt.

Lemma leaned in, forgetting for a moment the burning throb in her leg. "What?"

"Ovian was set on fire and killed, that's true. But the church twisted the story," Vinida said.

"Of course," Getonia murmured.

"Turned a high school fight into a case of religious persecution," Vinida said. "I wrote it all out in a book."

"An unpublished manuscript," Getonia scoffed.

"Which never made it past the review board, because it would be religious harassment to suggest that kid-ampers were anything other than poor, persecuted religious folk," Vinida retorted.

"Her manuscript was one of the sloppiest pieces of journalism I've ever had the displeasure to wipe my flaps with," Getonia said.

"Did you know that the official, state-approved story completely left out the testimony of the boys accused of bullying Ovian?" Vinida asked.

"Oh, as if we all need to hear from the twanks who set him on fire," Getonia shot back.

"Or that Ovian was never actually Tiresian?"

CHAPTER 64

SEEING, NEVER PERCEIVING

"What?" Lemma exclaimed, as Getonia scoffed.

Vinida raised her eyebrows and smirked knowingly. "The official story, as reported in Natisra's book, left out essential facts. The boys accused of bullying him were close friends of his. According to them, it was never about his religion."

"But he wore those glasses with dark lenses, to meditate. Natisra told me so," Lemma said.

Vinida rose triumphantly, and pulled a sheaf of pages from her purse.

"You keep a copy of your manuscript with you?" Getonia sneered. "How limp."

Vinida turned to a dog-eared page. There was a photo of Ovian Hodeft and several other boys, all wearing sunglasses, in front of a Tiresian Church.

"They wore them to mock the Tiresians. Each of the surviving bullies agreed. They also admitted to pranking actual Tiresians, things like tripping the blind ones, and calling out insults to the deaf ones."

Getonia rolled her eyes. "Of course the bullies said that."

"I verified it in school records. They'd been disciplined for it! Ovian too!" Vinida spat.

"They still set Ovian on fire," Lemma said, wiping sweat from her forehead as Nadia stitched up the last cut. The girl's time observing Schwartz at work had not gone to waste. "Bright, Nadia." Lemma patted her on the head. "Dr. Schwartz trained you well."

"True, but again, it had nothing to do with religion. Ovian and the other boy, the comatose one in the glass case—"

"Teskir Mong," Lemma said.

"Yes, Teskir. He and Ovian were close friends. Troublemakers, too. They got access to gasoline, and planned to start a fire in a Tiresian Church. Ovian accidentally spilled some on himself. His friends were idiots. One of them pulled out a lighter and lit it, as a joke. They swore to me they never intended to hurt him. But you know how gasoline fumes love a flame. Before they could stop it, Ovian was on fire. He died and Teskir went into a coma. Journalists pounced on the story. Natisra Fezz wrote her famous article, framing the narrative ever so perfectly. Suddenly, a fringe group of mentally disturbed self-harming twanks were now a persecuted band of martyrs. I was the only one who dared to question the official story, and the Truth Board made sure to shut me up. But you can read it," Vinida slid the manuscript to Lemma. "Unless Getonia's going to report us for possession of unliced printed materials?"

Lemma thumbed through the manuscript, which was titled *Seeing, Never Perceiving*, feeling icy fingers trail down her spine at photos of Ovian, Teskir Mong, and Ovian's mother, Quinn, who was smiling without any sunglasses.

'*Ovian and Teskir met when cast in Shakespeare's **A Comedy of Errors**, playing Dromio of Syracuse and Dromio of Ephesus, respectively*', one caption read. Another photo showed Ovian pointing a rifle at a target.

"Could I have some water? Talking about Tiresians makes me thirsty," Vinida asked Getonia.

"Some for me and Nadia too, please," Lemma added.

"Me too," Fremen murmured.

Getonia returned with a plate holding three glasses of water, pointedly ignoring Fremen.

"Thanks," Fremen grumbled. Lemma handed him hers.

Vinida downed hers in a second. "Read through that. Educate yourself." She proffered the manuscript to Lemma.

"Nadia, you want to wash up? Is it gel if I talk with you?" Getonia pointed to Nadia's bloody hands and tweezers.

"More water?" Vinida asked, waving her empty glass at Getonia. "And can we dim the heat in here?"

Getonia groaned. "Thermostat's on the wall. Water's in the kitchen, or the bathroom, get it yourself."

Vinida went to the wall and lowered the thermostat. Then she went into the bathroom.

"But even if you're right about Ovian, it doesn't explain any connection between Barreaux and the others," Lemma mused, loud enough so Vinida could hear. "You think he worked with Curio or Shwa Chinny?"

"Nadia, what's wrong?" Getonia interrupted.

Nadia's face had gone pale.

"You gel, Nadia?" Lemma asked. "Getonia, what did you do to her?"

"I didn't do anything."

"Who did you say?" Nadia asked Lemma.

"Curio? My boss at Balkon."

"The other one."

"Shwa Chinny."

Nadia put her hand over her mouth and bolted for the bathroom. She didn't make it across the room before vomiting onto the floor.

Lemma rushed to her side. "Nadia, did you know Shwa Chinny?" she asked. "Did he ever pay you for something?"

Nadia nodded, her expression miserable. "You went to his office, almost two weeks ago. I scoped you."

"You scoped me there?" Lemma asked.

"You were on the train. I wanted to say howsie, but I spected you wouldn't want to be recognized. I waited when you went in. Then you left. Didn't have time to catch your eye. He came out… I needed money. I pitched to him."

"And?"

Nadia's voice wavered. "So he paid me… told me to come back the next night. I started visiting him every other night. Then one day… you know the day I came to your apartment?"

Lemma nodded.

"I'd been with him. He was acting different. Had all the fans on, kept complaining it was too hot. Took out a bottle of lick and drank it all. Then he fell down and didn't move. His skin was blue. I ran… just ran. Ran all the way to your place."

Lemma and Getonia were silent. In the quiet, the sound of water pouring from the bathroom faucet was louder than ever.

"You gel in there?" Lemma called out to Vinida.

"Gonna wash off," she called back.

"And no one else was there with you and Chinny? The day he died?" Lemma asked Nadia.

"Just us. The door was locked when I left, don't spect anyone else could get in."

"Come here," Lemma said, pulling Nadia into a hug. "Shwa's death wasn't your fault. And you did the right thing, coming to my apartment that day."

"Lemma?" Nadia sniffed. "I'm sorry about Milligram. You told me not to say anything about what you told me. I shouldn't have. I'm sorry."

"Everything will be gel, Nadia. I promise. We'll find Milligram, and find out who's behind all this, and thanks for helping me with my leg. You did real bright."

With one hand still around Nadia, Lemma turned again to *Seeing, Never Perceiving* and flipped through it.

The pages stopped, almost of their own will, on a series of images of Ovian, Teskir Mong, and their parents.

She came to a chilling photo of Teskir Mong, tubes sticking out of his face, sometime after he had gone into a coma but before he was placed on display in the glass case. While his face and the upper half of his body were charred by burns, his legs and feet were pale and unscathed.

Lemma peered closer at the image.

Something was off. Lemma looked once more through the pictures of Ovian, Quinn, Teskir, and Ovian's circle of friends. There was the photo of Ovian with the rifle, and with the drama club. Frowning in concentration, Lemma tried to find the source of her restless suspicion.

Then she saw it.

CHAPTER 65

ROSY HALO

The manuscript dangled in Lemma's hand as she jumped up, knocking Nadia to the floor, and ran to the bathroom door, shouting Vinida's name.

She knocked. "I figured it out! Vinida?"

No answer.

Lemma looked back at Getonia and Nadia, whose faces bore identical expressions of unease.

"Vinida!" She knocked again. The only sound from the bathroom was water pouring from the bathtub faucet.

Lemma dropped the manuscript. "Vinida! Answer me, or I'm forcing the door in!"

No one answered. Nadia was whimpering and Getonia was trying to console her.

Lemma backed up and charged the door, planting her foot several inches away from the knob. The door splinted, tearing from the lock, and dangled pitifully from its hinges.

"Vinida! Oh, dear God, no!"

Lemma rushed to the bathtub as images poured into her mind. She had been here before, she knew this exact script, and the only action left before the final curtain was to call in vain to a body that had long lost the ability to hear.

"Vinida!"

Lemma bent over her, using her left arm to lift the woman's head out of the ice-cold tub, and slapping her cheeks.

"Getonia! Come here!"

Getonia entered and screamed at the sight of Vinida's lifeless body floating in her bathtub.

"Help me pull her out!" Lemma shouted.

The two heaved, but Vinida's wet clothes clung to her, dragging her down. Vinida's body slipped, landing on the bathroom floor with a dull splat. Water flowed over the edge of the tub, and a stream of blood trickled from the spot of Vinida's head where it had struck the tile.

Lemma collapsed beside her, unable to stop shaking.

"I'll give her this." Getonia pulled open a cabinet above the sink and took out a liquid-filled syringe. She quickly jammed it into Vinida's heart. Nothing happened.

"We need to call the police." Getonia's voice shook as she reached for her phone.

"Don't. Do not get the badges. We're calling Donovez." Lemma pulled out Donovez's phone, relieved the water hadn't damaged it.

"She's dead!" Getonia protested. "We have to call them."

"Badges are incompetent twanks. Donovez is head of Abadon, he needs to know." Lemma made the call, and waited for an answer.

Getonia could only stare at Vinida, whose hair swayed in the puddle of rosy water, crowning her like a Renaissance halo.

"Well, I'm calling the badges."

"No!" Lemma snarled. Before she even had time to think about it, her hand snapped out, grabbing one of the syringes from the cabinet and brandishing it at Getonia. "Stay away from her! Stay away from Nadia!"

"This is my apartment."

"It'll be your grave if you don't wipe off."

Getonia stumbled backwards, out of the bathroom.

"Get away from Nadia!"

Getonia went and stood on the opposite side of the room from the girl.

Lemma spoke into the phone. "Donovez. It's Lemma. Vinida's dead."

Donovez's response tore through Lemma's eardrum, even as she pulled the phone away from her head.

"I told you, people are still in danger. Vinida drowned in a bathtub, just like Wade Syan."

"Who else is there?"

"Getonia, Fremen, and Nadia."

"We'll send a team. Don't touch anything. All of you need to stay there for questioning. Do not contact the police."

"I can't stay," Lemma said.

"Did you not hear me, Lemma? You need to stay put."

"I need to stop them."

"Who, Curio?"

"No. Masidon Barreaux."

CHAPTER 66

THE GUTTER

"Who— why Masidon? He's on the list; he's one of the potential targets!"

"Trust me, Donovez."

"I don't want to trust you. I want you to squat at Getonia's until the team gets there."

"I'll call you back. Getonia! Nadia! Fremen!"

They stared at her.

"I'm going to bounce, and I can't tell you where. Abadon is sending death agents here to investigate."

"Why them?" Getonia demanded.

"Because while she was coming here, Vinida bought a death insurance policy from me, and now we have to venge her." Lemma said, waving the plastic bills Vinida had handed her only an hour before. "So, you are going to tell them exactly what happened, including the fact that she asked for multiple glasses of water, and complained that it was too warm in here, and turned down the thermostat, understand?"

"What does that have to do with anything?" Fremen asked.

"Because it's rimming relevant, that's why!" Lemma screamed. "And Nadia, you have to tell them everything about when Shwa Chinny died, because I think they died the same way."

"Lemma, please don't leave me here," the girl begged.

"Listen to me, Nadia! Do exactly as I tell you. I love you. I'll be back."

Lemma ran into the street, the wet manuscript stuffed into her jacket. Officer Garrity's handcuffs, key fob, and gun were still in her pocket. She ran past several CityBus stops, knowing better than to give them her thumbprint.

Signs on buildings leered at her, angry red letters taking the place of the usual ads and public notices. The messages all spelled out the same warning: Annalemma Quartz, wanted for the deaths of Officers Colburn and Shawl, as well as Citizens Shwa Chinny, Wade Syan, and Harriden Vik.

Lemma's profile picture glowed by each message. Lemma pulled the hood of her jacket over her face.

Her phone buzzed.

"Lemma, come in at once."

"Sorry, Donovez."

"We'll track your phone's location. I gave it to you, remember?"

"This phone doesn't do that." *Or does it?* She wasn't sure. She hoped not.

"The city just issued an alert."

"I scoped."

"Lemma, did you ghost them?"

"I ghosted two of the badges, with Fremen's help, I told you that."

"What about Shwa Chinny and Harriden Vik? You had met with both of them, and you were with Vinida when she died."

"Ask Getonia and Nadia. I wasn't anywhere near her."

"Lemma, I want to believe you."

"Wipe off."

"But you have to come into custody. Or I'll put out an alert of my own."

Lemma's flesh chilled at the thought. She sat down by a gutter, weighing how much to tell Donovez without giving away her location or her plan.

"You're one of my best agents, I don't want to have to ghost you," Donovez pleaded.

Near Lemma, a rat approached the gutter and began to lap water.

"Hear me out, Donovez. They all died the same way." Lemma reasoned. "Syan and Vinida both drowned in bathtubs. Perron Mills drowned in his toilet."

"Maybe another inmate did it."

"He had a cell to himself, I visited him. Fezz drowned in the fountain at the hospital."

"Because Mills pushed her!"

"I'm starting to doubt that. The fountain was on the other side of the room that night. And Mills was intent on going after the governor."

"Shwa Chinny died from alcohol poisoning."

"Nadia said he was acting weird. She said he complained about it being too hot and drank an entire bottle of lick. Vinida drank a jackload of water and cranked down the temperature."

"So?"

"Both of them felt thirsty, and hot. And Harriden went into a freezer. Maybe she also felt hot."

"What, they had a fever?" Donovez asked.

"It would explain why they all were thirsty. Vinida's bathwater was cold. So was Wade Syan's," Lemma said, suddenly remembering. "The night he died I put my hand in the water when his blink fell in. It was cold. Not even room temperature, freezing cold."

"I get fevers sometimes; they don't make me stick my head in the toilet or crawl into a rimming freezer. And what's Masidon have to do with this?"

"If I tell you, I'll give away where I'm going, and you'll find me and ghost me."

"That is correct."

"But if I can find out how Masidon made them drown…" Lemma murmured. She glanced at the rat. It was still at the gutter, still guzzling as much of the filthy water as it could. Her fingers traced the outline of Garrity's gun in her pocket as she recalled what he had said in her apartment.

Phronesis. Hydrate. Chill. Be avenged.

Rats.

Lemma suddenly understood. "Donovez, you still there?"

"Yes."

"I figured it out."

"Claps."

"Today, one of the badges who came to my apartment mentioned a rat poison. He said it makes them go outside before they die, so they don't rot in your home."

"I've heard of it."

"Why do the rats go outside?" Lemma asked.

"I spect the poison makes them scout for water. Makes them…" Donovez's voice trailed off as he realized what Lemma was saying.

"Thirsty," Lemma finished.

The rat continued to lap water.

Chapter 67

Webs

Lemma walked for an hour, then two. The images of her face did not stop staring at her from the public billboards, and more names had been added. She was now a suspect in the deaths of Vinida Entierez and Perron Mills.

She had tried to tell Donovez why she suspected Masidon, but there was no way to put her theory into words without sounding insane. She doubted it herself, stopping below city lamps to reexamine Vinida's manuscript, now warped from where it had touched the water that had killed her. There was only one way to confirm her theory, to determine whether it was true or a wild fantasy accessible only to the insane.

But Lemma was insane. The rest of the world could have all the sanity they wanted, and good for them, if it helped them get to sleep at night. Lemma, however, had long sacrificed sanity for Truth, from the moment she insisted Syan's death was no accident, to her refusal to accept that Shwa Chinny had acted alone. The only question now was how to convince Donovez, the rest of Abadon, and the entire city, to be insane like her.

Her feet were burning holes through the soles of her shoes when she arrived at the Wade Syan Hospital. It was quiet, a far contrast from the packed party the night of the dedication.

There was a glass slide on the door, but Lemma's thumbprint would surely trigger an alarm. She sat on the curb outside, waiting for a hospital worker to enter or exit. Finally, a nurse approached, touching his thumb to the slide, and entering. The door closed before Lemma could follow him through.

Next, a security guard approached, but instead of scanning his thumb, he pressed his bundle of keys to it. The scanner beeped, and the door opened.

Lemma stood, her heart pulsing. She looked around, and seeing no one, walked to the door and pulled out Garrity's keys. Between the metal keys hung a small black fob.

Lemma touched it to the scanner, which blinked green.

"Welcome, Officer Garrity."

The door opened.

She retraced her steps from the night of the dedication, passing the hologram of Wade Syan, going down the steps and navigating the same halls where she and Natisra Fezz had walked.

She passed doctors quietly talking to one another, and nurses pushing medication carts, and orderlies wheeling patients on gurneys.

"Excuse me?" a nurse asked.

Lemma remembered what Perron had told her. She ignored the nurse, feeling with her toes for the orange ridges along the hall, and continued walking.

"Are you vision non-dependent?" the nurse asked.

Lemma kept walking and didn't answer.

The nurse waved her hand in front of Lemma's face. Lemma didn't react.

The nurse reached for a radio. "We have a vision and hearing non-dependent woman with no gown or ID on floor zero. Scan the rooms for an empty bed."

Lemma continued to walk along the ridged path. She was almost at the glass box containing the comatose Teskir Mong.

The nurse tapped Lemma on the shoulder, and she tensed. The nurse gently reached for her hand, and tapped against Lemma's palm.

"Hmm?" the nurse said, tapping the same pattern again.

If only Masidon had given her ear plugs along with black lenses, she could have learned this language for the deaf and blind. Lemma nodded, hoping it had been a yes or no question.

The nurse tapped again. Lemma nodded.

The nurse tapped one more pattern, and Lemma nodded again. The nurse left. Lemma was alone.

Looking around she noticed a door slightly ajar. Inside a row of hooks held white gowns. Lemma put one on. Then she stepped cautiously back into the hallway and approached the glass case.

Inside the man lay motionless, an IV drip in his arm and a mask over his face. Plastic tubes and hoses protruded from his mouth and body. His chest moved slowly up and down. His waist and legs were draped with a sheet. His feet weren't visible, as they had been in one of the photos in *Seeing Without Perceiving*.

On the glass case was the metal plaque Lemma had read the night of the dedication. She leaned forward on the glass. There was a Thumb-Scan and keypad, but she had no idea what the entry code was. She swiped Officer Garrity's key fob against it, but it didn't allow access to the case.

"Access denied."

"Excuse me!"

Lemma forced herself to remain steady, as a male and a female nurse approached.

"This is where I left her. Unable to see or hear. She didn't have a gown on before." The female nurse walked up to Lemma, who was running her hands over the glass door to the case.

"Hey," the nurse said gently, nudging Lemma on the shoulder. She tapped a pattern on Lemma's palm. Lemma nodded, keeping her eyes down as she spied an ID badge clipped to the waist of the nurse's scrub pants.

"Come with me," the nurse said.

Lemma drove her knee into the nurse's belly, grabbing for her ID and swiping it on the keypad. The male nurse shouted, but Lemma moved too quickly, shoving the female nurse at him, and taking advantage of their combined fall to dash through the newly opened door and into the glass case.

The door closed after her. Both nurses were on their feet again, pounding on the glass and shouting at her. The male nurse was frantically swiping his ID.

"Access granted. Welcome, Nurse 245205."

Lemma charged the door, planting her foot in the man's groin as he entered the case. The nurse collapsed to the ground, and the door closed once more, leaving the female nurse helpless outside.

"Don't!" the male nurse coughed. Lemma knelt beside him, pressing the carotid arteries in his neck until he lost consciousness.

Then she approached the comatose young man. She pulled the white sheet off his legs, exposing the same toes she had seen in one of the photos in Vinida's manuscript. They were webbed, just as Quinn Hodeft's had been.

"Howsie, Ovian," she said.

CHAPTER 68

THE MAN IN THE GLASS BOX

The male nurse was still unconscious, but the female nurse was screaming into her radio for assistance. Within minutes, Lemma would be arrested. She pulled out Donovez's phone, but this deep in the hospital, there was no way to make a call.

She ran her fingers over Ovian's body, withered and skeletal after so many years lying in this bed. Locating an IV drip in the jungle of tubes, she twisted a dial, and tapped on his shoulder.

"Ovian?"

The man stirred.

She turned the dial on the drip as far as it would go.

His eyelids fluttered.

She pulled out the syringe she had taken from Getonia's apartment from her pocket, and inserted the needle into his inner elbow.

His whole body jerked. He opened his eyes and groaned.

"I'm here to help you. What's your name?" Lemma asked, removing the mask and pulling the tube from his mouth.

"They said— I'm… Who are you?" he fought against his restraints, threatening to tear the tubes in his arms out.

"My name is Lemma Quartz. They put you in a coma. I'm here to rescue you. What's your name?"

The man's face was deeply scarred. It was no wonder the doctors had mistaken him for Teskir Mong.

"Tell me your name."

"Ovian… I'm Ovian Hodeft. How long have I been… where am I?"

"Wade Syan Hospital."

"How did you know I'm Ovian?"

"What?"

"Everyone else thinks I'm my friend. They keep calling me Teskir."

Lemma felt a weight in her stomach. Everything about him, from his identity to his alleged brain damage and need for a coma, was a lie. "They said you were asleep."

"Everything was black, but I could hear. I could feel. I'm cold."

He started sobbing, and Lemma placed her hand on his cheek.

"Please be quiet, Ovian, or they'll catch us. I'll get you out of here. I'll get you to safety." Lemma breathed into her hands, and rubbed warmth into his bony arms.

"Is that better?"

"How long have I been here?"

"Ten years. Ever since the day that… do you remember what happened?"

"Teskir and I and some of our friends were playing around with gas. One of them lit it. There were flames everywhere. Then I'm here… can't move. Can't see. But I could hear everything. They think I'm Teskir. I couldn't speak. Couldn't move."

"Can you move now?"

His body had stopped shaking. He tilted his head to the side, and wiggled his shoulders.

"Almost. How did you get in here?"

"It's my job to break into places."

"How did you find me? Everyone else thinks I'm dead."

"Your mother had webbed toes. You got your toes from her."

"You know my mother?"

"I interviewed her."

"Where is she?"

"I'll find her. I'll get you out of here, and you can tell everyone what really happened, gel?"

"What… where are we going?"

"I'm going to get you out of here to a safe place. Can you sit up?"

The female nurse pounded the glass case.

"Who is that?" Ovian murmured.

"Don't worry about her. Can you sit up?"

Ovian raised his head slightly then he fell back on the pillow. "Can't… it's hard to move."

"I'm going to bring in a stretcher and carry you out."

"Where are we going?"

"There's a lot to explain, but the people who thought you died turned your death into a political movement. Lots of people are being hurt because of it, children, especially. If we can show everyone you're alive, maybe we can fix everything."

Ovian murmured.

"You want to come with us?"

"I want you to kill me. Before anyone finds us. Please, kill me. Please!"

"You're going to be safe. But I promise, if anyone does find us, I'll shoot you before they can bring you back here, gel?"

Lemma stepped over the unconscious nurse. Approaching the side of the glass box, she pulled out Garrity's gun. The female nurse stopped pounding on the glass and stepped back, her eyes wide. Lemma scanned the unconscious nurse's ID, and opened the door.

"Get your radio and call off the alarm. Tell them not to come," she ordered the female nurse.

"I—"

"Do it!"

The nurse spoke into the radio. "False alarm. Situation under control, no backup necessary."

"Now listen to me, Nurse— what's your name?"

"Jaggard." Nurse Jaggard was shaking.

"Nurse Jaggard, you're going to contact the state capitol, and demand to talk to Governor Kawling, you understand?"

"The governor?"

"Yes. Tell them that Lemma Quartz, who saved Governor Kawling's life at the Syan Hospital dedication, has a message for her."

"Lemma Quartz?"

"Yes. You saw the public notices outside? I'm wanted for murder. You get to be the one to turn me in and collect the reward."

"I do? Why?"

"Because the entire city needs to know this, and that's worth me going to the badges." The police would love to have the badge-killer in their hands, Lemma thought darkly.

"Need to know what?"

"Ovian Hodeft and Teskir Mong's bodies were switched. Ovian is alive and has been in this case the whole time. Teskir Mong is dead. He was buried in Ovian's grave. You know what I'm talking about?"

Nurse Jaggard nodded.

"And when you've told all this to Governor Kawling, then—"

Lemma's feet were jerked from under her, and she landed facedown on the floor.

CHAPTER 69

IDENTITY

Lemma fumbled for the gun, but it had fallen to the floor. She thrashed her feet, striking someone behind her, and crawled forward, her fingertips brushing against the gun.

Someone grabbed Lemma by a fistful of her hair, jerking her head and shoulders back.

"Don't move!" said the male nurse.

Lemma struggled, and he pulled her hair harder. Lemma grabbed his wrists, trying to pull herself to her feet, but her arms were exhausted.

"Call the governor," she gasped to Nurse Jaggard.

"She's delusional," noted the male nurse, yanking her hair harder.

"I'm not delusional! I'm Lemma Quartz, I'm wanted for murder!"

"What does this say?" Nurse Jaggard examined the adhesive paper label on the front of Lemma's gown. "Ms. Kells. She should be in Room 1023. Scheduled for dual leg removal."

"No," Lemma said fiercely. "I'm not a patient, my name is Lemma Quartz."

"Uncertain of identity," Jaggard said, shaking her head sadly. "Prone to panic, possible paranoia, aggressive tendencies."

"I'm not rimming aggressive!" Lemma screamed. She struggled, kicking and flailing her arms, as the male nurse pulled her roughly to her feet by her hair. Her scalp felt as if it was about to tear off her skull.

"Now, Ms. Kells, everything is going to be gel, you'll feel better after the procedure is over," the male nurse assured her,.

"I'm not Ms. Kells, give me my phone!"

"Patient is under delusion that she owns a phone," the male nurse said.

"Actually, she does have a phone, and a weapon." Nurse Jaggard pointed to the gun on the floor.

"Patient exhibits disregard for state and national laws," the male nurse said.

"Loose me!" Lemma screamed.

"Try to relax, gel? You'll feel better once this is all over and your legs are gone," Nurse Jaggard told her.

"I'm calm now. Look how calm I am," Lemma swallowed. "Scope me? I'm not struggling. I'm not even angry that you're about to cut off my legs."

"Well, scope at that," Nurse Jaggard said happily. "You're already feeling better, and we haven't even begun the procedure."

"It's— you can't— I'm not— I'm a criminal!" Lemma shouted. "I'm wanted for murder. You have to turn me in!"

"Ms. Kells, you have been in this hospital for… three weeks," Jaggard said, checking her notes. "You haven't killed anyone. Now please, are you going to be quiet, or will I have to sedate you?"

"Ovian Hodeft is alive!" Lemma shouted. "Read the manuscript in my jacket! Call the governor! Tell her Lemma Quartz wants to see her."

"We'll do that. Let me sedate you and I will contact the governor and tell her everything you said. Do we have a deal?" the male nurse asked in a crooning tone, the one he used to placate agitated mental patients.

The gun was several feet out of her reach. She had no choice.

"Deal." Lemma felt him let go of her hair.

"Lie on the floor."

Lemma's chest was flat against the cold floor tiles, as the male nurse pushed a needle into her neck.

Blackness swarmed around her, but she could hear and feel everything, from the cold floor on her cheek to the frantic whispers of Jaggard and the male nurse.

"She said Ovian Hodeft is alive."

"She's delusional, obviously."

"She wants us to contact the governor."

"Again, it's paranoia. I've scoped bad cases, but this is something else."

"So what do we do? You're not actually going to bother the governor with this?"

"Get her to a holding ward, and then prep her for surgery."

CHAPTER 70

DO NO HARM

It was like being injected with the paralysis medication all over again. The reality of what was about to happen washed over her, sending chills through her motionless body. Lemma tried to call out, to struggle, but she was unable to move.

The nurses' voices dissolved into whispers. She was lifted up by invisible hands, set on a cushioned surface, and rolled on shaky wheels, down a long hall, turning left, then right, then left again. There was the weightlessness of an elevator, then another elevator, and then Lemma was picked up and lowered onto a bed. Someone went through and emptied her pockets.

"We should restrain her."

"I sedated her, she's out."

Not true, Lemma thought. She tried to force her eyes to blink, her toes to wiggle. Nothing.

"What's this one in for?" These voices were new.

"Looks like…" Someone touched the front of Lemma's gown where the adhesive label was. "Type this in, would you? Scheduled for dual pedectomy."

Something wet was drawn across her thighs. She did not need anyone to explain what the lines were marking.

The smell of rubbing alcohol entered her nose, immediately followed by a cold sting as her thighs were sterilized.

"I can't imagine what this poor girl was going through," Nurse Jaggard said. "No wonder her husband signed her over."

"It's hardest on the families, I think," a male voice said. "They have to make the decision."

Lemma tried to move her mouth. Her mouth didn't obey.

"It's not much easier for us," another nurse said. "I have nightmares where we do a procedure and then the patient changes their mind. Could you imagine? Living with that?"

"I heard about one case," Jaggard said. From the sound of her voice she was standing close to Lemma. "A family signed over their elderly father. Said he was complaining of depression. Said he wanted it. After the operation, he woke up and changed his mind. Threatened to sue the hospital."

"That's awful!" a female voice gasped.

"But it turned out gel," Jaggard said. "After several weeks, he accepted it. Even said it made him happier. So he was better off for it. He joined the Tiresian Church and began a whole new life."

"It has tremendous therapeutic effects," the male voice agreed. "Like cosmetic surgery for someone with a poor body image. You see it in their eyes, hear it in their voice; they become a completely new person."

"Hold on," another voice said. "Are we sure this is Ms. Kells?"

"What, did her identity disorder spread to you too?" the male voice scoffed. "When we found her, she thought she was wanted by the state for murder."

"Yes, but Kells' chart says she's Caucasian. This one isn't Caucasian. She's what? Japanese? Chinese?"

"Democratic Monarchy of Central Korea, by the looks of her," one of the voices said.

"Do we have the wrong patient?" Jaggard asked.

"Must be."

There was an appalled silence.

"Then where is the real Ms. Kells? Why is this one wearing Kells' gown? Who is she?"

"Look out the window."

Lemma heard the window blinds rustle.

"Her face is on the billboards. I don't believe it. She really is the one they want. Send out a notice throughout the hospital to find the real Ms. Kells."

Lemma's heart fluttered. For the first time since she had been rendered unable to move, she had hope.

"So… should we contact the police?"

"She originally said she wanted to talk to the governor."

A nurse scoffed. "If she's wanted for murder, she's not going to be allowed to see the governor. Probably wants to ghost her."

Lemma was losing track of which nurses were saying what.

"We could turn her in to the police."

"What'll we say?"

"Huh?"

"They'd want to know how a fugitive wanted for murder broke into the hospital. They'll take us in for questioning, and then they'll find out we accidentally switched two people, and misplaced a patient."

"I'm getting an alert. They found the real Ms. Kells wandering the hospital."

"Claps to them, but what about us and this one?"

"It's an innocent mistake!"

"For you! You have tenure! You could spread a patient and they wouldn't fire you!"

"We haven't done anything yet. We can figure this out."

There was silence as they tried to come up with a solution.

Finally one of them said, "What if we say she turned herself in, and asked for the procedure?"

"What?"

"Think about it! If a criminal requests medical treatment based on religious grounds, it takes precedence over any legal process. We could say she wanted to convert to the Tiresian Church. Plenty of criminals get an independence surgery to avoid incarceration. I even found a set of corneal shields in one of her pockets. She was already experimenting with vision non-dependence."

"And when I found her," Jaggard said, eagerly chiming in, "she was feigning blindness and deafness. We have that on the surveillance tape. Clearly that's what she wanted."

"Switch the procedure? Leave her legs, remove her eyes and ears? And then turn her over to the badges?"

"It makes for a better story than saying she broke into our hospital while we were losing track of our patients."

"There won't even be an investigation if we do everything legally. All we need is her consent."

"Or a judge's consent. I know of several who'd approve this in a heartbeat, even in the middle of the night."

"Get their approval. Then give this poor woman the surgery she needs."

The nurses left the room.

CHAPTER 71

THE ALGORITHM

The seconds crawled like glaciers. Anger and panic boiled within Lemma. She could do nothing but wait, cursing herself for believing she could rescue Ovian so easily. Why hadn't she told Donovez? She hated herself for her stupidity, and hated the nurses even more, with their false care for their patients, ready to amp a whole hospital wing of people whether or not they wanted it, as long as they didn't get investigated.

Focus, she ordered her panicked brain.

I can't focus.

Focus. There has to be something. Someone who knows you're here, a signal you can give.

Perron Mills. What about him? His tricks had gotten her here. Could he also get her out?

Her fingers twitched. The darkness was fading, the room gradually appearing around her.

She groaned in frustration.

Wait.

She had groaned. Aloud. She groaned again.

"Help," she whispered.

Lemma's fingers and toes were dead. She was still in the grip of the paralytic medication, like Ovian had been for a decade, but now her voice was returning. If only she could call out to someone who could help.

Then she remembered the night Perron had broken in.

"Computer," she murmured.

There was a soft hum as a computer responded, "Enter or say passcode."

She had heard it, less than an hour before, when the male nurse had swiped into Ovian's glass display case.

"504524."

"Incorrect identification. Access denied."

Lemma cursed. "205245."

"Incorrect identification. Access denied."

Focus, you twank.

"Computer, input code 245205?"

"Access granted. What can I do for you?"

She breathed a sigh of relief. "Send a message to Governor Kawling."

"I apologize; I can't address messages to a specific person. If you want, I get send a message over the intercom to the entire hospital."

"What about the city? Can you send out a message to the city billboards?"

"I can if there is a public health crisis. Is there a public health crisis?"

"Yes."

"What do you want your message to say?"

"Computer, do you understand programmed scripts from voice translate?"

"Yes, I can convert verbal instructions into a programmable script."

"Gel. Input string: 'Ovian Hodeft alive in Teskir Mong glass box. Lemma Quartz trapped in Syan Hospital, room one zero two three, about to be amped.'"

"Very well. I have your string as: 'Ovian Hodeft alive in Teskir Mong glass box. Lemma Quartz trapped in Syan Hospital, Room 1023, about to be amped.' Is that correct?"

"No, only use characters. No numbers—"

"Very well. The numbers are represented as words. How should I save that string?"

"Uh— myMessage."

"Very well. I saved your string to myMessage."

"Convert myMessage to an array." Lemma's voice was stronger now, but her eyesight was still blurry. She fought to remember how Donovez explained the code.

"Very well. String myMessage is now an array."

"Remove all spaces and punctuation from myMessage."

"Very well."

"Create a new string, titled Fibonacci."

"All right. I've created a new string, titled Fibonacci."

"Set Fibonacci equal to the first ten thousand digits of Fibonacci's number phi."

"Very well."

"Read back the first five digits of Fibonacci."

"1-6-1-8-0."

"Bright. Now…" Lemma struggled to put the algorithm into words. "Create an array of numbers. Title it: myAlphabet."

"Very well."

"For each character in myMessage… convert it to the corresponding numeric position in the alphabet, and store the result in myAlphabet."

"I have done so."

"Read back the first five numbers in myAlphabet."

"15-22-9-1-14."

"That spells… Ovian. Bright. Now, for each number in… myAlphabet," Lemma paused, forcing herself to think clearly. "Find the numeric position of the first occurrence of that number in Fibonacci. Store that result in a new array of numbers, titled myCode."

"Very well."

"For each number in string myAlphabet, if it's a two-digit number, append a one to the end of the corresponding number in myCode."

"Very well. I've gone through myAlphabet and myCode, and put ones on the ends of numbers in myCode with the same position as every two-digit number in myAlphabet."

"Great. Now, for each number in myAlphabet, if it's a one-digit number, append a zero to the end of the corresponding number in my-Code."

"Very well."

"Now go through myCode, and for each number, if it has less than five digits, put zeroes on the front until it has five digits."

"Very well."

"That's great. Now, add the string 'NewTulip786 PHI' to the front of myCode."

"Done. I've added 'NewTulip786 PHI' to the front of myCode."

"Gel." Lemma breathed. If there was a single mistake in her algorithm, it would be unreadable to Donovez. But she had no time to check it. "Print myCode as a Public Health Crisis Warning."

"Done. Is there anything else?"

"No."

Lemma waited in silence and in darkness. Somewhere in Room 1023 a clock was ticking. She counted to ten, then fifty, then to a hundred.

She lost count around five hundred sixty. She began counting again. This time, she made it to nine hundred forty-six. Then she lost count.

Then the door opened.

"That was rimming eternal," Nurse Jaggard said with a yawn. "Prep her so we can get this done before dawn."

"Hey!" Lemma said.

A nurse screamed. Two others cursed.

"I don't want this procedure! I'm in my right mind, and I don't consent to any operations, so don't cucking touch me."

Someone covered her mouth with a cloth. Lemma felt a needle jab in her arm. Lemma's voice was gone once more.

"Never mind that." A nurse wiped cold alcohol on her face, around the eyes and ears. "Let's continue."

"Are you steady? The medication was wearing off; she said she didn't want any procedures," another nurse objected.

"We have the judge's order; it would be too suspicious if we backed out now. Get ready to make the first incision."

"Are you sure this is the right thing to do?" someone asked.

"If she is really a criminal, then trust me, this surgery will work wonders on her. She'll be a new person. I've seen them, in the hospitals, in pews at church. I know it sounds jacked up, but some people aren't really whole until part of them is removed. It's like a tumor for them. Imagine what kind of life she must have had, to go out and ghost people. She'll be happier this way. And she'll have an easier time in prison. She'll rehabilitate faster. I'm steady; this is the kindest thing we can do for her."

"And no one will investigate us?"

"Correct."

There was a scrape of metal on metal. Lemma felt hands grasp her face, and there was a tiny poke behind her ear. Then something cut across her scalp in a streak of white hot pain.

CHAPTER 72

GLIMMER OF LIGHT

Every part of Lemma's body was in silent pain. She wanted to writhe, to cry out, to die, but her body stayed in the bed, defenseless against the scalpel cutting into her face.

A wet cloth was placed on her face, and the surgeon made another cut. Lemma's skull was ringing with pain. Her paralyzed eyes leaked hot tears. Soon her eyes would be removed, and her ability to hear would be silenced. She could do nothing to stop it.

"Stop," a frantic male voice said. "We have to stop. Stop the procedure, right now. A call just came in."

The throbbing in her head nearly drowned out his voice. She was still in the dark.

"Who is it?"

"State capitol. We have to stop, right now."

"How do they know what's going on? Oh, cuck!"

A panicked voice said, "Rimming sew her up!"

Pins were stuck into her scalp. Her skull was on fire.

A furious voice came from down the hall, growing louder with each syllable.

"I swear, if you've hurt her, if you so much as gave her a paper cut, I will have your testicles on whole wheat toast, do you understand me?"

Lemma listened, unsure if she was hallucinating. That voice. She knew that voice.

"Did you hear me? What will I eat?"

"My testicles, Governor Kawling."

"And on what?"

"Toast."

"Whole wheat toast!"

The door burst open.

Nurse Jaggard cringed. "Governor Kawling, we found the fugitive," she said.

"What the cuck is this? You're amping her? Answer me, you little twanks!"

Nurse Jaggard stumbled over her words. "She asked us to. Really! It's true! Came in and said she wanted surgery before she was arrested."

"She asked for it?"

"Yes, Governor."

"Wake her up."

"Governor, this—" a man was speaking.

"Dr. Vallen, be quiet or I will investigate this hospital so hard your colon will dangle out your flaps, do you understand me?"

Dr. Vallen made no reply.

"Well? Did you hear me tell you to be quiet or not?"

"Yes, I did."

"Then be quiet!"

"Yes, Governor. Sorry, Governor."

"Take those rimming tubes out of her."

"Yes, Governor."

"Immediately! And be gentle!"

"Governor, do you want me to be gentle, or immediate?"

"Both!" Kawling screamed so violently that globs of spit fell on Lemma's skin. She never thought she'd be happy to be spit on, but she was. Kawling had arrived in the nick of time, impetuous, demanding, saving her from being blinded and rendered deaf.

A needle jabbed Lemma's arm, and the IV drip was pulled out.

Every part of Lemma's body ached.

Then, from the corner of the dark universe where her eyes had floated, a glimmer of light appeared. At first cloudy, then translucent, the room swam into focus.

Finally, she could move her head. She blinked, and stared at the face of Governor Raemin Kawling.

"She had an unliced manuscript, an illegal gun, and a phone," Nurse Jaggard said timidly.

"Plug it. All of you get out. You, what's your name?"

"Nurse Jaggard."

"Bring some coffee and a pitcher of water."

Everyone left.

Lemma began crying. Embarrassing, messy tears spilled down her face. Kawling gently dabbed her cheeks with a washcloth.

"Governor…"

"I'm Raemin."

"You need… everyone spects—"

"Lemma, I need you to answer one question. Did you kill any of those people?"

"What?"

"Officer Colburn, Officer Shawl…"

Lemma spoke in broken sobs.

"The badges… it was self-defense— but I didn't ghost Syan or anyone else. It was Masidon Barreaux. He's using rat poison. It makes you thirsty and that's why people are climbing into bathtubs and freezers."

"Masidon Barreaux?"

"I know it sounds insane. I can't prove it yet, but if you question him he'll tell you. Also, Ovian Hodeft is alive. Everyone thinks it's Teskir Mong in that glass case, but it was Ovian, this whole time. His feet are webbed, like his mom's. He has webbed toes."

"Lemma…"

"Masidon knows; that's why he's killing everyone, so he can keep it secret. And he had Shwa Chinny and Curio posting for him."

"Lemma, please calm down."

"You don't believe me."

"I do believe you. Oh, Lemma you are so close."

"Close?"

"They weren't working for Masidon. They were working for me."

CHAPTER 73

RAY OF SUNSHINE

"What?"

"I apologize for misleading you until now."

"No!"

"But I promise, I will explain everything."

"You ghosted Syan?"

"Patience!" Kawling hissed. "Let me give you the explanation you're entitled to."

Kawling pulled up a chair and sat down. Nurse Jaggard returned with a carafe of coffee, a pitcher of water and some cups. She placed them on the table beside Governor Kawling and scurried out of the room.

Kawking poured a glass of water. "Are you thirsty?"

"No. Tell me what's going on."

"Gel. I'll start at the beginning." Kawling cleared her throat.

"Once, there was a little girl who had parents that loved her, and wanted nothing but the best for her. They called her their little Rae of Sunshine and told her she could follow whatever dream she wanted.

"After I graduated law school, I pursued my dream: public service. I clerked, interned, worked on campaigns, and ran campaigns of my own. My first bid was the state legislature. I was a novice, naive. I believed that people wanted a leader with a commitment to the public good, someone who could inspire hope and optimism in the future of society.

"But I was wrong in my approach. My message was to be kind to the poor and make sure everyone was healthy and owned a garden where they could grow vegetables. My opponent ran a campaign based on fear, how there was no food left in the stores, hunger everywhere. Well, guess who people voted for? I learned a powerful lesson that day, Lemma. Hope is best left to greeting cards. Fear is what inspires action. If you want to sell someone a fire extinguisher, show them a man whose face has been burned off. If you want to sell a campaign, show a world where people are gnawing on wads of money to curb their hunger.

"When I next ran, I knew what my tactic would be. But what would be the angle? It couldn't be the food shortage; Wade Syan had already solved that problem. Society was finally progressing.

"I thought long and hard about what angle to sell. Better schools? Better hospitals? Every politician promises that. I needed to set myself apart.

"And then I got my answer. A group of silly twanks thought they could achieve enlightenment by cutting their arms off and scooping their eyes out. They were a cult with fewer than a dozen members, hardly a threat. We mocked them on late night comedy media.

"But then public perception shifted. It flipped in a single afternoon. I'd never seen minds change so quickly. Ovian Hodeft, a young boy who liked to wear dark glasses, like the Tiresians, was set on fire. By the time doctors realized they had accidentally switched the boy with one of his friends, Natisra Fezz had become famous around the world for her article on anti-Tiresian prejudice.

"I rode the waves resulting from Natisra's article. I promised to give their church every protection the law offered, and I was proudly photographed with Hodeft's crying mother, as well as church leader Masidon Barreaux. I was now the champion of the underdogs, the oppressed. The idea that Ovian was not a martyr but was alive would have ruined all of that. So the doctors kept their mouths shut. When I won in a landslide, I made sure to reward them for their loyalty."

Lemma coughed; her throat felt dry and rusty. "Did Masidon or Natisra know?"

"The doctors told only me." Kawling sipped from her cup. "I won the governor's seat. The Tiresian Church has blossomed, faster than any other religion. Their membership was once big enough to win me the governorship. Now it's grown large enough to win me the presidency."

Kawling drank from her cup, a faraway look on her face.

Then she frowned. "But it was still far from certain. Natisra knew too much about Ovian, and Vinida was dangerously close to discovering the truth, even after I had the Public Info Department shut down that book of hers. Shwa Chinny loved scraping data; he could have blackmailed me. And when I had Chinny scrape information on Syan, I realized Syan was also too dangerous to keep alive. If I am to advance, I need a clean slate. I needed a way to silence them from afar, to shut down my enemies without it ever being traced back to me.

"So I labored, using foreign scientists no one will ever find, until we came up with a method, a way to inflict such great thirst that a person would drown themselves to quench it. Just like a rat. Untraceable."

Lemma cleared her throat, and spoke for the first time. "So you poisoned them? You poisoned Syan? And Chinny? And Fezz?"

"It wasn't poison, Lemma, but an infection. A virus. And I only infected Syan."

Lemma squirmed. She was regaining power over her body. "Who infected the rest?"

"You did."

CHAPTER 74

HAIL MARY

The throbbing in Lemma's head was suddenly gone. "No. That's impossible. I didn't even know about it."

"That's the beauty of it."

"No!" Lemma said.

"I can prove it. The virus takes six days to incubate, then it kills swiftly. Every person you mentioned, other than Syan, died exactly six days after you first met them. Think about it. Fezz died at the Syan Hospital dedication, on Friday, May 18. So you must have met her and infected her on May 12. Shwa Chinny died on May 25, so you met with him on May 19. And you say Vinida died tonight? Six days ago was May 25. Did you meet Vinida the same day Shwa Chinny died?"

"What about Perron Mills? The badges said he died on May 24. I visited him on— on May 21, only three days before."

"But you first had contact with him at the dedication, didn't you? May 18? Twenty-four minus eighteen is six."

"No. You're making it up," Lemma insisted.

"I'm sorry, but it's the truth."

"But how did I infect them?"

"You're a carrier, but you're immune to it."

"How?"

"Would you like some coffee?" Kawling offered.

Lemma's eyes were heavy. "Yes."

"Milk?"

"No."

"Why not?" Kawling held a cup of coffee to Lemma's lips, which held just strength enough for her to drink.

299

"I'm allergic."

"To dairy. Exactly. One of a handful of people, out of almost nine billion. The rest of humanity had that gene edited out of them. That same gene that cursed you with your food allergies makes you able to carry my virus with being harmed by it. You ever heard of Typhoid Mary? She was a cook who worked in people's homes a long time ago, carrying and spreading typhus without ever succumbing to it. You are the Typhoid Mary of our age."

"How did you learn that?" Lemma asked.

"Through thousands of trials."

"No, how did you know I'm allergic to milk?"

"Because Wade Syan and I were friends. The night I infected him, six days before he died, of course, he and I met for drinks. He casually mentioned that a sex worker he employed as a spy had recently met a young woman who had saved her from being attacked by goons. She told Syan this woman had an unusual allergy and worked for Balkon Death Insurance Agency."

"Harriden Vik."

"Yes, Harriden Vik. She had no idea how valuable that information was, and neither did Syan. I never expected that someone with an allergy even existed anymore. You cannot imagine how excited I was to learn of you. Before, I had planned on infecting everyone myself. Now that you entered the picture, all I had to do was find a contact at Balkon and make sure that you were the one to investigate Syan's death. I observed you through his bathroom window that night. As soon as you were close enough to the blink, buzz buzz! I sent a coded message, easy enough to crack, which led you to each of my targets. Not only did you solve the code, you made great use of it. The Balkon data that you sent to Shwa, and your coded message tonight on the billboards. That was fortunate for you, or your eyes would have been ripped out by now."

"But Masidon... I visited him first, before anyone else. Why wasn't he infected?" Lemma asked.

"Masidon was the one who infected you. I needed to put as much distance between you and me as possible. Masidon didn't know the full extent of my plan, but I told him to expect a visit from you, and to make sure you ingested it."

"So, ever since I met with Masidon I've been infecting people?"

"You became contagious six days after Masidon infected you. Once the virus was incubated, Masidon set you up with Natisra. You did the rest. My perfect assassin. You played your part beautifully," Kawling said.

"But what about all the other people I met? Everyone at Balkon? People on the street? I've seen Masidon since I became infected. And what about you, right now?"

"Masidon and I have kept ourselves immune. You know Dipsocene? The medication the Tiresians take for their phantom pains? One of its side effects is defense against a number of viruses. Including mine."

"So every Tiresian that I met…"

"Is safe from it."

"What about others? People on the street? On public transit?"

"People on the street pass by you too quickly to get infected. As for public transit, you use the expectant mothers section, don't you? It's toxic for actual expectant mothers, so you had it all to yourself."

"What about Balkon?" Lemma asked.

"After Masidon infected you, I told Curio to start issuing Dipsocene to everyone at Balkon."

"So Curio was in on it?"

"Curio knew only what I told her. She didn't know that Syan was going to die. She never knew that you had an infection, or how the Dipsocene was protecting her and her employees from you."

"But she knew things about his apartment, like the bathroom window being jammed shut. She had to have been there," Lemma said.

"Certainly. I sent her to put that blink in the wall. Several days after I'd infected Syan, once I knew for certain you would be involved, Curio paid him a visit when his wife wasn't home, pretending to survey him about his satisfaction with Balkon's services."

Lemma slumped back on the bed, the weight of this new information crushing her into the mattress. Perron Mills, Harriden Vik… everyone except Syan had died because she had inserted herself into their lives, chasing clues without ever guessing that she was merely a pawn in someone else's game.

"And that," Kawling said, "Leads us to our next topic: my contract with Curio."

CHAPTER 75

INSURANCE

"What contract?"

"My agreement with Curio. She would assign you to the Wade Syan case, hide the blink in his bathroom wall, and she would make sure everyone at Balkon was taking Dipsocene daily. In return, I'd grant Balkon an exclusive contract to provide security and detective services for the state."

Lemma couldn't believe what she'd heard. "For the state?"

"Yes."

"But Curio said the contract was awarded to Axiom."

"Axiom's lobbyists were able to win over the rest of the state legislature before I could persuade them to go with Abadon. But now that you are aware of your abilities as an assassin, you can easily remove Axiom's allies, as well as Axiom's leaders. Then maybe Curio can stop ordering you to poison my tea."

Lemma flushed. "What makes you think I'll do that? Ghost Axiom?"

Kawling smiled. "I thought you would jump at the chance to eliminate your competitors. Or is murder suddenly beneath you?"

"Take it out of me!" Lemma shouted, pulling herself to a sitting position. "Whatever you did to me, cure me!"

"Cure you?" Kawling asked. "Listen to yourself! Without that antidote, no one can stand against you! You can eliminate world leaders with a single breath! You and I together, Lemma. I, the world's most powerful leader, and you, the world's most deadly assassin. No one will stop us. Journalists, lobbyists, drowned in their own tubs. Excess of immigrants?

302

Violent goons? Solved overnight. And I'll pay you well. Knife license, gun license, camera license. You wanted a new leg for that kid? Adoption papers? I'll help you adopt a million children with three legs each! And Balkon will worship you for years!"

"I'm not with Balkon anymore. I'm working for Abadon."

"Fine, then Abadon will get the contract. I don't care."

"Loose me, Raemin. I did your work; I ghosted everyone on your list. Cure me. Please!"

"Sorry, I've invested too much in you."

Lemma's hands balled into fists. "Then ghost me. I'm not helping you."

"I was afraid of that. I can do without you. Your mutated genes are valuable but not essential. I'll have you tried for those murders. The two children you want to adopt? They'll go to a nice Tiresian family. The state contract will go to Axiom."

"You'll never get away with it. You can try and ban us, but you'll never get away with it."

"I won't have to ban Abadon, Lemma. Once every citizen gets free, state-subsidized service from Axiom, neither Abadon nor Balkon will be able to compete. They'll wither away to nothing. That little neighborhood experiment of yours? Wilco? Yes, I know about that. It'll be bulldozed. Everything you have worked for, everyone you care about—undone."

The first glimmers of dawn were starting to trickle through the window. Lemma's head, body, and mind ached.

"Cheer up. We do have a cure. It's different from the Dipsocene. You won't have to be my personal assassin forever. Once I've attained my goals, I'll cure you. It won't be that long until you can retire. You'll still be young, and you'll be very, very wealthy."

Lemma clenched her teeth so hard her jaw almost shattered. Then she surrendered, and nodded.

"Wonderful, I knew you'd come around. Your first assignment will be tomorrow evening, at the Governor's Ball. There'll be quite a number of targets I'll need you to shake hands with."

"Yes."

"After that—"

There was a crash and the door to Room 1023 burst open.

"Lemma!" Jax was breathing hard, his hand clutching a scalpel. "Are you gel? Governor Kawling, what's going on?"

"Jax!" Lemma shouted. "Stab her! Rimming ghost her! Do it! Quick!"

Jax didn't think. He didn't pause to consider why Lemma was issuing the command to kill Kawling. He dove toward her without hesitation. She screamed, but it was too late. Jax was on top of her, raising the blade in his fist.

There was a crackle of electricity and his body convulsed. Two guards had burst in, waving blue batons.

"Stand down!" Governor Kawling ordered. "Bag his body and dump it."

Lemma's mouth was dry. She stared at Jax, limp on the floor, scalpel still in hand, hoping that he was feigning death, that he would strike Kawling any moment now.

"And you." Kawling turned to Lemma, as the guards dragged Jax's body from the room. "What was that you shouted? For him to kill me? I'm disappointed in you. Are we not partners anymore?"

Lemma barely heard Kawling's voice. Visions of Jax danced in her mind: when he stole Syan's blink from Curio for her, when they hugged after Fremen's trial, every time he lent her his jacket. Jax had died trying to help her. It was her fault.

"I wanted to trust you, Lemma, I really did. But I also know the value of insurance."

Kawling motioned, and a section of the wall displayed a live feed of a room in the hospital.

"We picked up the amped boy, Gram Mills, on one of the public buses. He's safe with us. As for the girl, Nadia, we found her at Getonia Orea's apartment. Unlike Gram, she's not Tiresian, so she wouldn't be taking Dipsocene. Let me guess. You first came into contact with her six days ago?"

Lemma didn't want to consider what Kawling was saying, but the thoughts forced themselves into her head. Nadia had come to her apartment hours after Lemma had met Vinida. And if Vinida had already succumbed to the virus…

The live feed showed Nadia strapped to a bed, jerking her body against her restraints.

"By now she would have drowned herself if we hadn't found her," Kawling said.

"Loose her!" Lemma screamed.

"If you insist." Kawling pulled a radio from her pocket. "Release her."

Security guards appeared in the feed, bending over Nadia. Nadia leapt off the bed. Running across the room, she thrust her head into a toilet.

"No, Nadia. Don't!" Lemma screamed.

"Are you going to be loyal to me?" Kawling asked. "I was very displeased by what happened with that young man just now. You won't try anything like that again, will you?"

"Please, I swear I'll ghost whoever you want. Just stop her! Please!"

Kawling hesitated, pursing her lips. "Absolutely sure you'll be loyal? I don't want any more surprises."

"Yes! I promise!"

"Put her under," Kawling said into the radio. The guards tackled the girl and pressed a syringe to her neck. Nadia's body went limp.

"I'll give you your list of targets. I'll see you at the Governor's Ball. Be sure and wear something nice."

The morning sun was shining as Governor Kawling left Room 1023.

CHAPTER 76

WOLF ON THE FOLD

Friday, June 1

The sun climbed to its apex, and the afternoon rolled on lazily.

A woman entered Wilco Residential Zone. Her black hair was cropped short, grazing her high cheekbones. She walked with a limp. A surgical mask hugged her bandaged face, and her right arm was bandaged as well.

She approached a cluster of goons in the middle of the street and resisted their initial threat for her to wipe off. She examined each of their mouths, noses, and ears. The goons made kissy noises at her, their fingers slithering towards her hips, retreating in haste when she displayed a Balkon Death Insurance Agency medallion.

The woman left the cluster of goons and visited each house along the street, spending ten or fifteen minutes in each, until she came to the house where Ennerd Vik had died a month prior. She knocked on the door, and Fremen Orea opened it.

"Lemma! You're alive!"

"That is a true statement."

"You cut your hair."

"Also a true statement. Harder to grab."

Fremen stared at her darkened eyes, and at the bandages and bloody stitches on her scalp and face. It looked like someone had tried to peel her face off. "Lemma, what happened to you?"

"Doctors nearly amped me. Eyes and ears both."

Fremen put a fist to his mouth. "Getonia called the badges last night. They took Nadia and Vinida's body. Didn't find me. I ran away. Sorry."

"It's gel. They ghosted Jax."

"Oh!" Fremem's voice cracked. "Lemma, that's awful. I'm sorry."

"Can I come in?"

"Yes. Why the mask?"

"Risk of infection. Can't be too careful. Germs everywhere."

Fremen held out his hand to her, but she refused to take it.

"You're housing someone, right?" she asked, breathing as shallowly as possible.

"You mean one of the Cobra pack?"

Lemma nodded, and Fremen pointed his thumb at a closed door. "He's in there."

"Can I speak with him?"

"He's asleep. Doesn't like to be edged."

Lemma pushed past Fremen, and rapped on the door. "Open up! Rep from Balkon here."

The door opened, and a man came out. He had a lean frame, with teeth of silver and gold. His bare chest displayed more ink than skin.

"What?" he asked.

Lemma removed her mask, and shook his hand. "Health inspection."

"I'm healthy," he said sullenly. "I was sleeping."

"If you're healthy then the inspection should go flash. You'll be back in bed in no time."

"What you looking for?" he asked.

"Just checking around your eyes and ears. You can keep your pants on."

"Sure you don't need to scope out my flaps?" he asked, grinning.

She led him into the living room, wincing as Fremen scowled at her. "Say 'ah'."

"Ah."

Lemma pushed on his tongue with her bare fingertips, then felt the metal teeth in his mouth.

"You going to check all of us out?" Fremen asked.

"No. Just employees of Cobra." Lemma rubbed his molars, trying to remember where she had seen him before.

"We're not important enough?" Fremen demanded. "Is that it?"

"Wipe off, twank," the squatter said, as Lemma whipped her fingers out of the path of his metal teeth as they snapped shut.

"Aw, sorry, sushi," he said, smiling. Lemma did not smile back.

"What's stringing you? Don't like jokes?"

"Couldn't say. Haven't heard any."

"Oh— oh! You made one just now, uh?"

"Sounds like it."

"Hey, is anyone inspecting you? Could I have a look?" He tried to reach for her mouth, but she pulled her head back.

"I'm under orders to give you a health checkup. If you make this procedure difficult for me, I will make it painful for you."

"Hey now! I'm a good boy, sushi. I'll behave."

Lemma took his pulse, and listened to his breathing.

"Hey, you're not one of the Reezys, are you?" the goon asked, suddenly alarmed.

"No. Why?"

"Last doctor to look me over was a Reezy. Tried to talk me into cutting my sack off."

"You steady that was a doctor? Not every girl you've ever talked to?"

"Hey! That's funny!" the man laughed, flashing his metal teeth. "You should be a comedian, sushi. Got a sharp tongue on you. Have I scoped you before?"

"Possibly." Then Lemma remembered. This was the third goon who had tried to assault Harriden that first night, the one who was protected by death insurance. Lemma bubbled with hatred, but she forced herself to smile at him. "Maybe I have one of those faces."

"Come back sometime, gel? What time you free?"

"Oh, I'll catch you in about six days."

When she had finished, Fremen followed her outside.

"Lemma, tell me what's going on. You're helping them? Giving them health checkups? What about me? Don't care about my health?"

"Fremen, listen—"

"No, you listen. What's the plan? How much longer is Cobra going to squat on our flaps?"

"Exactly six days."

"Why? What happens then?"

"They'll stop edging you."

"How?"

"They just will. You have to trust me."

"And what happened last night? Why did Vinida die?" Fremen grabbed her shoulders.

"Wipe off!" Lemma almost spat in his face. "Loose me, unless you want to die sucking a toilet." She shoved his sternum, and he released her. "I need you to trust me, instead of accusing me of cucking you out to Cobra, gel?"

Fremen glared at her.

"Now wash your hands. Take some Reezy meds, the Dipsocene. It's important that you do. I'll come back when I'm finished. I need your help tonight."

She left him standing on his porch. Seeing several Cobra goons up the street, she spat in her palms, rubbed them dry, and went to greet them.

Chapter 77

Face of the Foe

The Governor's Ball was packed with politicians, union representatives, and businesspeople. Cameras flashed like fireworks, and shoes polished to a mirror-like shine squeaked on the marble floor of the capitol ballroom.

Musicians dressed like fancy penguins played strings, and waiters as well as automated drones passed among the guests, carrying platters of food and drinks.

"Good evening, Senator, my name is Lemma Quartz."

"Pleased to meet you, Ms. Quartz."

They shook hands.

"May I join you for this dance?"

"I'd be delighted."

Lemma had thrown all her effort into her appearance, spending hours that afternoon with apparel consultants and beauticians. Her face had been carefully styled with brushes and pencils, makeup artfully covering the cut left from the incision the previous night. Her black eyeliner was so artfully applied that she could cut men in half with a single glance. She wore a tight dress of cobalt blue, the product of three hours of harassing store clerks, many of whom were certain they recognized her face from the public alerts the previous night. One had even contacted the State Police Force, but was met with a staunch assurance that Lemma Quartz was no longer a suspect.

Lemma danced with men as best as her bandaged right arm would allow, and conversed with women, snapping at the wait staff, and using her bare hands to share zebra-stuffed mushrooms with her new friends. She found Masidon Barreaux, sitting on the stage in his motorized chair, and gave him a warm hug. She laughed, flirted, asked for drinks, and offered drinks. She posed for pictures with the guests, demanding that the photographer take just one more photo, and this time catch the light off Lemma's necklace.

"Waiter, bring me a plate!"

"I'm sorry, Ms., we don't have plates here."

"How do you not have a plate? Get me a plate immediately!" Lemma demanded.

"State law, Ms. Quartz," a silver-haired senator explained. "We're not allowed to spend money on meals if there are lobbyists present. As long as there aren't plates, it doesn't count as a meal, see?"

"That's very clever," Lemma said, managing to smile at him and keep her eyeballs from rolling.

"But if you're intent on plates, I happen to have some at my apartment. Senator Tizola." He smiled, his dark goatee twisting hopefully.

"Just plates, or will they be accompanied by food?" Lemma asked.

"Food, drink, whatever you crave." Senator Tizola reached out, his finger brushing against Lemma's elbow. "I have a private car parked outside, ready to leave at a moment's notice. It has a full minibar stocked with ice, drinks, and garnishes."

"But no plates?"

"Not in the car. We'd need to go to my apartment for that," he said.

"What about your family, Senator? Would I be meeting them if I go to your apartment?" Lemma asked.

"My wife and children are visiting the coast. I'm not joining them until next week. It would just be you and me, with nothing to distract us."

"And your plates," Lemma corrected. "It would be just you and me, and your plates."

"Yes, it would be just the two of us, and my plates," he said eagerly. "Shall we go?"

Lemma leaned over and spoke softly in his ear. "That's a tempting offer, but I can't bounce yet. I need to speak with a few more people tonight."

"I can introduce you to whoever you want. I know nearly everyone here. Oh, Governor," the senator called, catching sight of Kawling.

Governor Kawling turned, paling as she saw Lemma with Tizola.

"Senator Tizola," Kawling said. "What a pleasure."

"Governor, have you met Lemma Quartz?" Tizola gestured to Lemma, who shook Kawling's hand.

"Governor Kawling, I'm honored to meet you," Lemma smiled boldly. "Senator Tizola was just telling me about his upcoming vacation next week to the coast. Sounds lovely, doesn't it?"

"It does indeed." Governor Kawling viewed Lemma shrewdly.

"So many riptides in that area… Senator, you do know how to swim, don't you?" Lemma asked with concern.

"Of course I do. Loved the water my whole life."

"Well, then all that water shouldn't pose a threat, should it?" Lemma said. "Oh, forgive me, Senator." She put a finger to the corner of his mouth and wiped, smiling at Kawling. "Bit of sauce. Governor Kawling, let's have a chat. Bye for now, Senator."

She threw her arm around Kawling's elbow, and pulled her away.

"We shouldn't be seen together like this," Kawling said in a low voice. "This is the opposite of subtle."

"I spected you would be happier to scope me."

"But not to be seen with you. There are photographers all around."

"So I'm hiding in plain sight. Here!" Lemma spun Kawling around, smiling as a photographer raised his camera.

"Lemma, you're being reckless."

"Let's dance, shall we?"

Lemma wrapped her arm behind Kawling, and they swayed to the music.

"You're tense," Lemma whispered, stroking the lavender jacket on Kawling's shoulders. "Under stress?"

"I'll relax when this is all over. Who else do you have?"

"I got everyone: Tizola, the journalist, both doctors—"

"Keep your voice down. You've never heard the phrase 'Loose lips sink ships?'"

"Funny. I learned it as 'Loose lips transmit viruses.'"

"Quiet!"

"Kawling," Lemma tightened her fingers around the woman's arms. "I did everyone you asked. You owe me."

"And I will repay. Give me several hours, and you can have both the boy and the girl."

"And the antidote?"

"I have enough for one person."

"What?" Lemma's body went rigid.

"Keep your voice down. I won't warn you again. I have enough to infect one person."

"Infect?"

"The antidote itself is contagious. You can transmit it and cure others via a blood transfusion."

"So it's like a benevirus?" Lemma said, remembering her conversation with Dr. Schwartz.

"What's a benevirus?"

"Never mind. What if Nadia and I don't have the same blood type?"

"We'll produce more of it. Patience, Lemma, we'll get you cured."

"How long does the antidote take to work? Six days, like your virus?"

"You'll be cured as soon as you take it," Kawling assured her.

"What if I accidentally infected someone and they don't have Dipsocene? Can people take the antidote instead?"

"The antidote is not a vaccine, Lemma. The antidote will only work if it's taken after the person shows symptoms, or in your case, becomes contagious."

"So if they get infected but they don't have Dipsocene, they need to wait until they get thirsty, then take the antidote, then they'll be cured immediately?"

"Yes. In the meantime, have you thought more about my offer of long-term employment?" Kawling asked.

"If I work for you long-term, if I stay infected, I want my photography lice."

"Granted. Along with a camera, a gun, and adoption forms for the two children."

Lemma inhaled cautiously. "I also want Ovian Hodeft released."

"Ovian? He's in a coma."

"I was able to wake him last night. I want him brought out of the coma and released from the hospital."

"And what am I going to tell the public? That Teskir Mong's body suddenly walked away?"

"Tell them he died. I don't care. Just get me Ovian."

"Wait a year," Kawling urged. "Work for me for a year, and I'll release him to you."

Lemma glared. "Yes."

"Any other demands?" Kawling asked. They began dancing again.

"I want an explanation."

"Of what?"

"You told me why each of those people were your targets, except for Wade Syan. Why did he have to die?"

"Wade Syan," Kawling sneered. "You really want to know?"

"Tell me and I'll ghost every target you have without question."

"Very well. You ever heard of Hydra?"

"Hydra? What's that?"

"It was Phronesis Tech's latest project."

The image of Perron Mill's cell popped into her mind, and Lemma realized she might have misread the writing on his wall.

"Syan was keeping it a secret, but thankfully, Shwa Chinny was able to help me out."

"The information Chinny stole from Syan. You asked him to?"

"Correct. It's why Chinny had to be eliminated. That and his tendency to monitor every little thing I did." Kawling smiled. "Then they blamed him for Syan's death. Even I never guessed it would work so smoothly."

"What was Hydra?"

"It would have allowed the regrowth of organs and other body parts," Kawling said.

"So?"

"Who do we know who might want to regrow missing body parts?"

"Someone who's Tiresian?"

"Anyone who's Tiresian, Lemma. Every Reezy who realized they were lied to, that cutting off their limbs or eyes is nothing more than pointless, empty mutilation. Every child who grew up and left that cult would finally be able to get their missing pieces back."

"And you wanted to stop that?"

"Of course! What would that look like for my presidential campaign? Or for Masidon and the church? What if half my voter base was openly renouncing the Tiresian Church?"

"You— you…" Lemma's skin was hot with anger. "You and Masidon ghosted Syan because he was going to cure Milligram? You are absolutely evil, you rimming twank."

"You flatter me, Lemma. You think I'm the only opportunist here? What about Syan? You think he donated to the church just to see his name on their wall? 'Thirsting for the Future?' He never wanted to quench thirst. He created the thirst one amputation at a time. Then he sold them pills to numb their stumps. And he would have sold them their limbs back as well."

Hatred was boiling in Lemma's stomach. "No."

"Oh, yes. I've said it a hundred times: a businessman would sell you the sunrise if he could stake a claim to it. And what about yourself?"

"What about me?"

"You said you are willing to ghost my targets for a year without question. You don't think that includes any doctor who tries to find a cure for amping?"

"*Was* willing," Lemma stopped dancing. "I was willing. But you've made up my mind."

Lemma threw her arms around Kawling's neck, pulling her into a kiss.

"What are you doing— Lemma!" Kawling's protest was smothered as Lemma's tongue jumped out, wetting the inside of her nostril.

Kawling pushed her away, spitting with rage.

"Cuck, Lemma, what was that?"

"Goodbye, Kawling. You won't see me again."

Kawling glared as Lemma disappeared into the crowd. She was aware that others were watching. From the flashing cameras she guessed that Lemma's brazen kiss had been captured. Kawling scowled and wiped her lips and nose.

"Get that camera out of my face," she hissed at a photographer. "And get me security."

Uniformed guards approached. Kawling fanned herself, removing her lavender jacket.

"Governor," a security guard asked. "You wanted to see me?" Beads of sweat were on his forehead, which he brushed at impatiently. Around them, others were fanning themselves, removing coats and undoing collars.

"No," Kawling murmured.

An electronic bell rang over the speaker system, and the musicians stopped playing. The crowd fell silent, as a magnified voice echoed throughout the capitol ballroom.

"Howsie, everyone. My name is Lemma Quartz."

CHAPTER 78

DEW ON HIS BROW

"Let me tell you a story. There was once a little girl, born to parents who didn't want her. When she was finally adopted, her life only got harder. She was one of the last babies who still suffered from allergies so intense she could only eat a few types of food.

"Then one day, an innovator named Wade Syan developed a new way of producing food. It was high quality, resilient without chemicals, safe for the world and especially for the little girl to eat. The little girl grew up to idolize him, and when he was eventually found dead in his own bathtub, that girl vowed to solve his death and venge him.

"One day, after five weeks of investigating and finding clues, she learned that Wade Syan's drowning was no accident. It was the result of a carefully calculated assassination, an infectious fever which made him so thirsty that he had no choice but to crawl into a tub of cold water to sooth his burning thirst. It was there that he died. And it is with this same virus that you all have been infected tonight."

Governor Kawling cursed, brushing sweat from her forehead. The security guards stared blankly at her, waiting for instructions, dark spots growing in the armpits of their gray uniforms. The crowd around them was murmuring, pleading, waving their hands through the air and fanning their glistening skin.

"There is an antidote to the virus," Lemma said. "But the only way to receive it is to remain here, in the ballroom. If any of you try to leave, you will succumb to it faster."

Kawling cleared her throat. "I need all of you to remain calm."

Her tactic might have worked, but for a single woman who screamed with a deep, agonizing cry, as if a dentist had drilled through her tooth without an anesthetic. She broke rank, and ran towards the entrance, tearing off her blouse and bra, her skin sticky and pasty. She fell to her knees in front of a water dispenser by one of the exits, gulping and gasping as water poured onto her cheeks, into her mouth, and up her nose. Then she collapsed to the floor, coughing out water, which spilled over her chin, towards the red flower tattooed on her chest.

Getonia Orea coughed once more, and stopped moving.

Senators screamed, and journalists pushed past each other, knocking over the wait staff as they retreated to the stage, fighting to get as far from the exits as they could.

"Governor?" a guard shouted. "We have to quarantine the room."

"Get me out of here," Kawling demanded. "Get me out of this rimming ballroom!"

But the guard had already given the command, and every door slammed shut in a blare of red lights and sirens. Bolts clacked within the door frames, and in seconds, the entire ballroom was on lockdown.

"Thank you for remaining." Lemma's cool voice sailed through the room. "It will be easier to cure you. Now, everyone must listen to me. There is only one way to save yourselves, and that is for Governor Kawling to tell me where the antidote to the virus is."

"Kawling, what is this?" Senator Tizola, his aged chest bare and sagging, fought his way to her side. "What's happening? What the cuck is happening?"

"It's Lemma Quartz. She's a death agent, and she's a rimming psychopath. You—" she grabbed a security guard. "Have the building sealed, and search every cucking room for her."

People were crying, weeping into their phones, if they had legal ones. A good number had pulled out unliced blinks as well.

"If Kawling doesn't reveal the location of the antidote to me, all of you will be dead within twenty minutes," Lemma continued. "Kawling, give me a ring, won't you?"

Men were pulling off their jackets, then shirts, then undershirts, pouring their cocktails over their chests in a frenzied effort to cool down. Women pulled off their dresses and held their sweating arms away from their bodies. The smell of sweat fermented in everyone's noses.

"Are people taking off their clothes?" Masidon Barreaux shouted from his motorized chair. "What is happening?"

"Governor, do something, please, I'm melting here!" a woman begged, her sequined dress puddled at her feet.

"Don't touch me! Don't touch me!" someone shouted.

Kawling pulled out her phone.

"Lemma, what have you done?"

"I spected our kiss was too sweet for you to ignore me." Lemma's voice was smug.

"What in the rimming cuck do you want?" Kawling yelled.

"I want Ovian, Nadia, and Milligram. Tonight."

"I was going to give them to you. We had an agreement, Lemma!"

"But this way is faster. Like you said, it helps to have insurance."

"I swear to God, you gutter squint, I will have you spread and rammed with a candlestick until your colon falls out!" Kawling screamed into her phone, not caring that every person in the ballroom could hear her.

"Save it for our honeymoon, love. Where's the antidote?"

"Lemma, if you don't call this off, I will have Nadia and Gram cut into little pieces."

"I can fix everything, if you tell me where the antidote is."

"And what then, you're going to waltz in here, and dish it out? I told you, there's enough for only one person."

"You said it can be transferred through blood. I know a universal donor. He'll take it, and give an ounce of blood."

Kawling screamed in frustration. "To everyone in the room? Even if we drained him dry, that's only enough for a handful."

"Not for everyone. For me, Nadia, and you. The rest can drown."

CHAPTER 79

FOAM OF HIS GASPING

The minutes passed. Kawling sat and waited, her gray hair disheveled and sticking to her sweating neck and forehead. Around her were the ball guests, two hundred naked businessmen, journalists, and representatives. They lay flat on the cool stone floor, having drunk every last drop of water and all the cocktails. Crawling over each other, they swarmed into the bathrooms, fighting to cool their faces in the sinks and toilets. Some felt their bladders get tight, but with the bathrooms already crowded, they had no choice but to squat and piss on the ballroom floor.

People shouted at security guards to do something, but the guards were as lost as they were, waving their electric batons at anyone who threatened to become too disorderly.

On the stage sat Masidon Barreaux, who called out helplessly for someone to tell him what was happening.

Kawling pulled out her phone. "Lemma, have you found them?"

***

Outside the state research center, Donovez stood with five agents, guns aimed at the door. Silhouettes appeared at the windows, opening the lab, and beckoning them in.

"Stay low, and keep your guns ready," Donovez warned. "Do not hit the package."

"Which one has it?" another agent asked.

Each of the four figures in the glass window was holding a box.

"They all do," Donovez said, with equals parts resentment and admiration.

***

Another unit of Abadon agents appeared at the doors of State Minor Aid Facility 9342. Three workers stood at the door, and one led out a boy with one leg, walking on crutches. He was crying.

"We have the boy," an agent said into a radio.

"Lemma?" the boy asked, his voice shaking. "Where's Lemma?"

"Lemma's going to meet us," one of the agents promised.

Another squad of agents approached the Syan Hospital. They were met by a team of nurses, and a unit of State Police.

"You have Ovian and the girl?" one of the agents asked.

A nurse whose name tag read "Nurse Jaggard" answered. "We have the girl here. Teskir Mong is in the glass case. You're going to take him out yourself."

The nurses pushed forward a gurney with an unconscious girl on it, as the agents wheeled her into their car.

Then the agents entered the hospital.

***

Donovez stepped into the state research center and approached the four men. "Give them to me."

"Have your men put down their weapons."

Donovez gestured, and agents lowered their weapons. "The package?"

Each of the four men held out their boxes.

Someone's gun fired.

***

An agent shone a light on Gram Mill's face, comparing it to an image on a tablet. "We have him," he said into a radio. "Mr. Mills, you want to talk to your friend?"

"Lemma?"

"Yes, Lemma."

The boy took the radio. "Lemma?" he whispered into it.

"Milligram! Oh thank God! Thank God you're gel. Milligram, go with the men, and I'll scope you in an hour, gel?"

"Lemma, they said my mom—"

"I know, Milligram. I'm so sorry about that. I'll explain everything to you. And make sure you take your Dipsocene, gel?"

"Lemma, Nadia said that you knew about my leg… and that—"

"Milligram, I'll explain everything to you later. I will tell you everything you want to know. I love you, gel?"

"I love you too, Mom."

***

Donovez fell to his knees, his hands shielding the back of his neck as a tornado of glass shards blew over him. Crouching, he retreated from the lab workers, who were only blurred smudges in his tightly squinted eyes.

"Reverse!" he coughed, as one of his agents grabbed his shoulders, pulling him out of the doorway, glass crunching under their feet.

The agents looked at the glass display case with the metal plaque.

"Oh!" Nurse Jaggard exclaimed.

Lying on the floor in front of the case was a nurse. His eyes were open, and foam was trickling out of the corner of his mouth.

"Oh, cuck!" Nurse Jaggard said, and put her hands to her face.

The bed in the glass case, which had held the presumed body of Teskir Mong for ten years, was empty.

***

Kawling cursed into her phone. "I don't care if someone's ghosting you, ghost them back!"

"Governor, the attack was from inside the research center." At that, the voice cut off.

Then her phone buzzed with another call. "What?" she hissed.

"Tell them to stop." It was Lemma.

"Tell who to stop?"

"Your twanks in the research center are shooting at Abadon! Call them off, and give us the antidote."

"My men? Yours shot first!"

"And tell the hospital workers to find Ovian."

"What do you mean, find Ovian?"

Lemma screamed out a long string of curses. "Stop rimming lying to me!"

"How am I lying? Ovian's in a glass case, he's not hard to find."

"He's missing, Kawling. Where did you put him?"

***

Donovez lay on the ground, breathing in short bursts. Every part of him ached, but he hadn't been injured.

The lab workers were on their knees, their hands in the air.

"Donovez," One of his agents cautioned. "Donovez, look!"

A figure in a wheelchair had appeared from behind the four kneeling men. The glint of a gun appeared in his left hand. He motioned for one of the lab workers to pick up the four boxes and hand them to him. He looked though the boxes, and pulled out two vials.

"Who is that? Stop!" an agent pointed his gun at the figure in the wheelchair, who was now holding the vials up in the air.

"Don't shoot! If you shoot he'll drop them! Stop!" Donovez shouted.

But the person in the wheelchair didn't stop. With his left arm and an amped right wrist, he wheeled himself away and out of sight.

"Get him! Find him and get those rimming vials," Donovez hissed.

***

"Get me security," Governor Kawling barked into her phone. She brushed sweat from her forehead, stepping over Senator Tizola, who was lying on the floor in his underwear, whimpering pitifully. "Send fifty officers! Yes, you heard me! Send fifty rimming officers to Balkon headquarters. It's disguised as a decommissioned refrigerator factory, Facility Nine-Three-Eight-One. Do it now!"

***

"Kawling!" Lemma's voice echoed from the ballroom loudspeaker. "You promised me the antidote! You promised, but you haven't given it. Everyone in that room, including you, is going to die unless you give it."

Shouts of protest broke out. People were crowding around Kawling, demanding to know if it was true.

"Governor, tell her!"

"Do something!"

Then Lemma's voice entered the room once more. "While we are waiting for Governor Kawling, I'd like to tell you all a story about a boy named Ovian Hodeft."

Kawling cursed, and pulled out her phone. "Listen to me, squint!"

"We have Nadia and Milligram safely. Where is Ovian, and where is the antidote?" Lemma asked.

Lemma's voice continued over the loudspeaker, a recorded clip that described in painful detail the truth about Ovian, Teskir, and the glass case.

"Lemma, I don't know where they are!" Kawling shouted, trying to drown out Lemma's voice. Everyone in the ballroom was staring at her in horror. Masidon Barreaux's face was twisted and downcast, wishing he was deaf as well as blind, as Lemma's accusations against him and Kawling seared his ears.

"Masidon, did you know?" Lemma's recorded voice asked. "Did you know that Ovian was alive, trapped within his own paralyzed but conscious body? Did you know that Kawling wanted Syan dead?"

"Ovian… Ovian," Masidon muttered, trembling and sweating. "Not Ovian."

Kawling was climbing onto the stage, finding Masidon's motorized chair. She ignored his pleas for an explanation, forcing open a lid of a side compartment and retrieving a bottle of Dipsocene.

"Raemin is that you? What are you doing?" Masidon panted. "Talk to me."

"Get me Ovian and the antidote," Lemma hissed through Kawling's phone. "You will be dead in minutes if you don't."

"How did you do it, Lemma?" Kawling asked, opening the bottle and leaving the stage where Masidon's chair was parked. "You infected all of us. How? Symptoms—" she coughed, lying down and pressing her cheek against the cool marble floor. "Symptoms don't appear for six days, and we have the pills."

She poured the entire bottle of Masidon's Dipsocene into her mouth, chewing the bitter tablets. "How?"

"Like you said; I'm the world's deadliest assassin."

Kawling didn't answer. Her limbs were shaking, her face was rigid, and lathery white foam spilled from her lips.

CHAPTER 80

IDOLS ARE BROKE

"Kawling?" Lemma shouted into her phone. "Kawling!"

"Scope," Fremen said, pointing to one of the surveillance screens in the maintenance closet.

Lemma leaned in, fanning herself. Kawling was on the ground, shaking.

"What happened to her?" Fremen asked. "Is she dead?"

"I don't know— wait." Lemma's blink had buzzed with a message. "It's Curio. She wants me at Balkon."

"Does she know what's happening here?"

"I don't know, Fremen I don't know! Oh!" Lemma dug her fingernails into the sides of her neck in frustration.

Her phone buzzed with a call from Donovez.

"Donovez!" Lemma said. "Kawling's dropped."

"What?"

"Kawling's dropped; she can't help us anymore."

"How?"

"It doesn't matter how; you need to scout the antidote."

"I looked every-cucking-where."

"Did you get a chance to scope who stole the vials?" Lemma asked.

"Negative, but their right arm was amped at the wrist and they were in a wheelchair."

Lemma forced herself to remember if she knew any Tiresians with an amped arm.

Then Lemma received another message from Curio: [*Report to Balkon immediately*]

"Where's Milligram and Nadia?" Lemma asked Donovez.

"Milligram's in a car, Nadia's in an ambulance. The girl's sedated."

"And Ovian?" Lemma asked.

"They searched the hospital. Couldn't find him."

Then her blink buzzed with another message from Curio: [*I know what's happening at the ballroom. I have your antidote. We have a safe place for you at Balkon.*]

"Curio has the antidote," Lemma read aloud. "Donovez, forget the research center. You have a car close to the capitol?"

"We have an ambulance less than five miles away. It's carrying Nadia."

"Have them pick me up."

"At the capitol? Aren't there badges shielding it?"

"Then drive through them."

***

Lemma and Fremen waited and watched from the closet. Badges paced the hall outside the door.

"Kawling's out. Ovian's gone. Curio has the antidote," Lemma said. "Fremen, when we get to Balkon, you'll take the antidote then donate blood to Nadia and me. Schwartz said you were O negative, right?"

"What happens to me when I take the antidote? Will I be immune?"

"The antidote only works on people who are already thirsty. If you take the antidote while healthy, nothing will happen to you. But if you get infected after you've already taken the antidote, you're cucked. So make sure you're popping Dipsocene when you're around me. But not too much," Lemma added, glancing at Kawling's body on the surveillance screen.

"If you want my blood, get me out of here without spilling any. We need a diversion," Fremen said, fanning his neck and sweating. "Badges won't let us get two feet without dropping us."

"Tell them to clear out?" Lemma pointed to the microphone. "Threaten to infect them?"

"They're wearing gas masks." Fremen gestured to one of the surveillance screens.

"Attention," Lemma grabbed the microphone. "Every security guard report to the third floor."

"Claps, Lemma," Fremen said. None of the guards had moved. "And what about the people in the ballroom?"

"We don't have time to worry about them, let them roast."

"Lemma!" Fremen threw her a look of disgust.

"Senators, businessmen, corrupt journalists. All twanks. The world's brighter without them," she said.

"My wife is in there!" Fremen spat. "Doing what you told her!"

"Now you're concerned for your wife? The wife you cucked with Harriden?"

"Wipe off!"

"Wait…" Lemma said. "We can make this work. We can save them and get the badges off our flaps. Give me that." She reached for the microphone. "Listen to me," she ordered. "At my signal, all of you must evacuate the ballroom. Go to the ground floor and exit out there. Do not stop running until you are outside the capitol building."

"You have to tell them about the virus," Fremen said.

Lemma groaned. "Pay attention, because this next part is important. All of you must ingest exactly one dose of Dipsocene as soon as you can. The chemie the Reezys take. Then you'll be immune."

"Should I open the doors?" Fremen asked, but Lemma shook her head and continued.

"But none of you can ever eat anything containing dairy. If you do, you'll die immediately."

She smirked, as Fremen rolled his eyes and hit several switches. The temperature display, which had been set at 33 degrees Celsius ever since Lemma had left the ballroom, began to decrease. Every door in the ballroom opened.

"Run and find Dipsocene. Go!" Lemma shouted into the microphone.

Naked, sweating, and sticky, men and women ran out of the room, jostling each other in their haste and leaving behind Kawling's motionless body. One of the runners pushed past Masidon Barreaux's wheelchair on the stage, which began spinning in circles despite his desperate attempts to apply the brakes.

"Now what?" Fremen asked.

"Blend in," Lemma said, pulling off her dress.

She had never run naked in public before. It was like one of those dreams where one realizes their pants are off, but that no one around cares because they are also part of the dream. So Lemma and Fremen ran without shame, their bodies slick and sweaty, pressed in a crowd of reeking, panicking, journalists and politicians.

"Getonia!" Fremen shouted. "This way!"

Getonia got up and followed him.

The security guards raised their weapons, threatened to shoot, but the naked horde ran past, clamoring through the halls, forcing their way into the cool air outside, too relieved to wonder about the ambulance that approached them, or why three people climbed into it before it drove away. No one even looked back to see a single motorized wheelchair spinning in circles on the stage of the ballroom as its lone occupant flailed his arms pitifully, begging someone to turn it off, until the chair drove over the edge of the stage.

The ballroom was silent, except for the fizzing of Kawling's mouth, the dying whir of Masidon's wheelchair motor, and the sound of two ivory eyeballs rolling across the floor.

CHAPTER 81

MELTED LIKE SNOW

"Donovez didn't say you'd be flapping." One of the agents tossed three hospital gowns to Lemma, Fremen, and Getonia, who fought to keep their balance as the ambulance skidded around a corner.

The gown clung to Lemma's body, still running with sweat from the heat in the capitol building, as she bent to touch Nadia. "She gel?" Lemma dared to ask.

"She's alive, and sedated."

Nadia's eyes were rolled up, white and motionless in her sockets, swaying with the motion of the stretcher whenever the vehicle made a turn.

"Stay strong, Nadia," Lemma whispered. "Stay strong for me."

***

Senator Tizola was shaking, sweat sliding down his back and pooling on the black leather seat. His hands gripped the moist steering wheel, his bare feet shook with the vibrations of the accelerator. The minibar in the backseat rattled with loose bottles and spilled ice cubes.

"Dipsocene, Dipsocene," he muttered, his eyes bulging, sweat dripping down his face. "I need a capsule of Dipsocene. There's been an attack, they poisoned me, infected me. I need to take Dipsocene, it's the med the Reezys use. Must find a nurse, get Dipsocene…"

The car bounced over a curb, sailing into the air and landing with a bone-shaking thud. It skidded to the entrance of Syan Hospital. Someone in a hospital gown was staggering towards his car, waving at him.

"Dipsocene, get me Dipsocene!" Tizola begged, throwing open the door on the passenger side.

***

Curio was standing outside Balkon when Donovez' ambulance drove up, parking next to the same Balkon ambulance that had once collected the goons who had attacked Harriden Vik.

"Is she alive?" Curio asked, as Balkon agents took the stretcher with Nadia from the ambulance.

"Just a mite. You have the antidote?" Lemma asked.

"Inside and upstairs. The triage unit." Curio directed her agents into the building.

Lemma turned to Fremen and Getonia. "You did bright. Both of you did real bright. Get to Donovez. Stay with him and Milligram, I'll find you all after Nadia recovers, gel?"

Fremen nodded, and the ambulance left. Lemma was alone with Curio.

***

Balkon was unusually crowded for so late at night. Agents stood around holding knives or guns if they owned them, waiting for directions from Curio.

"Why are they here?" Lemma asked.

"We're on top alert," Curio explained. "Even though Kawling is down, we're still Schedule One."

"You know about Kawling?"

"It's all on the CityNews live feed. They're showing everything. I'm impressed, Lemma. You managed to hold the entire city hostage."

As Lemma walked past the agents, some covered their mouths with their hands.

"They know I'm contagious?"

"That's what your rambling story seemed to imply. What exactly is it?"

331

"A virus," Lemma said. "Makes you thirsty so you drown yourself like a rat. I'm a silent carrier, so I can infect people. Kawling used it to ghost Syan, and had Masidon infect me with it, that's why everyone's been drowning. As long as everyone here took their Dipsocene from Schwartz, they'll be safe."

"The Dipsocene is the antidote?"

"No. Dipsocene prevents you from getting infected if you are exposed. If it's been more than a few hours since you've been exposed, you need to wait until you get thirsty and then take the antidote. It takes six days from exposure until you get thirsty, or in my case, contagious."

"What if you take the antidote when you are first exposed?"

"It won't help."

Curio sighed. "It all makes sense now."

"How much did Kawling tell you?" Lemma asked.

"The bare minimum. Three weeks ago, Kawling told me to start giving Dipsocene to everyone at Balkon daily. She promised me she'd appoint Balkon to shield the entire state. I had no idea what the Dipsocene was for, or that you were infected."

"Did you know she was going to ghost Syan?"

"She told me to visit him and hide the blink in his bathroom. The night Syan died, Kawling contacted me and insisted I put you on the case. I was able to guess that she was involved in his death."

"I was right," Lemma said. "You only knew about the window because you'd been in his bathroom."

Curio scoffed. "But I didn't ghost him. I accept what should have been your apology."

They had approached the upstairs triage room. The agents placed Nadia carefully on a bed.

"What's that?" Curio asked, as Lemma set a box of syringes on the counter.

"Sedative. Until we get her the antidote, she has to be kept under. Where is it?"

"Mm?"

"The antidote, where is it?" Lemma said. "Nadia and I need the antidote."

Curio said nothing. Instead she sat on the bed next to Nadia.

"Curio? Are your ears broken? Give me the antidote."

"Ask your friends at Abadon."

Lemma was startled. "Abadon— who— how do you know about them?"

Curio sneered and held up a phone. "Kawling told me earlier to-night, while you were holding everyone in the ballroom hostage. She called to say you were going to cuck me out. You're working for Abadon, you cucking traitor."

"I'm the traitor?" Lemma shouted. "You tried to have me ghost her!"

Curio popped a pill in her mouth, and picked up the box of syringes. "Where is the antidote? Not the Dipsocene, the antidote!"

"I had to say something to get you here," Curio said. "I need to punish you."

Lemma gritted her teeth. "You're going to kill me?" Lemma looked at Nadia's limp body. The girl would be nothing but dead weight if she tried to flee with her.

"Not yet."

"You want something? What?" Lemma asked.

"Not me. Jax." Curio's eyes glinted.

"Jax is dead. He broke into the hospital to rescue me, and Kawling's badges ghosted him."

"He survived. He escaped, and he wants you."

"What? Why?"

"Lemma," Curio scoffed. "He's always wanted you."

"Curio, you're not making sense."

"So I'm going to give you to him." Curio rolled a syringe between her fingers. "Punishment from me, and revenge from Kawling."

"Jax doesn't— he wouldn't."

"Not yet. You don't know him like I do."

"I know him pretty rimming well."

"Did you know he smells your jacket when you're away from your desk?"

"Wipe off!"

"He looks at you when you're at your desk," Curio continued. "You don't see him, but I do."

"Wipe off!"

"He has an unliced picture of you. He brings it into the restroom on his bathroom breaks. Want to know what he does with it?"

"Plug it! Shut your rimming mouth!"

Curio bent and lowered the syringe over Nadia's right eyelid. Lemma snapped to the girl's defense with such speed that she had no time to realize it was a trap. As Lemma lunged towards Curio's wrist, Curio jerked the syringe away from Nadia's face. Lemma gasped at the stinging pain above her left breast and collapsed on top of Nadia like a rag doll, the needle sticking out of her chest.

She breathed in short gasps as a sensation of dark emptiness swallowed her.

"Shall we make a wager?" Curio whispered, ripping the syringe out of Lemma's skin, and rolling her on her back. "Let's bet on Jax's self-control. If he can keep away from you, he'll be safe. If not, he'll die in a tub of water, just like Wade Syan."

Lemma tried to crawl off the bed, but her limbs refused to cooperate. She couldn't move, couldn't see.

"So we have a deal." Curio pulled on Lemma's feet, straightened out her body, and left her on the bed next to Nadia. Then Curio left the room. The minutes dragged by, Lemma's heart pulsing faintly, sending throbs of pain against the puncture left by the needle. She would be able to feel everything that was about to happen, and this time there was no computer to send anyone a message.

Then the door opened and someone spoke.

"Is she here?"

It was Jax Yedra.

CHAPTER 82

EYES OF THE SLEEPERS

"She's right there."

Lemma hated Curio's voice; she hated its smugness, its satisfaction; every syllable dripped acid onto her ears.

"Who's that?" Jax asked. "That's Lemma's friend, right? Nadia?"

"You can have her, too. But be flash."

"They're asleep?" Jax's voice moved closer to the bed.

"They're both unconscious."

"Unconscious?"

"Correct. Neither one can hear you, or remember what you do to them."

"Gel."

"That's what you wanted, isn't it? Being alone with Lemma? You said you wanted to be with her where she couldn't escape."

"I didn't mean it like this."

"Well, that's how it is. She's going to wake up soon, so either flash it, or bounce."

"If I could wait for her to wake up…?"

"You think she'd agree? Didn't she tell you she never wanted to scope you again?"

Please, Lemma prayed. *Wait. I'll listen to you as much as you want, if you just wait for me to wake up. I'll forget about everything else. Don't do this, Jax, please.*

"I have to do it as soon I can. Before I run out of time," Jax said.

"Very good."

"You… you said she won't be awake for a while?"

Jax, don't. Please, Jax, Lemma thought.

"She won't know anything."

Lemma screamed inside her skull. But nothing came out.

"Then maybe I should. I can tell her what happened afterwards. Just so she'll understand."

Jax, what's wrong with you? Lemma wondered. *Why the rimming cuck would you possibly want to tell me? You're a twanking limp coward, that's why. Please Jax!*

Jax bent over her. She could feel his warm breath on her face, and smell it too. She could smell his sweat, the residue of his Blue Iceberg deodorant. That smell would haunt her forever, would always remind her of this night, when she lay helpless, pleading silently for Jax to come to his senses, or else die suddenly of a heart attack, or be distracted, anything that would prevent this from happening.

Please, someone come in and stop this. Ghost me, or ghost Jax, or ghost all of us. Jax, don't do this!

"Shall I leave you alone?" Curio asked, her voice gloating.

"Yes."

The door shut. All Lemma could hear was his breathing. She waited, in the infinite expanse of darkness that surrounded her.

"I know Curio said you can't hear me or scope me," Jax said hesitantly.

Don't believe her, Jax. You know this is wrong; don't do it.

"I would never do this, please believe me, but I have to. It's the only way."

Jax, don't.

"I'm sorry. I promise, I'll explain everything."

Don't.

He still hadn't touched her. Lemma wished he would get it over with.

Then she heard a wet, smacking noise. It was the sound of someone chewing, or licking, or kissing. The sound was coming from the other side of the bed where Nadia lay. Suddenly, she reversed all of her prayers.

Don't touch her, come over here to me. Do whatever you want to me, just leave Nadia alone!

Lemma strained her ears. Jax was moving, from the side of the bed where Nadia was, around to Lemma.

If you touched Nadia, I'll… I'll…

"I'm sorry," Jax mumbled.

She could feel his panting breath as he leaned over her. She was no longer afraid.

Touch me, Jax. Do it. I dare you. You already touched Nadia, come touch me so I can ghost you. I want you to do it. Do it, Jax. Pin me. Then die sucking piss out of a toilet.

That awful wet noise returned. It was as if a horse was licking sugar right above her face.

And then, as Lemma lay helpless, Jax pulled her jaw open. Two warm, salty slugs slithered into her mouth and rubbed against her taste buds. His fingertips ran between her gums and lips, scraping over the chip in her front tooth in a flash of white-hot pain.

Her fingers and toes tingled as motion began to return. The dose of paralyzing drug Curio gave her had been small. Lemma's vision was coming back. She could see Jax's stupid, cowardly face in front of her.

Bite down, she ordered herself.

Her jaw twitched.

Her toes moved.

She bit down, but she was too slow. Jax pulled his fingers out of her mouth before she could clamp her teeth on them.

"I'm sorry," he murmured as he quit the room, leaving Lemma to burn with the fiercest hatred she had ever felt, so hot she feared it would dissolve her.

The door closed, and she lay there, the salty taste of Jax's fingers lingering on her tongue.

CHAPTER 83

WAXED DEADLY AND CHILL

"Well?" Curio asked, once Jax had left the triage room and joined her in the hall. "Are you satisfied?"

"Not yet," Jax replied from his wheelchair, staring into his boss's eyes.

Curio's blink buzzed. "Badges are here. Someone spilled where Balkon is."

"Who did?" Jax asked.

"Don't know. Maybe your girlfriend told Kawling."

From downstairs came the muted sound of gunshots.

"Wait it out," Curio murmured, touching the gun at her waist. "Wait it out."

"Give me your gun," Jax said. "Just in case."

"Can you even shoot with your left hand?" Curio laughed mockingly, and stared at Jax in his wheelchair. His right foot was missing, his shin hanging limp and bandaged. His right wrist ended in a stump. It was bleeding through the bandages wrapped around it.

Jax glared at her, and examined his wrist.

"It wasn't my fault you were arrested in a hospital," Curio said. "So the state amped you. Don't worry; you can get a new hand and foot. Schwartz gets new limbs every week. In the meantime, you can go meditate with the Reezys. See if you get enlightened."

"It doesn't matter," Jax said. "In six days, I'll be dead anyway."

"Dead?"

"Yes, dead. You probably have it too, if you touched Lemma in there."

338

"You know about the virus? How do you know about it?" Curio asked, narrowing her eyes at him.

There were more gunshots. Someone messaged Curio again. She cursed.

"Badges cut off the exits. We're trapped."

"What do they want?" Jax asked.

"What do you think they want with a business that ghosts civilians without allowing them the due process of a trial? I have no rimming idea," Curio said bitterly. "How'd you know about Lemma's virus?"

"I have friends at the hospital."

"Friends that couldn't stop you from being amped?"

"They found me after I was amped, told me what was happening at the Governor's Ball, told me about the virus and antidote, helped me escape. What about you? How do you know?"

"Kawling told me, earlier tonight."

"Then why'd go near Lemma if you knew she'd be infected?"

Curio shook the empty vial of Reezy meds. "No more left, but that's gel. I'm immune. Everyone in Balkon's immune. Did they give you Dipsocene when they amped you?"

Jax shook his head. "You're all out?"

"There's some downstairs in my office," Curio said. "Maybe if you move fast enough you can get to it before the badges shoot you."

The gunshots were growing louder.

"You knew Lemma was infected, but you let me in the room with her?" Jax asked incredulously. "You wanted me to get sick?"

"You and Lemma shouldn't have cucked me to Abadon." Curio shrugged. "What I don't understand is why you went in there knowing she was contagious. You'd risk dying just to pin her one time?"

"Pin her?" Jax's face contorted with revulsion. "You spected that's what I wanted? You spect I could pin her from this rimming chair?"

"You asked to me to bring her to Balkon so she couldn't escape. Forgive me for assuming the obvious."

"So you wanted me to die?"

"You clearly want to die! You knew about the virus, and you went into the same room as her! Twank. Doesn't matter. Lemma infected you, all the Dipsocene is downstairs, and Lemma said they lost the antidote. So you'll die soon enough either way."

Jax looked up at her and smiled. His expression made Curio take a step backward. "Lemma didn't infect me. I infected myself."

There was a colossal explosion from downstairs. The entire building shook.

Curio flinched. "There goes your Dipsocene. Wait! Jax—"

Jax had used his left hand and the stump of his right wrist to roll his wheelchair into Curio's shin. She pulled out her gun.

"You're going to shoot me?" Jax asked. "You only have ten bullets; you'll need those if the badges come up here."

"Then don't make me waste any on you. Bounce. Wheel yourself to a nice bathtub and drown yourself."

There was a panicked cry from the triage room, followed by another voice speaking soothingly.

"They're waking up," Jax said.

"Lemma was already awake, just temporarily paralyzed."

"Lemma was awake? You said she wouldn't know what was going on."

Curio smirked. "I showed her who you really are. She was aware during the whole time, during everything you did to her."

Jax yelled and threw his body out of the wheelchair and against Curio's thighs. She lost her balance, and they both fell to the ground. Curio clawed at Jax's face with her free hand, her other hand clutching the gun. Jax crawled over her, reaching for her face as Curio wrapped her free hand around his neck and squeezed.

"You're rimming insane," she hissed, gripping Jax's neck. "I have a gun, and both my hands." She threw herself forward, putting Jax on his back and kneeling on him with her whole weight.

His left hand gripped her wrist as the gun fired again and again, the bullets screaming past Jax's ear and into the floor.

With a yell, Jax knocked the gun out of her hand and drove the stump of his right arm up into her eye. Curio screamed and Jax struck again, thrusting his bandaged wrist into her mouth.

Curio gagged, and tried to breathe, but as her throat opened, Jax's arm slid farther in. She dropped the gun, clawed at his face with both hands, trying to push herself off of him. But no matter how hard she pushed, his stumped wrist was still long and slender enough to reach all the way to the back of her throat. Her knees held her entire body weight. Her balance was off; there was no way for her to stand. Curio bit his wrist, her eyes rolling back in her head.

Her body went limp, and her jaws loosened.

She collapsed onto Jax, who pulled his bloody wrist from her throat and wormed his way out from under his boss's corpse.

CHAPTER 84

LOUD IN THEIR WAIL

"Lemma! You're awake. I can explain, I swear. I'll explain everything, please," Jax begged. "Here, take it!"

Lemma had come out into the hallway. Using his left hand, Jax slid Curio's gun on the floor to her. She picked it up and almost dropped it, her fingers still weak from the sedative.

"Lemma, I want you to listen to me," Jax pleaded.

"Lemma?" Nadia sounded drowsy. "What's... who's out there?"

Lemma stared at Jax. He was on the floor, panting and shaking, between the wheelchair and Curio's body. His right arm and leg had been amped. The bandage from his right wrist had come off in Curio's mouth and trailed from her lifeless face. His stitches had torn open and he was bleeding. Bullet casings, still warm, lay scattered around him.

Lemma's lips twisted in a snarl. "I was paralyzed and you came in and—"

"Curio told me you were asleep."

"And that makes it gel?" Lemma shouted. Her hand holding the gun shook as she pointed it at Jax.

"Don't shoot, please! Hear me out first; then you can shoot me."

"I don't need to shoot you, Jax. You're dead. When you..." her voice quavered. "When you stuck your filthy, rimming fingers in my mouth, because you're a cowardly little twank, you infected yourself."

"No, Lemma."

"You're going to die like Wade Syan."

"I infected myself."

"Lemma?" Nadia stood in the doorway.

"She's all cured, scope her." Jax reached for Nadia.

"Don't!" Lemma shouted. Her finger squeezed the trigger, and the hall echoed with the sound of the first gunshot Lemma had ever fired. Jax's body shook, and Nadia screamed.

A dark stain spread across Jax's shirt. "Lemma! I was trying to tell you… the antidote… I took it."

Donovez's description of the one-armed figure in a wheelchair flashed into Lemma's mind.

"That was you?"

Nadia, still shaking, pulled the jacket off of Curio's body and pressed it against Jax's chest.

"Good girl. Good Nadia," he said hoarsely. "That's bright. Press down; you're doing bright." Jax's eyes crossed.

"You have the antidote?" Lemma asked.

"Injected it. It's contagious. You had the virus, I cured you; you're both cured."

"You knew about the virus? And the antidote?" Lemma's stomach twisted.

"Yes," Jax coughed, his chest convulsing even as Nadia pressed the jacket against it. "Stole both from the lab. I didn't know which was which. Couldn't risk anyone taking them from me."

"You popped the virus too?"

"Had to be steady… antidote works right away… virus won't kill me for six days… take my blood, take my spit, cure them…"

"That's what you were doing to Nadia and me? Oh dear God, Jax, I'm so sorry. Jax, the antidote won't shield you— You need to pop Dipsocene right now—"

The door to the hall blew open.

Lemma turned and shouted, squeezing the trigger again and again, refusing to accept that she had already used the last bullet on Jax.

CHAPTER 85

WITHERED

The badges muttered to each other, and one with a round piggish face pulled the empty gun from her hand. It was Officer Garrity.

"Fits the description," he said. "Print her."

Another badge pressed her thumb against cool glass, which beeped and said, "Annalemma Quartz. CityLink: 7214853."

Jax's breathing was slowing down. Nadia frantically looked up at the badges.

"He's been shot! He needs medical attention and Dipsocene! No!" Lemma shouted, but thick fingers dug into her armpits, dragging her to her feet. Handcuffs snapped around her wrists.

"Nadia, find Donovez! Get a blink and message Donovez. I'll be right back, stay here."

The badges dragged Lemma away from Nadia and Jax.

"Where are you taking me? Please, Jax needs help!"

A badge rapped his knuckles against the back of her skull, and she fell silent, limping along with them down the stairs to the main floor.

Balkon had become a war zone. Cubicles had been shattered, and the floor was littered with fallen Balkon agents and state badges, wine-dark stains soaking the carpet under each body.

"I'm a doctor. Don't touch me," Schwartz was pleading. "Whatever you want, I have gold, silver, kidneys, livers, eyes; you name it! Just don't— Lemma!" Schwartz was bleeding from a cut on his eye, and was also handcuffed. "Loose me, I need to talk to her," he begged.

A badge kicked him in the chest, and he fell silent.

"We have the target, alert the chief," said the badge who had hand-cuffed Lemma.

"We lost contact with the governor half an hour ago," another badge said.

"Escort the target to the door."

They led her past the remains of a cubicle, where light glimmered off a silver name plaque which read "Agent Jax Yedra."

Then the badges dropped Lemma to the floor, shouting as they pointed guns and electric batons at what used to be the front door.

"Stand down! Hands up! Stop!"

"Who the rim is that?"

"He's unarmed."

"Who are you? Stop or get ghosted!"

Lemma twisted her head and looked at the newcomer. It was a man, withered and slender as a skeleton, crawling on all fours, feeling the ground in front of him.

"He's blind," Officer Garrity said. "He's a Reezy."

"Hey, Reezy!" another shouted, walking up to the man. "Can you hear me? Spect he's deaf?" The badge bent down. "Hey, Reezy!" he waved his hand in front of the man's face. "Hey!"

He drew his gun, and pointed it directly at the man's forehead. "Talk to me, twank. You want to get ghosted?"

"Sarge, he can't hear you!"

The man crawled forward, running his fingers over the floor in front of him.

The gun fired. Bits of tile sprayed where the bullet stuck the floor inches from the crawling man's head. He didn't react.

"Deaf and blind," the badge said.

"Why the rim is he here?"

The man crawled past the officer's legs. Then Lemma saw his scarred face.

"Ovian," she murmured. "Ovian, no!"

Ovian's knees and palms were dark red from crawling past bodies so disfigured he was fortunate not to see them.

The officers laughed, and Lemma felt another boiling surge of hatred.

"Help him! He needs your help?" she begged.

But the badges were laughing harder than before. The badge closest to Ovian threw out his foot, and Ovian toppled to the ground, hands and feet flailing as he tried to protect himself from the invisible attacker.

"Carry him back to the office! Put the cuck on a leash," Garrity laughed.

"Toss out some dog bits for him!" another badge said, bending over with laughter.

"His name is Ovian Hodeft!" Lemma forced the words out of his mouth. "He's been alive all these years, and you have to tell the press. You have to tell people he's alive!"

Garrity kicked her in the ribs. "Get up."

"Ghost me," she said. It was a dare and a plea all in one.

"You're coming— with— us," he grunted, pressing the heel of his boot on her knuckles. Her fingers snapped like branches, and she screamed.

"Ghost the squint," another officer said, as Garrity put his gun to Lemma's ear.

The gunshot echoed through the room.

CHAPTER 86

HEARTS BUT ONCE HEAVED

The gun fired six more times, drowning out the screams of badges, shattering glass and metal and bones.

The noise stopped. Schwartz was sobbing in the distance.

Lemma's eyes had cemented themselves shut, but she forced herself to blink. She was hot and wet, she had pissed and soiled herself, and the stench burned in her nose.

The badges were spread out on the floor, gasping, torn, bleeding out. Someone was walking towards her.

"No, don't!" she cried.

The figure fumbled with keys. Her wrists clicked apart.

"Can you hear me?" the man whispered.

She stared upward into his scarred face.

"Ovian," she murmured. "You can see."

"I can see and hear just fine. Are you okay?"

"How did you get here?"

"You're safe with us, Lemma. You! Go back to the car and get ice!" Ovian turned to a man with a goatee and almost no clothes. Senator Tizola left the building and returned, holding a piece of ice to his forehead and dropping a bag of ice next to Ovian. He stared at Lemma with a mixture of fear and awe.

"Tell Tizola to take Dipsocene," Lemma murmured. "Everyone has to take Dipsocene. Schwartz has Dipsocene. There's a phone in my pocket. Call Haydis Donovez. Find Jax; pop him Dipsocene. The antidote's in Jax's saliva. It's in my saliva." She was crying dry tears. "Call Donovez," she repeated. "Tell him— Jax— saliva— antidote's in his and my saliva."

Ovian was putting bony arms around her, holding ice to her broken fingers.

"Tell Milligram—" Lemma collapsed into blackness.

CHAPTER 87

FOREVER GREW STILL

Wednesday, June 6

She was in blackness.

Slowly memories trickled back. How long had she laid here?

"Can you hear me?" a familiar voice asked.

She tried to open her eyes, but the lids wouldn't move.

"I spect you can hear me. I'd ask you to move if you could, but the doctors say you can't."

She recognized that voice. It was that girl. How she hated that girl.

"So…" the girl said lazily. "Spected I'd drop by. Scope how you're doing. I spected you'd died. But don't string. We prefer you this way."

"She can hear us, right?" an unfamiliar man's voice said.

"I spect so. Overdosed on Dipsocene. She can't move, but she can hear and feel everything."

"So if I stick my finger in her eye…?" The man asked. His voice came from a lower angle than the girl; he was sitting down.

"She'll feel everything, but don't do it; the nurses will scope us," the girl replied.

"How long is she going to be dropped?"

"Well…" the girl's voice was now very close. "Doctors say it might be permanent. Don't jack around with Dipsocene."

Permanent? She chilled at the thought.

"Forever. Scary, isn't it?" the girl said, as if she'd read her mind. "Also, Masidon's dead. Crashed his wheelchair in the ballroom. Curio's dead too. You really don't have anyone left."

Several agonizing minutes passed.

"Maybe you're wondering," the girl continued, "how I got the virus to work so quickly in the ballroom? Surprise, surprise! It wasn't the virus. Had a friend crank up the boiler. Fooled everybody. You dropped yourself for no reason."

"Ovian's alive and recovering," the girl added. "They're going to publish an interview with him soon. Don't string out, we'll have the doctors read it to you. He'll spill everything about the Reezys. We went through your office. Found some contras. Nadia and I were cured. And Senator Tizola and everyone else at the ball popped Dipsocene that same night. I win. You lose."

"Now what?" the man asked.

"Well," the girl replied smugly. "In order to make her as comfortable as possible we should probably play her favorite music."

There were several clicks of a button, and Aenna Mei's voice began to sing.

"You said this was your favorite music, right? Goodbye, Raemin," Lemma Quartz said, and left her in the dark.

CHAPTER 88

SUNSETS FOR SALE

Lemma pushed Jax's wheelchair through the hospital, past the fountain where arcs of water danced in graceful parabolas.

"How are you? Warm? Cold?" Lemma asked.

"I'm gel." Jax stared out the window, where the sun was dipping into the horizon. "Lemma?"

"Mm?"

"I like that sunsets are free. Every evening, we get a free show, and we never sit back to appreciate it."

"If I had known you'd become philosophical, I'd have shot you twice."

Jax's laugh turned into a weak cough.

"You know what Abadon should do?" Lemma said. "We should find a way to monetize sunsets."

Jax looked at her.

"Why not?" Lemma said. "Maybe not the sunset itself, but the experience. Build a large porch, high above the city. Have warm sand to dig their toes into, serve them drinks."

Jax stared at her in shock.

"You're scoping me like I'm a monster! I'm just saying, if we sell murder, we should also sell something nice once in a while."

"Why pay to watch a sunset?" Jax asked. "The best things in life are free."

"Wrong. The best things in life bring a high return on investment," Lemma said with a smile.

She pushed Jax's chair to the window.

351

"What's on your mind, Jax?" She locked the chair's brakes, and sat on a bench, facing him.

"It's been five days. If Schwartz hadn't popped me the Dipsocene, then tomorrow would be the day I drown." Jax glanced back at the fountain.

"If you suddenly get thirsty, let me know and I'll just do this—" Lemma licked her pinky and stuck in his ear. Jax snorted, jerking his head away in playful irritation, and rubbed his ear on his shoulder.

Then Jax became serious again.

"Lemma, I'm really sorry about what happened that night at Balkon, when you and Nadia were dropped. I was only trying to save you."

"It's gel. It worked."

"I was trying to find the best way to cure you. I spected, maybe a kiss, like some sort of cucked fairy tale, but I knew you wouldn't want me to do that."

"A kiss would have been less rimming creepy than sticking your fingers in my mouth."

Jax grimaced. "Again, sorry."

"I'm sorry too. For shooting you, and for hating you, hoping you'd catch the virus and die. I'm sorry you lost your arm and leg trying to find me."

"It's gel. Schwartz is already scouting for new limbs."

"And a new leg for Milligram," Lemma said.

One of the billboards displayed an image of Wade Syan's face with the caption: "HYDRA: Leaked files hint at next generation of Phronesis Tech?" Below it was an image of Ovian Hodeft, with the words "Back from the Dead."

"Lemma?" Jax asked.

Lemma turned from the billboards and stared at Jax.

"I'll talk steady. Before we got assigned to Wade Syan, you and I didn't know each other that well."

"I knew you enough to hate you."

Jax snorted. "But you don't hate me anymore, right?"

Lemma smiled stiffly, knowing where this was leading.

"Is there… is there any chance of us ever being more than work partners or friends?"

Lemma's head spun with a thousand thoughts she could never put into words. It was easy to joke about saliva and fingers now, during the daytime. But every night since Jax saved her she had wrenched herself awake, slick with panicked sweat, certain Jax's fingers were on her teeth again.

"I don't spect— there's too much choking me right now."

"Gel." Jax swallowed, and pretended to look at the sunset.

"Jax, you're a rimming solid friend."

He nodded. "Friends it is."

Lemma pulled out the contra camera that Donovez had found in Kawling's home. She held it to her eyes, as the date flashed in the corner of the view. It was five days since she had performed her health inspection of the Cobra goons at Wilco.

"You've juggled that for days. Still haven't seen you use it," Jax said.

Lemma nudged the shutter button, allowing the fading sun to sharpen. "I've wanted a camera for five years. I'm only using it for special memories."

"Like?"

"I took one of Nadia and me, and one of Milligram and me, popping broccoli." Lemma smiled, remembering the boy's funny expression. "And one of Quinn being reunited with Ovian." Quinn had run trembling fingers over her son's scarred face and webbed toes, and then burst into a cry of joy. Mother and son had embraced, neither one letting go for a long time.

Lemma held her breath, drinking in the moment with Jax and the sunset, feeling the buzz by her hip as Donovez blinked her, wondering what he would say to installing a commercial sun terrace on the roof of the new Abadon headquarters.

She exhaled, and pressed the button.